"*The Pleasure Model Repairman* is like the best sex: mind-blowing and reality-altering. Wangersen's ingenious debut novel transports us to a very believable future where, for a price, android-like pleasure models satisfy human desires ranging from the vanilla to the perverse. This is one for Philip K. Dick fans-or anyone who wonders what sex will be like not too many years from now."

David Massengill, author of *Red Swarm*

"*The Pleasure Model Repairman* weaves a psychedelic tapestry far beyond the fringes of *Do Androids Dream of Electric Sheep.*"

Jason Rizos, author of *Supercenter*

"Shocking, rattling, disturbing, this will have you laughing out loud, and exploring curiosities that will make you blush. You're in for the roller coaster of your wettest dystopian dreams."

Kevin Downey, author of *The Intricate Trap*

"Just like that mad accordionist at your aunt's fourth wedding—that slick mook whose fingers drizzled the ivories like pink Bakelite rain—Wangersen will waltz you into a bourbon clanking, smoke-drunk daze. Down these weird streets a rocket mind must go."

Ron Dakron, author of *Hello Devilfish!*

First Montag Press E-Book and Paperback Original Edition February 2018

Montag Press
ISBN: 978-1-940233-49-9
Design © 2018 Rick Febré
Author photo © 2018 Arabella Radienne-Plum

Montag Press Team:
Project Editor – Charlie Franco
Managing Director – Charlie Franco

A Montag Press Book
www.montagpress.com
Montag Press
1066 47th Ave. Unit #9
Oakland CA 94601 USA

Montag Press, the burning book with the hatchet cover, the skewed word mark and the portrayal of the long-suffering fireman mascot are trademarks of Montag Press.

Printed & Digitally Originated in the United States of America
10 9 8 7 6 5 4 3 2 1

THE
PLEASURE MODEL REPAIRMAN

For Arabella

RUUF WANGERSEN

THE
PLEASURE MODEL
REPAIRMAN

Reality wears the collar, fantasy grips the leash.

Dr. Flavorian,
Eros and the Artificial:
1001 Imprintable Kinks

Inge-Borghesa-TetX40

Lust is the enemy. That was the rule.

A pretty funny rule when you find yourself in the lust business, but there you have it. Break it right down, it's not even a rule. It's more like some vague warning, some cautionary dictum. Like the easy-to-remember slogan of a corny Globo-Health abstinence initiative. Four block-letter words on a pop-up PSA or a Morality First poster peeling from the cinderblock of a public toilet in the Low Flats. Or even better still, it's the hook of a sermon shouted by that tattered substreet preacher gesticulating from atop the mount of his overturned bucket.

Lust is the enemy! Believe, ye faithless and weak in spirit and repent! Beware the horned one! Beware and repent! Repent!!

Word.

Go tell it on the mountain, preacher man. The whole thing was laughable, hilarious, really. Or it should've been. The only problem was he was right. It was right. To us in equipment repair at Fant Fixers, Inc., the lust rule was some serious stuff, and yes, even a religion of sorts, and we FF techs the penitent and the observant. Lust *was* our enemy, the only enemy we cared about, because it was the only one that could kick you where it counts—in the job. Fall hard for a dec and it was a real career buster. And that was no fucking joke.

In workaday action the rule played out something like this: When on a service call, the qualified tech keeps the lust rule front of mind at all times. You do not even look at the equipment if you can possibly help it. You certainly do not touch the equipment, except in an appropriate, techno-mechanical and repair-oriented way. And you (god forbid) most definitely do not sniff the equipment. Or taste it for that matter. Or lick, chew, nibble, bite, suck, slurp or gnaw it. No! You do none of those human-all-too-human things the average ordinary lustful sap of a john or a jane could and would be expected to do in the same ultra-inviting circumstances. What you, the certified tech, do is rise above, and only and exactly what you are there to do—and that is perform the services that we at Fant Fixers Pleasure Model Repair Division (69-Frame, Rat City branch) are handsomely compensated to provide. You fix the problem.

I followed the no-lust protocol for seven long years without a hitch. How? Because I was the best. I don't mean for that to sound cocky or pumped-up or self-aggrandizing, there were close calls, plenty of them, lots of opportunity for sex in the plastisex business. The repair game is risky that way. Not for everybody. But me, I planned to last, and to do that I had to be good. I observed the rule religiously. So confident was I in my professionalism, so certain was my faith in my methods and procedures, my meticulous a2d and top-bonus-earning technical prowess, that when it finally, actually, really *happened*, I didn't even know it. I hadn't looked, hadn't touched (not in *that* way) I didn't sniff or taste, didn't lick, chew, nibble, bite, suck, slurp or gnaw. It didn't make any difference. Maybe that's how it always goes down. You don't know the knife is in until you feel the twist.

Shit, I mean, all we did was talk …

I should've known better. The basics, Garl Motts, remember the freaking basics.

Don't converse, do the reverse.
Don't do more, effect restore.
Don't solve, resolve.

In my defense, meager as it is, it wasn't your typical service call. It was a *special*, and right from the get-go it cracked off like one. For starters, I hadn't been that close to the surface in years. It was all the way up in ParisGestalt City. 3-Frame. Two slender levels from the penthouse itself. The elevation alone had to be a factor. *Had to be.* The scrubbed quality of the air on 3 must have put the zap on my senses. Way up high where the oxygen is rich and sweet, along with everything else. No smog, no haze, no streeters looking for a handout, no graffiti to drag at your eye, or reeking piles of steaming garbage, no holo-meez jumping out to pester you with their HOVO-razzle and cracklepop ads—cigarettes, transplant insurance, *Bud Light®*, *Extrudos®* … everywhere damned *Extrudos®*. But not up top, not on 3, there was none of it. Nothing to bring you down down *down*.

Xec was there, of course. Patrols on foot, in cruisers, lurking on every block. But it's not the same Xec you find in the way down below. Up on 3 they're the polite sort of cop, all officer-friendly on it, just there to make sure you feel safe and secure, the better to focus and spend big on the über ritz and mondo charm of ParisGC (*the* Paris) with its boutiques, patisseries, lead-paned windows at every turn, quaint cafés with striped awnings, racks of oysters packed in ice, and doll-faced dec flower girls with their pails of long-stemmed roses. Real flowers, madames et monsieurs, mais oui, naturellement. Ooo la la, it was la vie en roses on trois-plates, top-shelf living in the supple world of monied style and the luxury brand. Oberan®, Tantradolce®, Patek Philippe®, Lamborghini®, Louis Vuitton®, Tobias Chen®, Umeki®, McQueen®, Punkd®, Aazura®, Vladavani®, Salomé®, Destradyne®, Mobili-Nerisi®, Normal Gene®.

What's in a name? Anything. Everything. The alpha and omega, it's the *all* that matters on 3. Jesus-H., go up that high it even snows on Christmas.

Clearly, I didn't belong. The company van stuck out like a cockroach on a supermodel's hydraform cheek. But knowing that I was going topside, I took the necessary precautions. I put on a fresh uniform, all pressed and crisp. It was my good one, too, with my name stitched in red script over the pen pocket. I took the time to hang my work order from the rearview for ease of scanning. This particular detail wasn't overkill. Five seconds after I pulled off the ML, a Xec cruiser swerved in behind me, locked on and lit me up. The cop would've yanked me over, too. Would've made me set my rig down on the street – "Please step out of the vehicle, sir …" – and then it's open up the back doors so he/she/it could take hizzerit's sweet time checking every part box and tool, followed by a full W.A.L.T.E.R. scan, my timetable blown to hell—only none of that happened because my work order passed muster. I was legit. The cop peeled off and I flowed on, and every Xec goon I went by after that acted like they didn't even see me. I was as good-to-go as any other highroller. For a whole four-hour appointment window I had a first class ticket to the world of the rich and heinous, and I could come and go as I damned well pleased.

The address was on Belle Epoque, a boulevard renowned for its Sunday promenades and impossibly high rents (even by 3-Frame standards) with architecture from a bygone era and general opulence run amok. The building even had a human doorman (named Bernie) who opened the door with his own hand instead of buzzing you in from a cage. The lobby was an embarrassment of empty space. Luxuriating in it, I took my time striding across the expanse of gleaming marble that stretched on to the elevator. I entered the shiny lift and the golden doors slid shut in front of me before I noticed there were only three buttons on the panel. Only three flats in the whole monolithic structure. That's class. When the little number 2 lit up, the doors opened again and I stepped out directly into a living room, supposing that's what the owners would call it, though it was far bigger than any living room I'd ever been in before. In the center was a long reflecting pond with orange and white and speckled koi gliding languorously under lily pads and the arch of a decorative bridge. I couldn't tell if the fish were real or decs, but either way they were impressive. I'd never heard of koi decs. The room was ringed by floor-to-ceiling windows that looked out onto a formal garden. The sculpted trees and shrubberies appeared to stretch into the lingering mist of an idyllic distance, the whole vista an aggregate perceptual space of a 1000-to-one if it was anything at all. Visual enhancements of this kind were known among interior designers as *versailling*, and you only found them in the wealthiest of enclaves. I stood there for a full minute, soaking in the sheer, humming amplitude of the posh in all its free air and velvety trappings, a world and a life so far beyond the imaginings of a down-frame dreamer it might as well not exist at all. I gazed at the disc of the setting sun where it hovered, framed, poised and shimmering in a dusk so heart-stoppingly stunning it was impossible not to see it as real. Even at 8:59 a.m. Apparently, some people didn't find mornings to their taste. And if you're rich enough (and they were) apparently you didn't need to have them.

"Are you the repairman?"

Time to snap out of it. Time to wake up, pay attention and earn my gruel. I turned and looked at her just long enough to establish that she was the subject and not the client, before I quickly averted my gaze.

"Where's the client?"

She hesitated.

"He is not here."

"Get him."

"I cannot, because I do not know where he is. He does not

announce his comings and goings, at least, not to me. He prefers that I remain in the dark on that note."

This was highly irregular, almost unheard of on an FF service call, especially one as high up as 3-Frame. Techs dealt with the client and only the client. He, she, they or (in lots of cases) it was required to be present at all times throughout the session for any number of reasons, all of them good ones. I took another look at the work order. Again I noted that dispatch had tagged the job a *special*, a general advisory to expect the unexpected, and it was starting to feel like one. I glanced up at the subject (without *looking* at her, obviously) and decided that the best course was to proceed with the repair. I pulled my gloves on, acutely aware that she was watching my every move.

"Find a comfortable chair," I said.

"I would prefer to stand."

Her tone was polite, her accent almost imperceptible. Was it French? That made a certain straightforward sort of sense, it being Paris and all. But I wasn't sure it was accurate.

"I'd prefer that you sit," I said. "Preferably in an area that's easy to clean up. No fine upholstery, no art that might get trashed, no rugs of oriental extraction that might get urinated, drooled, squirted or defecated on."

Her breath caught at this last regal detail. I realized I was running the risk of offending her sensibilities, finely-honed, *expensive* sensibilities that I could ill afford to offend.

"Please, it's really for the best," I added, in an exceptionally civil tone, though it was an obvious afterthought.

"Then the sitting room will have to do," she said, in a choked whisper.

Ah. It was not a living room, it was a *sitting* room. Mais bien sur.

"This will be fine," I said.

Establishing rapport with the subject wasn't always necessary, or even advised, but it seemed prudent in the circumstances.

She propped delicately on the edge of a settee that was
pricier than one I would have selected for the task, but there
weren't any shabby ones in the area. I moved around behind
her and opened my kit. This was how I worked, always from the
back, to minimize the opportunity for incidental eye contact. I'd
already smeared a liberal dose of NOF gel under each of my
nostrils on the elevator ride up. Standard operating procedure.
We techs carried tins of the stuff stashed in the zip pockets of our
coveralls. *Nofera®* was my brand of choice, extra strong because
I was extra careful. Without a liberal dollop of NOF even the
most experienced tech would be a sitting duck for equipment of
her caliber, existing as she did in a veritable monster's pool of
exuded pheromones out of which any one of her fragrant tentacles might slither, snatch you by the olfactory nerve, thrash you
around a bit (for fun) and then down you'd go. Boom. Bye-bye,
poor sap. Another repair tech dragged into the murky depths of
carnal abandon, lust winning, sap losing, game over. There was
no faster and more direct autostrata to the amygdala than a whiff
of lab perfected, high-octane pheromone cocktail.

As I leaned in to pop the hood, to my surprise she popped it
for me. She dipped her head forward and the nape of her slender
neck and lissome scapulae slid apart in different directions, opening right down her spine, each thin rib withdrawing and retract-
ing in a display somewhere between a blooming chrysanthemum
and a trick Chinese box. She opened herself up to me in this way,
exotic merchandise revealing itself exotically.

"Will this hurt much?" she asked. She was awake and alert,
another piece of startling news, almost as unusual as her being
alone in the apartment, or popping her own hood voluntarily.
Decs are designed to shut down once they're open. They fall into

the hypnogogic twilight, a waking trance we professionals called the *twink*. You could ask them things regarding their repair needs and they would answer without remembering any of it afterwards. But they never initiated conversations.

"No, you won't feel a thing," I said.

From the discreet logo tattooed on an inner fold of her paraderm I noted that she was a Cyrenex product, 6000 series. I managed to suppress a surge of excitement and awe as I reached down into my kit and dug out my Cyrenex adjusted tool roll. I untied the roll and flopped it open with what I confess was a measure of pride, being the only tech at FF who had a complete set of the prized items. To most in the industry they were more a collector's rarity than anything else, since there was hardly ever any call for them. I, myself, had only used them on one previous occasion, and that was a simulated evaluation.

But my excitement was tinged with a flash of irritation. The make-and-model details should have been on the work order. Why weren't they? Why nobody down at dispatch took the time to tell me it was a *Cyrenex* unit – let alone a *6K series* – that I'd be tinkering with, I had absolutely no clue. Someone must've known, though, and that's why they sent me in the first place, the man with the tools for the job. Letting it be a surprise was just one more thing *extra special* about the call. I did my best to push these distractions from my mind. There was work to do, she was wide open in front of me and it was time to get down to it.

I drew my airkey, tapped up the model number, and entered my access credentials. The projection flickered and displayed her specs. I scrolled as fast as I could read.

Well, well, well.

Even among the vaunted 6000 series this beauty was in a class all her own, an Inge-Borghesa-TetX40, the fabled *IBTetX* in the clipped lingo of the decarati. She was custom on top of custom, a full hypertissue superfit from head-to-toe. There wasn't an off-the-shelf factory cell anywhere in her gorgeous frame. Being something of a Cyrenex fanboy, I knew more about their lofty line of exotics than most. I even sat through a remote training module (more out of curiosity than anything else) but I never thought I'd actually come across one, not up close and personal, not in the flesh. This was because the IBTetX was practically a creature of myth. If the rumors were true, no two were exactly alike, they were real *individual* individuals, like fingerprints and irises, each a one-of-a-kind cast of a broken mold. It goes without saying that all that intricate design effort, all the concept-to-incept blood sweat and tears was driven by powerful market forces. There was strong demand in the slender market niche occupied by the few for whom price is no object. And for good reason. Each IBTetX unit was thoroughly and inextricably tagged to its owner, a triple layer imprint that enabled optimal specificity, so as to perfectly attend to the owner's private and inscrutable set of needs and desires.

Cyrenex was only the finishing house for this sultry and seductive work of art, the final assembly breakout for whatever micropod, chop shop or ejeet atelier she came out of, the details of which I wasn't going to find in a casual perusal of the specs. Designers at that level prefer anonymous notoriety to outright fame. They don't want to be found *too* easily. And yet, the realities of the business model meant they had to be findable by the right people, customers, benefactors, the ardent and wealthy appreciators of the most inspired of works. Unfortunately, if the right people could find you, the wrong ones could, too. Such was the lot and quandary of a superstar dec designer.

The subject sighed, demurely, almost inaudibly. I was taking too long.

"My name is Agrafena," she said. "What is yours?"

"No names," I blurted, too quickly, and of course too late.

"My apologies, I did not know that was one of the rules."

"It's not a rule," I said. No, there's only one rule. But with the introduction half made it was openly rude not to close the loop. "The name's Garl, ma'am, Garl with a G. It's best if you would proceed to clear your mind."

"Clear my mind … not such an easy thing to do."

I selected a 40-watt idolator and probed for hot spots. With luck, I'd pick up the pace, make short work of the repair, and be back in the van and on my way down home within the hour. ParisGC was a nice place to visit, but I didn't want to stick around any longer than I had to. Besides, I was getting a strange feeling of urgency, one I couldn't place, which meant it was time to get the job done and get out.

"Somehow you do not seem …" she said, her voice trailing off.

"Don't seem what?"

"You do not seem like a *Garl* to me."

I had an urge to move around in front of her and let her see the name stitched on my uniform. Instead, I bit my lip and kept on task. It was best not to engage in this kind of banter, especially with a unit of her qualities, unpredictable, mysterious, dangerous qualities.

Don't converse, do the reverse.

Don't do more, effect restore.

"No, you seem much more like a … *Ben*," she added. "That is not insulting, is it, to suggest such a thing?"

Struggling to concentrate, I chose not to answer.

"Tell me, would you mind very much if I called you Ben?"

"You can call me whatever you like," I said, as genially as I could muster, and kept working my line, moving faster now.

"My friends call me Grushenka, or sometimes Grushka, or

even Grusha. And given our, how shall I put it, proximity? I certainly hope that I can call you a friend. Are we friends, Ben?"

"Sure, we can be friends."

"Do you mean that?"

What was I supposed to say?

"Sure, I mean it," I said.

"That makes me very happy to hear that, Ben. Tell me, as a friend, do I seem like a Grusha to you?"

"I've never been good with names." My vision suddenly blurred and I blinked to clear it. What was happening to me?

"I do not believe that for one second," she said. "I suspect that you are very good at every single thing that you do."

I wasn't finding any simple deviances, or anything else wrong in her mains or secondaries, and that wasn't good. It meant this wasn't going to be a routine fix, not even close. And with no client around to tell me what it was that required fixing, it was up to me to figure it out. I re-checked the D.O. cheat sheet. There had to be something useful on it. But it was all standard stuff with one diagnostic call out: GM-1. General malaise-1. The code was as run-of-the-mill as they came. It was a catchall that by itself told me nothing because it was supposed to be listed in combination with one or more other codes, for one or more *specific* issues. I scrolled deeper into the specs, searched for clues, anything that might help me piece together what it was I was supposed to be doing. For a second I thought I was actually getting somewhere, but then I saw something that made the hairs go up on the back of my neck, right up on end, the full sizzling tingle. She picked up on it, too. Sensitive equipment always does.

"Are you all right, Ben?"

"Yeah, um … I'm fine. Listen—"

"Grusha."

"Grusha, seeing as how you're trying to help, you wouldn't

happen to know why your gen-specs are encrypted, would you?"

"Gen-specs? Encrypted? … I am afraid that I do not understand."

"Uh … nevermind."

Why I even asked such a question was a mystery in itself. I was forgetting my tech fundamentals. Units were designed not to hear things that might bring on an existential crisis, caused, say, by auto-referential neuronal stripping brought on by stupid questions about encrypted gen-specs. Induced psychosis was almost never the fix the client wanted from a Fant Fixers house call. What was wrong with me? And why were the deep specs not accessible? There were too many open questions, with not nearly enough answers. My best move, right then and there, would've been to grab my kit and bug out. But instead I soldiered on. Maybe I already knew it was too late.

"You asked me a question, Ben, but I'm having trouble coming up with an acceptable response …"

"I asked you something I shouldn't have. Ignore me."

I was about to say more, something fake and reassuring, when I had the sudden, disquieting thought that the real reason the client wasn't around to lend me his valued perspective was that his corpse was lying in a pool of congealed blood in one of the other splendid chambers in the flat. Maybe she was a *fatale* type (she had the look) but decs weren't supposed to carry out the murderous (aka suicidal) fantasies of their owners. Not all the way out. But then again, maybe that's what was wrong with her. Maybe that's the repair that was needed. The don't-kill-your-owner fix. My very next thought was to wonder if the corpse had a smile on its face, as in, it had all been well worth it. Not a good sign, me wondering that. *Run, you idiot*, some part of me screamed from atop a bucket in some downstreet alley. But the screaming part of me was low in my brain, way down in the primitive regions of the gray meatstick, the parts that always know the right answers, if only we'd listen. Lust is the enemy. Of course it is. But my eyes and hands kept working my line as if nothing was the matter. In desperation, having already broken the first unspoken code of the good dec tech, I decided to do more, and see if I could solve the mystery of what service I had been summoned to render.

"Ma'am, why am I here?"

There was a long pause.

"You are the repairman ..."

She said it matter-of-factly, her voice uninflected, as if it were all the answer either one of us should need.

"Yes, that's true, it's just ..."

"Just what, Ben? What is wrong? Tell me."

"Wrong? I didn't say anything's wrong."

I blinked and, just like that, I had activity up and down the line, the bands of my idolator lighting up like a Christmas tree. Whole sectors were popping, when not one second earlier every tab on the nuplex was nominal, latent, quiet as death. I used an interleaver to do a metacat redex and bleed off some of the stray-node kDz, but that caused Riggs oscillation, then tensor instability, which is never good. I tried to compensate down line but that sparked Riemann-Bhosarian blowback, which qualifies as a full-blown problem. All of a sudden I couldn't keep up with the fireworks. In the famous words of Marcus Vranes, the most famous dec designer who ever lived, in his infamous training HOVO for first-year techs (*Unit Repair No-No's*): "Once the plex devolves into a kDz noval state, what you have on your hands is a Hammurabi Hailstorm, which means, dear colleague, it's time to pack it up and go home." But I wasn't ready to give up and go home. It was the classic HH I had going, all right, but it came on too fast, way too fast. How? It didn't make any sense.

The subject hunched over her knees, gripped her legs and moaned. Not a sound I wanted to hear.

"You said that I was not ... was not going to ... feel ... to feel ..."

"You're not supposed to *feel* anything. None of this should be happening."

I reached into my kit and pulled out my resolver.

Somehow she sensed that, too, and she knew what was coming next.

"No, Ben! Do not resolve me, please do not do this! It is not the answer. You know this."

I hesitated.

Don't solve, resolve ...

I lowered the hated thing and jammed it back into its holster, wondering ... *was this my last mistake?*

She shuddered.

"Help me, Ben ... oh ... oh, please ... please help me!"

She gasped and moaned again, longer and louder this time. Then her neck and back closed up in front of me, the facets and flaps folding and tucking themselves in, sealing up her mysteries. It happened so fast I barely had time to get my tools out. Trembling and hyperventilating, she turned to face me. She tried to say something, and from the look on her face whatever it was it was damned important, too, but instead of speaking she clutched herself, hard and low, and lurched right off the chair. I caught her in mid-air and eased her to the floor where she convulsed, wracked by one spasm after another until − quite suddenly − she went still, her back arched, her body rigid as steel. Her mouth was open wide, lips locked in this perfect square O, as if she were frozen in the penultimate instant of agony, or ecstasy, or some cataclysmic collision of both antipodal states.

I leaned over her, cautiously, to check for a pulse and make sure she was still breathing, and right then ... that's when she went Samson Gorilla on me.

Rat City

I was in deep. That much I knew. But I figured I could handle it. Maybe I was in denial, but I figured I could handle that, too. I just needed the right perspective is all. Looking down from above, you know there's a thorny issue to contend with, sure, but you're on it, in fact you're all over it. You got this. This sort of cowboy confidence came naturally to me. I'd been in some tight corners in my day, yet somehow I'd always managed to wriggle my way free. The trick, as I saw it, was not to lose your frosty. You had to hang in, and stay loose, let the attitude see you through. This was how I chose to see the little situation that I found myself in.

After the job up on 3-Frame, I did four more service calls on four different levels, then caught the ML back down to 69. On a normal day, it was an hour and a half commute from the mega-lift waygate to Rat City, but tunnel traffic was surprisingly light and I made it back in fifty minutes. I dropped the work van at the motor pool garage, settled hard into the saddle of my Harley and lit out for the Lem Bar. This was the usual routine. Like most techs, I needed to unwind after a long day under the hood, and the Lem was our unofficial clubhouse, the place we pros converged and congregated for an after-work pop and the gossip of the day. It was the rare happy hour when somebody didn't have a crazy war story to share around.

On the way, I enjoyed the rumble of my bike between my legs, sucking in deep lungfulls of Rat City's greasy, unscrubbed air and relaxed for the first time all day. One by one, I passed my favorite haunts: Verna's diner, Proletariat Pizza, Mangy's gym, the Sit'n'Spin, Richlin's conveno with its flickering neon sign for Kickin' Chicken. I blew past my own crumbling apartment building and, as always, I shot a look back at the old *Torridreemz®* hot box on the street below my window. It was an out-of-date vDrome unit, with its big, fat footprint taking up way too much pavement and the faded, swoopy-font graphics like a throwback off a throwback. Old-school pleasure tech to say the least. The ancient fant coffin had probably been there since the last days of the infrax crews, it was the kind of street model people hardly seemed to notice anymore, and almost never used. And yet, the happy light on top was spinning. Occupado! Jesus-H., somebody was actually in the godforsaken thing, paying good nucoin to escape reality through synapse-sizzling n-feed. Will wonders never cease? I had an urge to kick it around the block, and make a close pass just to be sure my eyes weren't deceiving me. But the events of the day took up all the space in my fragged head, so I rode on, hit the gas, and to the comforting growl and pop of my straight pipes I let the rest of the town slide past me in a blur.

I wouldn't go so far as to call Rat City home. But somehow I knew it was as close as I was ever going to get. Years ago, while on a magtrain out of High Center (I have no memory of what I was even doing up there) I was seated next to an elderly zone planner. Normally, I don't talk to seat mates on trains, but he spoke first, and in the exchange of pleasantries, I revealed my destination. The Rat. The old guy smiled in recognition. Told me he worked the deep zones back in the day, and according to the regional core plan, Rat City wasn't even supposed to exist. It was supposed to be a no-name substation in the tunnel arc between New Fargo and Black Meadow, and would have been just that, if not for the massive gas explosion that carved a gallery right out of the substrate. It was a bad accident, he said, but it happened back in the glory years of Exploratory Reclamation, when such incidents were commonplace, and it was decs doing all of the work and most of the dying. They were the early-version 2000s back then, of course, and it was all about progress in the end. So long as it didn't impact the bottom line, or derail a project, nobody much cared. A smudge on a ledger and a minor mishap in the great unilevel subterranean scheme, the ever-steady march of One Destiny. As the planner told it, his dig teams moved on, with the road and power crews following close behind. They chiseled away and drove deeper, and in the huge hole they left behind, a tent city sprouted, lean-tos, huts and hootchs, then push-up buildings, real brick'n'mortar banks, barber shops, fastfood and whiskey bars, it covered the ground like some fungal bloom, the tendrils of development stretching and spreading until they occupied the available space. And for a time the place thrived, a little boom-boom town in the wake of the *Prow of the Future®*, until it was left farther and farther behind to become what it became, and aptly named. But that was a long time ago, ancient history, in fact, and aside from an aging planner, nobody much remembered, if they ever knew at all. These days, the Rat City I knew and loved didn't thrive so much as it scratched and subsisted in that giant hellhole, where it did only one thing well, it survived.

"G-Narly!"

My eyes hadn't even adjusted to the perpetual red midnight of the Lem Bar when Hana called out to me. There was a good crowd going, but she held our usual spot at the bar with one leg straddling my stool. Hana was my best bud and one of the top techs in the business. There wasn't much she hadn't seen. She was also incredibly hot, by anyone's standards of hot, and I was the only person in the whole FF office, among those inclined toward attraction to the human female form, anyway, who hadn't made a move on her. It was the basis for our early friendship; she liked me, and liked that I liked her without it being a ruse to get into her coveralls.

"Where the hell you been, Prudence? I'm one big beer and two shots in already. Ain't like you to fall this far behind this early."

"Look out below," I said. "Here I come."

I caught Patch's solitary eye and raised two fingers. Patch was the owner of the Lem and he worked the bar himself. Nobody messed with Patch, at least not without dire Cyclopean consequences.

"One of those days, huh?"

"Not anymore," I said, and fired back the first shot just as Patch finished pouring, and relished the cactus burn going down. He glared at me, briefly, and poured the other.

"Whatever story you got, G, gonna have to be good to top the freakshow I rezo-ed on 22."

"Bring it," I said.

She looked off, her eyes slipping out of focus as she gathered the details.

"Picture yourself on my last call," she said.

"Dispatch saved the best for last?"

"Like they do. So here's me, I got my rubber monkey open wide, in him up to my flippin' elbows, when, quite unexpectedly, I feel a strange sensation."

"Uh-oh."

"My reaction exactly. But it's real tender-like, right down there between my knees. So I pay it no nevermind."

"You're focused."

"Laser."

"A true professional."

"There's only one me. But there it is again, tickly, workin' its way up my inner thigh. So I pull out from under the hood, I look down, and sure as shit, plastic boy's got a prick like an anaconda, an extremely flexible anaconda."

"Please say no."

"Yes, sirree."

"Not a Trunkshow," I said.

"With a capital T."

Trunkshow Johnson, in the pidgin of the tech world, was a male unit Bias-Gittes came out with a few years back, so nicknamed because they came with the standard option of a prehensile member. Everyone wanted the novelty option. It was a design feature ahead of its time, way back when, but like so many of the vanguard innovations of those heady days of discovery, the first couple model years were real lemons. Techs cringed at the thought of working on a Trunkshow.

"So I tell him, knock it off, wingnut," she said. "Well, I might as well be talkin' to the wall, 'cause dickboy is down."

"He's out cold."

"Twinkin' and winkin'."

"Like you want him."

"Like he's supposed to be. Except peter pumpkin eater did not get the memo. It's up and at'em, bright-eyed."

"Bushy-tailed?"

"Bullwhip bingo gettin' friskier by the second."

"Frisky's a problem."

"Frisky's always a problem. So I push it away, it comes back. I shove it again, one eye's at my doorstep. Me?"

"You?"

"I'm back under the hood, working my line, but banjo peckerwood just won't quit."

"That had to be distracting."

"I ain't no snake charmer, G!"

"I'll vouch for that."

"Shut up. I got a situation, here. I reach up and snatch the first thing I put my hand on."

"Hammer? Cleaver? Brick?"

She shook her head.

"A ping pong paddle."

I laughed.

"No way."

"Kid you not. I'm like—*smack!* And this ain't no love tap, I hit that beanpole hard. But all it did was encourage the sucker."

"Yikes," I said.

"Yep. Unit's a hit-me-baby custom on top of his everything else. Mister jester wants more hot slappy action. Which I give him, only this time, dipstick hornsicle smacks me back."

"Oh no he didn't."

"We're game on, now. Me tryin' to resolve his defunctified ass with one hand, and with the other it's match table tennis with Tallywhacker the Saltwater Chub."

I cracked up. It was a classic tale.

"It was touch-and-go for a little while," she said. "But I slammed the prick home, got my job done and got out."

"Another happy customer?"

"Another happy customer."

We clinked beers. I tossed back my second shot and signaled Patch for another set up, then stared off into the purple glow of the juke box.

"All right, out with it," Hana said.

"Huh?"

"That was good material."

"Good as it gets."

"Then you should be on the floor beggin' for mercy. Cough it up, numb nuts. What's eatin' you?"

I took a long pull off my beer, and despite knowing that I shouldn't, I decided to level with Hana.

"Today ... well ... I had a deal."

It was bad, I knew that much (I mean, I pretended not to, with the B.S. about me not losing my frosty, and all) but I didn't know how bad until I saw Hana stare right through me with this totally blank expression. After an unnerving eight seconds, at least, she coughed and glanced casually down the bar to check who might be listening in. Seeing the rest of the gang engaged in their own stories of the day, their drinks and jokes and wild laughter, she drained her beer, set the bottle down on its side and slowly twirled it on the bar, one full time around, then another.

Having a *deal* was tech speak for forgetting the rule, for losing your objectivity about the subject, for giving the equipment the upper hand, for letting the enemy win. Having a *deal* meant you were just like every average ordinary lustful sap in the world, you were a mark, stupid and gullible and needy enough to actually fall in "love" with a pleasure model. We techs were supposed to be different. We were supposed to rise above, and when you couldn't do that, you were worthless to the industry. Having a *deal* was almost always a career buster. The best you could hope for was an ignominious rotation back to the home office, some menial desk job, the rest of your life spent in a cubicle processing service requests, or sending orders over to dispatch. And that was if you were lucky. Most techs who had a *deal* were fired the very next day.

"Oh crap, Garl Motts, not you ..."

That's how bad it was. To Hana I was always Prudence, or Cupidwrench, or G-Narly, or plain old G., never my real name, never Garl Motts. Which meant, in her eyes, I was already one foot out the door.

"When? Where?"

"First call of the day. Way up on 3, of all freakin' places."

"Who else knows?"

"Nobody but you, and the subject, of course."

"It happened on the call?"

"Partly, not really. I left the building, I think. I mean, sort of."

"You think? Sort of?"

The truth was I was in a bit of a fog about what exactly happened.

"I left and I went back."

"You went back? Never!"

"I know."

"Never ever go back!"

"Never."

"Never!"

"Ever."

"Never ever!"

"Never ever."

"Stupid."

"Dumb."

"So dumb."

"Stupid."

Patch must've picked up on the negative energy in our little stretch of the bar, because he set down two more beers and a liter of Kadavra® tequila, grabbed the dead soldiers and turned away. Hana waited until he was out of earshot.

"So what was it that did you? Was it a dude, a chick, a tran, a whatnot? Tell me it wasn't fuzzy. Please."

Hana hated fuzz and fur.

"It was a chick."

"Old? Young?"

I shrugged.

"Somewhere in the middle."

She eyed me in cold appraisal.

"What do you know, a plain old lady dec for Cupidwrench Motts. I always figured you for more interesting trade. Sorta disappointing to hear you're just a vanilla-ass dork."

"That's me, I'm 'fraid."

Her comment actually hurt my feelings, which was surprising. I guess I really was a mess. Techs, even the best of buds, tended to avoid the subject of their own orientation (there being so many) and any related exxtra-curricular activities. It was bad form to bring it up, because even talking about it swerved too close to the line none of us could afford to cross. So even my best friend Hana didn't know very much about me. Not that part, anyway. The subject of my preferences only mattered now that I'd crossed the line. She looked at me and shook her head, real sadness in her eyes.

"She must've been somethin' special, this dec bitch, to get to you."

"She was."

Hana's brief lapse into compassion flashed in disgust.

"You fucking moron."

"She's an IBTetX," I said.

Hana froze, then let out a bitter laugh.

"Right."

"She is."

"What, are you telling me that *you* have class, that you suddenly developed *taste*, on top of shit for brains?"

"No, I know better than that, H. But here's the really weird thing."

"Oh, the *really* weird thing."

"She wasn't some random exotic lupa some rich guy had made for himself. I know how crazy this sounds, but … it's like she was waiting there."

"Waiting for what?"

"For me."

Hana swiveled on her stool, turned full at me, no trace of humor left in her eyes. I could tell she wanted to scream in my face, so I appreciated that she kept her tone conversational.

"*Waiting* for you? An IBTetX custom-ass bitch is just sitting there, in ParisGC, waiting for you? As in, what, she's tagged to you? This *nobody* repair geek from Fant Fixers down in ratfuck Rat City? How's that gonna happen?"

"Hell if I know."

"You tell me."

"I don't know."

"It just ain't gonna happen. That's the answer. It ain't. And it didn't."

"I know this all sounds a tad off the wall."

"A tad, boo? Off the wall? It's off the freakin' channel!"

"I shouldn't have told you."

"Well you did. Too late for that." She stared off down the bar, refusing to even look at me. I'd never seen her so hacked off. "I s'pose you think you're gonna get through this with attitude, right? Not gonna tell the company. Just gonna gut it out?"

"That's pretty much the plan."

"That's the plan?"

"That's the plan."

"Here he sits, the man with the plan."

"I can handle this."

"You can handle this?"

"I can."

"Sure, you can."

"I can."

"That's what they all say, G. That's what each and every one of them all say."

The Booty Dharma

We were both T5s, senior dec techs, but for some reason, Hana had more tug down at dispatch than I did. She always had. All it took was one quick text from her and she set the whole thing up. We were going to be partners for the rest of the week, just like it used to be, back when we rolled together as greenstick rookies. She made up some lame excuse about wanting to get checked out on my custom tool sets. The truth was, she had as many odd-ball tools as I did, it was part of why we were so tight. We were both nuts for exotic equipment and fanatical collectors of the impossible-to-find sets you needed to get under the more custom hoods. So if anybody had been paying attention down at dispatch, they would've known her request was pure B.S. But paying attention wasn't exactly the strong suit of the geniuses in admin. Nobody even questioned it.

The next morning, we showed up at the motorpool, with our commuter mugs and our kits, and for the first time in years, we walked side by side to the same van. Funny thing is we both headed for the driver's door, since back in the day I did all the driving, but that was then, this was now, and Hana was having none of it.

"You're the problem child," she said. "I drive."

I nodded, my nose slightly out of joint, but what could I say? She was right, I was the problem child.

Hana's plan, such as it was, came together after she heard my own stupid idea of a plan over last call shots in the Lem. Hers was simple and straightforward, the way all good plans are, and it was this: she wasn't going to let me out of her sight, not for one nanosecond. So when we tore out of the dirt lot behind the Lem, me on my hardtail and Hana behind the wheel of her old Ducannon, she followed me home, cruising three inches off the road the whole way, her front bumper on my rear wheel like she was stuck there. She parked in my building garage, chained my bike to her car and crashed on my couch. With her head propped on my favorite cushion, and her eyes already half closed, she tied it all up in a bow.

"If we're going to nip this thing in the bud, the next 48 hours are critical," she said. "You just need to put some time and distance between you and the wicked hoodoo spell that 6000 series bitch put on you. You'll get her out of your brain, once we leech her out of your head, that's when you'll be free and clear of her fucked up mojo."

"Brain, head, fucked up mojo," I summarized. I thought she was asleep, but Hana lifted her head off the cushion and squinted up at me.

"You just watch, G-Narly. I'm gonna save your sorry lovedrunk ass."

Our first service call of the new morning certainly satisfied the distance part of Hana's equation. Dispatch routed us to the outer edge of our territory, a two-hour run just to reach the location. The client was a frequent and preferred customer of FF. His name was Clive "The Mangler" Galloway, an ex-professional cage fighter of modest fame, he'd been the manager of the Booty Dharma in Filter Rapids for as long as I could remember. These days there were Booty Dharmas popping up all over the place. It was a highly successful, mostly reputable chain of casino-strip-kyabakura clubs that spread-eagled across the ore patch from Redetroit to New Perdition. Each location was a full-service establishment catering to the johns, janes and whatnots who couldn't afford a dec of their own. Practically every dust hole town and pissant subjunction has one on its backtrack. The Mangler's Booty Dharma was bigger and grander than most others I'd been in, though they all stuck to the same tried-and-true formula: a central game floor that's basically an enormous labyrinth where the clientele could genuinely get lost, and frequently did, all while their senses were blasted mercilessly. The walls of the maze were the slots, alternating row-upon-oblique-row with rattling pachinko machines, forcing patrons to zig-zag their way toward the buzzing center, where the rows got shorter, bent inward, curved outward, and delineated semi-circular aisles where the gambling devices intermingled with soundproofed couples bars and private rooms tucked here and there between *Sens-U-Riders®*, *Squeeze Pods®*, other hot boxes and v-dromes of countless variety with offerings catering to every imaginable proclivity. There was even an old *Torridreemz®* of the same vintage and styling as the one outside my building, which was a real shocker.

As we approached closer to the central hub, we passed the islands of high stakes tables and, situated strategically above and around them, the mini-stages equipped with pop lifts that brought the menu-selected pleasure models up from the tech levels below. Once on station, the decs pole danced, lap danced, swiveled hips, whipped hair and writhed in various stages of undress and lasciviated pose, and all the while the nucoins chimed, chips clacked, jackpots dinged, sirens whooped, and every face in the place was bathed in a garish, pulsing neon glaze.

All of that was to be expected, but what I couldn't abide was the constant onslaught of ads, pushes, and hard-sell-sex. You couldn't take more than two steps in a Booty Dharma without a holo-me hawker leaping into your carpeted path to coax you into one trashy fantasy or another, with 'hot' dreams priced for every pocketbook.

What puts the shang in Shangri La? Find out, friend! This way, this way!

You think you've seen tits? You hain't seen hooters 'til you've seen these mongo-balloongahs!

Come quick, chiquita, or you sir, we've got a Bernardo. He just got out of jail and he want you … HE NEED YOU! …

The cut rate HOVOs crackled and buzzed out the second you walked through them, only to be replaced by the next flickering vision of tattered decadence.

Hana and I had been in the Mangler's Booty Dharma so many times we barely noticed the sensory blitz and so we never broke stride across the floor. But this time, I couldn't help but feel a jolt of pity for the average customers I passed, marks, every one of them, hapless punters and companion-starved suckers of all persuasions who somehow wandered into the Mangler's club only to be dazzled by the lights, the booze, the cheap flesh and the endless tales of tawdry possibility. Most of them were human (human still counted for something) fresh off a team train from somewhere in towards the core, or on R&R off a deep rig or some distant job site, with a few days to kill between re-ups and a fistful of payday cash. Heaven only knew what depths they would plumb 24, 36, 48 hours later, when they finally emerged, bleary-eyed, headspun and dead broke, stumbling back out through the pleated vinyl doors into the permanent morning light. Whenever I found myself on a Booty Dharma call, I couldn't get out of the godforsaken place fast enough.

Hana and I reached the center of the slot maze and a dec hostess came up and greeted us (she was a brand new Marvex Shay) and she guided us to the far side of the main stage where the Mangler was waiting. With a wave of his huge hand he motioned that it was too noisy to talk, so he led and we followed

him down a caged ramp that led into a tunnel, past the dressing rooms, break rooms, the pop lift staging areas, the lockers
and maintenance bays that made up the bowels of the club. We
ducked through the costume area, rounded a bend and came to
the armored door of Clive's own executive suite. Two hulking,
human bouncers eyed us suspiciously as we approached, but with
a nod from the Mangler, they let us pass without a bioscan or
even a pat down. Now that's some trust.

"Goddamn, I'm glad to see the cavalry arrive," Clive said,
as we entered the serenity of his inner sanctum.

"But yo, I didn't ask for no double coverage. I ain't gonna
get charged twice for this call, am I?"

"Two pros for the price of one today, Clive," Hana said.
"It's double-team Tuesday."

Clive grinned, flashing his famous mangler grill.

"Love my freebies. And it could be a good thing you showed
with backup. This wig might just take the two a'yous."

"Is that so?" Hana replied.

"Let's just say, I'm frickin' countin' on you two had your
Wheaties this morning."

Clive was no newb. He'd been around the block more times
than most FF customers put together. *Wig* was tech speak for
an extremely twerky or poorly-refurbished dec, units that could
cause all kinds of trouble, or simply weren't good for business.
Worst of all were the kind that scared people.

He led us past a wall of security cam monitors to a door in
back that I'd seen on previous calls, but had never gone through
and assumed it to be the gateway to Clive's executive shitter, or
possibly the club safe, or maybe both. The door didn't have a
scanner or code pad anywhere on or near it, just an old-fashioned keyhole below an antique door knob. Clive took out a big
brass skeleton key that hung on a leather thong around his neck.

He pulled it over his head, slipped the key into the lock, gave it a crank and heavy gauge bolts retracted all the way round the frame. It was old-school security, the kind of door that wasn't openable by digital means, especially not by anyone on the outside, like W.A.L.T.E.R. in some DarXec snoop op or, worse yet, some 400 pound hacker kid from the DBs. The only way to be sure it was safe was to hold the only physical key in the meathook of your own hand, a real flesh-on-steel guarantee. Clive hauled the slab of a door open and we saw that it led not to a vault, but into a dank, concrete corridor. He entered and we followed him past a row of dark and empty holding cells.

"Jesus H., Clive," Hana said. "What are you running here, a Booty Dharma or a max-sec lockup?"

He turned to Hana with a look of mild bereavement.

"Since when did you get so judgmental? I need a place to put rowdies and creeps, that's all. The diligent manager must be prepared for any hospitality-related incident, especially when it takes TLE forever to respond to house calls." TLE, Tri-Level Enforcement, a Xec subcontractor with a very shady rep.

In Clive's last creep tank down the line, the only one that was lit, stood a solitary female dec. She was in the center of the cell with her back to us, and stood with the perfect prim posture that was a factory default in, say, a high end domestic unit, not an exotic dancer in a low-frame club. Her hands were clasped in front of her and she wore a long, plain dress of an Amish or Mennonite style, with elbow-length sleeves and a peter pan collar, her head covered by an Old Order River Brethern bonnet. I recognized this last obscure detail only because of a job I'd done that involved some period-correct adjustments for a very particular fetishist over in the Wongmarket Bowery. It wasn't something I ever expected to find in a Booty Dharma.

"Angelique, these are the repair folks I told you about.

They're here to help you."

"I told you my name," she said, without moving.

"Your name's Angelique, and I'm going to get you fixed up so that you can get back to work."

She half turned, enough to see that her face had flushed with anger. That was unusual in itself.

"My name is Hester, and I don't require fixing."

Even in profile, I recognized right away that she was an 808 series, one of the *Galloping Goddess* models that Chromus-Chace pumped out by the thousands every year. I'd serviced plenty of them in my time, we all had, and you couldn't get any more straightforward than her type. To begin with, the 808s only came with a handful of options. For the gender female, you had skin tone, height, hips, cup-size, figure ("athletic" or "cushy"), eye color, hair color, hair length, pubic hair (shaved or bushy), voice and breath flavor. That was it, everything else came standard. The age was always 22, sexual orientation set to universal. 808s didn't even have an attitude calibrator.

That was the weird thing about the presenting unit, the distinct note of attitude. I'd never heard of an 808 saying that he, she or it didn't require fixing. The hallmark of any Chromus-Chace product was its safety-and-consistency guarantee. Safe-Con®. It was right there in the jingle of the commercials you heard ten times a day, the stupid little song that got stuck in your head.

Safe-Con made, Safe-Con's great, go with the best, go Chromus-Chace.

If an 808 wigged, which happened more frequently than the company wanted people to know, the ailing unit would do a soft shut down. It was an automatic. Threshold filters kicked in on any paraemotive response exceeding the standard deviations. You could bank on it. So when we got called in for an 808 it was always a recal-res, a recalibrate and restart. The one thing

808s didn't do was go and develop whole new personalities and change their names, and they definitely didn't espouse modesty or find religion.

As I sifted through these thoughts, the Angelique-slash-Hester slowly turned round to face us and glared at Clive. She'd sewn a big red *A* on the front of her dress, and seeing it Clive clapped his heavy hands together.

"*A* is for Angelique, there you go, girl. See? You do know your own self!" He chortled, baring his big metallic grin, as if he'd just solved the *Level Up*® riddle.

"A is for adulteress, fool," she said.

Clive's grin went all lippy, and he raised his hands in a helpless gesture.

"See what I'm workin' with. She was one of my best earners, too, until she came up the pop lift looking like this. She even sunk her teeth in a customer when he tried to pull that headdress thing off."

"It's not a headdress, you imbecile," she hissed. "And I didn't bite him hard enough."

"Good thing for me the chooch was so turned on he thought he paid for the extra action. Obviously, I went ahead and charged him a biting fee. But that was a close call. I can't have no more of it. I'm not gonna get sued by some Deep Co. union steward. Look, once in a blue moon I get a jackweed in here wants a school teacher, or a librarian, or a nun in that habit and shit. But here in knucklehead-ville that brand of kink is very rare, and there's zero call for this, this, whatever she is."

"Plain," I said.

Hester glanced at me in surprise, as if she wasn't expecting anyone to understand. Then her expression changed. She stared at me, intently, with a look I can only describe as a combination of shock, sudden recognition, and an almost instantaneous effort to hide these reactions. I didn't know her, beyond the make and model, and I was very good with faces. I remembered every dec I'd ever worked on. But in that one look I was certain that she thought she knew me, and not in some casual, offhand way, either. She took a step toward the bars. I thought she was going to say something, but she seemed to think better of it and pursed her lips, as if determined to keep whatever it was inside.

"All's I'm sayin'," Clive said, "Is I don't want to have to do a *schedule* here. So I'm seriously hoping you two can work your FF magic and put her back like she was."

A *schedule* was shorthand for what happened to decs who couldn't be resolved. Technically, it meant scheduled for a FR3, a factory-return-for-refit-and-repair, but everyone knew that automated assembly plants like the massive ones Chromus-Chace operated had no time to perform repairs on defective units. Time is money, after all, and *scheduled* units were never heard from again.

"We'll see what we can do, Clive," Hana said.

Hester's eyes flicked to Hana, then back to me. In an abundance of caution, I averted my own so as not to meet her gaze head-on. But with the 808s it wasn't much of an issue. Most techs weren't susceptible to their bawdy, pole-dancer charms, and this one wasn't making any effort to be charming. Not in the least.

We approached the cell door.

"Open it up and give us a bit of room to work, if you would," I said.

Clive pulled out his master key, unlocked the cell and stepped back to the wall. The Mangler actually looked a touch nervous.

Hester stood her ground.

"If you try to resolve me, I'll scream."

Although she was staring at me when she said it, I got the strong impression that she was talking to my partner. Hana ignored her. "I'll take this one," she said. "You got next."

Hester stepped close to the bars, her eyes still locked on me.

"I want him. I won't complain. I won't make any fuss no matter what you do to me, so long as it's him, and him only."

I glanced at Hana and shrugged.

"Looks like it's me, partner," I said.

"You sure, G?"

"Yeah, I got this."

I pulled the heavy steel door open and entered the cell.

A Little Me in Hester

We had a busy day after we left the strobe-blinding, flesh-jig-gling pulse of the Booty Dharma. From there we went up to 36 and an easy recal-res on a Rebel Cause 900 leather stud for a stylish geezer in Havana Lovedo. Then it was on to a straight-up resolve job on an old-model Metrixa Sugar Girl at a dingy casino called Kenny's Palace in Boxcar Beach on 44, way out at the end of the boardwalk. On the way we grabbed a quick bite at a food truck we both loved called My Outrageous Pink Taco, then it was back to Filter Rapids for a call at a private residence, a libido check on a CC Clonus Color-Me-Badd Hari, which went surprisingly smoothly given how those jobs could eat up a whole afternoon, especially with a jukey Hari on your hands. The last call of the day was a GZS-cell change out on a Bias-Gittes male, a custom mod, lightduty construction chassis with High Plains Drifter styling, a unit B-G marketed under the name Cliff Spring-er, but of course we knew and loved as none other than a Trunk-show Johnson. It was a funny coincidence, seeing as how Hana had recently played and won a ping pong match with a dec just like him. So I didn't argue when she offered to take the lead on the cohabitual cowboy. Besides, I needed time to meditate on the message I'd received on our first call of the day.

It happened while I was in the holding cell in Clive the Mangler's back-office gulag. I had Hester's hood popped (the 808s were flex-c-open and split-lateral in the lumbar region, very handy for ease of access, always a plus) and I was working to diagnose the problem and, with any luck, reverse her new-found modesty and turn her back into Clive's top-earning go-go dancer, Angelique. I was making good progress on the fix, when the specs I was perusing suddenly flickered and went dark. In their place, a hologram appeared and nearly shattered what fragile poise I still possessed. It wasn't the fact of a projection inside Hester that blew my mind, I'd seen HOVOs in decs before (sometimes you even got ads in those body cavities, which was really aggravating). No, what got to me was that the glowing hologram inside her was *me*, a tiny vision of me, right there in front of me, looking up at me; and the message he/I delivered was for me, from me, to me.

"Be cool …" he/I said. "Whoever's with you, they're watching. And even if they're friends, you can't trust them. Right now, you can't even trust yourself. Oh and, you might want to keep doing whatever it is you're doing, so they don't think you're suddenly prone to talking to yourself."

I did as I was told, and pretended to keep working, noting that the hologram me was better dressed than I ever remembered dressing. He also looked younger and was apparently in better shape, too. I couldn't help feeling a twinge of jealousy, however bizarre that might sound given the circumstances. But seeing as how I was already contending with some pretty heavy personal issues (vis-à-vis nascent/forbidden dec crush) to have a "winner" version of myself suddenly show up and start giving me advice from inside the torso of a repair job wasn't exactly what the doctor ordered. Especially when the doctor, my partner, was clocking my every move for any sign that I might be backsliding. On that note, it was just pure dumb luck that from where she stood, Hana couldn't see the little emcee that I saw on the stage of Hester's thoracic cavity.

"I know you got a lot of questions racing through your fucked-up noggin right about now," the diminutive hologram said. "Like who is this little fucker who looks like me, or how is this possible, or maybe you're thinking it's some kind of trick, some special-delivery mindfuck. I don't care. I'm not here to coddle your lobotomized ass, or try to convince you that I'm legit. For one thing—we have no time. So listen up, *Garl*, and take what I give you or leave it, it's your call. The message. Here it comes. Wait for it. Some important people inside the Xec apparatus, high-level, dangerous, extremely nasty people, know everything there is to know about you, your past, your present, your future. They *think* they do, anyway. What they don't know is they're missing some key information along that timeline. Right now, the way things stand, they're convinced that everything is totally under control. But when they find out what's happening to you – and they *will* find out – they'll realize that they were dead wrong, and they'll come after you with everything they've got. To fuck. You. Up. And that means me. You, me, whoever "we" are, they're going to *do* all of us, and collect the volume discount. We don't want that, now, do we?" When I didn't answer right away, the little he/I scowled up at me. "Nod to yourself, like you just found whatever's wrong with this twerky 808 you've got open here." I did as I was told, I nodded, sagely. "Good," He/I said, noting my response. Very sophisticated HOVO. Not cheap. "Now, there's only one way to prevent the getting-fucked-up part of your/my future. Find Grusha. Get with her, A-SAP. She can help us. Go where she tells you to go, do what she says to do and who knows? We might just pull this out of the hat." The little sharp dresser shrugged and his image crackled. "Well, that brings us to the end of our broadcast. It's time to snap out of it, my brother, time to wake up—or we both go down. The race is on. *Go repairman, go.*"

The image sizzled, popped and was gone. In its place, Hester's specs appeared again, a blur of scrolling CC metrics, as if they'd been there all along, as if the whole interlude was just what he called it: me talking to myself. I briefly considered that I was not only backsliding (per Dr. Hana's concerns) but that I'd already slid, slipped and fallen all the way down into whatever dark hole sanity goes when it has no plans of coming back, no return ticket, no trail of bread crumbs. But I had no opportunity to ponder this thought, or the freaky message from the mini-me, because my idolator suddenly lit up, along with Hester's whole biotree, bright and hot as a Taylor Screw on a redrock run. It happened just like it did up on 3-Frame, just like with *her*, except a Chromus-Chace 808 is no IBTetX, I had no chance to try a metacat redex, and Hester didn't go Samson Gorilla or get anywhere close, because her whole nervos overloaded, and before the Hystrom bolus even had a chance to skein, the displacement went asymmetric, then retrograde, like a wobbling mass of luminous lemon jello, it collapsed and imploded to a bright yellow pinprick, 20,000 kDz down to zilcho and poof in no time flat.

Hester sat up straight.

"I'm plain," she said.

And that was that. She shut down on me, all the way down, hard black. There was nothing I could do but watch it happen and stare down at the sad little heart-shaped tattoo on the back of her hand. I closed her up and put my tools away. It wasn't possible to do a cold start in the field, not with the lightweight kits we carried, which meant Hester had officially become more expensive than she was worth. If a unit did a hard shutdown it was an automatic schedule. And though Clive was none too happy about it, he took it in stride, he was a businessman, after all. In his big, smashmouth scheme of things this would be but a minor fiscal fubar. As we were on our way out the door, with Hester in tow in a trom bag on NoG lifts (reclamation for schedule was part of FF's Gold Customer service package), the Mangler was already on the horn to the nearest Chromus-Chace dealership, checking on his warranty status and asking what they had on the showroom floor. With luck and perseverance, he'd have another 808 Angelique, a Leesha, or a Joseen on the pop lift doing lap dances for C-notes by happy hour.

But it wasn't Clive's problems I was worried about.

For the rest of the day, even while trying to keep my over-stuffed Outrageous Pink Taco from exploding hotsauce all over my uni, I replayed the strange message over and over in my head, backwards, forwards, trying to dissect its message on each pass. Assuming that I hadn't imagined the whole thing and, assuming further, that it wasn't some bizarre set up, or worse yet, some elaborate prank (there were a couple of tube-famous pranksters among the tech pool at FF) I had one overriding question. What in Jesus H. was the little hologram trying to tell me? I knew my own past well enough to know there wasn't some vast swath of time that I'd spent lounging around in designer suits, respectable footwear and annual-salary-costing watches, all while making mortal enemies of people in the upper echelons of Xec (in my spare time, no doubt) or "getting with" sultry-eyed Inge-Borghe-sa call girls. The fact was, I didn't know anybody in Xec and (surprise, surprise) I didn't want to. Hell, I didn't even know the name of the thug cop in crapdunk Rat City whose palm I greased every time he caught me speeding on my Harley. The little me said something was *happening* to me, and he made it sound like whatever it was, it was happening in the here and now. But the only thing I could figure was any different about my life from any other wonderful day, or week, or year, was my recent *deal* with the very dec female he was urging me to "get with" (assuming, further still, there wasn't more than one IBTetX named *Grusha* that I was supposed to run into in the world of my wanderings). Which meant that I'd either already *got* with her, and as far as I remembered (as far as recall in those situations can be trusted) she hadn't told me to *do* anything, or go anywhere, she didn't give any advice, or offer anything else, besides going Samson Gorilla and having an orgasm that nearly broke the floor (and me) (best not to think too hard about that ... yeah, better not to think about *her* at all). So as for mini me's precious advice, *getting* with Grusha only served to mess me up. Beyond that conclusion, I didn't know what to make of it. Though it didn't take a great leap of the imagination to know what Hana would have to say if I was stupid enough to tell her. So for my first smart move in a long time I kept my trap shut.

I stood there and watched while she made short work of our last service call, the riled-up wrangler of a Trunkshow and his look-alive lariat of a Johnson. Faster than you can say re-cal-res Hana was packing up her kit, and we were back in the van, leaving another happy customer in our dusty wake. Unfortunately, once we merged onto the UB, traffic slowed to a creep and it was stop-and-go all the way back to the ML, two solid hours until we reached the Rat City limits, and we still had Hester to deal with, her shutdown body a lumpy shape in the trom bag in back. So we made a quick detour and dropped her at the morgue. It wasn't a *real* morgue, of course, calling it that was just another bit of tech gallows humor. What we called the morgue was in reality a poorly lit loading dock on the back side of a nameless warehouse on Runciter. We all knew full well what went on in that warehouse, though nobody liked to think too hard about it, not any more than you absolutely had to, and it never came up in conversation. What was the point? With the package delivered, we pushed on into town, dropped the van at the motor pool and at long last found ourselves in the cruising comfort of Hana's '46 Ducannon where I fully enjoyed the *blub blub* of its Magnaflo® jets, with genuine TesterPac® rumble. And though the two of us hadn't spoken more than three words between us all the way home, now that we could practically taste that first ice cold beer, the mood lightened and the Lem Bar was just ahead. Hana looked over at me with a knowing grin.

"You didn't think about that dec bitch once all day, did you, G-Narly?"

I hesitated, for maximum effect.

"Think about *what?*"

Hana cackled and punched it: *blubblubblubblubrrrRAAAWW-WRRR.*

So, I'm Having This Dream …

I don't dream much, not that I remember, anyway. When I wake up there's nothing there, not a moment, not a face, no ghosts or echoes. But this one particular dream was so razor-line clear and lasting, I couldn't get it out of my head. I don't want to come off sounding all histrionic, but it really was more than just plain memorable, as dreams go, anyway. It was so real it was like it wasn't a dream at all, even though it had to be.

But I'm getting ahead of myself, here.

Before I had the dream, I did something I shouldn't have done, several things, in fact. It started after happy hour with Hana at the Lem, both of us in fine form, loose and laughing like old times, until last call, when I slipped four milligrams of Procoma® into her last shot of Kadavra®. Two would've done the trick, what with all the tequila we were freighting, but I needed to be sure. Hana was my best friend in the world, maybe my only friend, and the last thing I wanted to do was slip her a mickey. Friends don't knock friends out cold. But I couldn't see any way around it. When we first took our stools at the bar, I tried, I really did. I assured her I was out of the danger zone, and she agreed. The spell of the high-plate bitch was broken, she said, busted up, mojo dead, my *deal* behind me. So I told her I might as well go home alone, but Hana said, No fuckin' way, Jose. She insisted on seeing her prescribed plan all the way through, taking me home again, crashing on the couch again, camping in my hip pocket for the rest of the week. It was a labor of *un*-love, she called it, and she wasn't about to let up on me until she was absolutely positively sure that I was cured, over it, over *her*. *In the clear*. I didn't have the nerve or the heart to break it to her that I was a lost cause where *un*-love was concerned. Who knows, maybe I still clung to a shred of hope myself.

I cut the timing pretty fine, given the dose I slipped her, because as usual Hana insisted on driving and the Procoma® took effect about half a second after we pulled into the spot in my building garage. She got the car stopped, at least, reached for the kill switch, but slumped onto the console instead. I carried her to my apartment, got her cozy on the couch, then went back and borrowed her Ducannon for another spin. First stop, the Fant Fixers branch office on the other side of town. The place was locked up tight for the night, but I had a key and a balaclava, for the cams, in case anybody arrived in the A.M. hopped up enough on morning java to actually take note of the after-hours entry log. Not much risk of that, since nobody at FF cared in the first place, and I was cautious not to do anything that might arouse suspicion. All I did was use Big John's authenticator to reset the 3-Frame access codes on the work order I still had from my service call up top. Then it was back in the Ducannon, cruising fast in the nocto light, where I made excellent time to the ML and was back up on 3 inside the hour. Back in ParisGC.

A Xec cruiser did pull right in behind me and tail me for a block or two, but when my codes checked out, and given the lateness of the hour, I was more likely some important person's intimate liaison than an unauthorized access. The aged Ducannon worked in my favor, being so totally out of place, so wrong, so obviously *not* belonging that it *had* to belong. At least that's what I figured the cop was thinking, and it must've been close to right, because the cruiser swung off me and disappeared down a side street, and I was left to flow at great speed down the Champs-Elysees-Nouveau. Not that I had any idea what I was going to do when I reached my destination. I worked up a couple half-baked ideas, but they fell apart in their respective mental dry-run stages. Jesus H., if I couldn't even think up a way to circumvent security systems in the lobby, how was I supposed to make it to the elevator? And actually getting inside her flat seemed ridiculously impossible. The building was like a fortress. And what about Bernie the doorman? What was I supposed to tell him? Back for some midnight repairs? Don't worry, I'm a professional? And if I did somehow manage to get inside, and "get with" this Grusha? What then? What was I supposed to say, or ask, or do? How was some dec courtesan supposed to help me when she was the cause of all my problems? It felt like it was all some kind of sick joke I was playing on myself.

With that thought I was jolted by a sudden suspicion that the hologram messenger me inside Hester really *was* me, an inventive hallucination conjured by my subconscious, in order to spin an explanation just crazy enough to convince me (the sane me) to engineer a way out from under Hana's watchful and protective eye, so I could beat a path right back to 3-Frame and the luscious lap of the femme fatale who now owned me, body, mind, soul and any other parts that mattered. Quite obviously, even harboring such a thought meant there was no sane me left. But some *me* had driven me to this reckless end, and come morning, after I lost my job and my only friend, and found myself in restraints in the rubberized interior of a white van on my way to The Pines, Rat City's favorite, best kept and only loony bin, I would at last receive all the electro-shock treatments and heavy-duty anti-psychotics that I so clearly deserved.

But all of my frantic ruminations on faulty plans and fears of madness turned out to be for naught, or at least inconsequential, for when I turned onto Belle Epoque, her street, the first thing I saw was the criss-cross of police tape and the laser wire everywhere. The building lobby was dark, with piles of shattered glass, broken bits of furniture, picture frames and pulverized masonry, all neatly shoveled and swept up into dusty heaps at curb side. This was 3-Frame, after all, where appearances must be maintained. Although the entrance was sealed off by the black-and-yellow tape, a matrix of lasers and flashing Xec pop-ups *warning warning* that this was a Restricted Area, the building itself looked perfectly normal (though with no sign of Bernie). It wasn't until I stopped the car, set it down on the pavement, got out and looked up that I saw the reason for the barriers.

The whole floor where her flat had been was gone. In its place was a blackened ceiling above cavernous dead space and the twisted curls of heat-warped rebar. It was a well-executed job, as far as that sort of thing goes, which was apparent in the minimized collateral damage to the upper and lower floors. The structural and load-bearing beams were untouched, merely stripped naked, as if readied for cleaning. The apartments above and below hadn't even suffered cracked windows. The blast was focused, surgical, and utterly devastating, precisely and only where it meant to be, a full layer removed from a tiered cake without so much as a smudge to the frosting. I stared in total shock even as I mused that the aftermath was entirely predictable. Xec investigators would do their poking around, but they'd see (had already seen) the signature stamp of a professional hit, and with no actual crime scene left to investigate, it would be easy to find nothing in the way of leads, and a whole lot safer that way, too. Some cases didn't lend themselves to cracking. Besides, it wasn't even a homicide if the victim was a dec, only aggravated property damage. And if there was no deep-pocketed client around to press the matter (and I certainly hadn't found any sign of one) the investigation was already DOA. Building contractors, salivating at the prospect, would be in with their bids before the tape came down. They'd repair, renovate, and two months later, the bright white smiles of realtors would show a sparkling new flat. As if it never happened. As if she never existed.

I looked down at the nearest pile of bombed-out refuse, and there on top, in plain view, was the embroidered back of the designer settee she propped on while I worked on her ... while I walked her right into a hailstorm ... worked on and fell for ... fell for ... no ... I didn't fall because there was nothing to fall for. She was gone. And I could now be cured because she was gone.

She was gone ...

"Hello, there."

The voice was behind me and I spun around to find its owner standing closer than I liked, but he had his hands out in an open-palmed gesture of friendly, non-weapon-wielding innocence.

"I didn't mean to startle you," he said. He wore a fedora and trenchcoat, and for a second, I thought he might be one of the Xec investigators, lingering after-hours for some classic return to the scene urge of the criminal mind. But Xec agents didn't come at you empty handed. Whoever he was, he wasn't Xec.

"Who are you?" I asked.

"One might ask you the same thing." He cocked his head. "Do you mean to say you really don't know?"

"If I did, I wouldn't have asked."

"The name is Tang, Gavin Tang," he said, emphasizing the last name as if I should recognize it instantly. I didn't. Again, the innocent hands were right where I could see them. He paused like that, and eyed me, as if finally, really seeing me.

"No, no, my error, entirely, I'm 'fraid, I mistook you for an old friend." He looked up to the black chasm of destruction two stories up. "Though it is perhaps coincidental that we have a mutual acquaintance, a female of studied charm and exquisite countenance, who resided very near the epicenter of that remnant of a conflagration."

I stared at him and he stared back.

"I don't know any females on this frame," I said.

He blinked, and quickly smiled.

"Then, regrettably, we have no tangible connection whatsoever. Good night, sir."

He raised his hat, ever so slightly, and walked away without looking back.

I exhaled, realizing I'd been holding my breath. I pulled the car door open and slumped back in behind the wheel and got out of there. I made it back to Rat City without incident, apparently, though I don't remember anything about the drive, nothing but the tunnel lights, dripping into me through the smear of the windshield. I parked the Ducannon in the building garage, taking care to chain it to my bike, exactly the way Hana would've done it. Somehow I had the presence of mind to do that much. In my apartment, I stumbled down the side of the hall that didn't creak, past the couch where Hana lay softly snoring, and to my own bed where I collapsed. All I could see, on the road, on my feet, in my bed, was Grusha, her face, her eyes, her lips, and now she was gone. Blown up, obliterated, out of my life forever. Who would want her dead? And why should I even wonder why? How could I possibly know a thing like that? I didn't travel in those circles. I didn't know the first thing about her *real* artificial life, not about her business, or her owner, or her debts. Still, I dwelt on it, my head a spinning reel of questions, and phantom answers that led to more idiotic, unanswerable questions, until I was senseless and empty, turned inside out. I closed my eyes and that should have been it, exhausted as I was, it should have been a night of sleep like death (I really *was* that tired) but it wasn't. And this is where the promised dream kicked in.

Indeterminate passage of time.

I was up and back in the hallway without remembering getting up or moving at all, I just ended up there. My apartment, being a boxcar layout, had a long stretch between front door and living area, with no closets or windows to either side, just a plain corridor with cracked walls, peeling paint and an old sealed off heat register. It was simply a passage, to and fro, and I never so much as hung a picture or gave the stretch a second thought beyond the footsteps needed to go from one end to the other, until I found myself standing in the middle of it, staring at my boots and feeling very wide awake for a guy who knew he was sound asleep.

Then the scene shifted (I know this sounds strangely convenient, but that's what happened). One moment I was in the hall and the next, in a blur of motion, I moved into the wall, through it, somehow, and into another hallway. This other space was the same length as the corridor in my apartment, only half as wide. It dead ended in the direction of the front door, so I went the other way, made a sharp left, then a right, and proceeded down a steep set of stairs illuminated by tiny pocket lights. As I descended, I noticed that in place of my work boots I wore shoes, brogues, expensive ones from the look of it, shoes I'd never seen before in my life and certainly didn't own. I ran my hands over the quality material of my trousers and suit jacket, a tailored shirt and tie. Though I couldn't see the clothes in the dim light, I knew (just knew) they were the same designer duds the little hologram me sported inside Hester the scheduled 808. Maybe the clothes do make the man, I thought, as I walked and noted that I carried myself with a suave confidence that Garl the repairman did not possess. It was the walk of a man who had somewhere to go, something important to attend to, the sort of man who thought time was money.

The stairway ended at a landing with a door that swung open at my approach and I was on the street, on the lonely side of my building, all brick walls and caged windows. The old *Torridreemz®* hot box was up ahead on the corner. I used the whirring, clicking jalopy, from time to time (I admit). FF rules encouraged techs to bleed off "tension" in impersonal ways. *Where there's no want, there's no need.* The manual actually said that. But, in the moment, I was curious as to why the sharp-dressed me was headed right for it.

Normally, you inserted nucoin or flashed a credit card at the scanner to open and enter the form-fitting bed of any vDrome unit. It's what I'd always done. But not here in dreamtime. In dreamtime, the clamshell-like box opened on its own at my approach. I ducked to get in and lie down but before I could there was another jittery blur, things in motion, me in motion (I know, I know, ludicrous, lame) but when the dream world slowed to normal again I wasn't in the box at all, instead I stood at a threshold, a simple, cut-out doorway, over which hung slender cords of amber beads, a fragile, iridescent barrier that winked and reflected a rippling light from whatever was on the other side. Parting the beads I passed through.

Going in was slightly dizzying and disorienting (even by dream standards) especially with all the *exiting, entering* and *blurring* through this's and that's. Here I felt I should be on the "inside" of a place, but instead I stood outside, at the edge of a manicured lawn to one side of a large, angular house, with a flat, overhanging roof, the structure below all glass windows and steel beams. I vaguely recognized it as a Neutra house I'd seen in a HOVO once, though I seem to recall that the famous original stood somewhere in the hills and chaparral canyons in the Mulhollandia theme park overlooking the urban sprawl of Reprocity on 9-Frame. But

I knew I couldn't be on 9. Could I? I focused on my immediate surroundings. At the edge of the lawn, there was a swath of patio that led to the blue glow of an infinity pool, beyond which stars winked in a perfect night sky (a little too perfect to my taste) and I walked across the lawn to the patio and looked out at the city lights, an oblong smear of sparkling jam in the distance far below. And then I realized why it was too perfect. Even in my dream the city wasn't real. But it was good sim, very good. Good enough to make me think it might be real, which seemed a strange bit of detail for any dream. I followed the patio around the pool and I was suddenly aware of her. I hadn't seen her, at first, where she stood so still she nearly blended with the night. She was at the rail at the edge of the rocky drop-off, facing away and staring out at the same starry view, her bare shoulders softly rounded in a backless dress. Who else but her? ... *Grusha.*

Absurdly, I considered averting my eyes, the way a good tech should, and even patted my pockets, instinctively searching for a tin of NOF gel. But then some smarter, cooler-headed part of me thought ... *What the fuck are you doing, dummy?* She's already got you, man. What more damage can she do? Besides, she can't be here in the first place, not really and truly, not in the flesh, because this is a dream and, let's face it, the girl is dead. You saw what's left of where she lived.

I kept walking (to my credit, I thought) approached her, my heels clicking on the tiles, and though I knew she heard me, she didn't turn. I stopped behind her and eyed her figure. How was it that he described her, the mystery man on 3? (Gavin Tang, he called himself): A female of studied charm and exquisite countenance. She was every bit of that, and more. Formidable. I think I even said so aloud.

"It appears that the clothing does not make the man," she said. "You were you. You were my Ben, coming to me. I *had* you.

And now look at what has happened. You have gone away and left me again."

I didn't have the slightest idea what she was talking about, or how she could even know all this (whatever it was she was talking about) since she wasn't even looking at me when she said it. She spoke as if she were talking, not to me, but to the night itself. The sim night, anyway. Then she did turn. And when her eyes fell on me, I sensed behind that gaze a sudden and desperate hope, an almost explosive yearning (this is what I took her expression to mean, mind you) but as those eyes searched my face, the hope (or whatever it was) drained away. One perfect brow arched and tears welled in the place of searching.

"I have power over your heart. You feel my power, I know you do. Tell me that you feel it," she said.

I nodded.

"I feel it, I do …"

"You are a poor liar. Another sign that you are not my Ben."

I badly wanted to be her Ben. And I did feel something, like some part of me was knocking, pounding on the door, but whoever he was I wasn't letting him in.

"If you feel it, how is it that you resist me? Explain this to me," she said.

"Lady, I wish to god I knew."

She shook her head, dismissing my words, as if we were speaking two different languages and, try as she might, she couldn't make me understand a word of hers. So instead she stepped closer, and the perfume of her, her skin, her hair, her, well, her everything-about-her enveloped me for a brief, heavenly, land-of-silk-and-whiskey kind of moment. I even caught and savored the impossible sweetness of her breath.

She reached out and took hold of my wrist and coaxed my fingers open until my hand lay flat, as if she were about to perform some bit of palmistry, some prestidigitory act. But instead, she pointed to a tiny blue dot in the center of my hand. It had always been there, I never gave it much thought, always figured it was just a mole or a birthmark. But then she opened her right hand to show me the identical mark on her palm. She hovered her hand over mine, raised it, and in the space between them a HOVO image sprang to life, merging in the center, like two halves of a broken crystal, rejoined. It was a shimmering sculpture in light—Mauro Skarpenthia's famous *The Entwined*.

The split HOVO was a cheap trick, a bit of devotional body art you'd see on a daily basis, lots of different shapes and versions. It was the sort of thing young lovers did together when drunk and giddy ("Let's get tattoos!") then duck inside a 3-D hink parlor to pick out matching designs (*The Entwined* was a classic) (cliché, even) and kiss sweetly while the tabs were lased (though rarely on the palms) (far more frequently they were zapped onto other, nether body regions) so that when the lovers emerged again, the perfect intimate secret was theirs alone. Hink art only materializes when one tab is aligned in precise proximity to its mate. The surprising part, as I stood at poolside under a gorgeous sim night with an Inge-Borghesa-TetX40 who wanted me to feel her power, wasn't the hink itself, it was that we shared such a secret. But then, dreams can be weird that way.

Her gaze shifted from the glowing image to me.

"Apparently, you know me better than you think."

I swallowed, and let out an insipid little laugh.

"I'll have to admit it's pretty hard to explain," I said.

The look in her eyes shifted.

"Who would you explain it to?"

"Good question."

"You must come back to me, my love. I will die without you."

"Ma'am, I, um …" I stammered.

"You know this, within yourself you know it."

"I'm not sure how to put this, but, uh … I think you're already dead."

She snatched my hand up, the hink between us fizzled and disappeared, as with her free hand she swept her dress aside, exposing a magnificent breast (the left one) (I think) which hung like a pendulous, creamy fruit of some as yet unknown genus. She pulled my hand to it, pressing it firmly to her flesh, the rigid nipple and the startling softness of the mound it nestled in. She held me like that, pressed to her until I felt her heart beating in the delicate hollow of her chest. Her lips parted, as if she were about to speak, but gasped instead, softly and breathlessly. A tremor ran through her, as if this one touch, our skin-to-skin, pulse to heartbeat contact, nearly overwhelmed her.

"Does this, do I … feel *dead* to you?"

I had to admit she didn't.

We stood there like that, long enough for the moment to become awkward, and I realized that she was waiting for something. She stared into my mouth, expectantly, but then sighed, with a profound sadness in her lidded gaze.

"Even now you do not feel me … not as I feel you."

What was I supposed to say?

"Tell me," she whispered. "Can the repairman repair himself?"

Suddenly, and I mean lightning fast, something changed, like there was a part of me who stood outside and behind the loser who stood there with his hand pressed into the bosom of this insanely beautiful woman, gripped there, *by her*, all but literally clutching her heart, and in that switch the other me didn't want to be detached anymore, didn't want to focus on technical thoughts and observations, he wanted to be there, really *be* there. I felt him force his way in, battering down the door, like the real me invading the fake me (or vice versa, depending on the perspective) and with his jarring intrusion, or extrusion, or psychic intervention, everything in me came together in wanting her, wanting to pull her close, closer than close, wanting to taste her lips with my whole mouth and breathe her in, her entire body, wanting to inhale every atom of her being, and right then and there, really and truly (all at once) *get with Grusha*.

I mean, Jesus H., what the fuck good is a dream like that if you can't do that kind of stuff *in* the dream? It's worthless! And worst of all was me, being the worst part of a worthless dream. Because even as this massive wave of want crashed through me I couldn't bring myself to act. I stood there like a vestigial limb. I honestly couldn't move. It was like there was a force field surrounding me, *protecting* me (for lack of a better ridiculous word) from the other me, my better self and his desire for her, keeping us both from connecting with her in every hot-monkey, Samson-Gorilla-worthy capacity that my billion cells screamed for me to unleash.

I had a sudden, pitiful urge to try to explain all this to her, to convey the gist of the bizarre predicament we found ourselves in, and get it across that it wasn't her (not at all) it was my fault, I was to blame (or part of me, anyway) (but the whole me would take the fall) yet before I could utter a single word of this, or even draw a breath, the dream world shifted. Grusha, the house, the pool, the view, the whole vignette was ripped away like a magician's cloak, and I was alone again.

Behind the wheel of a large automobile, driving somewhere else (somewhere fucking else) in the night. I was still in the grip of the vision of her and of my longing to be with her. But I recognized and accepted that I was in another segment of the dream, and even in the dream I knew that I wasn't driving *to* her. I was driving away from her. It was a cruel trick, but at least the vehicle I was driving was upscale. It wasn't Hana's old Ducannon this time, it was a car I couldn't have afforded in a thousand lifetimes on my FF salary, a make and model I recognized only because I'd once joked with Hana it was the whip I'd buy if I won the GloboLotto®, a real dream car, an Aston Martin Aqualine. But even in the supple confines of a luxury sedan I wasn't touring some ritzy top plate boulevard, I was still in deepest bumfuck Rat City, retracing the back streets and byways I'd traveled with Hana that very day. I pulled around behind the warehouse on Runciter, entered the dark alley and stopped at the central loading dock, the place we called the morgue.

Another blur of dream motion, and somehow (I don't know how) I gained entry to the warehouse itself. I remember a swipe of card, a click of lock, and I was in, moving again with the speed and confidence of a guy who knows where he's going and what he's doing. Inside, the lights were low and cast a bluish tinge. From the empty workstations, HOVOs glowed in sleep mode. It was the middle of the night, after all (for a dream, this was a strikingly realistic temporal detail, if you think about it) and as I walked I saw no one. I passed through a barrier of hanging plastic slats, the kind used in cold storage to separate temperature zones, then entered the "factory" itself. The place was a disturbing combination of medical lab and industrial facility. There were multiple procedure bays, situated like spokes of a wheel off a central control hub. Each bay had a tilted steel table fitted with clamps, blinking monitors, and tool pods on reticulated arms and gimbals, while under them ran lines of catchment ducts and fluid gutters. Along the periphery walls stood gleaming tanks and translucent carboys of different shapes and sizes, some cylindrical, conical, others with stanchions, stairs and ladders, and all around, a vast array of pipes, hoses, tubes, valves and drains with connecting junctions overhead and below. It was like some nightmarish brewery. But I knew what it was they brewed here. I looked down and stopped, mid-stride, noticing a bit of scalp and clump of hair caught in the mesh of a strainer. Sloppy cleanup, even by horrific dream standards.

I moved on, my pace quickening, as I slipped between rows of open vats full of milky fluids, opaque and swirling, some a sickly jaundiced hue, others a phosphorescent greenish white. After a distance, the vats gave way to pressure vessels with winking status lights, humming gauges and escaping wisps of fume. I passed the open doors of an autoclave and on the far side I came upon a sprawling parts and assembly area, then recognized it was the final *disassembly* area of the plant's workflow, with hundreds of carbon-fiber bones dangling on wire frames and tag racks, femurs, fibulas, tibias, costae, vertebrae, all arranged by size and type for inventory, laser marking and packaging. Beyond I entered a zone where there was an audible bubbling and gurgling. The light was low and purple-hued, and I stopped to let my eyes adjust (another oddly realistic detail for a dream) and then turned to see shelves upon shelves of uniform glass vessels that contained the reclaimed organs, muscle fiber, strands of tendon and eyes, hundreds and hundreds of eyes, all slowly churning and tumbling in gently aerated, temperature controlled saline baths, fed by nutrient tubes and latent biomonitors. The alternating focus in their softly spinning, somersaulting pupils gave me pause, as they seemed at turns to catch sight of me, hold and witness my approach.

Against the farthest wall lay a single trom bag on its own cold table. I reached for the bag's head and unzipped it from there, slowly and carefully, to find Hester inside. She looked cold and dead, until her eyes snapped open and she blinked up at me with a brave smile.

"I knew you would come, sir. I never gave up."

Cave Canem

People and their damned dogs. Holy flippin' fido frick. Every time I did a service call and I thought, hey, it just can't get any weirder than this, I mean, we're talking right out on the freaky, loose-thread edge of fetishistic fringeville, a week or two would go by, and dispatch would send me on a run that topped it somehow, some way, in sheer, eye-punching, whango, out-there, brain-sizzling *whoa* factor; and invariably, it had something to do with goddamned dogs and their demented scratch-happy owners.

When you applied for a job at Fant Fixers, the first thing the company wanted to know wasn't about your experience, or your aptitude, or skillset, or all the fancy-pants tech shit you thought you knew. No, what they wanted to know, right off the bat, were the things you *wouldn't* do. I suppose they figured if you wouldn't do a thing, you couldn't fix it.

The stuff I wouldn't do was an easy enough box to check because for me it was a visceral response. I flat-out refused to work on underage decs. Of course, "underage" was a bit of a misnomer where decs were concerned. Technically speaking, all decs were manufactured to be a certain age, it was purely a matter of design, a product feature, so to speak, and although some models were sophisticated enough to actually *age* in a way that replicated natural human aging, every dec started out brand-spanking new at whatever age he or she or it appeared to be. Hence, a dec kid could be pushing a hundred-and-fifty, while a gracefully aged zaftig milf could be eighteen months old. Only an expert could read the signs of actual age, and even we were stumped from time to time. Now, I know and appreciate that people want all sorts of things, for all kinds of reasons, and generally speaking, I tried hard not to judge. But anything to do with kids, dec or human, simulated or otherwise, it didn't matter, if the equipment even appeared child-like, it triggered my mental gag reflex. I found it to be twisted, the wrong way twisted; hence, underage was one of the two job types I simply wouldn't touch. And so I checked *won't* on that one.

My other big *won't* was snuff (Deathgrat, Able is Cain, the Bathorites, the Nosfos and all their ilk). The idea of getting off on killing, or watching a thing be killed and die, and the further idea that the thing being killed, being artificial, made the act of killing it perfectly A-Ok, well, anything in that vein turned my stomach almost as much as the pedophiliacs and the 'lestors. So, no minors, and no death or dismemberment, those were my two big cross-offs. The point here being, there was a fairly steep downside to all this prudery (long before Hana called me "G-Narly" her nickname for me was "Dear Prudence") said downside being that anyone who wanted a career at FF with those two major blackouts had to work on pretty much every other category of sexploitable jizzfactor you could name (and many that I, for one, couldn't even fathom before I met them face-to-whatnot). We're talking about a sizable range of paraphilias, obsessions, kinks and kooks and the decs designed to match them. It was customized and customizable equipment across a swath that went deep (*very deep*) into the purple and black on both ends of the spectrum.

There were the classic stylized mods, tops, bottoms, switchblades, rabbit ears and antlers (some things just never went out of style), wetlook, latex-vinyl-PVC retrofits, leather, suede, organic strapons, klisma-quipped units (too many pre-accessorized models to even try to name them all), there were somnos, hypnos, morphos, revirgins, weepers, gappers, faux-necro, vapors, channelers, freakish mutantmods, tentacletops (all sorts of tentacle options), exos, tudes, dowagercon, footbinders, pasiphaers, dismantlers, hazmatters, creeps and crawlies. There were the rubbabooties, that noblest of noble street names for the wannabe decs, humans who desperately yearned to become artificial, and the subset who tried in every way to be mistaken for pleasure models, and who (parenthetically) were almost always trans (the whole idea of *trans* has very little meaning, anymore) or cross, and were typically inclined toward the milieu of extreme degradation (but not always) and listed as *plasticusimitatiophilia* in Dr. Flavorian's codex. We FF professionals got those calls too, because of the dec parts they used, modifiers, implants, change-outs, and because so many of the pretenders' deepest desire was to be worked on by a "real" dec tech, a rite of passage of sorts (I surmise) and very often they got their wish, because where there's a will there's a way. We certainly found ourselves servicing them (very polite customers in the main, who almost always offered to tip, which of course I refused as it was against FF policy). There were the DHM, Dentition, Horns and Mandibles, including the fang thing that was big here a few years back, and the furries (always lots of fur) (an ungodly amount of fur, really) (Hana's favorite) animals and animalian mods, large, small, very small, terrestrial, aquatic, mythic, proto-mythic, extraterrestrial probing, and, of course, "other." Working with all these types, including my required *willingness* to work with animals, meant, of course (here I cringe) working with dogs. Dec-freaking-canines and their bowser-lovin' owners. Jesus H.

To be fair, my rant here should not give the impression that there wasn't plenty of plain vanilla in the pleasure dec world. There was (to be sure) and that vanilla was our bread and butter. For Fant Fixers, as a company, as the gross margins were concerned, vanilla was by far the hottest color in the fantasy rainbow, the bright beige sweet spot, the bullseye of the sexual attraction dart board. The same was true industry-wide, where the overwhelming majority of enjoyment-leisure-and-hospitality models pumped out by the Big Three manufacturers fell into the eminently predictable categories. Cheerleaders, proball players, actors, idols, rockers, rappers, royals, pop stars, news anchors, supermodels, "beefcake" and porn stars. There was more ass, tits, ripped abs, bulging biceps, luscious locks and ultra-white smiles in the vanilla swath of the spectrum than you could shake a thick stick at. Practically every service call I made was for a Marvex Brandi, or a Kelli, a Bree or a Gina-Marie, a Bradley, a Christophe, a Domingo, all the famous faces in the rock-bodied cheer squad of the ever-winning Miamicita Profins. We called those jobs *pom-pom runs*. There wasn't a week went by you didn't see at least one Chromus-Chace Anthony Lake, or a Cyberbell Gabriella Strandberg, a Marvex Young Elvis (units the HOVO bloggers liked to call Elvis Repersonators). There were plenty of runs to do a recal-res, or a sensitivity scan, or a straight libido check on the Juan Dongs, the Nikki Zhangs, a Meena Tabu here, a Tyler Morningwood there, and of course, Cyberbell's ultra-high maintenance Miles de Steele, units every bit as twerky and unreliable as they were insanely popular.

But whether the unit was vanilla factory-direct, or an option-ladened custom, there was always another factor potentially in play, an item where the successful tech had to be quick on the uptake. On half the jobs Fant Fixers, Inc. was called out to "fix" the dec in question didn't have anything wrong with it. It was the client who needed the adjustment. You just knew it was going to be one of *those* calls if it boiled down to some lame-ass, technically-vague complaint. The work order usually said it all, that and the tone of Angie the dispatcher's voice when she drawled over the radio ... client says the tits are too soft ... says they're too springy ... too spongy ... too floppy ... too flat ... says the pussy doesn't smell right ... it's too tight ... too roomy ... dry like the desert ... wet like a swamp ... says the butt feels like rubber ... like wood ... like tofu ... like a softshell crab ... says the dick doesn't get hard enough ... it gets too hard ... gets hard then soft again ... says it sproings to a funny shape ... says the body odor is blinding (body odor was always described as "blinding") ... says the hair isn't silky enough ... not curly enough ... straight enough ... long enough ... isn't lustrous ... has no shine ... no body ... no bounce ... says the eyes don't look straight ... don't blink at the same time ... aren't brown enough ... green enough ... they're not true blue ... and, best and most famous of them all: client says the eyes don't stare deeply into my soul.

We'd seen it all, we'd heard it all. We were jaded as all get-out. But seriously, you had to be both an able equipment diagnostician *and* a pretty darned good street psychologist on every call you made, and a polite one, at that, especially if the unit was still under warranty. Manufacturers didn't want their decs scheduled for return for reasons of simple "i-con-specs," a.k.a. individual-consumer specifics, a.k.a. good old reliable human frailty.

On the other hand, it could be a delicate matter to address the heartbreak of erectile dysfunction with a brand new client, or say, the vagaries of a post-menopausal hypoactive sex drive, or worse still, broach the touchy subject of a client's actual needs, and even orientation, not being quite perfectly in line with their habits or expectations or commitments based upon life or purchase decisions. You don't know what you don't know (my hero Marcus Vranes said that). The way I figured it, most times people couldn't help who they were, or where they ended up, or what they wanted out of life. No matter the repair situation, I made a genuine effort to be respectful, attentive, a good solid tech. It

was a matter of pride with me. But that approach definitely had
its drawbacks.

Which brings me back to my dog issue.

One full week had gone by since my *deal* on 3-Frame, and
the bizarre holo-mail I received from the action-figure-sized
me inside the twerky 808 Hester (née Angelique) and my ill-ad-
vised late-night run to see the IBTetX vixen herself (who was
either the cause of all my troubles, or my redeemer, depending
on which *me* you listened to) but instead of finding her, what I
found was a bombed-out flat, then met a mystery man (Gavin
Tang) who seemed to know her well (*how well?*) after which I had
a dream close encounter with the very same *temptress* poolside at
an opulent safe house somewhere below street level directly outside my apartment building (accessed via the tawdry fixture of a
Torridreemz® hot box, no less) followed by *Dream – Act II* wherein
repairman, now dressed to the nines, takes road trip in fancy car
to the dec morgue only to find Hester lying awake and alert in
her trom bag waiting for *me*. Best or worst of all, the dream part
seemed more real than the real part, more like a living memory
than any dream should. The rest of the week was uneventful,
remarkably boring, by contrast. The good news is there weren't
any other dreams, none I remembered anyway, and as good luck
had it, Hana wasn't any the wiser about my nocturnal activities.
So after the week we spent joined at the hip as partners, when
she didn't observe any signs of obvious recidivism, lovesickness,
moonstruckness, whirly-gig-eyes or symptoms of me being otherwise libidinously impaired, Hana pronounced me cured and
I was either blind or fool enough to think she was right. In the
days that followed she continued to watch me like a hawk, but
she gave up doing the guard sleep on my sunken couch and went
back to rolling service calls in her own van. Thus it was that I was
dispatched on my first solo trip as the "new" me. It was an ob-

vious bad omen that the first call to pop up on my FF scheduler was a *dog* job.

The location was at another high-hat address, way up on 10, the farthest up I'd been since my illicit midnight run. 10-Frame was no tony 3, but it was living the sweet life by my deep plate, cave-dweller standards. The building itself was new construction, thick walls adorned with coils of concertina wire on the outside, slabs of crap art hanging in the lobby. It had all the charm of a supermax lockup. I thought I also detected the off-gassing chemical stench of the sort of place lifer cops and Xec brass might want to retire. That should've been another bad sign. Still I went through the main checkpoint, it took freaking-forever, then two more security stops once I was inside the compound, both with bomb-proof glass separation, human guards in body armor and drive-thru scanners. I was half an hour behind schedule when I finally found myself in the elevator.

I got off on the floor I had a service pass for, padded down a corridor lined with green turf to the apartment with the number that matched the number on my work order. I rang the buzzer. No answer. I double checked the address on my butt set. I was at the right place (according to dispatch) and I was about to buzz again when I noticed a crack of light from the lowest panel on the door. I nudged it inward with the toe of my boot and it gave. It was a dog door on hinges, the very sight of which put a knot in my stomach. I glanced back up the corridor, the green turf, the hinged slats in the doors of the other apartments, and it all came together: I was in fucking poochville. But I had a job to do, so I crouched down and eased my beloved client's dog door open just enough to call through.

"Fant Fixers! Service call! Anybody home?"

There was a groan from within.

"In here ... help ... I need help."

Whoever it was, he didn't sound to be in any acute state of panic. His tone was more disgusted than frightened or distraught. His voice was very low, with an unusual growling quality to it, which should've been a tip off. The dog door was sized for a large animal, so I pushed it all the way open and crawled through. Once inside, I reached back for my kit and hauled it in after me. I stood up and remained very still.

Even though the work order said it was a dog job, on the elevator ride I took care to apply a liberal smear of NOF gel under each blow hole, a good thing, as it turned out, but not for the usual reasons. I was in a spacious foyer, but from what I could see around me, and in the adjoining rooms, the place looked more like a kennel than an apartment, and a filthy one at that. You could practically see the sour dog smell hanging in the air. There was no human furniture anywhere in sight, and the few objects scattered around looked like they were custom built for dogs and doggish activities. I cleared my throat to announce my presence. The answer came immediately.

"I said I'm in here goddammit!"

I followed the voice into the adjacent room, which was lit by a single jaundiced lamp. I saw the two dogs right away and looked around in confusion for the owner of the voice, until I realized that he was one of the canines. I'd heard about this sort of thing while trading tech war stories at the Lem Bar, but I hadn't encountered it personally. Not up close, anyway. Most of my wacky dec dog experiences had to do with what people liked to do *to* their dogs, or *with* their dogs, or in the company *of* them, not the few and the proud who went the extra distance to actually *become* one.

Even in the bare light I could see that the fellow had been significantly and expensively modified to the point that he was more Doberman Pinscher than human male. There was heavy facial reconstruction, limb removal and mod replacement, torso-scaping and implantation of a full coat of short black and brown hair, breed-pattern specific. I wouldn't say it was an attractive sight, but it was impressive, if you went in for that sort of thing. *Divine mutilation,* as the Moreauvians liked to call it. Yet for all his carefully constructed visage of canine ferocity, his moxie was being severely compromised by the fact that he was stuck to the hind quarters of his Doberman paramour, having taken her doggy style (of course) and the two of them were wedged in that position under an item of furniture that looked to be some kind of gymnastic vault underneath which, from all appearances, they had inadvertently migrated in the ecstatic humping throes of their amorous gambol and frolic.

"What are you lookin' at?" the dog man barked.

I held my tongue, figuring anything I said would be taken as unwanted commentary.

"Don't just stand there, get this fucking thing off me," he growled.

I always carried an electric screwdriver in my kit, just in case, call it superstition (if you didn't bring it, you were certainly going to end up needing it) and this was that rare occasion when it came in handy. The pommel vault was secured to the floor by heavyduty screws, which meant the good fellow probably hadn't foreseen the possibility of finding himself in an embarrassing predicament beneath it. All I did was unscrew the mount on one end of the vault, which allowed him to arch his powerful back, raise the whole apparatus, sidle sideways and separate from his partner. One of the reasons they'd gotten so inextricably stuck was that both she-dog and owner were wearing choke chains, which had tightened around them in their flailing ardor. I reached to help untangle them but pulled back fast when the female snapped at me.

"Yeah, pro'ly not a good idea," the altered man said. "I ain't gonna bite you, but she will."

He got up with a deep-throated groan, and snatched the chain of his sleek mate when she snarled and lunged at me again. I was happy to see that he still had one human hand, though it was also covered from forearm to fingernails in coarse brown hair.

"What in fuck's name took you so long? We were in that goddamn tie for hours."

"You were my first call of the day. I got here as fast as I could."

"Well that's not good enough. Do you have any idea what it's like, waiting there like that?"

I hesitated.

"No," I finally said.

They stood side-by-side and stared at me with those mean brown eyes, the Dober Man and his dec-Dober-bitch.

"No, the man says, girl. Definitely not my favorite answer."

The elongation of his face into a prosthetic snout made it hard for him to enunciate clearly, especially words like *definitely* and *favorite*, which came out of his curled black lips as if formed around a mouthful of raw gristle.

Effanuhleee … faayboarut …

His mate leapt and strained to come at me, but he jerked her back with a brutal yank on the chain.

"Easy, Tomba, he's just the repairman. He helped us, a'member? Even if he was very, very, *very* late."

He squinted as he eyed me, hard enough that it wrinkled the fuzzy ridges of his sloped brow.

"Yeah … a very familiar looking repairman," he muttered.

I clapped my hands and rubbed them together in conclusory fashion.

"Well, if you don't have any more technical issues, I'd best be getting on to my next call. Once you get behind it can be a real howler to make up the time."

"Did I say that?"

"Say what?"

"That I don't have any more technical issues."

Taaknuckle hishoos ...

"Well, sir," I said. "How can Fant Fixers be of further assistance?"

He took a step toward me, and so did his dog, in lock step, now, right at his heel. She wasn't lunging anymore, but her eyes were focused, riveted and expectant, as if she knew the hunt was on.

"Call Dieter," he said.

"Calling Dieter ..." his home system responded.

"Who's Dieter?" I asked, with the phone warbling over the room speakers, but the Dober Man just stood there.

There was an audible chirp as someone picked up, presumably Dieter.

"Max! How you been, ole buddy?"

"Getting over a bad case of the cramps. Listen, D, you 'member that perp we glassed for months on end way back when, tag-team op with Task Force Torino?"

"Yeah ... dec runner, a real operator, ran his own crew. Edgely was his name."

"Edgely, that's it."

"We had the bible on that scumbag, 'til that fuck Serpas gave us the NFA. Piece of shit still stinks. What about him?"

"He's standing right in front of me."

Yippee-Yo ... Yippee-Yay

It's really sort of surprising, but people still harbor a whole lot of misconceptions about decs. Silly things, lots of times, basic stuff. Like even after decades of co-habitation with artificial lifeforms, you'd be talking to some random guy about something totally run-of-the-mill, like maybe you're wondering about an after-market part for your motorcycle, or standing at a counter ordering toppings for a pizza, and right there out of the blue the ignorance bubbles up and pops in your face. We're talking nutty, baseless, off-the-wall opinions and preconceived notions that couldn't be further from the truth.

Here's one: a lot of people still think decs don't eat real food. Maybe the earliest models didn't, or maybe they could chew but not swallow, I don't know, I've never actually encountered any plasties from the dark ages. Maybe they exist somewhere, hidden away in some private collection. Nowadays you couldn't find a working version of an A200-series, or a Soover ZTZ9, or a GrozziTech Rosella, not even in a museum. The truth is, modern decs not only eat food, most have appetites every bit as big as a proball flanker, sometimes bigger, you just don't see them eating because they don't like to masticate in front of people. I've never heard a good explanation for why that is, probably an app echo, or a soc-filter holdover carrying the preferences of some long-dead DuGrodyne designer who couldn't stand to see his prototypes stuffing their faces, so he gave them a complex about it, a shame response rooted in their need for sustenance and that triggered modesty verging on open embarrassment around the act of eating.

Here's another weird one: a lot of people, mostly kids in their late teens and early twenties (in my observation) firmly believe you can't contract VD from a dec, because, *as everyone knows*, decs are self-cleansing/self-disinfecting units and therefore basically "immune" to all diseases. This was true, up to a certain point, which is what made it such a dangerous myth. Decs are synthegenically designed to counteract a broad menu of viral, bacterial and parasitic afflictions, and although they're susceptible to their own infections and diseases, it's highly unusual for a human to pick up any of the more common STDs, Chlamydia, herpes, syphilis, HIV, HPV, genital warts, the clap, scabies, prangs, crabs, etc. from a dec in any one-on-one sexual encounter. Trouble is, people in the younger demographic tend to pool resources for a good time, say, all the fellas in a fraterment going in sharesies on a Marvex Kelli (or whatever model they can all agree on) so that on any given Saturday night as the turns go round, in what can often be fairly rapid succession, the boys also go in sharesies on their own bodily fluids and whatever else they might be bringing to the party, in what amounts to a practically perfect clinical exchange as, one for all and all for one, they skinny dip in the same frictious plunge pool.

The more abstract the subject matter, the wilder and more certain the opinions surrounding it. Take the ever popular conviction that most of the decs manufactured sector wide were combat models. You'd hear that "fact" expressed with great bombast and authority. It's a total fiction. PCPs, pleasure models, companions and pets outnumbered all other categories put together ten-to-one. Next came food service, then clerical, ag, health care, domestic, the special-option LCAM chassis with feature splits for labor-maintenance-construction-mining, and only after that, way down the list in terms of total physical units, came CCS, combat-crowdcontrol-and-security. It wasn't that DoD and Xec didn't have monster-bloated budgets, they did. But 90% of their production needs were met by factory ship output for development-world applications, which made good sense to the Standing Committee, the resident puppets of the Junta, for a variety of reasons, almost all of them wrapped up in complicated graft schemes, but rendered possible because the evolution of armed conflict had reached a point that it was both logistically feasible and far more economical to enable warfighter unit fulfillment at the tactical point of greatest need. Let's face it, ever since the advent of the earliest TGS Elites there just wasn't much competition anymore, certainly no realistic chance of an uprising, which meant "security" at home had basically become a non-issue.

How and why I knew these things (or cultivated my own cherished certainties) I do not know. It was strange and getting stranger. Disconnected globules of detailed information were breaking off and plopping into the commode basin of my conscious mind with increasing regularity. It was happening all the time, now, and at the stupidest of moments, too. Take just the one example: Here I was with my wrists and ankles zip-tied as I struggled to stay upright in the backseat of a Hunda Tactica® with heavy tints and an almost overpowering smell of dog, mainly because it was being driven (at great speed, I might add) by the Dober Man himself, with his sweet, snarling, chicken-biscuit-loving better half strapped-in up front on the passenger side and snapping back at me over the headrest, all while I tried my level best not to bleed to death from the lacerations her toothy mouthings had already left in the tasty meat of my lower right extremity. The point being, in the dire rear seat automotive and exsanguinating circumstances, you'd think I'd have a few more pressing things to ponder than casual human ignorance about artificial gastronomy, dSTD myths or obscure GLOBO-military-industrial stats, all told a passel of data points most people don't care about, least of all me. But what was even more irritating than finding myself focused on arcane snippets of so-called knowledge, while being abducted by a dog-faced Xec retiree, one who almost certainly had designs on taking me to some rendezvous point with ex-goon colleagues who planned to finish the job they had *interruptus* on way back when, despite my vigorous protestations of mistaken identity in the here-and-now, what really got my goat was the sneaking suspicion that it might not be mistaken identity after all, because the little dickweed prick of a hologram inside Hester's inner works (who claimed to be me) was starting to sound a bit too right about a few too many things, and the recent cavalcade of off-subject info defecating into my brain in vast, alarming clumps, like, say, cute factoid-licious tidbits about factory ship capacities, or combat model output stats, or, say, verbatim transcripts of intercepted communiqués of the Standing Committee and their droning indigestions, or the secret peccadilloes and sexual preferences of an aging oligarch (lovingly nicknamed the Jolly Rancher, no less) or access codes for all the unmanned checkpoints on 2-Frame, or the precise sequence of digits of a fistful of numbered Rivieran bank accounts, or the names and faces of people and decs I'm quite certain I've never met, and coursing through it all like a mean constant, like invasive dark matter, were the endless thoughts about *her* ... lots of wicked, forbidden, entirely inappropriate and unacceptable thoughts about *her* ... the sum of which, *in toto*, seemed like the sorts of thoughts the well-dressed mini-fuck of a laser projection might be entitled to have crammed inside his micro noggin, but not me, not the *real* me. I was just a freaking fucking *repairman*. That was the pisser. What if *the little guy* really was me, except *he* was the one having all the fun?

The practical part of me tried to set aside these ruinous agitations and focus on being the simple man that I was in the straightforward, if distressing, predicament of the present. I was being taken for a ride, no more, no less. And based upon my captor's misconceptions, the destination would doubtless be remote, painful and all-but-certainly terminal. It was in that moment that I had the thought that finally got my repairman back up. I mean, Xec attitudes, extreme canine retrofits, domination, bestiality and bad dog behavior (in general) all of that came with the job. But being screwed over by a client on a standard service call, a client who didn't even have a legitimate fantasy-related technical issue, well, that was just plain unacceptable. The call wasn't even a *special*.

In the final analysis (as they say) I don't know which one of us underestimated me more, the dobey-faced ex-lieutenant, or me, myself (*whoever* I was) but it was readily apparent that neither one of us expected what happened next. Somehow, and I mean, I'm not sure exactly how, in one spasmodic contortion that I genuinely believe I am not physically capable of, I houdinied my zip-strapped hands from behind my back, down under my ass, up behind the toes of my boots and out front, all before Detective Liver Breath had a chance to check his rearview. In the next move, or maybe the same move, I was up and over the back of the passenger seat where I popped the release on the safety belt that held his foamy-mouthed vault partner in barely checked restraint. Now, dogs are good at some things, and just plain not all that terrific at others. One thing a dog isn't great at is any display of equipoise, balance and nimble grace in a moving vehicle. My lunge over the seat happened so fast the vicious animal didn't even have time to bite me before I hurled myself back again into the rear compartment. The dec dobey, now freed of her bindings, scrambled after me, all four legs going in a frenzy of leather-scratching motion. Yelling something or other, her master grabbed for the chain too late, because she was already between the seats coming straight at me, trailing strands of whipping slobber, her whole carnivorous being hellbent on joining me in back, to clamp jaws, thrash neck, and rip and tear me to kibble-sized hunks of viscera, pulp and sinew, all the better to snack on later when the mood was right, which would have happened, except that I popped the latch on the left side door, kicked it open, gave a little hip check to my assailant, and let her salivating momentum do the rest as, with a yelp of doggy surprise, out of the car she flew.

The Dober Man's Tactica wasn't traveling more than a meter or so above the road surface (you weren't supposed to drive any higher than that) but he was moving at a clip that easily trebled the speed limit, it being the Tactica driver's god-given birthright to speed and, as ex-Xec, he could always count on professional courtesy if he ever got pulled over. At that hurtling rate of progress over tarmac I didn't have to look back to see the result of stepping out at such mad velocity. No, I saw all I needed to in those wide, bloodshot eyes of his.

"Oops," I think I said.

My guess is he didn't hear, so riveted was he on whatever ugly somersaulting episode was happening on the asphalt of our dust.

"*Tomba!*"

Hearing the raw desperation in his scream I almost felt sorry for the Dober Man, but there was no time to indulge empathy, traveling at the speed we were traveling, *unforgiving* is perhaps the word that best captures any prolonged bout of distraction on the part of the driver, especially when he's facing the wrong way, howling and cranking the wheel all at the same time. Over we went. Over and over and over. The car rolled fifteen — I tried to keep count — maybe twenty times. It was pure dumb luck that the first time around slammed the back door shut or I'd have been jetsam for sure. But with the compartment closed up tight the experience was a claustrophobe's Chinese New Year, with airbag detonations cracking off, it was damn-near symphonic, timpani to the left of me, tom-toms to the right, volleyed and thundered, with secondary and tertiary panel bags popping and billowing in place of the collapsing first movement. I was punched, pummeled and slapped around by inflated sumo wrestlers in fat-hand gloves, until we flipped the last time, a slo-mo, straight up end over end, and down hard, the car skidding some distance on its roof, spinning one time round the clockface and stopping in a gurgling, clicking, buzzing silence.

Ironically, it might have been better that I wasn't belted in, because as I lay there against the headliner in a powdery tangle of spent airbags, marveling at automotive safety in the modern age, I did one of those mental body checks you do when you just know you're hurt, it's not a matter of if, it's where and how bad. You're braced for the jolt of pain, the spiral fracture, compound and comminuted, the dead flop of a limb connected only by a cord of tendon and a puppet of skin, only to be happily surprised to find that all systems check out A-OK, nothing broken, nothing out of place. The blood that I was alarmed to see smeared everywhere in the glow of the dome light (which had somehow stuck on) was indeed from me, but it was just the bites to my calf and ankle, the lacerations so lovingly administered by the dearly departed robo canine back at Sir Dobey's dog house. Good old oozing puncture wounds, I was almost happy to see them, given the last twenty seconds of luxury car turned industrial blender. So with no fresh injuries beyond a bad case of the spins, I fumbled with my zip-strapped hands, found the door release, nudged the door open and shimmied my way out onto the pavement.

I made a full circuit of the vehicle (hopping, because of my zip-strapped ankles) before I crouched down next to the driver's side window and saw that the Dober Man wasn't as lucky. The pointy-ness of his surgically-shaped head may have been the root of the problem. From the looks of it, he slipped the shoulder of his seatbelt while looking back, so when the rollover started he somehow got his snout caught and stuck in the steering wheel. The *sport* package of a model like the Tactica is designed to allow the driver maximum *feel* and control. But if the onboard sensors detect an imminent collision, or other vehicular mishap, the car's advanced apps take over to try to avert disaster, which was probably how it autosteered with his snout wedged in the column and snapped his neck. From the nasty angle he presented, the wheel had torqued him around at least one full turn. He stared up at me, glazed eyes half-lidded and leering, as if promising this thing wasn't over, not by a long shot, not even close, perp.

I hauled myself up onto the gel-coat of the undercarriage and sawed the zip straps off using the jagged edge of a splintered quarter panel. I noticed the wheels were only half descended; yet another onboard system that performed questionably in the wipeout. The upshot: I wasn't all that impressed with the vehicle's road score, given all the commercials, splash screens and HOVO trax you were forced to endure touting the car's *preeminence*, the famous voice with the UKinc accent, dripping with droll sophistication … *Hunda Tactica, armored sport sedan … security … luxury … preeminence … because there's only one you …*

One thing I was sure of was that I wouldn't be taking the carcass of preeminence on any joyrides anytime soon, even if I could somehow manage to get it upright. *Totaled* was the actuarial term of art. I twisted off a piece of inverter and used it to pry the trunk open. Inside I found and retrieved my FF kit. The Dober Man apparently brought it along to dispose of in whatever shallow resting place he planned to leave what was left of me. It was good to have my tools back. I just didn't feel quite put together without my kit at my side. Feeling around inside the trunk I found a large-caliber handgun hidden in a *secret* panel. I added it to my gear, along with four clips of ammo and a flash grenade. I felt a little nauseous just touching the stuff. I wasn't much for weapons, hell, just the opposite. I was a certified dec tech. I wondered how I was ever going to reconcile having the tools of harm in my kit with the dictates of my Synthetic-Alternate-Hippocratic oath. Especially after what happened in the car. I was now responsible for one dec animal turned roadkill, and at least partially to blame for a human death. I shrugged and packed the weaponry, figuring I'd have plenty of time on my hands to tear myself up over the issue. I breathed in the darkness. The only direction I could see was the stretch of wasteland where the headlights plunged, twin conicoids of light pointed half-on and half-off the highway. The rest of the night was so black it tugged at my pupils as if jealous of their light. I had absolutely no idea where I was. All I knew was that we'd spent a long time dropping on the ML, far enough down there were no road signs or landmarks. The dog man had taken me deep, and if I wanted to find out how deep, I'd have to survive until morning. The Low Flats could be a challenging environment, whatever vehicle you were traveling in. But walking? Nobody walks in the Low Flats. Not for long, anyway.

The Lizard Wizard

I guess I should be thankful. Levels existed way down low that had fully worked up infrastructure, highways, power and sewer, plumbed cul de sacs in developments laid out with community access roads, driveways, house pads, except nobody ever saw any of it, because the simsun never rose down there, never did its slow, diffused arc across the false sky. It was lights out, permanently. There was no need for light. The Dwell Deep land rush was long (long) over, and it was a bust, no more suckers to sell to, the distant dreams of market demand un-ending broken, shattered, the many bubbles popped, their labors dried to flint chips in the silent and empty night. If the dead canine man had taken me down that far to *do* me, my chances of getting out again would have been slender to nilch, and I couldn't know for sure whether he had or hadn't until the simsun either came up or the darkness refused to budge.

It's sort of funny that we still refer to our days and nights by solar cues, *dawn, dusk, sun up, sunrise, sundown, sunset,* even though nobody I know has ever seen the real thing, the genuine nuclear fireball pitching through the cosmos. Stubborn nostalgia and linguistic inertia had us marking our days by the old descriptors even when all that happens on any given plate is the lights come on in an opaque overhead sometimes called the false sky, aka the frame top, aka the ceiling. So I was happy (something of an understatement) to sense the old rods and cones tingling, and I even stopped and watched the oblong blur spike and rise and stretch the horizon. Within minutes the fade up was at full bright, so even in quarterlight I knew where I was. One of the experimental deep-agro projects, a level far enough down to be considered low, but not so way down deep as to be in perpetual darkness.

Great yawning fields pressed the road on either side, hectare upon hectare, as far as the eye could see, and all of it barren, fallow, the gray-stubble of some miracle grain that hadn't turned out quite miraculous enough, or the market failed out from under it, or something else killed it off. All the deep-agro projects were in trouble, had been for years, but the lights still came on, the diurnal cycle and sinusoidal temperature variations kept on without missing a beat, exactly the way they did when the grain, or the perfect earth protein venture was brand new. No doubt it would rain soon, the acidity modulated to maintain the perfect pH. Why lights and water for dead fields? Like so many things that on their face made little-or-no sense, the real reasons had nothing to do with making sense and everything to do with money and power. Like maybe the deep-ag projects were supposed to fail all along, incur massive losses, creating juicy offsets for some zaibatsu's grand tax strategies. Or maybe it was all about making somebody look bad, a blood rival in the lethal game of claw and scratch to the top box on the org chart. Then again, maybe it was as simple as the old standard—it was going to cost more to change things than to leave them be. Why not? Nobody gave a rat's ass about energy use anymore. ViroCon's fixed costs for the whole deep stack were negligible. Once the Junta was comfortably ensconced in its untouchability, the stasis of permanent hegemony for the oligarchs, the old energy wars were no longer necessary, and the tech titans and captains of industry were permitted to release the cold fusion and related discoveries they'd paranoically kept a lid on for decades. Maybe longer. Who knew? Their calculated delay in releasing the technology, though costing billions of lives (human and dec) and cementing billions more in the scrimp cellar of abject poverty, was nevertheless all very wise and prudent and good from the lofty perspective of power and greed. After all, plentiful, dirt-cheap energy way back in the early days of One Destiny could have upset the balance, even toppled regimes, thus discombobulating the proper order of things. But with the advent of the TGS Elite combat series, security was a given and the status quo enshrined. With that sort of fool-proof stability, licenses for revolutionary new tech could be policed, price controls maintained and patent protections enforced. Payment through the customary channels was ensured. With all that in place, it was finally OK to let it be known that near limitless energy could be generated from a single glass of water.

My reverie was jolted by a sound.

My mind had wandered far afield, another stupid fit of abstraction. Here I was worrying over inequities in trans-global, multi-frame economies and a host of other people's problems, the little freak of a homunculus once again trying to run my show, all while the *real* me, the only me that mattered stumbled along on a dusty highway, getting thirstier by the step and not paying nearly enough attention to what else might go wrong.

What *was* that sound?

I spun around wondering how fast I could get the handgun out of my kit. But it was only a tumbleweed, skittering along in a big gust of wind that paralleled the road. Strange that, though. There wasn't supposed to be any wind down on the deep frames, not that I'd heard about, anyway. Fully controlled atmospheric conditions. Still, weirder things had been known to happen. Since there was only the one tumbleweed, rolling and bouncing into the distance, I turned and headed the way I was going, though just as I picked up the pace, so did the wind. It whipped at my back and nudged me into a shuffling jog. At least it wasn't in my face, I thought. But then it swung round until it was directly in my face, then shifted again, a confused blast, coming from different directions. Lightning flashed and there was an immediate crack of thunder. It occurred to me that I was the tallest thing I'd seen all morning, and the only thing resembling a lightning rod anywhere in sight. I considered lying down, that is until I looked back, squinting into a haze of flying straw and grit, and immediately jettisoned the bad information I had received about no wind on the low plates.

As I looked on, the vortex of a funnel cloud arced out of the ceiling and stretched groundward like the tail of some mythic, nasty-tempered beast. The whirlwind dropped faster than I thought it should, as if it had a will of its own, as more lightning burst around and within it. And just that fast the pointy tip of the cloud touched down in a field three, maybe four hundred meters behind me, and instantly it was on the move. It zigged across the road, sliced through a ditch sending a wake of dust flying, then zagged back over the road again, chewed the field over there like a walking drill bit, swung wide, reversing direction yet again, then snaked back and popped up onto the highway. This time it stayed there. There was no more S-turning or veering off. It followed the road, right down the centerline, like somebody was driving the vicious twirling tentacle—straight at me.

I ran.

I yelled as I did, too, something totally idiotic like, *This can't be happening!* though I couldn't hear the sound of my own voice over the howling roar of the wind. I shot a look back only to be startled by how fast the twister was coming on. It was a hundred meters and closing, with no deviation, still moving toward me with an uncanny sense of lethal direction. I dodged left to shake it, then cut hard right off the road into a field, my knees kicking through the dead shoots for all I was worth. I looked back again, relieved to see that the cloud had taken my bait. It whipped left, spun off the road away from me, but only fleetingly, before it changed its mind and swerved around again. It jumped the road to my side and came on, now, fifty meters and closing, no zigging, no zagging, it plowed the dry ground, scoring it deeply as it threw up walls of dirt and bore down on me with craftsman-like precision.

An airhorn bleated. It was an unexpected sound, probably ear-splitting anyplace else, but here at ground zero it was a squeaky whisper over the growling rumble of the storm. In the next second, from out of nowhere, a tracked vehicle sped into view, hopped the lip of a small knoll, cantilevered toward me and cranked sideways, its spinning orange beacon like the halo of an angel. The passenger door flew open and a great bearded face thrust out of the cab.

"Need a lift?"

In my haste to sprint to the open door, the handle of my kit slipped from my sweaty grasp and I dropped it.

"Leave it, man!" the beard screamed.

But a dec tech is nothing without his kit. I reversed course and darted back to retrieve it, but as I reached down, I was sand-blasted by a physical wall of wind. The front edge of the vortex was so close I could feel its sucking tug. The ground caved under my feet, my kit sliding away from me, until I caught the handle, snatched it up and hurled myself toward the vehicle. For one, two, three heart-clenching seconds, I lost sight of the man and his rig in the suffocating churn of the cloud, but then the flashing light was there, the beard, the open door. I clawed my way to him, hauled up onto the track and his outstretched hand. I lunged for it, he caught me and held on in a ripping down draft so fierce I lost sight of him again right there, but he pulled and I jumped and into the cab I flew.

"Mel," he shouted. "Get the door!" The door slammed shut and latched on its own. "Put your spikes in, baby! Go deep!"

The vehicle seemed to know what to do. I felt it settle and hunch, as if burrowing crab-like into the dirt. In the same moment, the storm was on us, over us, driving right through us.

"Hang on, mate!"

I didn't need to be told twice.

We bucked and rocked, the wind screaming around us, and from the tortious bending groans and shriek of the mechanical stresses, I was sure the cab was being torn off its tracks and we were about to take a ride up inside the drain pipe to be splattered on the big top like a bug on a windshield. But the whole time we rattled and shook the bearded guy next to me whooped and cackled with the abandon of a lunatic. Then it was over. The twister passed beyond us and everything went still. We stared after it as it swirled away across the field and a few seconds later flew apart, dispersed to nothing, and the only signs it had been there at all were the deep ruts in the ground and the drifting dust that lingered.

"That's what I call close!" the man said, grinning. He looked over at me, and though his smile held, his eyes were piercing. "Well, I'll be buggered," he said. Before I could respond, he stuck his hand out. "Dave Rambeaut, at your service."

I shook it, feeling a little dizzy.

"Wait a minute," I said. "*The* Dave Rambeaut? The Lizard Wizard?"

He laughed.

"Now, there's a name I haven't heard in many a moon. Right, I reckon so, he was me, and I was he. I think, anyways! No man splashes in the same septic twice, eh? You okay, mate? You don't look so peachy."

"I'm just … trying to get my head around the fact that I was saved from a freak tornado by Dave Rambeaut.

"That was no freak willy willy chased you down out there, mate. That was my burglar alarm."

"Burglar alarm?"

"Twisted, right? Bit of mistaken tridentity, I'm 'fraid. I never would've switched the swinger on if I'd known it was you. You're many things, but you're no burglar."

The dizziness was getting worse.

"You know me?"

He pumped his eyebrows, still grinning.

"Let's just say I know *about* you."

As if to change the subject, he jammed the vehicle in gear and in response it moaned. I don't mean the transmission balked or he ground the gears, but his thrust of the shift lever caused a human sound to emit from somewhere inside the cab. Female, slightly husky, vocalizing a mild protest that was more akin to pleasure than pain.

"You need to warn me when you're going to do that, my darling," the voice scolded.

"Sorry, baby-bushka, I'll be more gingerly."

"By the way, your friend sounds thirsty."

Dave looked over at me.

"That's what it is! How long you been on the highway?"

"Fifteen hours, give or take," I said.

"You got the rasp of parchment, mate! Let's get you back to the station for some low-dration? Are you ready now, boops?"

"Ready, my love," the cab said.

Dave pulled another lever, more gently and persuasively this time, and I felt the vehicle retract its anchors and rise out of its hydraulic crouch. With the roar of a powerful engine, we lurched into motion across the furrows. I glanced around the cab and saw that the dash and steering column, gear levers and knobs, even the bench seat under us, all had an odd, organic quality, as if the whole machine was constructed of sens-trans fibers.

"Jesus H., this vehicle is a Class Six dec," I said, trying not to sound too amazed.

Dave shook his head.

"Oh, no, mate. She's in a class all by herself. Melody, sweetness and lux, I'd like to formally introduce you to ..."

"Garl Motts," I blurted.

"Right ... *Garl Motts.*"

"Nice to meet you, Garl Motts," the machine said.

"Likewise," I muttered.

Dave laughed again. It was a raucous, carefree guffaw. He seemed the happiest man alive. I just couldn't believe I was sitting next to him. Dave "The Lizard Wizard" Rambeaut was a living legend, a serious o-o-g, and (next to Marcus Vranes, anyway) he was hands down the most famous dec designer of all time. He'd spent his career with Marvex in the ultra-secretive lab known to the decarati as *Table Twelve.* There, together with his hand-picked R&D dream team, Rambeaut was responsible for innovations considered some of the greatest leaps forward in optigenetics and biomimetics history. Before he left, in an equally famous and ugly public falling out (a nasty spat with everyone who was anyone in the c-suite at Marvex) his team had developed the neuronal snapstrand and HTR spindle grafting techniques that leveled the development playing field, and made it so any dabbler with half a lobe and a filthy chop shop could call him-or-her-or-itself a "designer" and kick out creatures great, small and hideous beyond all reckoning. The Moreauvians took Dave's ball and ran with it the farthest, scurrying hip-hoppity off into the deep and freakish corners of their altered (and very fuzzy) underworld. And then, of course, there was the loose-knit band of brothers, sisters and others that called itself Tera-Anima, growing their faces-of-ears, transkin creations, exo-organs, magnisense (and et-cetera) (don't even get me started on those Tera-Anima maniacs). But those were fringe acts and side shows. It was the Big Three manufacturers that divvied up the ripest and juiciest fruits of Dave's genius and let him ride off into the sunset, and although he did not go softly into that dark retirement, the Lizard Wizard fell off the face of the mainstream nex all but entirely. You knew he wasn't dead, or suspected he might not be, if you were in the niche circles that kept abreast of such things as bleeding-edge mutagenetics, because evidence of his signature activities would pop up in odd places, like snippets on obscure designer forums, or oblique mentions in trade rags like *Receptor* and *Hypertissue*. I remembered an FF clinic on advanced exotics where the HOVO host even mentioned Dave by name. But he subsisted in the shadows and apparently he liked it like that.

What I couldn't shake, in the here and now, was Dave Rambeaut saying that he knew me, or had heard *of* me. It didn't make any sense. I was a repairman from Rat City, a *nobody*, as Hana had so affectionately pointed out. It was more than a little unsettling.

Up ahead of us a big hole in the ground came into view. It was completely invisible until we were right up on it, and Dave made no attempt to brake or swerve away, and we plunged in. We went airborne for a second or two, me weightless over my seat. I grabbed the dash to brace for impact and the vehicle let out a playful squeal.

"Easy, big fella!" Melody said.

There was no impact. The hole turned out to be a steep ramp and we banged down onto it and rolled, accelerating into the subterranean darkness. I looked back through the rear window and saw the hole close up behind us, and realized that the outlet was the way Dave appeared seemingly out of nowhere to rescue me. The passage ahead of us leveled off in a long stretch of tunnel and we drove some distance until Melody's headlights fell on a large, corrugated steel door. She rolled to a stop and we waited as it clanked open in front of us and we drove across the threshold into an industrial garage. Behind us, the door lurched into reverse and slid shut with a bang.

"Wanna try and guess where we are?" Dave asked.

I shook my head.

"You might be surprised."

I was pretty sure I couldn't handle any more surprises.

Dave popped his door and got out, brushing the dashboard tenderly as he did so. The vehicle gave a little Mmmmm of pleasure.

"Secure yourself, tiki tonga, and travel with us, if you would."

"But you know I don't like the big room, Dave," she said.

"Righto. We'll see you on the inside, fluffy puffy."

"'kay. Don't be long, Big D. I mean … don't *take* long."

He winked and motioned for me to follow him. I got out on my side, careful to exit without any unnecessary caressing movements, then took my kit and shambled after him toward a red door on the far wall. Dave turned the knob and shoved it open just a crack. I heard the smooth whir and buzzing din of factory sounds beyond. Dave pumped his eyebrows.

"Welcome, my friend, to the machine."

He shoved the door wide and we entered the biggest room I have ever seen.

Melody

"It's a twitch house," I said.

"Twitchy as they come, mate." Dave was still grinning, though his smile was tight and even a bit forced.

"I call it the Grand Ole Meat Opry, elsewise known round the wide rim as TENDER-IZ® Packing Co., Livestock Building Number 5. Supposably, it's the biggest T-barn on the whole F.O.E.Yo, if there's a bigger one out there somewheres, I do not want to know about it."

"I see what you mean," I said.

Back in the day, most of the meat on the market was grown in culture vats in highly efficient and profitable operations. That was all well and good except for one thing: the cultured product didn't satisfy the porterhouse, t-bone and filet mignon-loving taste buds of the upper crust. Market research confirmed it. The people who could afford more (aka, those who mattered) didn't want their meat cultured, they wanted it reared and grown the old-fashioned way. They wanted real steak for dinner. Grain fed, watered, exercised, organic and *all natural*. But there was one snag. The Presumed Sentience movement had joined forces with PETA and together they put tremendous pressure on the few remaining mega-ranches and slaughterhouses that dotted the planet. The solution for the monied market (because the monied market always finds a solution) was the twitch house.

The "room" where we stood was a mass-scale, stim-growth plant. It had a ceiling at least a hundred meters high and though

I thought I could make out a wall in the distance to the right, the opposite end was too far away to see. The entire space was taken up by one continuous and winding maze of an overhead production line with gleaming tracks, pipes and nests of tubing under which hung thousands upon thousands of living cattle *primes*, the headless, hoofless, hair-and-skinless product known variously in the twitch world as "dogies," "sticks," or "shorthorns," (whereas the T-techs themselves, whether for reasons of backchannel marketing, nostalgia or flat irony were called "buckaroos").

The primes traveled, ever so slowly, on their hooks under kilometers of winding track, each "animal" with a feeder pod full of protein-rich slurry above it and, slung alongside, a monitor rack with its tangle of zaplines that migrated over the plump bands of muscle tissue like electrified tentacles delivering their stimulating jolts and eliciting the responsive *twitch twitch twitch*. We were clearly at the mature end of the circuit, because the dangling primes were enormous, hormone bulked heifers, close to slaughter size. In contrast, at the other end of the factory growth cycle the "cattle" were no more than fist-sized pouches of starter cells, sticky clumps the buckaroos called "gobits," "goobers" or "mash." I knew all this from a grainy documentary HOVO I'd seen in high school, one of those standard vocation-and-industry type flicks. More stuff I didn't want or need to know.

The Lizard Wizard looked vaguely disgusted by the whole enterprise.

"We're doing Wagyu primes this cycle, buffalo backstraps the next go round. We can change out and set up for hens, turkeys, turducken. Whole headless, breast solos or DMOs. Dark meat only. We're nothing if not flexible here at Building 5."

"So … what exactly is it you do here, Dave?"

"Facilities Manager and resident science guy."

"Of a twitch house? You?"

"Always wanted my own abattoir. Joking. TENDER-IZ needed a geneticist, I needed a place to lay low. It was a marriage made in carne asada. You probably heard about my little flap with Marvex."

"I don't know anybody who didn't," I said. "'Creative differences' was how the news cycle spun it, as I recall."

"Creative differences, my ass. It was my new stuff! Management didn't like it, not one bit, that's what caused the kafuffle. I scared'em, mate, scared'em bad. But that's all sewage under the bridge, now. I'm here, out-of-sight, out-of-mind, and most importantly, left to my own de-vious-vices. That's the beauty of this place. Far as the factory bullshit goes, I don't lift a finger. The buckaroos do it all, hook, starts, slaughter, flashfreeze, packing, distro. That all happens at the other end of the house, three-point-five klicks that direction. Nobody comes down to my way 'cept custodial and repair units, scoots and hovers, mostly, a few lobotomized 808s. Why? Those are my orders. At this dude ranch, I am *the Dude*."

I opened my mouth to say something but couldn't think of what it should be. I tried to lick my lips, but only succeeded in making a dry, chapped, smacking sound. I was getting lightheaded.

"Look at me, yabberin' your flippin' ears off while you're there dyin' of desiccation. C'mon, let's get you fed and watered. This hanging carno show is not what I brought you here to see."

Dave led me through a set of swinging double doors and down a long corridor that led to a vestibule with an open freight elevator. There were no buttons, only an up-and-down lever. He hauled the cage shut, leaned his hip on the lever and down we went. We passed through other floors, equipment and storage levels, most of them dark, until we hit bottom with a soft clunk. Dave pulled back the cage and I followed him into another featureless corridor, struggling to keep up with his determined stride. The passage descended at a slight angle and the quality of the light changed. It went from the harsh fluorescent overheads to a diffused glow where the passageway itself was the source of the luminescence. As we continued downward, the shape and texture of the walls changed, as well. It went from slab concrete to a translucent, organic material that rounded off the sharp angles until we were in what appeared to be a shaft or tube. It took me several steps before I noticed that the substance of the walls wasn't static, it throbbed and undulated all but imperceptibly around us, its subtle motion more a sensory suspicion than anything you could focus on, like the migration of a sunfish, or the slithering crawl of a snail. The tube appeared to be made of *living* tissue. I wanted to stop and examine it more closely, but we went by an intersecting passage and I realized I might lose Dave in the maze if I did, so I kept on moving, careful to keep him in sight. After a minute or so of the gradual descent, the passage leveled off and we entered a central junction or hub, roughly oblong in shape, like some huge, organic, atrial chamber. The undular movement in the wall lining was more pronounced here and I could feel its tremulous, rippling motion in my legs, pulsing gently up from the floor, though "floor" is a crude word for the supple material we stood on, and gravity keeping our feet in that direction was the only thing that distinguished what was underneath us from the walls or ceiling, all of it one iridescent, swimming cytoplasm around us. There were several open passages leading out of the hub, each of them identical to the one we emerged from in appearance, and interspersed among these openings were a number of thresholds with 'doors' of hanging, diaphanous, skin-like bands.

    Dave stopped in front of one of the thresholds and turned to me with steepled fingers thrust into his beard, an oddly contemplative pose.

"What say we hit the beach, pour a pig's ear into us?"

"I'm not sure what you mean," I said.

"Every good lab's got a beach and a tap handle. Marcus Vranes said that."

Vranes. The Lizard Wizard was quoting my personal hero, and it was a quote I hadn't heard. I was getting dizzy again.

"Are you saying this place is a lab?"

Dave's grin went supernova.

"With a beach and a bar."

He beckoned me to the doorway and held the flaps aside.

"Après voodoo," he said.

I stepped through into a short tunnel of the same organic material and instantly felt the warmth of the air, humid, tropical warmth. I breathed it in and even tasted it, the balmy tang of salt air, and a few steps farther in I heard the wash of a calm surf. Then we were out of the tunnel and into the blazing sunlight. It was so bright all I could do was squint and peer under my visored hands over an azure swath of ocean and the lighter blue of the sky with one or two innocent puff ball clouds floating in it.

A few years ago, I spent a long weekend at a tech convention at the Coastest Mostest resort in Marina del Fuego on 33, so I knew what a beach was supposed to look and smell like, and what fine-grained sand felt like between your toes. But the Coastest Mostest was a holoproj, a pretense of an approximation, and of a quality (if that's the right word) that made itself known in its absence at every turn. Dave's beach wasn't the real thing, either, but for a handful of magical seconds, I couldn't tell one way or the other. The sensation *of* the real was everywhere, it permeated the experience, we're talking so real it doesn't matter that it's not, to dredge up another quote of the famouser-than-God Marcus Vranes. Standing where I stood, even Vranes would have been impressed.

When my eyes adjusted a bit, I saw the promised bar down the beach, a silhouette of grass roof and bamboo posts under a stand of perfect palms. Dave went by me with a friendly clap on my shoulder and I followed him across the hot sand. It was an open-air cantina, its hanging fronds rustling lazily in the delicious breeze. There were a few scattered tables and stools around a horseshoe counter, and inside, a low back bar with a row of the promised tap handles, some old photos tacked up, knick-knacks, straw hats and a greasy black grill that looked hot and ready for cooking. It was anyone's version of paradise.

Dave handed me some dark shades and slipped on a pair of his own, then ducked behind the bar, snatched up, flipped and caught two pint-sized glasses, and perused the beer selection.

"Ah, let us see … an ice cold lager, no? For the sheer thirst-quench-ability."

"Anything works," I croaked.

He filled a glass to foamy overflow and slid it my way.

"Try that on for size, amigo. We'll adjust as the mood steers us."

I guzzled the beer and most of its golden salvation coursed down my throat, though twin streams trickled over my cheeks and onto my neck. God was it good.

"Dangerous to hydrate with beer," a voice said. It was her, the sweet, husky voice of the tracked vehicle. Melody.

I lowered my glass and turned to see her step into the shade of the cantina from the direction of the water, sun-bleached hair, hypnotic green eyes and a honey-toned tan. She was nineteen, maybe twenty, the perceived age of most impossibly beautiful dec females, but the weird thing was, for one, two, three skipping thumps of my heart, I thought she was human. Now, I'm no amateur at making such calls, it's an area where I am an undisputed expert. I can spot a dec, any make or model, with one flashing glance across a crowded room. But like our tropical, oceanside surroundings, Melody was of a quality that wasn't supposed to exist. The shock of this, combined with the glorious effects of the beer, led me to stare at her far longer than I should have, before I remembered myself and hastily averted my gaze. I even patted my pockets for a tin of NOF gel.

"You're very depleted," she said. "Have some water next."

"Water? Gud förbjude!" Dave exclaimed.

"He needs something to eat, too. After that, the two of you can have as much beer as you want."

Dave raised his hands in protest.

"Why am *I* on rations?"

She ignored him, and kept her kind eyes on me.

"Do you like mahi-mahi?"

"Love it," I said, distractedly, still looking everywhere but straight at her. I held my breath, too, and finally located a trusty tin of NOF.

"Spare yourself, mate. She ain't gonna sic a pheromone on you. You're basically bulletproof, anyways. You are a special case, fully non-seducible."

"I wish that were true. If only you knew how much I wished it," I said.

"It *is* true. Trust the Wizard on this point. Breathe freely, feast your bleary eyes and rest your weary soul. You're quite safe here. And remember, lest we forget, beauty's in the eye of the beer holder."

He held out a fresh pint of lager in one hand and a much smaller glass of water in the other. I accepted both. I decided it was absurd not to trust Dave Rambeaut, both given who he was and all that had happened since I practically jumped into his lap. I raised my gaze and looked straight at Melody. I must have had a very funny look on my face, because she laughed, her whole face beaming this huge, warm, ethereally gorgeous smile, and yet, taking in the vision of her loveliness, I didn't feel myself drawn to her, or losing control of my senses, or dissolving into a simpering salmagundi of carnal conniption, all of which meant, to the best of my ability to judge, anyway, I was still myself. Not that this was any great reassurance.

"You're cuter than I thought you'd be," she said, still smiling.

"I am?"

"Much. My cab optics in the sand rat aren't exactly up to snuff." She shot a scolding look at Dave. "Thanks to Mister Deferred Maintenance here."

"I got a big honey-do list, babiguana. I'll get to it. Promise."

"Without my optics, I couldn't see you riding inside me. But I liked the sound of your voice. You have a kind voice, Garl. Amazing how much you tell about a person from the sound of his voice."

I was confused.

"You're the same Melody as the vehicle?"

She nodded.

"One in the same. We're pescetarians, by the way. I hope that's okay."

"We don't eat meat," Dave said, glancing upward into the bamboo rafters, with a grimace for the twitch house that was somewhere above us. "Go figure."

"We don't eat real fish, either," Melody said. "Real fish have feelings. But the mahi mahi we serve is so good you won't know the difference."

"I believe it," I said.

She reached out and brushed my forearm with her fingertips, and gave it a reassuring squeeze. Then she turned and joined Dave behind the bar, the sway of her hips as she moved every bit as mesmerizing as her eyes.

I tried to get my head around her being both the sand rat vehicle *and* the tanned beauty tossing fresh tortillas on the grill. I looked to Dave for help, but he merely pumped his eyebrows, apparently his signature deflection.

"Let the concept filter in slow," he said. "Don't try and snap it up all at once. It's bigger than it seems." He took a sip of beer and wiped the foam from his mustache with a sweep of his fingers. Melody worked the grill and in no time I heard a welcome sizzle and caught the inviting aromas of newly fried corn flour and blackened fish. The meal was even more delicious than it smelled, and I noticed, as I ate, Melody's easy manner as she chewed contemplatively and her eyes strayed out to the sunlight that winked in the shifting blinds of the trees. Every few moments, her eyelids fluttered, and she shuddered as if from a slight chill, though the air was warm to the point of hot, and I was left wondering what else she was feeling, seeing and doing while she sat and dined so serenely with us. Dave didn't appear to notice, or was too busy eating to pay any attention. He moaned, grunted and gawd-ed over every bite.

"You outdid yourself, chef lovey dove, like you always do."

"They're simple tacos, Dave."

"No such thing as *simple*, not with you, mysteriosita. She's magic, my friend, everything she does, everything she touches, says, gazes on. Magically *magic* magic."

Melody rolled her eyes and giggled, a musical sound that seemed amplified somehow by the tropical air.

"He makes such a scene."

Dave pointed his half-eaten taco at me.

"This fellow, here, he's magic, too, Mel. A bit of livin' black magic right here in our midst, with a powderin' of pixie dust behind the ole ears."

"I'm afraid you're mistaken. I'm just an ordinary—"

"—repairman, yeah, I know. Just a lowly, phantasm-fixin' tick-nician, you."

Melody pursed her luscious lips and made a face.

"Don't listen to him, Garl. He gets one beer in him and he'll say almost anything."

Dave stuffed the rest of the taco into his mouth, shoved his chair back and stood.

"When you've had your fill, I want to show you the rest of the lab."

"Uh-oh, here goes," she said. She reached over and gripped my arm again. "Just don't think of it as any big thing."

"Move with us, if you would, peaches-and-dreamy," Dave said.

"I'm with you," she said, softly, and gazed off over the ocean, though she made no move to rise.

I stood up.

"I'm ready," I said.

"Right," Dave said.

He headed for the tunnel without looking back. I followed after him back through the barrier of strands into the central hub, where suddenly it hit me. I stopped cold. Dave noticed, turned and waited. I stepped to the curved and luminous wall of the hub, reached out and touched it, very carefully. It undulated, rippling outward from the point of contact.

"It's her," I said. "The whole place is her. It's all Melody."

Dave looked giddy to the point of madness.

"*Yes* ..." she said, her voice everywhere and nowhere. "It's me."

Dave grabbed my hand and pulled me after him.

"C'mon, man, we need to keep on truckin'. The pièce de la resistance lies within."

He led down another one of the passages. It twisted and wound its way like some circulatory vessel, narrowing the farther in we went, the walls closing around us until my shoulders practically brushed them as we moved. Dave was going so fast I could barely keep him in sight, and when eventually I did lose him, before I could even register what that meant, I rounded a bend and there he stood, waiting for me. He was outside another threshold, one with a smaller opening, and like the others it had a barrier of skin-like strands. Dave parted them and held them aside.

"Entre, s'il vous plais."

"That's what you said last time."

"Last time I said voodoo. This time it's *you-do*."

I didn't know what he was talking about, but I entered (I didn't see what else I could do) and like before I was struck by the dramatic shift in the atmosphere. Unlike the ambient air of the passage, or the balmy salt breeze of the ocean, here the air was hot and heavy, and every bit as humid as the reptile house in the Redetroit Zoo. There was a subtle hint of musk, as well, not unpleasant in any way, but rather intriguing, and to be honest, maybe a bit more pleasant than I wanted to admit. The room (if that's what it was) was dark, but not completely, just enough so that it took my eyes a long moment to adjust. When they did, I detected a diffused red-lit glow with no obvious source of emanation. After several more blinking seconds, I finally made out the first outlines of detail. We stood at one end of a very large, low-ceilinged space, and although I didn't trust my sense of distance or dimension in the bare light, I guessed the area to be roughly the size of a sports arena or conventioneer's pavilion, enormous and roughly oval in shape (I couldn't be sure about this last detail, it was just the impression I had). The surface of the space (I won't even use the word floor this time) had a subtle convexity, so that its center was slightly higher than the edges all round, while the matting, if you could call it that, was highly textured, like a strangely uniform moonscape, apparently constructed of the same smooth, skin-like material as the strands over the thresholds throughout the Melody complex, except that here there were visible folds, bumps and creases, tucks and mounds, not like some rough or craggy meteor-struck planetoid, more like the smooth underside of some bottom-dwelling sea creature, incredibly supple, yet tactile and reactive at the same time. As my eyes continued to adjust, I made out other features, and saw that I was not mistaken about the uniform scheme of the surface, whatever it was, for there was a repeating pattern of crevices, slender dips and soft rising bumps that gave the overall impression of a sculptural knoll on a farm field, freshly plowed, yet strangely in its row upon inward twisting row, fecund in the rift and ready for the planting, and then I knew it, I saw it, in a blazing flash I realized what it was I was looking at …

"My god … it's full of vulvas."

Svadhisthana-hana-bobanna-
mi-my-mo-manna

"Correctamundo," Dave said. "I would point out they're full torsos. But as you keenly observe, each is of the female sextraction. See the pattern they make, the way it flows, one body into the next, the apparent chaos of the map but an illusion. Let your eyes find the taxonomic topography. Start from the middle top of the rise, there in the center, follow it down the curve. Look at the way they mandelbrot out, lying head-to-toe, as if holding hands, one goddess folded into the next, all connected, all one, enormous, flesh-and-blood Matrikas frieze of a multiform mamacita."

"Head-to-toe? They're headless," I said.

"Technically, yes. Footless, too. But the heads are implied. Can't you see it? It's animated statuary! They're living visions of your classic marble Aphrodites of Antiquity. Lying down, of course, winsome in their supinage, eh? Sometimes I lose the pattern myself. There it is. Yoni, navel, tit, tit, yoni, navel, tit, tit, yoni, yoni, navel, navel, and then yoni, navel, tit again, and so on and so forth, every one with a full set of supporting organs, spine, ribs, pelvis, hips, thighs, glutes, whilst necks, shoulders, knees and toes, knees and toes are sublimated in the substrate. You can't see'em when she's at rest, but trust me, mate, those legs can get open when they want to, and those bellies will catch a rhythm and make themselves known. I'm a witness."

"Jesus H., Dave ..."

"I call it the venuscape, or the goddesscape, or sometimes even the great escape, depending on my whim du jour."

"Jesus-fucking-H."

"A legitimate sentiment. I mean, you wanna talk about objectifying the female form, you can't get any more *mondo*-jectified than this. It's like Siamese gigatuplets in a sisterhood soufflé."

"How ... how many are there?"

"No idea. I lose track whenever I try'n make a tally. I know it's a factor of four, because, let's face it, all good deities are."

"Wait a minute, you said *when she's at rest*. Do you mean to tell me it's all *her*. They're *all* Melody?"

"Every last calla lily. Yes sir, that's my baby, no sir, don't mean maybe. Sorta makes you want to get out there and roll around, doesn't it? Unfortunately, we don't have time for that kind of horseplay. 'sides, Mel needs a shad more "attention" than either one of us gents is presently equipped to provide. Not underestimating you, mind."

He motioned me to a fixture in the wall that looked like a human-shaped shadow.

"Join me over this a'way, if you'd be so kind."

At first I thought it was another tunnel entrance, until I stood close enough to see that it was only slightly inset. The blackness was a coating of obsidian facets, hundreds of them, like winking jet sequins. I knew what it was—an array of microsensors. But I didn't know the purpose.

"Step right up, don't be shy! Place yourself in close proximity to the sensory pad, if you would, please."

"Why?"

"Why not?"

"I want to know what you're going to do."

"You trusted me this far, didn't you? Won't take but a second, and you won't feel a thing. You have my word on that."

If I hadn't been in a state of shock, I might've asked more questions. But as things stood, I simply did as he wanted. I stepped up to the array and leaned into it. The instant I made contact, the pad latched onto me and sucked me close, like soft, dextrous limpets. The whole panel spun, taking me with it, like those false walls in old-time monster HOVOs, the kind that transferred the victim into a hidden room behind, only Dave's version of the spinning wall took me all the way round and released me again. I stepped away with a tingling sensation in my limbs and a slight wooziness. The whole thing took no more than a second or two.

Dave stared at the glowing screen of an oddly-shaped handheld device.

"There we are ... got you. That'll do nicely, yes. The point here is the girl's grown tired of my jiggly love handles, lovable as they are. But you, you're a fine, strapping specimen. Everyone needs a little variety, now and again, even one such as her. Are you catching my drift, here?"

"I'm not sure," I said.

He stepped to the edge of the whatever-*scape* he was calling it. I joined him there and watched as his fingers moved fluently over the screen of his device, which, from the quick glimpse I caught, appeared to show levels like a miniature mixing board.

"Do you really think this is a good idea, Dave?" Melody asked, her voice reverberating softly from all directions.

"It's the only way, puka shell. We need to make a believer out of him."

"But ... the *big* one? You remember what happened last time."

"Go big or go home, am I right?" He looked at me. "Size counts, sure, but this here, this is purely a numbers game. Over-whelming, whelming, *whelming* numbers."

His fingers tapped and swiped the screen and the room responded with changing light and a thrust in the power hum, as conical nodes descended from hidden recesses in the ceiling.

"What are those things?"

"Speakers," he said. "It's all done with directional sound. This is going to be a tad vicarious from your perspective, I'm 'fraid. But it won't be boring. Promise."

"What won't be boring? What are you doing?"

"Not me. You. Your aural signature is about to make sweet music with my multi-talented wahine."

"Dave, I'm a certified Fant Fixers repairman. I'm under contract. There are rules, specific codes of conduct. I can't get involved, I'm not allowed to be part of anything like this. Nothing even close to this."

"Consider it a repair then, if that helps. Better yet, call it an *installation*. Log it as whatever you want. A rose is a rose is a rose. You say tomato, I say tah-maw-to, let's call the whole thing off, on, off, on. Hey, that's digital. That makes you the binary in the coalmine."

"I have no idea what you're talking about."

"Neither do I, it's all nonsense, only nominally sensical, anyway. Truth is, words can be so imprecise, so let's let the bodies do the talking. Let's us get out of the way and let you two get it on."

He made another adjustment, and the frequency of the tone modulated sharply as the volume grew, accompanied by a powerful droning bass that reverberated right through me, and I felt an instinctive urge to cover my ears, but resisted it. Somehow Melody's voice cut through the penetrating layers of echoing decibels.

"Wait," she said.

"Yes, wait," I shouted.

"Yes ... *wait* ..." she echoed, but with a slight gasp this time.

"You want me to wait, do you? Is that what you want?"

Dave said. He wasn't talking to me.

"Don't ... no, don't ... *don't* ..."

I was about to throw myself at him and pry the creepy device from his bony fingers, when something about the tone of Melody's voice changed and held me in check.

"Don't turn me on, Dave," she said.

"If you *really* want me to stop ..." he paused and let the reverberations linger. "You know what you have to say."

"Don't ... *stop* ... oh, god ... *don't stop!* ... *DON'T STOP!*"

Dave nodded with a manic grin and cranked the volume up. The ceiling lurched downward a whole level lower, like some dance club special effect, then it dropped again, and fell into position right over the fleshy dance floor, where it hovered, and the sound hammered, thumped and zoned, then groaned with a long, drawn-out guttural buzz. In response, the floor heaved and shook, a rhythmic spasm that resounded in vibrations from the center outward as, one and all, the many knees thrust up and the legs spread wide, breasts heaving, nipples like diamonds, as the thighs went wider still, the manifold labia open, inviting, like a seabed of anemones set to feed, one and all they received the piercing, inundating sound, all of the torsos writhing together, caught in the gummy substrate, like bodies swimming in a viscous glue, humping as it held them fast, stretching, arching, the combined visual effect a synchronized wave that rippled across the surface, like the upraised arms of a frenzied concert crowd, the movement sailed inward from two sides and met in a mounting collision of tides, then split, canted and swerved, rolling outward again, heading toward the edges, straight at us and coming hard in a churning, oceanic force that drove me back and threw me into the wall, but somehow Dave kept his feet, leaning into the rushing tsunami with a surfer's wide stance, he rode the gyrations, as he worked the volume and keyed the pitch, and when the swell reached its pulsing, pummeling apogee he raised his elbows, a longboarder on the boiling crest of a storm surge, he rode it in, wherever *in* was, and with that, the floor of Melody's bodies (*all* of her) rocked and rumbled in a violent, twerking pussyquake as she let out a scream of such primal, such feral and ecstatic release that my hands shot to my ears (no choice about it this time) as the whole silk-skinned surface clenched, puckered and sprayed, geysers exploding, gushing, squirting, on every side and all the way across, the lights flashed bright, a flaring nova in the cascading mist and within it, I had a fleeting glimpse of rainbow and a final retina-singed image of Dave, launched sideways into the air, fully horizontal, bucked right off the back of the joy-raging *she*-beast of his own creation in the split second before everything went black.

I breathed.

My respiration, fast and deep, was the only sound I heard. Beyond that, there was the heat of the air, drenched and sticky.

I heard a click and a flashlight came on. It was Dave. He got up with a groan, rubbing his hip, then shined the beam around until he found me and blinded me with it. He strode over, put a hand out and hauled me to my feet.

"You all right?"

"I think so."

He swung the light to the room at large.

"Melody? Can you hear me, floopy-moopy? Talk at me, babe."

"… *oooohhhhh* …"

"A good sound, me thinks, do you agree? Are you still with us, honey bunny?"

"I told you what would happen, mister … *know-it-all* …"

"Point taken. But was it worth it? *That* is the question."

"Oh god … god, *yes* … *forever yes.*"

"Forever yes, the principessa says. Now, that's a good'un, good as I've heard."

"But now the power's out, and just look at me. I'm one big wet spot."

His light swept here and there over the plain of glistening breasts, bellies and loins, all open, relaxed and still, while paraurethral fluid trickled and flowed in rivulets between and around them, like desert flowers after a drenching cloudburst. I had sudden appreciation for the convexity of Dave's surface design. Melody's supple statuary was a living aqueduct, draining quickly and efficiently toward its edges.

"Jawohl!" Dave shouted. "Wet spots and polka dots, ja, ja, ja, mai oui, oui, oui. Cost of doing business mein schatz, mes belles escargots."

He looked at me. "I haven't seen her this happy in a quite a spell. But look, mate, don't let it go to your head."

"Go right ahead and let it, Garl," Melody said, her voice reverberating from the humid expanse of darkness. "You marked me deep … *soooooo* deep …"

"Hey, I was the one doin' the driving," Dave complained.

"And you were great, honey. Don't be jealous."

"Jealous?"

As I listened to them I realized I wasn't breathing. I couldn't breathe.

"I need to get out of here," I said.

Dave swung his light in my direction, and in the backglow I saw his grin, curious, knowing.

"Oh, right, I almost forgot. Our faithful repairmensch already has a steady girl."

"I don't know what you're talking about," I said.

"Confused, the fixer man is. Used, he feels. Bonded, they are. He's in thrall to his inamoratic Shelagh, almost as bad as she is to him. Holy dooley, it's like they were made for each other."

"Oh, Garl, don't worry," Melody said. "What happened here didn't mean anything, not in that way."

"Didn't *mean* anything?" Dave cried. "Crikey, baby, it meant everything!"

"I've got to go, I'm … right now, I'm … leaving," I stammered. I felt ridiculous saying it. I had no concept of why I was so upset, and certainly no idea where I thought I was going. I only knew I needed to move, and quickly. I turned for the threshold and parted the strands. Dave hurried after me, shining the light ahead of us.

"Fine, fine, you go, it's cool. I'll even show you the way out. But do me one itsy-bitsy little favor first, that's all I ask. You owe me one, right? Not that I'm countin'. As you may recall, I didn't leave you out there to twist in the breeze. Could have, didn't. Saved your bacon, I did. So did Mel. Blame me, not her."

I stopped and stood there with my back to him, the blood pounding in my temples.

"It was your own *burglar alarm* you sent after me."

"True. But it was untested until you came along. Damn thing scared the hell outta me."

"What is it you want?"

"Just and only that you should understand the singular purpose behind all that … uh … periaqueductal pandemonium."

I noticed a faint sparkle in the supple walls of the passage. Apparently, Melody didn't need an external power source to emit her own dancing glow. It also meant that I didn't need Dave's flashlight to find my way out. I kept moving. He trotted after me.

"Please," he said. "It's important."

I stopped again.

"Now you're toying with me," I said.

"Oh no, mate. No, no, no. Simple survival that there that.

For you would be the absolute wrong *muthafucka* to toy with in any circumstance. But! Indeed! I am toying with Mother Nature. Give me one terasecond and I will show you how."

I turned around and met his eyes. He nodded, slowly and meaningfully, then turned and hurried back to a spot outside the threshold where he bent low and pulled up a fleshy panel near the floor, removing a lattice of some other organic material that looked like beeswax. The compartment he opened bathed him in a flickering blue light. He reached in, nearly to his shoulder and pulled out a small object. He cradled it in his palm, then raised it with his fingertips and tilted it slowly. It was a tiny ampule containing an even smaller quantity of radiant blue liquid. Yet it was the source of the sparkling light.

"Gaze upon the veritable verity the two of you hath wrought. What color is *your* orgasm?" Obviously, it wasn't a question he expected me to answer. "Hers are always like this, electric sapphire, and chock full of *the stuff*."

"The stuff?"

He walked to me and held it up between us.

"*The stuff*, man. Jizz of the gods. Collect enough of this rocket fuel in one tank and a person could change the world. All of them. I'm speaking literally, here, of course." Dave flashed his craziest grin yet. "Mel is the generator."

"The what?"

"The *sexengine*, mate. Please tell me you understand."

"I can't tell you that, because I don't understand."

"You need to. Very important."

"The sexengine?"

"Look, it doesn't matter what you call her, call her whatever you want, but the basic design is encoded right here in the book."

"What book?"

"*This* book."

He wasn't holding any book. And I really didn't know what he was talking about. He shook his head, still grinning, but with a weariness in his eyes that I hadn't seen before.

"Someday, maybe. Maybe someday," he said.

My head felt like it was splitting into sections, actually breaking apart in a skull-rending episode that was about to make the walls around us a very messy place. Dave must've seen it, because he brushed past me without another word and headed with long strides back up the passage. Once again, I followed after him, trudging to the beat of my own pounding cranium. We went back through the central hub, retraced the winding route up through Melody's core until we reached the place where the organic walls thinned and her shimmering glow faded to featureless, grey concrete, and then we were outside her again, back in the industrial corridor of the factory sublevel.

"Farewell, Ben," she said, a softly echoing whisper from the pulsing tunnel behind me.

I stopped and turned.

"Why did you call me that?" My voice was flat and toneless.

"It's your original self. But the best you is yet to come."

"I don't know what you mean."

"Don't be troubled. You have what you need. We'll meet again, you and I. Our paths are entwined. I've seen it."

Dave rested a hand on my shoulder. It was an oddly paternal gesture.

"C'mon, man. I don't know how much more of this revelatory shit your poor sprained brain can absorb."

A short distance up the passage and we were back at the elevator. Dave slid the cage home and held the lever up. We rose, and watched Melody's level disappear below us. We passed the other floors, passed through the twitch house level and kept on rising, continuing up until we reached the top, where the car lurched to a clunky stop. Dave pulled back the cage and we exited into a plain concrete vault, not much bigger than the elevator itself. There was a hatch in the ceiling and a narrow ladder that led up to it. A dusty rucksack sat at the base of it.

"My getaway bag. You're welcome to it. Some water, stale energy bars, electric torch. Suffish supplies they just might be enough to get you somewheres, if somewhere's you want to go. On foot, I'm 'fraid. I think you appreciate I can't spare my vehicle." He pointed to the hatch. "That's the way out. I'll turn off my willy willy machine long enough for you to get clear. But don't dally, mate. I can't leave it off for long, times bein' what they are."

"Okay," I said. The last thing I planned to do was dally.

He held up the ampule of sparkling liquid.

"I want you to take this."

I shook my head, but he pressed it into my hand, closed my fingers on it, and clasped his hands around mine.

"Meditate on this in your wanderings: Can there be a true zenith of pleasure without its defining opposite, aka the prospect, aka the counterreality of ultimate pain? I'm not talkin' about *fantasy* pain, here, I mean the wicked stuff of night terrors and the black shadow. Many believe the one cannot exist without the other, the light won't shine without the darkness. Not me. I think the light can shine all on its own. Heaven exists, paradise, real elysium, for all of us, and if we can't locate it and get there, we'll just have to make it ourselves right here. Build the fucker out. That's where the work is going."

"I don't follow," I said. It was true, though I felt like it was all I was saying.

He pressed my fist more tightly around the ampule, as if it were some crucible.

"It's here," he said. "Hypergasmic energy is the key. A permanent state of ecstasy can be achieved, without loss of sensation or desire, one sustained, mind-and-soul-blowing, spirit-releasing climax without end amen. I'm talkin' about bliss, mate. Bliss, with a capitol B. Wherein Icarus flies right up to the sun and he does not tumble, because his wings are true. He climbs, he soars, he joins with fire, no longer the stardust, but the star. When that happens, we see the door, we approach it as light, light as light as yin devours yang and at long last we become as gods and make good our escape."

I was having a hard time keeping up with his ramble, much less understanding it.

"Escape from …?"

"This."

"This."

"The. Way. Out."

He wasn't grinning anymore. There were tears in his eyes. He let go of my hand and shook his head, and from the pain in his expression I knew there was more he wanted to say, critical details he needed to impart, but instead he threw back his bearded head and laughed, a real crazy man's laugh.

"Go on, now, before I change your mind," he said.

I picked up the pack. It was reassuringly heavy. I slipped it over my shoulder and reached for the ladder, but looked back at Dave and held up the glowing ampule.

"What am supposed to do with this?"

He shrugged.

"Don't know. But don't lose it. That shit might come in real handy some pisser of a day."

He slid the cage shut, leaned back on the lever and the elevator started down.

"Wait," I said. "I meant to ask you—how did you know *about* me?"

"You need to get to the bridge, mate. Find it, reach it."

"What bridge? What are you talking about?"

Instead of stopping, he smiled and began to sing, as the tears flowed freely, now.

"*I'm gonna let it shine ... this little light of mine, I'm gonna let it shine ...*"

"Dave!"

"*... let it shine, let it shine, let it shiiiiinnnne.*"

The cage disappeared from view. He was gone and I was alone again.

Revelations

The Low Flats are a big place. They stretched. On and on they stretched. They're mostly flat, too (as one might expect) but not all flat. It was said, by those who cared enough to say such things, that the flats ran clear round the globe, the full circuit, the total wrap. This factoid I knew. When I first heard it, I understood it in the abstract way we can be said to *understand* dimension, the concept of distance as perceived in a nature HOVO, say, one featuring an arid plain way down deep, or a picture postcard of a famous wasteland, the carefully staged foreground blending to a beige blur in the epic beyond. Now that I was actually on that barren plain, a tiny pixel in the HOVO, a microscopic fleck on the postcard, all but certainly overlooked and incredibly insignificant in the yawning immensity of the place, my *understanding* of its size took on a dimension of its own. I needed to make the place small. The smaller I could make it the better, if I had any hope of making the reality of walking across it work. Walking across it? What did that even mean? What if there was no *across* it, but only around it? And what was I doing walking in the first place, on foot (*again!*) in the desolation of the Low Flats? How in the Jesus H. did I let that happen? I tried to recall all the steps and missteps that brought me to where I now stumbled.

When I emerged from the Lizard Wizard's secret back door, a camouflaged hatch that opened into a sandy patch of agromix, I stood in the middle of a bone-dry megafarm. In one direction, just over a shallow rise, I glimpsed the expansive roofline of the monstrous **TENDER-IZ®** Packing Co. Building No. 5. So I headed the other way, out and into and across the hectares of agronomic nothingness. The place wasn't technically a desert but it played out like one, all parched grit and endless horizon of sameness. I took the first road I happened upon and followed it to where it ended in a sign bolted to a stubby, pitted length of guardrail. ROAD END. No doubt. The other two roads I came upon and followed both petered out in dirt tailings that emptied into fields of scrabble rock and sand, *bed layer* the engineers called it, the ground not even prepped for agro. I imagined the luckless road crew that was originally dispatched to cut and level the surface grade this far out, finally and collectively coming to their senses, singing *What the fuck are we doing? No one's ever going to come this way!* before calling it good enough for government work and turning back. I empathized. But I couldn't sing along, because I had come this way, and I couldn't turn back.

Hours later, I staggered upon a road that was two full-blown highways intersecting in the middle of nowhere. I stepped out of the desert onto the asphalt and stood at the center of that crossroads. I shifted through quarter turns to gaze long and hard in each direction. But the highways were indistinguishable, broken yellow lines on flat black ribbons that disappeared where they met the faux sky. I chose the one that followed the arc of the simsun, as best I could track it. Though why I thought that was a good idea I can't say for sure. There was no helpful signage. No signage of any kind. The planners probably figured you didn't need any stupid signs. If you didn't know where you were already, way down this a'way, you weren't supposed to be here in the first place. But then, in the distance up ahead, I saw that sure enough, there was a sign. I couldn't read it, not at first, it was too far off, just a tiny rectangle by the side of the road. Just knowing it was there, though, and with my eyes locked on it, I had some fresh spring in my step. And after what took longer than I thought it should I finally reached it, and stood below it and stared. It was one of those giant, elevated roadside billboards. Despite the badly faded graphics and print, the ad was still ghostly visible:

Extrudos® … fun to eat, snuffin' snack pangs where they sleep

I took that same highway for many more hours, until it ended, ominously, in the black mound of a lava field. It wasn't a huge surprise. From time to time, more often than "they" wanted you to know, Famous Original Earth would vomit up molten bile out of whatever abscess it felt like vomiting out of to spoil your works, your plans, your roads, and if the timing was just right, maybe even your day. It was another bracing slap of reality in the face of the *Dwell Deep* fantasy. My own particular swath of pyroclastic regurgitate was cold and hard, though. It resembled a bad case of geothermal indigestion that happened long ago, years, maybe even decades, when it swept over the highway, covering everything to either side, and leaving the mounded flow that cut across my path. The only thing I could think to do was to go up and over. The climb wasn't easy, as the pumice broke and crumbled away, turning to scree under my weight, and I scrambled and nearly fell on the last step of the steepest shot. Once I was on top the going was easier, but slow, as I made my across the crusted surface of the lava with its ropey organic textures, sworls, lips, ridges and deep folds. It reminded me of an immense petrified version of Melody's fleshy moonscape, and that thought led to a flash of embarrassment at the way I'd behaved during Dave's *sound check* of her exultant capacities, a thoroughly prudish reaction on my part toward something I knew to be artificial. It should've been no big deal, given the million insane things I'd seen and done as a repairman. Maybe it was the mere concept of Melody's sprawling multiplexity that was too much for me to handle. Or maybe I really was "in thrall" to Grusha, the Parisienne vixen who – dead or alive – had no intention of releasing her grip on my heart. How did Dave know about her? Why didn't I ask him that question? And did she have me *this* messed up? God knows, my troubles started when I met her. Whatever the answers, whatever was *really* going on, it was no excuse for me behaving like a child. No excuse to leave Dave's company in a huff. So why had I? Where did I think I was escaping to, anyway? I was scattered and dispersing in my own head, my mental state a subcommittee of cross purposes, with all the voting members wanting to ram through their own self-destructive agendas. The only consensus seemed to be that I needed to keep moving, keep shucking, keep on keepin' on.

When I finally reached the far side of the lava field and scrambled down off of it, the underneath highway that I thought I was following was nowhere in sight. It must have made a turn somewhere back under the flow, or else it just stopped like the other roads I'd followed. Either way, the path ahead was roadless, another undifferentiated plain of bed layer that made the lava mound behind me look like an ambulatory theme park.

Night came fast as the simsun dipped, oozed long and disappeared. I used the last of the light to dig through the contents of Dave's rucksack and find that he had the foresight to include a little, foil emergency blanket, which I shook open and went fetal under in the pitch dark when the cold came and I shivered the whole nocto through. I was thankful to be up with the simrise and washed some of the dust down my throat with one of Dave's juice pouches, even though it started out an icy brick, and I had to warm it to slush with my own frozen hands. I took a few nibbles of an energy bar and it was back to aimless trekking. I walked all day into another night, with collapse into another fetal nest on the ground under a roof of flimsy foil, and then through another simrise and another day into night. Though I encountered no more lava fields, I did come upon and follow other roads, all of them less traveled. So it wasn't with any great and lingering astonishment that I never saw another traveler. Though I once spied a dust trail in the distance that might've been a low flowing truck or a freight skimmer, but it was too far away to tell. On one road I crossed a narrow bridge over a dry irrigation canal. Later on, when the road forked, again without signs, I took the fork that struck nearest the direction I thought I should go, though the road ended like all the others, and I was greeted by the open arms of another frigid night. There was another simrise, then another, other roads. I lost track of how many I'd taken. One ended in a refuse pile, with the extra-added insult of no good, usable garbage, even though I took the precious time to scavenge and sift. Another road, made of fist-sized, angular rock that was clearly designed to inflict maximum pain on the foot-bound traveler ended in a tumulus berm that appeared to serve no purpose beyond shielding the view of the vast plain of bed layer that stretched on the other side of it. But the best road ending, hands down, in terms of sheer, potential drama, was the high quality asphalt spur that led to a circular helipad with a faded white 'H' at its center. Call me an inveterate optimist, but I actually stood on that 'H' for a long time, slowly turning to scan the horizon for any sign of an inbound air ambulance. I was ready for my evac. But it wasn't ready for me.

There were other roads and other endings, none worth relating here. Though along the way I did develop a convivial and even intimate connection with the big-shouldered character of the flats. I felt like I was really getting to know the place, and not in some aloof, standoffish way, but on a close, bosom and meaningful level. Sure, it started out formal enough, some casual conversation, small talk about the weather and the like, but we kept things lively with clever asides, and a winking recognition of the flinty-dry sense of humor we shared, us two, and this led quite naturally to a running, tit-for-tat repartee, inside jokes and familiar routines. It wasn't long before the first name basis lapsed into pet names and easy giggles, and then, to my honest surprise (though I should've seen it coming) to that first dusty kiss. It was a good hard one, and right down on the ground we went. No one ever forgets the first one, it was something we shared, and always would. After that we were a genuine item, complete with public displays of affection and our own cutesy language. We had secret names for things, signals and moods no one else could ever guess. We settled in, we got comfortable, us two, unabashedly naked in each other's sight. The flats knew every inch of me better than I knew myself, and I certainly came to know and appreciate that big-boned body, its gullies, trenches and washouts, the entertaining patches of talus at the base of an otherwise unremarkable dip, the uneven rock, here, the unexpected hole, there, always good for belly laugh when a foot goes in wrong and an ankle rolls. Oh, and the sounds we made, the two of us moving together, as one, our signature scuff, crunch and scrape, we had legs, we did, that was how you knew (you just knew) we were going to last, we were in for the long haul. We mellowed, god knows we did, we grew old together, the flats and me, finished one another's sentences, ate off each other's plates, you take my carrots, I'll eat your peas, we stared off into space, together, never needing to ask what the other was thinking, how the other was feeling. It was there. All of it, right there.

Still, no matter how close I thought we were, I had the sneaking suspicion the flats were holding something back. There was the unspoken issue of the wall of opaque distance ahead that never drew any nearer. And here, I thought I was demonstrably devoted, especially when I looked down and watched myself walk right out of the sole-less carcass of what used to be my left boot.

If that's not commitment, and when you get right down to it, real devotion, then I don't know what is. Hours later, when the right foot, imitating the bloody, blistered martyr of the left, followed its ascetic example and carriage sacrifice, and stepped out of its own useless cocoon, that dried and shredded chrysalis, dragging the husk for some distance before it, too, was free, looking fresh and new, the skin of a babe, of a podiatrist's desk model, and plodded and soldiered on, humping after its twin, until it caught up and they were indistinguishable as blood brothers, two paws of ragged meat, pilgrims marching, wandering at times to find the path, and once on it, hobbling toward the gleaming shrine where I might offer up the very last, the bitter distillate, drizzled over my fetid stumps, offering up all that was left, arranged upon that altar in the proper way so as to finally open the true heart of the flats, the secret, innermost organ of accord and acceptance, of me, and my sincerity.

I stopped on a piece of a road that I knew just had to lead to another taste of nowhere, and I suddenly became agitated over our *supposed* relationship. It was then I realized it wasn't the flats that was holding out on me. The problem started back before I ever took my first step into the wasteland. Something else had spoiled my relationship with the ground I would cover. Poisoned it, in fact. I wasn't getting anywhere because there wasn't anywhere for me to go, because a certain *person* wanted me to think there was *somewhere's* to go, because *he* wanted me out. My thoughts sped back all the way to Dave and in a flash I realized that he'd planned the whole thing. Every action, every word, all of it was perfectly calculated to goad me into taking every step that I took, every pulpy, bloody plod, Dave was the arch matchmaker in a relationship that was going nowhere, because it was meant to go nowhere, me and the flats (what was I thinking?) with its *you'll-never-be-good-enough-for-me* attitude and its hot and cold shiftiness, blazing one moment frigid the next affections, ever dangling the pretense of a way forward when there was none, and never would be. Dave the genius, the master, the Wizard, always four steps ahead (*all good deities are*) got exactly what he wanted from me, told me what he wanted me to hear, then ushered me to Jacob's Ladder, Garl's hatch. Welcome to the dead zone, Ben. Dave wound me up like a toy, set me down on the ground and watched me waddle, buzz and click off and away from him and his living labyrinth of a girlfriend. He was jealous (*just like she said!*) and that's all there is to it, the why-he-done-it, why he said "Go on, now, before I change your mind," and I did and he didn't. He let me wander off into the lonely low-low, into the great parched beyond, and on and on, into love and gravel kisses, beyond the beyond, no turning back (*why would you?*) so irretrievably past the point of no return, which has no point (it never did) not when you're not who you think you are (and I wasn't) so obviously I was the perfect person to ask directions of, and give directions to (*can't get there from here*) (*that's what I really said*) and it all led to the precise stretch of moveable non-place where I moved without moving (you're moving, you're just not *moving*) and where I knew (in my crumbling bones) that where I was wasn't going to become somewhere just because I was there, because, let's face it, as a nobody in the making (*already made*) not being around for much longer was a good, healthy stretch of the way towards not being around long enough to matter at all.

So there it was, plain as day. The Lizard Wizard had marched me to my death to get rid of me.

This revelation blew in on the same demon breath of wind that saw my ceiling-directed fist shaking rants and cotton-mouthed railing, the rage spilling out of me, vented outward and upward to merge with the smeared clouds of spectral bile already spouted and spilt, nimbus pillars of rumbling acid and hate, one unspeakable revenge scenario spiraling into thunder-ous convergence with the next, a supercell that made a mockery of Dave's little wind machine, a quadrillion times more powerful, sucking it up and devouring it, along with the twitch house and the *Gizzard*'s sprawling muta-genie of an oversexed club house, yes, her too (nobody's spared) vacuumed right out of the ground, the dirt, the dreams, the flats, the world itself, pulled inside out, level after level, until the whole shiteating *all-of-it* is properly mangled in the chamber of compressed horrors until the only thing left is you (*me*) because it's all inside me now (*you*) but that's our problem right there, it's too much to hold, and, anyway, we're going in after it (*being part of it, and all*) falling, tumbling, the pull so strong it's tearing us apart, and because the gravity isn't me (*or you*) (*we're us, remember?*) the same me that thought I could control it (*what vanity*) (*what hubris!*) as we endure my just comeuppance, sucked in, slurped up—*wuffslphfphfwuffwuffwuffwfff!* and spit out, right where I am, facedown on a gritty patch of bed layer.

Everything looks exactly as it did, as if we hadn't been sucked up into me even though I now realize it wasn't me (not the gravity part, or the place, only the falling) and this realization forced me to roll sideways on that hard scrabble patch and look back across the days, where I can almost follow the trail of my remnant leavings. A crumpled *CarboTurd*® energy bar wrapper here, a squeezed hydro pouch there, its pokey straw sticking up like an antenna, relaying the signal, but it's faint, so weak and scratchy that I can't quite make out the words, if they are words (*or even language?*) but I hear the rhythm, the word-*like* rhythm, and that's enough for us, because we know that communications are being attempted, someone somewhere is sitting there in a lonely chair in the humming dark of some distant echo station transmit-ting, because they haven't given up on us (*the only one who hasn't*) (*and it's getting harder*) so we can't give up on them, and so I listen, patiently (*one has to be patient*) and I walk and decipher and decode, the movement one with the work, and it's hard work, tedious work, but I can't take a break or I'll lose my place, the progress I've made, so I keep on right through the night because I know she's worth it (*so worth it*) and her message, when I finally get it down, when it's all there, when at last I see the whole of it and comprehend, the message is the goddess, she's what this is all about, what it was always all about, and even as my feet catch and I falter, crawling, to get up, to crawl again, my hands and knees shredded maps, I am rewarded for the purity of my vision, by a gift. I can see it just ahead, and I even know what it is, a k-box survival kit of the kind the deep road crews were issued to leave in place, at intervals, so that a team stranded by equipment failure could walk back out of desolation, maybe even make it all the way home, on a yellowed plastic bladder of stale water and dry bricks of protein crackers. I give thanks to my benefactress as I fumble to open the tab and drink, the strong taint of degraded polymer lining, and I tear into and eat the ancient crackers that crumble to a chalky meal in my hands, a mason's mortar paste in my mouth. I fashion a bindle from the split and torn remnant of my rucksack (long emptied of its original contents) and fill it with these new provisions, this manna placed into the desert for me, awaiting my arrival, my path leading me to it to stumble upon it and take and eat, drink and live, yes, live, to walk another day, for her, for my goddess, and another day after that (*willingly!*) and however much longer and farther she will have me walk until I reach the next k-box, and the next, until I stop measuring time in anything like the way I used to do it, because it isn't necessary any more, the meaning of the measure lost because I'm no longer walking to something, not even to the next box, for that would be inexcusable short term thinking, having been given the great gift of the long view, the devout and thankful view, the vision of one who hopes and prays for more walking, because I do so hope it will not end, verily, for *destination* is a dangerous illusion. It smacks of heresy, antithetical, blasphemous impulses of the worst kind, corrupt to its core and corrupting, for the road is all that's needed, it's all that matters, and the mere notion of a terminus is to be fended off with my last strength, my last breath, but not yet, there's more breathing to do, inhaling, exhaling, respirating, one foot dragged and levered forward, followed by the other, I can't tell them apart any longer because they're one moving stick, a metronome, the pendulum, tick tock, walk, tick tock, walk. We know about delirium, yes, yes, I do, the important differences, like where the lines lie between what is and what isn't, and why that matters. I'm aware of the mirage, but we don't stray toward it, even as it moves with us, and my companions, with me, beside me helping me to stay on the path, stoic in countenance as they stop and wait for me when I fall. This I know even though I don't see their faces, for they won't look back, always the eyes are on and ahead to the road we must travel, just like they won't speak because any talk would be breath that's needed, wasted, but they're with me, those fellow travelers, generous with their patience, and despite their resounding silence I know exactly what they're thinking. They think they want me to prove myself, a stones-to-bread sort of proof that none of us can sink his teeth into, but I know what it would mean to try, a second, third and fourth coming, so I keep my own silence and I kiss them, those companions who would vie for my living soul, and who fold and meld and fold in and over again, replacing cell by cell that person I thought to be me but now recognize as us, until the former is but a memory of an offhand remark from those luscious lips, her lips (*the goddess*) in a dream that was itself a mirage, and still, it's me I cling to, me I cleave to, in order that we might save them and to accomplish that, I must resurrect my own purpose in order to absolve them in the origin and center of their corruption. That is why I grip the kit, the Fant Fixers kit, yes, that was what we called it once, a kit, and although it's a little dusty, scratched and dented in places, forgotten for long stretches, even in my clutch, I've hauled it a long way, as if it were a part of me, and when I go down, it goes down, and when I rise, it comes with us. *Why?* Because I'm ready, willing and able to work when there's work to be done, when a need arises, when a call comes through, even though it's getting hard to remember why there might be such a call, or what the need could possibly be for the assemblage, the collection of sinful things, the means to ends, the tools for the job, to repair the subject, to recalibrate motivations, to *fix* the problem, urges, yearning, don't try to solve, resolve, but you didn't do it, did you, you didn't alter that which is already perfect and thereby corrupt it and subvert the goddess, and so we walk in circles, we circumscribe the ruins and raise the walls anew, my path the sign and the truth of its dimension, my footsteps the chiseled glyphs that mark the tabernacle and intone the sacred voices, so that others might hear and follow out of the shivering darkness, into the reliquary, and there find the chalice, and there immerse, wherein nothing else matters, as we approach the sign on the shoulder of the highway ...

REST AREA – NEXT EXIT

My shuffling steps are the motions of a prisoner released who no longer seeks release, who moves as if bound though he is no longer bound. I take the gently curving exit off the roadway and proceed to the open doorway marked by the universal symbol of the male, for that is good and proper. I enter and there ascend the pulpit of the bucket Mount and preach the Word spoken for those who will come, for in their absence is the promise of a presence. For as surely as they are hungry to be saved, they will be drawn to the light, as once I was, so that which is spoken to the air alone is not spoken in vain, nay, it is prefatory to redemption. The first are always the four, as all good things are, for they were here upon the wall long before my arrival and will be long after my departure, to be shouted to the great spiraling body of the heavens (verily) to be heard and taken and cherished within the bosom and known the best: *Lust is the Enemy!*

Moreauvians

I suppose they thought it was funny. Moreauvians find all sorts of weird stuff funny, always giggling, making faces, sashaying about, cranking hips to strike poses, and putting on their frisky little spot dramas and so-called jungle puppet comedies. Every band was some mix of troubadours, streeters, the lost-lost, punks, junkies and vagabonds, fused together in an unholy alliance, usually around a seamy clique of fallen academics, or one charismatic designer with a taste for the Mo-Mo creed and the life of the ever-traveling gypsy circus. *Modifly* was what they called their code of radical alteration, *divine mutilation*, the shifting seasons of the body, conscious change, become what you are, ever high and fly. They were do-it-yourselfers, you had to give them that much, from the homemade liquid-razor-blades they called *bitey* cooked in their dribbling stills or squeezed drip by drip from filthy dosed rags, to the perpetual haze of the *mavala* of blue shrooms they grew in the dark and dried on the tops of their rickety painted wagons, and packed and smoked in their fluted horns, to the whole arc of spooky mod operations they performed on one another and on themselves in the grungy "parlors" they set up wherever they encamped.

Dr. Flavorian's *Codex of Eroticisme and the Known Fetishes* placed Moreauvians under the phylum Fur Lovers. In my own experience I found that definition too narrow, though I had to admit wherever I encountered Moreauvians (there was never only one, and you were wise to keep your distance however many there were) there tended to be a lot of fuzzy hair and furriness in the mods they fancied. The big cats were the ever popular meme, leopard faces, lions manes, tiger tales, sculpted cat noses of every shape and pucture, paws, pads, twitchy fuzzcup ears, and, of course, feline jaws and claws.

The rag tag band that had gathered around the public toilet in the vicinity of the lonely Niter Pines Rest Area on the outskirts of Lowden included several cat types, but also a number of other creature mods. There was a chubby capybara, an impressive baboon mod, a clutch of meercat girls, a tapir, a powerful-looking croc body and a hizzerit with a full-sized rhino horn and retrofitted neck brace. The group was most definitely a mixed bag, but true to Flavorian's category, general furriness was a quality they all appeared to share, even the croc. They camped in the rest area's empty parking lot and came every day to laugh and clap at the sermons delivered with great sweaty-browed intensity and fervor by the bearded preacher in rags who emerged from the cave of the Men's Room four times a day, like clockwork, clutching his bucket, to place it on the ground with great solemnity and stand upon it and deliver the Word and anoint the congregants with his rant and babble.

It was only when one of the fuzzy bunch, a skinny mavala kitty named Zooth, crept into the Men's Room bearing gifts of two crushed Chick-O-Sticks® still in their crinkly packages that I had a crisis of faith. I guess that's what you'd call it, the moment I realized I was the preacher, or perhaps better stated, a man who desperately wants to believe and make some sense of the divine in the corporeal and who wears the mantle of that calling, and simultaneously resumes consciousness that I (he/me) was also a fully certified pleasure model repair tech, recently in the employ of Fant Fixers LLC, Rat City branch office. For a handful of tantalizing seconds, I held these disparate personalities within me and tolerated the duality of their combination, before the fixer man took me all the way back and the preacher retreated into his shadows. That's how it came to be that it was the FF tech alone who glared down at Zooth, the blinking cheetah-boy, whose padded fingers and retractable claws walked his arms where he junk-scratched his bald kitty cat elbows. He mumbled just intelligibly enough for me to comprehend that he'd been in the Men's Room before, during one of my sermons, snuck in and rifled through the remnants of my ruck and spotted my FF kit against the wall under the torn and curled corners of the Morality First poster. He confessed that he was fixin' to "promote it" (Moreauvians were famous thieves) but changed his mind when it hit him that if he left the kit with me, maybe I could use the tools, maybe I possessed skills beyond those of a crazy bucket sermonizer. Maybe I could help him with his issue.

Zooth revealed that he was a dec and not a mod, though I'd already divined this. He explained that he started his life some thirty-odd years before, incepted as a boy toy in a sprawling retirement community called Heche en Sol. I'd not heard of the place, but I knew plenty like it. There were lots of them scattered up through the 10s and 20s, entertainment package living, theme parklets and walled fantasy enclaves. The kid had escaped the compound he was assigned to "all accidento," he said, while looking for an extra piece of cake after a "big ol' pawty," he found his way into the industrial kitchen, gorged himself on leftover desserts, then curled up for a nap inside a waiter's push cart. But the door of the cart shut and latched on him, somehow, and food service had packed it into a container and trucked it off premises. Zooth would've spent the rest of this short, artificial life locked in the dark of that steel box if a maintenance dec hadn't heard him banging on the walls and let him out. He passed on the chance to return to the old folks *pawty* zone from whence he came and escaped into the great, wide underworld. He scrounged out an existence as a streeter, stealing food and dumpster diving, but the hunger almost killed him.

"Awmos' wen out fom dey cramps," he explained.

But he got lucky, if it can be called luck, and crossed paths with a band of Moreauvians, Marcos-and-Grange, quatro-deuce, Deep Claw Alley band, as he identified them. The troupes had names like that. Zooth pulled down his tank to show me a crap tattoo on a fuzzy pec. MG-42.

The leader at the time liked his face, and so jumped him into the band, took him as his personal bitch and set about modifying the kid to suit his tastes. That was how it worked, strict hierarchy with no choice for the bottom about the mods, not at first. But within a month top cat was dead, gut ripped open in a "slash battle," and Zooth, left to his own devices, hooked up with another cheetah boy he liked. The only problem was one of the early mods they performed had left Zooth with severe erectile dysfunction. It was amateur hour 24/7 in the butcher tents and filthy hootches of the Moreauvian "tailors" and that sort of mishap was not uncommon. But that's where the preacher in rags and his mysterious FF kit came into the picture. The way Zooth saw it, maybe the babbling substreet minister had the touch and the tools to put his flaccid catprick back on bona fide firmament. Or as he put it, maybe his problem wasn't so much "physico" as it was, like, "zike-logico."

Seeing as how Zooth was the one who jolted me from my own *zike-logico* issues, and was generous with his snacks, I decided to try and help him. I fished my kit out of the garbage pile that had been my cozy nest, my prayer mat and home sweet home for days, if not weeks … months? I set up in a clear spot on the cold tile, knelt in front of the box and opened it. It was like my first time all over again. The contents seemed foreign, strange and somehow wonderful. I brushed my fingertips over the tools of my trade, the resonators, inhibitors, flowmeters, tines, clamps, arc forks, strayfield drives, the meds and tintures in their labeled cartridges, and beneath the hinged trays in the deepest well, the tied rolls of the special sets, each emblazoned with its brand.

"How long have I been here, Zooth?"

"Wiao know. Wen weez got hee yafew daze 'go youz alray hee."

"A few days ago. But I've been here longer than that."

"Yey, ah denk so, too, lookso tangs, yey."

I picked up my transfixer in one hand and my resolver in the other, and my palms felt calloused and my grip clumsy around the graceful instruments that they were. But there was a hint of recognition in the feel. Something to work with, maybe. Something to build on. And something's better than nothing.

"Come over here and sit down with your back to me," I said, the authority in my voice sounding familiar, different, but familiar.

Zooth did as he was told, without hesitation, as I carefully tore open the end of one of the slender Chick-O-Sticks® packages. I raised it to my chapped lips and tapped it, ever so gingerly, causing a tiny avalanche of blaze orange flakelets to slide into my mouth. I chewed slowly to make it last. Crunched and chewed. It wasn't real food, but it was the best I'd had in weeks. Unexpectedly, one of the sinks in the restroom let forth a trickle of brown water, and I hurried to it to wash the fluorescent manna down. No cupping from the toilets to hydrate, and something in my belly, too. Providence.

Feeling like I was on a roll, I opened Zooth up. The cramped access revealed him to be a Cyberbell Dax8 Eagerpro, which I'd already surmised, judging from the slight hitch in his gait, though he had several factory mods, a Jacoby-Ryser skillset upgrade, a Squiremusk® pheramixer and a few other quasi-exotic enhancements. We called them 'Deezies' in the biz. Supposed quality merchandise marketed to people for whom supposed quality was good enough.

There was a mini-conspiracy theory that made the rounds in decarati circles that *Deezy limpdickedness*, which was not at all uncommon, and typically experienced right around the 30-year mark, was a bit of pre-engineered obsolescence. A built-in johnson jinxer, not bad enough to warrant a recall, and eminently fixable, which meant plenty of work for the fix tech community, essentially a big whopping favor to the industry, with expected return favors, brand pushing, kickbacks and other under-the-table arrangements all part of the purported scheme. It was widely believed that Cyberbell engaged in these sorts of shenanigans more than the other big players. Me, I just figured it was shoddy design, defective assembly or both. Cyberbell's real problem was cheapness, and if there was a true conspiracy in the mix it was that Cyberbell's own marketing people spun the whole favor-to-the-industry rumor to build b2b buzz and keep people's eyes off the genuine nugget: that Cyberbell product was utter crap.

So I fixed the cheetah-kid up. I even told him he was right about his condition, it was all *zike-logico* after all, that it was an easy repair for me (which was true) and that he was good to go. He was so happy he leapt and pranced and sprang from wall to wall, handling and exciting himself enough in the process to do a spot test drive on his substantial equipment right then and there (garish proportion was another Cyberbell shtick, all in keeping with its *Size isn't everything, but ...* campaign) and in record time Zooth's rock hard sproing was on proud display, bursting through his threadbare jammers like a shiny new hood ornament on a clapped out Maverac. But then he stopped, abruptly, mid-skip, mid-fap, still giddily clutching his protuberant yamcicle and stared at me, panting and trying hard to look serious around his toothy feline grin.

"Samiz dat det you sayed, upan det bucket."

"Oh. The sermons, you mean."

"Yey, de saymens. I layke det, yey. Et make me tink out loud. On de aynside, yunoh? Out loud aynside."

"Loud thinking, that's good, Zooth. It makes me feel good to hear it. Thank you for telling me."

"Yey, yey … um … dey goon eat you, yunoh det? Das wha dis awl bout. Das wha dey waitin on out dey."

I nodded and started repacking my kit, carefully, methodically, reverently.

"I know," I said. "They're going to eat me."

Vore. Moreauvians veered over into that sweet, smacking bit of politesse along with their other animalistic peculiarities. Of course it was only isolated fringe groups that did so, but there'd been enough incidents to brand the whole tribe as notorious for saturnalian romps that had a disturbing tendency to wind up in cannibalistic feeding frenzies. Victims were selected seemingly at random, when opportunity knocked, or when the mood took hold of the clan. Why they did it no one seemed to know, and those few Moreauvians who were caught and arrested after the fact didn't seem to remember anything about their barbarous behavior, or so the news cycle spun it. I had my own suspicions. Like maybe it was all that fur. Or maybe it was that you couldn't be a real beast unless you ate out animal-style every now and again, and coughed up a few genuine-product hairballs. Or maybe it was only and merely that with cats and dogs and crocs and baboons living together, sooner or later you didn't need to go looking for the jungle. It came to you.

Samson Gorilla

Technically speaking, decs have a limitless libido. This was by design, even the early hospitality drones were eventually made that way because, after a great deal of trial and error, manufacturers realized that it's easier to start with a full blown kDz power package at inception and scale back from there to optimal levels, than it is to build out that sort of dopaminergic capacity on demand. Hence, the designer axiom that it's better to establish and inhibit than it is to generate to establish. Besides, let's face it, many folks in the custom after market wanted their decs oversexed. For those others who preferred a more prim and proper carnal demeanor, there were layers of failsafes and limbic governors that kept the potential flood safely behind the dam. But all those neurofilters, skeins and dampeners relied on one single, off-the-shelf bioelectric switch to remain active. On rare occasions, the switch would trip itself in response to some highly specific external stimulus, instantly removing all artificial inhibitors, as I had witnessed exactly once. A trained pleasure model repair tech could trip the bioswitch manually (as it were) by introducing a Daxo-boost spawn-phased omix cambion, not a *real* cambion, of course, you couldn't pull that off with a field kit, but with a little perseverance the Dhianni-Haymaker workaround was doable. Essentially, by sparking the D-H projection you replicated the external stimulus that would've elicited the response condition and caused the switch to flip all on its own. It was surprisingly straightforward once you knew the steps.

When the switch went off, the curtain came up. The triggered episode was what we in the trade called going *Samson Gorilla*. The moniker was in honor of a designer named Rema Delectra Samson. RDS was a minor leaguer in the dec design world, as far as it went with any technical genius or biomimetic accomplishments, but she definitely made it to the bigtime when she went off the deep end, turned performance artist and tubed herself (dozens of times) wearing a gorilla suit while locked in a padded cell with one or more pleasure models when the bioswitch was tripped. Just as dogs, given an endless supply of food, will eat themselves into gastro-intestinal rupture, pleasure models with the gt88216ee binary Maxey-Nubar bundle deactivated will literally fornicate themselves and/or anyone and/or anything in the vicinity unto extinction, including any demented designer-turned-artist who happens to be wearing a selectively protective and very hairy bombsquad bodysuit.

Cruelty to decs is not in itself a crime, it having been deemed by the Powers-that-Be far too complicated, legislatively and jurisprudentially speaking, to criminalize the full spectrum of conceivable abuses, especially in light of the reality that far too many of the Powers-that-Be were deeply immersed and invested in many of the most abhorrent categories of the same, acts wherein the term *cruelty* didn't even begin to scratch the surface. Bizarre acts of "artistic abasement" on the other hand, weren't good for business, especially where the subtext of the offending vids, tubes and HOVOs focused popular attention on the very issue of cruelty to decs, which many believe was RDS's real purpose and certainly her only crime. The following message flashed at the end of every Hairy Mountain Gorilla production: "No living decs were harmed in the making of this tube." The PtB decided the attention wasn't wanted and therefore wasn't to be tolerated, so the perpetrator was ferreted out, arrested in her underground "studio" and made an example of, via prosecution for various infractions that were pressed into service whenever necessary: lewd acts in the fourth degree, simulated sodomy, tantamount to bestiality, depravity with intent to enlighten to name but a few. The last news blurb I caught on the subject of Rema Delectra Samson reported the now-celebrity artist was headed for incarceration in the maximum security detention complex at Lako Baines Deep Core. She would be in solitary, of course, because of the number of decs, mods and Resistance sympathizers in that overcrowded lockup, and because no padded suit can protect you in the LBDC. But I digress.

Before I closed Zooth up after fixing his malfunctive cob, I rigged his gt88216ee bioswitch for a 26-second triggered deactivation, after which Zooth would go right back to being what he perceived to be normal. I set the trigger on a four minute delay. I didn't need a full four minutes to pack up what little I had with me in the Gentlemen's, but I wanted to account for the time it would take to usher Zooth out of my workshop and get him back to milling with the herd. Three minutes and fifty seconds after he left, I peeked around the corner at the entrance, and realized it was a good thing that I hadn't set him on a five minute timer, because the heavily muscled croc bodied Moreauvian, who I guessed to be approximately female and the new alpha of the mangy bunch, was on her way toward me. Something in her reptilian expression told me she was suspicious and hungry (a bad combo) and the others were gathering behind her in salivating anticipation of what was about to commence—it was time for the all-you-can-eat preacher buffet.

The big croc only made it three more steps before Zooth's switch flipped, and his response didn't disappoint. Going Samson-G with a brand-spanking-new sprocky was like streaming ape shit into a skimjet engine on proburner. Fortunately for me,

Zooth's eyes were locked on the alpha croc when the juice kicked, so he went for her first, although "first" doesn't really do justice to the phased impression of time-bending sequence, as the blur formerly known as Zooth did his hyperdriving, powerdrilling best to simultaneously peg every orifice of every animate thing (and a few inanimate ones, to boot) within a sizable blast radius of his exploding libido. The other Moreauvians, helplessly caught up in the supersexed frenzy, quickly responded in kind, and the result was a vicious caterwauling juggernaut scrum of an animal orgy the likes of which I couldn't have imagined and would not have believed even if related to me by Hana in the Lem Bar (with her serious face on) she the ultimate yarn spinner of true-to-God parasexual confabulation.

At the eight second mark I made my move from cover, betting that by then the bugged eyes would all be inward leering. The tumbling ball of pandemonic activity had migrated a few degrees to my left, so I cut hard right and spotted what I was hoping for across the lot, the only powered vehicle mongst the sprawling caravan of painted wagons: a beat-up old VespaNova with a vestigial sidecar crudely attached. I hurried to it, tossed my kit in the buddy hole and took the saddle. The crazed preacher me, the one who prays all the time when left to his own devices (a constant muttering jabberstream) doesn't pray *for* things so much as he prays *to* things, as best I can figure, anyway. Whereas the Garl in me ditched the preacher's bat-shit monomania for a far more pragmatic agenda. I was praying hard in that moment as I sat astride that jetbike—*for* something. With every stringy fiber of my jerk-dried frame, I prayed *for* the little crapheap of a machine to start.

And who knows? Maybe some winged hizzerit in some astral thin place even heard and answered my plea, because with a coughing sputter the dented gen-set kicked over on the very first try, and the thing shook like it wanted to rattle right off its rusty frame. But it didn't, and it didn't die on me, either. It kept on running, spewing gray smoke from its pock-holed pipes. I slammed the shifter into *Flow* and the bike lurched forward, whining in shrill complaint. I wobbled and weaved left and right through the barricades of gypsified carts, barrel fires and heaped detritus, going slow enough that any one of the ravenous band could have disengaged from their coitating crush and caught me at an easy lope. But a few seconds later, I cleared the last of the obstacles and pointed for the highway. Even at full throttle the scooter took a scary-long time to get up to anything approaching a respectable speed, and it wouldn't flow higher than a stripped hair's breadth off the ground. With the onramp in sight, the bike sputtered and my breath caught. The mangy thugs could've still caught me if they came at a sprint, and I cringed when one of them, the baboon, looked my way out of the pack-sexing rabble and his eyes registered with genuine distress what was happening: the preacher meat was escaping. He just had time to stretch his primate lips and bare his hideous yellow teeth, his jaw yawning wide to shriek a baboonish alarm when he was abruptly yanked back into the humping thrusting fur-splitting buck-sweat-and-slobber-flinging transcopulation of a yowling feral fleshstorm. The bike coughed one last time, then zoomed. I was out on the open road. I was away.

Subspace Frequency

The little VespaNova ran better and longer than I thought it would and I was luckier than I had any right to be. A tattered downstreet preacher with a crazy beard in bug-flecked rags propped on the banana seat of a smoky rustbucket bike should have attracted plenty of police attention. I never should have made it half as far as I did. Maybe it was a sign of the times. Anymore, security was simply taken for granted down on the levels where it no longer mattered. So whether it was luck or numbers, I didn't encounter a Xec cruiser or one single jackedbooted goon through any of the 149 levels it took me the rest of the day and all through the night to transit. With the proper EZpass you could take the ML all the way from the Low Flats straight up to the penthouse. And if your business on both ends was vertically proximated you could make the trip door-to-door in under an hour. That was to be the beauty of Dwell Deep, when V-P, silo chic and the promise of a cakewalk commute were all-the-rage leading to widespread gentrification of the lower frames. But after the notorious *downers*, the pit riots and height flight, the EZpasses got harder to come by, freezing out those bold souls who invested everything in a future that didn't turn out to be. With no pass it was a different story getting from down low to anywhere up top, and silo living wasn't nearly so chic. For the same reason, my own trip was on lonely back roads, a zig-zagging, gerrymandering circuit of byways, detours and long, lateral stretches of hydroponic ag access routes. More times than I cared to count I had to go down in order to go up. I sneaked onto rattling one-truck freight lifts, creaking shuttles and funiculars, the infrastructure left over from the early boom days and the era of heavy lifting. I took utility tunnels and siding shafts so steep I had to get off and push the squeaky-wheeled machine to make any headway at all.

Still, I wasn't about to let a little rough headway stop me, not after the odyssey of the flats, no, not after the desert. I was confident the lowest lows were behind me, or so my ragged, bearded faith told me. They had to be. Best of all, I could feel myself waking up, really coming to, and though I wasn't at all sure what the open eyes of daylight would mean or what I would see, I didn't want the new glow of my tweaked consciousness blinkered. The connections were too compelling. Things were just getting interesting.

Near the halfway mark of my halting rise from the down below, there was a brief but important encounter that's worth mentioning. It was 88-Frame, and though I had no intention of giving up, my body was saying otherwise. I was depleted, sapped, breaking down physically. The Chick-O-Stick buzz was long past and my ride was steadily losing power beneath me. In that moment of exhaustion, in a dark alley in the industrial sprawl of that level, I got off the scooter and pushed, tripping over my own feet, really staggering. With every faltering step I took, the pavement reached up and tugged hard at my knees, to make that one spot the claiming spot where I would drop, fall, fail, and never get up again. We, all of us (whoever we were) would lie there together, the ground and us, and listen, as the last breath went out. I stared into the dimming crystal of the VespaNova's headlight, its dying filament pulsing in synch with my own imminent demise, when the distant sound of a four-stroke finjet engine cut through my twilight reverie.

I raised my head to watch the approach of a pair of riders on a solitary offroad machine, a man and a woman, both in black leathers. They swung around behind me and stopped. I squinted at them through my tunneling vision, saw the kickstand snap down and four boots take the pavement. The man strode up to me first, and with kind eyes and a reassuring nod, he took the handlebars of my runty scooter, gently unfingered my rigored grasp. As I stood there, wavering, he wheeled it over to their idling Norton and connected it to a power-take-off. The woman approached me next. Without a word spoken, she lifted the flap of her shoulder bag, took out a green bottle and a round loaf of black bread and offered them to me. When I accepted the gifts, she pressed her hands together flat in front of her face and bowed.

"Namaste," she said.

The man had the VespaNova charged in a matter of seconds, the restored brightness of the headlight made the little rig look good as new. He disconnected it, wheeled it back over to me and propped it on its stand. He too pressed his hands before his face and bowed. I dipped my own chin in a feeble pantomime of the gesture, but he didn't seem to care. They got back on their bike, the woman in front, her man behind. The gleaming, oversized gas tank had their names scrawled across it in fancy gold script: *Madam & Yves.* The kickstand clapped up and, with a last nod to me, she steered the bike around and accelerated away, gaining flow as they grew smaller.

I stared after them until the smell of the fresh bread reached me, and I sank my teeth into the loaf. It was dense and hearty, still warm in the middle, and as I chewed, wanting it inside me faster than I could get it there, I tore at the cap of the bottle. The beverage turned out to be wine, a pinot noir, maybe (I don't know) it made no difference as I poured it past my chapped lips and swollen tongue. I drank deeply and the alcohol set my head to spinning, but I finished half of it, and a good chunk of the bread, too, before I thought to save a little for the road. Whether it was their own picnic the riders gifted me when they saw me dying on the road or whether it was their plan to give it away all along, I'll never know. But I know that angels exist, I'm certain of that, now, for I am the living proof of their concomitance.

With the strength of the food and drink I rode on. Higher and higher I traveled. I made better decisions with every level I achieved and left behind. There were fewer wrong turns, no more going down to go up and I began to recognize things. There was a busy streeter intersection on 60 we techs called the Tramps-Elysées that I never could have imagined would be a reassuring sight. Half an hour later, I passed by the address of a notorious FF client and kinbaku artist who went by the moniker Sir Drake Kobi. I'd been to Sir Drake's palazzo many times and knew the area well enough that I remembered a secret shortcut up a condemned, through-level bridge that my scooter just had power enough to climb. Once I was up to speed again I blew past Hana's favorite midtunnel smoothie stand. I was making real progress. Yes, I was on the move.

I made it all the way to 41 before I finally crossed paths with a cop. She saw me and decided that a lunatic preacher flying by on a bent bike was worth interrupting the important business of her day. She tore out after me, siren blaring and flashers whirling, giving me the whole berry show. I pulled over, set down and she screeched up within a micron of my fragile rear fender, trained her hot light on the back of my head, and left the flashers going for full effect. She even left her cruiser in flow, hovering a full meter above the street, as if the bulked-up ride was barely reined in from its champing desire to run me down. I watched in my rearview as the driver's door hissed open and a cute set of modular stairs folded down, on which a pair of shiny black boots descended heavily. The cop took her sweet time, too, pulling first one glove on, then the other, hitching her belt high on well-breakfasted haunches, then nudging her mirrored shades up on the bridge of her nose, and finally resting her right hand on the butt of her gun, as if it were the natural place for a hand to go. She was a piece of work, all right, every Xec cliché there was stuffed into one tight blue package. But I quickly identified (to my great relief) that she wasn't even Xec. She was one of the semi-deputized rent-a-cops the mid-frame developments gave a badge and gun to in order to ensure that at least the neighborhood thug was on the payroll. Maybe she planned to shake me down. If that was the case, looking the way I looked, local law enforcement was having a slow week. But as she drew closer I got a better look at her face and realized I'd been speed trapped by the new sheriff in town, *new* being the operative word, here. As I clocked her sauntering approach, I noted other signs of her rookie status. One, her gun looked *brand-spanking*-new, as in, quite possibly never fired. Her web gear was also heavily laden with lots of optional enforcer add-ons, some in duplicate, which meant she wasn't going to be exactly fleet of foot. The steel taps on her boots weren't going to help, either. Finally, the showboat posture of her parking job was going take precious seconds to reorigami itself back into shape for any resumption of a high-speed pursuit. In the end, the decision for me was an easy one.

I waited until her babyface was four clickety steps off my shoulder before I twisted the accelerator. I was practiced at coaxing the little bike to high revs before dropping it into gear. I revved it once, twice, and kicked it, lurching away as I tracked her reaction. It was nothing less than spectacular. First her mouth dropped open, as she registered the impossibility of me attempting such a thing. Then she started after me on foot, big lumbering steps as she struggled to draw her sidearm on the move. But as I edged away from her, she reversed course, too abruptly, slipped on her heels and went down. Her pistol jerked free of its sticky holster, at just the wrong angle, discharged on impact with the pavement and put a large caliber hole in the front Hy-Gen® cowl of the patrol cruiser. It was perfect placement, the one-in-a-million shot you can only dream about. The car spurted hot green liquid through the bullet hole like arterial blood, immediately lost flow, dipped sideways and settled onto the road surface with a thump, crumpling the cute modular stairway in the process.

I didn't let up on the throttle for a long time. As I raced away from the rookie rent-a-cop I finally figured out where it was I was going. Call it rote recollection, or residual disorientation, or the simple, rigid inability of a repairman-joe to leave a job half finished. On the morning I left Rat City on my ill-fated service call to the Dober Man's beware-of-dog house, a second appointment flashed up on my FF scheduler. The address was still frozen on the little screen of the butt set in my kit: Jagabrew. 117 Albatro Cntr. Circle 5-8. Obismo 33-1342. Within the hour of my encounter with the green cop, I found myself on 33, in Obismo, directly outside the security gates of the very address and (this next detail is almost too incredible to relate) no sooner did I brake and stop than the micro gen-set of my trusty VespaNova rattled hard, snapped off its corroded bracket and exploded to smoking pieces on impact with the pavement. My brave little steed gave up the ghost the moment it delivered me to my destination. I fished my kit out of the sidecar and set off to do my duty, and finish the job I had been dispatched to undertake.

Despite the formidable gate, there wasn't any security to be seen, which was unusual for a mid-frame complex, but another stroke of fortune for me. Being out of uniform (to say the least) no guard would have let me anywhere near the place. I found the name on the plate and pressed the button. The client was understandably surprised to hear me over the intercom. And I guessed that he probably didn't have high-res HOVO on his sec-pad or he never would have buzzed me in. When he did, I took the elevator to the 8th floor and found him waiting in the corridor outside the open door of his apartment. As I approached, he looked me up and down with the hard squint of incredulous disbelief.

"What the hell *are* you?"

"Fant Fixers tech, Mr. Jagabrew. Do you still have a service-related issue?"

"You must be fucking joking. I gave up on your sorry ass. Flakey-ass fako fixers, anyway."

I paused.

"If you'd prefer that I leave, sir …"

He squinted harder still, with such facial force that his eyes seemed to disappear backwards into his head, leaving only slits of extraocular flesh.

"Poofer? I poof-fer what I called *fer.*"

"I'm afraid I don't follow, sir," I said.

"The piece of shit ain't gonna fix itself, now, is it?"

I'd dealt with curmudgeony clients many times and was undaunted by the task.

"Why don't we see if we can remedy your situation. I do apologize for the extended delay."

He looked me up and down again, still blocking the doorway with his substantial frame. I was suddenly self-conscious about my own appearance, the unruly beard and rags. I must've been quite a sight to behold. Not to mention the olfactory component.

"Tell me this ain't how you repair boys are s'posed to look."

I had to think fast.

"No, sir. It was a bit of role play, you see. My last service call required it. At Fant Fixers we go the extra distance, do whatever it takes to ensure that the client is satisfied. If we can't fix it, the fix is on us, that's our motto. Please excuse the inappropriate attire, I had no opportunity to change."

He rocked his head side to side, his greasy lips pursed in a face that managed to be both flabby and pinched at the same time, and was locked in an expression that seemed to mimic my pitiful excuses. But he stepped aside, and with a jab of a stubby thumb motioned for me to go on in. So on in I went.

All it took was one sweeping glance at Mr. Jagabrew's studied décor to recognize the sort of client I was dealing with. Not the worst of them, but far from the best. He had a steady source of income, that was clear, and he obviously didn't need to go anywhere to earn it, that too was clear. The apartment looked and stank of his permanent presence. The kitchenette was full of dirty dishes. The living room had a sunken couch and coffee table cluttered with beer cans, food delivery containers, scattered Bic® lighters and a blackened glass pipe. Situated in front of the couch was a new home theater system with the latest in expanded HOVO and surround sound. I knew it was new because the boxes and packaging were shoved against the wall. Judging from the nearby carton of expensive cigarettes (Dunhill®) and the brand new system (Trivid®) juxtaposed with the crap couch and reeking carpet, I guessed there'd been a recent infusion of large money into the man's life. Though what he did for a living wasn't readily apparent. He obviously used the Trivid system to both record and stream, because there was a life-size HOVO of himself paused and jittering on the propad, while on the image fringe was another person who didn't look like he was having nearly as good a time as Mr. Jagabrew in the magical moment.

I finally allowed my eyes to venture to the far end of the apartment, the area I'd been instinctively avoiding in the visual exploration of Jagabrew's crib. It was back there that the laser-cams were positioned to record *the show*. His dec, my subject, was in the midst of Mr. Jagabrew's other defining lifestyle choices which were on proud display. The entire back half of the apartment was a dungeon, fully tricked out in every way.

My work with FF had taken me into a lot of dungeons. Over that time, I developed the opinion that there were good dungeons and bad dungeons. There was a lot of tasteful stuff in the bdsm milieu, plenty of class acts. Mr. Jagabrew was not one of them.

It was evident that he styled himself a "Dom" on the forums he was certain to frequent and where he posted his tubes. But how he saw himself and what he was were different things, for it was also readily apparent, there in the back half of his lair, that the man was an aggressive and unimaginative vanilla sadist, and there was not a classy bone anywhere in his body.

Normally, I would've suppressed this sort of a running interior critique, I would've kept it buried somewhere below the level of conscious operations, seeing as how it might distract me, indeed, might interfere with my ability to be fully present and the best, most attentive FF tech I could possibly be for my valued client. I'm not sure why it was any different this time. Maybe it was the cumulative effect of the sojourn up from the way down below, the long, strange trip across the Low Flats, or the hiatus at the Niter Pines Rest Area. Or maybe it was something else. Like maybe it was the sight of the thick dossier on Jagabrew's coffee table, an actual hard copy file (if you believe that) embossed with the eagle of Xec and a printed name that I recognized, even as Jagabrew tried to block my view with his thick frame, then casually turned the folder over and set a plate of greasy wing bones on top of it. Or maybe, just maybe, it was the expressionless eyes with dark hollows in the skeletal head of the emaciated and contused dec teen who was secured by his wrists and ankles in wall-mounted cuffs at the dungeon studio's center stage.

One of my very first clients, way back when I was an FF newb, was a grizzled old pimp who ran a stable of semiexotics and harbored a wide philosophic streak. He once asked what I thought had changed in the world since artificials came on the scene, not that either one of us knew what life was really like back in the days before plastic minds and Presumed Sentience. Still, it was an interesting question to ponder. I told him I thought decs took away any real meaning to the word inhibition. They weren't human under the law, despite the presumption, so there weren't any real limits to what you could or couldn't do with them or to them. The darkest, dankest, most illicit and extreme fantasies could be acted out, and with the right kind of money, acted out over and over again. That's not to say those sorts of things didn't happen in the days before decs, they certainly did. But once the big three manufacturers started cranking them out in numbers, there was huge proliferation and a marked improvement in affordability. When that happened the questionable behaviors became more prevalent, pervasive, commonplace, even, and largely accepted, or at least tolerated. Decs weren't people, however real they might seem to be. They were fabricated, like appliances, the work of human hands, and so they fell in the pecking order somewhere below natural pets. Cats, dogs, rabbits, rats, iguanas, frogs, ferrets. You could be cruel to an animal, but decs were machines, and let's face it, you can't hurt a machine, no matter how much it says it feels the pain. The response to stimulus was simulated and, by definition, *un*felt. Or that was the dominant thinking, and even though the Presumed Sentience Movement tried to alter it, or at least mitigate it, that historic thinking persisted. Decs didn't get an out, they didn't get a safe word, because they weren't real.

I said all this to the flesh monger. It was a bit of a rant, I admit, and I didn't stop there. I told the pimp I thought humans were emotional adolescents, in the main, and that our evolution-ary progeny (if we were lucky enough to have any) would judge us as such. We were a world of cruel, needy and dangerous pricks. And it wasn't that we'd regressed into that state, we'd always been that way, and had never grown out of it. We weren't ready for zero inhibitions, I said, and if we were ever going to be, things would need to be different. We would need to be different. It's go-ing to have to be a whole new ball game, I declared, a brand new paradigm. Let's go ahead and call it *true empathy* in a fully-shared neuro-electrified grid, or some such thing. Until that day, if it ever came, society works (or if "works" is too lofty a word, at least it doesn't self-extinguish) because and only because of inherited and/or instilled repression, our persistent and nagging inhibi-tions, the emotional barriers and parapsychologic forcefields that wrap us up and keep us, or most of us anyway, from committing the many unspeakable acts that zip through our minds. With-out those inhibitions, our pumped up monkey brains would go cattywampus haywire, they'd liquefy to toxic mush in our gourds, and spill out of our ear holes in crimes of species wide self-im-molation. Inhibitions are the *what* that holds the *this* together, I exclaimed. Inhibitions are the strange angels of our better nature.

Indulging my rapturous disquisition, the contemplative pimp heard me out, and he surprised me too, because rather than decamp in the face of my meandering screed, he engaged and probed.

"I hear you," he said. "But what am I supposed to do with all that mess? If what you say is accurate, even in part, where does it leave me? What actions must I take? What further actions must I abjure?"

We held this dialogue, and the talk slid north and south, as it were, with sliding puffs of a hookah mouth, and all the while I stayed on task (I was there on a job, after all) and worked diligently to reset the libido governor on his prized androgyne. The prostitute was a Nebulosa Ze-Sylph Trans-Cis 2.0, better known in the tech pigeon as a TC 2-Way. It was a beta version, no less, a Marvex factory-custom one-off that none other than Table 12 and possibly even the Lizard Wizard himself had a hand in making. He/She was work of a quality that Marvex was no longer capable of producing. Quality was its problem, as in too much of it. The thing was over-engineered right out to the edge of human frailty. It keeps wanting to fuck itself, the pimp complained. I know the feeling, I quipped, flashing a winning smile (being so *new* at the time, I had a new tech's lame idea of benchside manner) but it was only after I told the pimp that the dec's radical mood swings and near constant self-pleasuring were symptoms of a bug I could easily fix that the old monger relaxed again and leered back at me with what I took to be an expression of vague amusement. I was nearly finished with the adjustments to his TC 2-Way, when I floated a sort of an answer to his normative queries.

I don't know where it leaves you, or any of us, I said. But I believe that what we do to *them* we do to ourselves. If decs are used and abused until they become dead to meaningful sensation, or lost to hope, or both, there we follow. We travel together in this, whatever-*this*-is, and there's no running from it, the condition or the connection, no hiding from the truth, or pretending it doesn't exist. It finds us because it's already in us. Forsake our inhibitions altogether and we become the monster that's lost any ability to feel. Figuring that as a pimp the old guy was probably inured to harsh language, I even waxed profane (a big no-no in the manual). Jesus H., I said, sex doesn't even work right without inhibitions. The point is, limits equals intensity, and the tighter the aperture the higher the pressure. It's better to be with them than without them. The whole framework of conformance and trespass are the lines of play on the field. They are the inbounds, and the out-of-bounds, experience, inexperience, the full ranging spectrum of desire, shame, freedom, repression, smeared across a million flavor range, from the brush of fingertips or the shared glance of the subtlest order, to the criss-crossing contours of strap-bound, blindfolded and ass-clenching flying in the dark.

I said all this, or something like it, and the pimp pondered the words for a long moment in nodding, goatee-stroking silence, before he said, "You're not givin' me that lust-is-the-enemy turd all dolled up in a fancy new wrapper, now, are you?"

"Nope," I said. "Lust is more complicated than that one turd. It can be a friend, an enemy, either, neither, both, or something that transcends those hobbled definitions. But if it's to be a friend, it's a far better friend when in harness. I guess what I'm saying is—we have to have limits. We need them. It's a matter of survival for us and them."

The pimp grinned, then chuckled, then laughed his head off, his diamond teeth sparkling in the cold streetlight.

"A better friend when in harness. I like that, I do, yes indeed. And call me strapped to disagree, my fine feathered fabricateur."

Like most philosophizing, any epiphanies gleaned in the moment were left behind in the fading glow of discourse, as he signed the FF work order and I gave him his pink copy, life resumed its shifting shape and went on as before, the pimp back to pimping, gently easing his newly-repaired TC-2 into the velvet cush of his purple stretch El Cid, and me, I went on to my next service call of the night, and the next one after that, I was new after all, and the newbie always gets the shit schedule.

And so, although it may seem the stuff of tangled up digression, I related this story to the new client Mr. Jagabrew, told him of my dialogue with the pleasure merchant and of our agreement as to its conclusion, and though I spoke quickly and mumbled much of what I said, it didn't matter, because Jagabrew wasn't listening, anyway. He didn't care what I had to say as he talked over me and casually tortured the skin-and-bones dec he had cuffed to his "hobby board" which was his name for the dungeon wall. The thing was fully equipped with shelving, straps, mounts, carabiners and toys, lots of toys. But it was your standard, cliché collection of domination-and-submission related accoutrements. Pretty damned tedious, all of it, really.

The dec was a Sweetech® *Barely Legal*® 16GNO17 Jhett. Sweetech was an arms-length subsidiary of Cyberbell, a shadow division that was embedded in contracts, corporate licenses and tax records, that Cyberbell, with its squeaky-clean image and famously skittish execs, could pretend didn't exist. There was simply too much money to be made in the sweet-dec trade, way too much demand in the marketplace to leave it all on the table for the other big players to gobble up. Therefore, it was the shadow division, and not Cyberbell itself, that kicked out thousands of decs just like Jhett, with his trademark streeter punk styling, lank hair, pale skin, plenty of ink (the tawdry template art that was a Sweetech standard option) and various and sundry piercings and spacers (the female and hermaphroditic versions of the model, the Jordin and the Jules, were nearly identical in appearance) (as a group, "Team Jailbait" to us repair techs). Jhett was factory set to be eighteen, supposedly all the 16GNO17s had to be (some Cyberbell bylaw) though the design concept was that he should *appear* to be much younger. Ironically, Jagabrew's Jhett looked older, as if putting up with the dungeon master's daily doses of vicious kink had physically aged him, something I didn't think was even possible.

"Look me in the damn eye, Jhett, you piece of shit," Jagabrew growled.

Jhett did as he was told, then quickly averted his strung-out gaze, apparently conditioned to anticipate that his master didn't really want him to look him in the eye. Jhett, eh? Anyone with a scintilla of self respect would've changed the standard model name to a custom name that suited his or her fancy. It was the first thing you did on unboxing and activation. But my cherished client hadn't even done that much. God only knew how long Jerkabrew had the kid in his amateur pain palace, Jhett playing the part of the foil to the archkeeper of clamps, probes, ball gags and doo-hickeys, the victim waif in the overlord's febrile fantasy arena.

"See what I'm talkin' about," Jagabrew whined. "Nothin' there. Lights out, ain't nobody home. All's I'm askin' for's a ent-sy-weentsy flinch once in a blue-fuckin'-moon. Purty please? What I gotta do to get this sissy to wake up and smell the bull-whip? I'm tryin' to get off here, yo!"

"Decs don't get a safe word," I whispered.

Who was I talking to? ...

Jagabrew's face did that pinched thing again. He was wondering the same thing.

"What did you say, repairfuck?"

I shook my head. Tried to shake off what I was about to think.

"I understand the issue, is what I meant to say," I said.

I was having difficulty concentrating. I crouched and made a show of opening my kit and searching for the right tool. I was playing for time. According to the codes on the FF work order, I was cache-dispatched (however many weeks ago it was) to fix the Sweetech unit's problem, do a dermal refab and/or change-out on the neck, portions of the anterior scalp, upper back, wrists, forearms, shins and ankles, where the cigarette burns and weeping lesions wouldn't *rehabilitate* the way they were supposed to. With decs, you didn't call it *healing*, but that's what it was, and the upshot was that this unit wasn't healing up properly after Jagabrew's continual loving attentions. The job was all very routine. It was supposed to be, anyway. Standard stuff in the most standard sense of the word, and normally I would've made short work of the repair, even taken the opportunity to amplify the kDz-endorphin volumes right up to Overjoy and tweak the variances on the dec's submissive response set so as to make him a more agile bottom to Jagabrew's intemperate top. But that was the old me. The new me knew that these adjustments would only be a temporary fix, a band-aid on a gushing wound, one that would fall off as soon as I left the premises, because Jockitchbrew was a mean-spirited, ultraviolent and destructive personality, by nature, really a very negative individual, and his Sweetech purchase, the presenting article of fabricated chattel, Jhett, *our* Jhett, was failing and wasn't long for this world.

I asked Jagabrew to stop pulling the subject's head back by his hair. To my surprise he did stop. He even stepped back, thinking I was about to perform some repair-related task, until he realized with a look of fury that I simply wanted him to stop. Jhett's chin dipped to his chest and Jagabrew shook his head in disgust.

"How much you wanna bet there was a factory recall I didn't get notice on? Not like your type's ever gonna tell me, anyways."

"My type …"

"Everybody knows FF's in bed with the fuckin' manufactures [sic], and the little guy's left to suck hind tit, per usual."

"Per usual …"

Jhett lifted his head and looked at me with those methadone-kitty eyes of his, eyes Jagabrew had paid good money for, eyes that he had every right under the law to see looking at him longingly, fearfully, however comefuckmefully Jagabrew wanted to be seen, and I was there to fix things so they did. Fix the problem, Garl. But right then, with his eyes still on mine, Jhett breathed words meant only for me. *Help me.* It was a phrase a model of his type could and would be expected to utter in the circumstances, something he was factory set to say. Just playing the part. On an average, ordinary service call I would've smeared on a little more *Nofera®* and gone about my business, ignoring his desperate plea for the act it certainly was. It was what I was supposed to do, what I was trained to do—*Don't converse, do the reverse.* Fix the problem, Garl. Except I didn't do that. Something about the tone of Jhett's voice told me that he had stepped outside of his parameters. He really wanted my help. He wanted to stop hurting. He wanted to live. He wanted out. I glanced at a nearby inset shelf, a built-in featurette of Jagabrew's prefab *Harmers Wallmanax®* grotto, and there caught sight of a newly opened *SoSlayMe®* erophernalia shipping box, the end torn open just enough to reveal the shiny new BenzOmatic® hand torch inside, still nestled in its display-form plastic. Staring at the nozzle of the torch, I swear I saw it ignite (*though I couldn't have*) and there was loud, cracking sound somewhere inside my head, as if something very heavy that surrounded me, a crustal skin of enormous weight was suddenly breaking, parting, sheering, calving and crumbling away from me, leaving me naked and sailing free, so airy and so light that I closed my eyes and sighed.

"You're right about the factory recall," I said. "I'm not supposed to tell you this, but I'm going to, because I need to take this unit with me."

"Say what? How'zat s'posed to work? You ain't even opened him up yet, find out what's wrong."

"Not necessary, I recognize the model. Like you say, it was an NTT, notice to techs, strictly back door stuff. Sweetech didn't want the word to get out to the general purchasing public. They tried to keep it on the downlow."

"Keep *what* on the downlow?"

"The need for the recall, of course. But you, sir, you saw right through their nefarious pivot. It's the smart consumer they fear most, always has been. Yes, that would be you, Mr. Jagabrew. Unfortunately, this isn't a fix that I can perform in the field."

"Not a fix I can pooform in the feel," he mocked. "That how it works? That how you do it there at Phony Fuxers? Say, *I recognize the model.* Say, *I'm gonna take your property.*"

"I assure you, my motives are honorable."

"That's a good one. Tell you what, *fixed-boy*, you take your *whore*norable-motives ass and you get the fuck out."

"Please don't do this, sir … it's not an optional repair, you see. It's a mandatory recall."

"Oh, I do see. You need sump'um for your troubles. Okay, yeah, I got a little sump'um sump'um for you right here."

He lurched at me with startling speed and I felt it before I saw or heard it, the sharp, rippling buzz that channeled through me. There it was in his grasp, a PyroWhip® Taser, the most powerful brand on the market, now shoved and digging into my ribcage, a good clean contact, too, sparking, click-clicking, and I should've gone down hard to the floor in a spasm of agony. Only I didn't. The charge went through me, harmlessly, and by a path to ground where I directed and willed it to go (*I know how crazy this sounds*) and in the next instant, there was a blur of arms and hands in the space between us. It took a portion of a second for me to realize it was my own arms and hands in rapid motion. In the mix the taser was plucked from Jagabrew's grip, it flew and hit the wall at high velocity, its hard plastic case shattered on impact, knocking other things off the hobby board. I watched each object fall, in turn, as if it were the star of its own art film, the chrome crutch plug, the peg-leg strap on, the diamond gag, and I could take my sweet time screening each scene, frame by frame, and truly appreciate its allusions and nuances, because I was operating in a dimension of speed that could scarcely tolerate the oozing *slowness* of everything happening around me, and so needed diversions to fill the yawning vacant spaces between events. I watched a clawed anal hook pirouette to the floor, tumbling a three-quarter turn before it hit, even muttering the equation of its rotational arc. A black spandex hood fluttered as it fell, like a graceful manta ray in the sun streaked ocean deep. A double-pronged donkey dildo bounced when it hit, like a dancer with as much spirit as flair, despite its one long leg and one short. But the black ceramic butt plug with the furry, skunk-striped tail was the festival winner, for it demonstrated such poetry and pathos in the lyrical ambivalence of its descent.

There was another sound, a wet, bone-crunching thud, and Jagabrew grunted sharply, it was almost a bark, like some large animal threatening to charge, but instead he hunched forward, bent over, and when he straightened again, I registered the look of surprise on his face, and then saw that he was fingering the edges of a deep, gurgling dent in the hollow of his chest. We both noticed, at the exact same time, that I held between us the squishy lump of his pinkish-white heart in my outstretched palm. It was sheathed in a purple veil of dripping viscera, and the way it was proffered it looked as though I was trying to give it back.

"That's ... mine!" he croaked.

"Yes," I said. "Sorry."

Jagabrew coughed once, spraying a geyser of blood, he took one heavy step toward me and collapsed in a pool of exsanguinating offal. It was a terrible mess. And I really *was* sorry. Killing the client wasn't even addressed in the Fant Fixers manual, probably because, at some level, a few basic commonsensical assumptions had to be made about what was and wasn't good and bad for business, not to mention just plain old right and wrong. I crouched down and carefully placed the heart next to him and wiggled my fingers. They ached the way you'd expect them to after using them to puncture a large man's sternum. I wiped my hand on his shirt, not to be disrespectful, that wasn't the intent. It was more that I was leaving all traces of Jagabrew on and around his body. I stood and went to Jhett. He looked back and forth from me to the leaking mound of his former master in what was pretty obviously a state of deep shock. I worked as gently as I could to unbuckle and remove his restraints, taking great care because his wrists and ankles were oozing bracelets of infected wound.

"But … Jag's *dead?*"

"I think that's a fair assumption, Jhett. From the looks of things, he died of extracted heart failure, compounded by a terminal lack of imagination."

I don't think Jhett heard me. A big part of the issue was that Jhett didn't know he was a dec. Many decs didn't, or if they did, they didn't dwell on the issue. Filters, it was all in the filters. If Cyberbell was good at anything it was in the development and core engineering of directed neuronal habituation and synaptic filtration. Jhett focused only on what he was supposed to know and do, what he'd always known and done, securely fastened in the certainty that his owner was his master and the center of his world, and all he needed to do was everything and anything that he could to please him and excite him and all that sort of business. Having the rug of his reality yanked out from under him was more than a bit disorienting, and the filters didn't help, in fact they made it worse.

"I … I don't understand."

"I know," I said. "You're going to sleep for a little while, now. When you wake up, everything's going to be better. I promise."

Skip This Chapter
(It's Really for the Best)

Keys in hand, it didn't take me long to find Jagabrew's pickup truck in the parking garage of the residential complex. I would've been happy with any old junk heap of a rig, so long as it flowed. Vehicular beggars can't be choosers. But his truck turned out to be brand new, a GMF-Trebant-2550 with king cab, Nitroglide® and the Supertow-Gator Hangtime® suspension package. I'd seen the commercials and, clearly, so had the heartless Jagabrew. I gently situated the sleeping Jhett in the rear compartment, trying my level best not to disturb the bandage job I'd done on his wrists, ankles and various other lesions. Killers on the run don't usually have time for luxuries like careful dressing of wounds, or infusion of IV-liquids, but Jhett urgently needed the care, so I gambled that his ex-owner wasn't going to be missed by anybody anytime soon. I slipped behind the wheel of the truck, pushed start, and maneuvered the tricked-out rig toward the nearest exit. To my relief, I saw nobody in the garage, and no one on the street, either, as I pulled out of the compound and rolled slowly past my deceased two-wheeler. I bid adieu to the little scooter that could, then leaned back into the lumbar caress of the bucket seat, inhaled the off-gassing polymers of that new-truck smell, set the autotint to midnight, accelerated to glide, went wheels up and put the truck in cruise at 10 klicks over the speed limit, pointing the hood ornament in the direction of the nearest megalift.

I knew where I was going.

Many things were now clear.

Perhaps not coincidentally, the "wet" episode with Jaga-brew brought me the rest of the way back to being me, the *all-of-me* me, at least as far as I could tell, as far as anyone can be said to know that they are themselves, being themselves. I'm not sure whether it was the sight of Jhett strapped and dying on the wall, or the homicidal act itself, or the dead man's slick blood on my fingers. Whatever it was, in that handful of gruesome seconds, with Jagabrew's fatty heart still twitching in my open palm, all the identity-related questions that gnawed at the walls of my consciousness for seven long years finally ate their way out of the placental sac and screamed upward into the cold morning light.

I knew with absolute certainty that up to that point I had been three people in one, a trio of distinct and separate person-alities: 1) the half-crazed downstreet preacher, who called him-self nothing, but whom others variously knew as Obidiah Fareye, John Highlife, Barker Rags, or simply, the preacher man; 2) the fantasy unit repairman named Garl "Cupidwrench" Motts, the meticulous, professional, service-oriented tech whose best friend Hana liked to call G-Narly or Prudence or simply numb nuts; and 3) the crime-lord-cum-resistance-subcommander-and-public-en-emy-numbering-in-the-low-single-digits, Ben Edgely, aka Praxis. All three of these individuals were packed, wound, wrapped and twisted tight in one very fucked up wanton dumpling of a deep-fried cranium.

I also saw, with the same quasar clarity, how it came to pass that it was so damnably crowded in my own head. It was not by accident. I wasn't born like that, not as all three of us anyway. Ben Edgely was the original me, the first head resident in my dome. The extra-added personalities was what happens to you when somebody turns a GegrilleMax® high-intensity resolver on a human being's head. Induced psychosis was a given. That it manifested in a form of multiple-personality disorder wasn't entirely out of the ordinary. The unusual part was that I was functioning at all.

Here's the way it happened (as best I can piece it together):

Edgely, operating in the underground as the much-feared resistance figure Praxis had been on their hitlist for years. When he was finally cornered and captured (following an *et-tu-brute* betrayal that's a whole 'nother story in itself) he was interrogated for days, unsuccessfully, until Archbishop Castiff came up with the brilliant idea of placing a resolver to Ben's temple and pressing *REZ*. The archbishop acted out of fury and frustration, but his move was later proclaimed a stroke of pure genius, when the leader of the Junta, Colonel Serpas, saw an opportunity and took the lead. In the hours and days that followed, he convinced his partners, and they all came to see and realize how much more fun it was going to be than simply being "rid" of Edgely. Garl Motts was nothing more (and nothing less) than a personality the Junta created, right there in the interrogation room during the post-resolution trance, the sweet, supple phase of maximum suggestibility. Garl was induced into me, rubbed hard into the malleable gray goo of what was left of me, until he took me over all but completely. Killing Ben Edgely would have been way too easy, and that's why it would not do, and why the archbishop was lauded for his bit of kneejerk inspiration. One pulse from that resolver set the stage for a far tastier drama, for it enabled them to send "the vile bastard Edgely" into exile in his own head, sentencing him to a permanent vacation in the lowest lands of servitude and humiliation. Oh, what a wonderful jape it was, how scrumptious for those bigwigs, and how they lapped it up, the oligarch, the administrator, the colonel and the archbishop, the full quorum of plutocrats all gathered together to sample the broth of sweet revenge, adding a dash of this drama and a pinch of that conspiracy to the recipe until the course they were serving was so satisfying, so rich, so exquisitely ironic, it was too delicious for words. That Edgely, *the* Ben Edgely, Praxis himself, operator of operators and prickliest thorn in their sides for years, should be trapped in a prison of his own mind—and as a lowly dec repair tech, no less. It was just *sooooooooo* good.

Here, a brief but important side note; it was precisely because the nabobs collectively believed that Ben Edgely was given to legendary sexploits, seductions and impossible conquests of the heart (and loins) that were every bit the equal to his mythic reputation in the underground that they deemed it the ultimate coup de grâce to turn him into a *pleasure model* repairman, thus (hilariously) rendering him a technical eunuch; not a one of them ever suspecting (until much later) that Edgely was in the grip of a monolithic and rapturous love for a single female unit—the afore-and-multimentioned Inge-Borghesa courtesan, Grushenka. But this minor oversight was of little consequence in that juicy moment because once they were done with their mental manipulations, everything Edgely owned, everyone he knew, everything he was, his entire reality was stripped from him, and replaced with a persona that was spoon-fed into him like pabulum, reducing him from rebel mastermind and underworld icon to a lowly service tech who would live (if you could call it living) way down on one of the deep frames (*Why not Rat City? It's the worst place I've ever seen! Yes, very nice choice, Colonel Serpas, we readily concur!*) employed in a dead-end job in the mildewy branch office of a barely solvent company (*There's a Fant Fixers in that rotten hole that might do nicely. Excellent suggestion, your eminence. Archbishop Castiff comes through again!*)

Of course, the Junta couldn't trumpet their miraculous victory. They couldn't breathe a word of it to the rest of the Xec hierarchy, or the Standing Committee, or any of their legion of thugs and minions, for if they did, their enfeebled pet would be dead within a single dicycle and all their good fun spoiled. So it remained their little secret. Edgely – now Garl Motts – would live his warped and pitiful little life. He would be checked in on from time to time, paid a visit to by one or another of the foursome, for the sheer entertainment value, if nothing else, to enjoy and cackle over his plight all over again (*truly, it would never grow old*) watching Garl the dutiful employee (*how Edgely would have gagged on that one*) Garl the hard worker (*their former archnemesis would've vomited at the thought*) Garl with his scrupulous ways, his tool collections, his earnest, client-first resolve (*Resolve, yes! Yes!*) Why, great galloping geldings, folks! Garl Motts is a darned good contributor to society! He's an upstanding citizen! A stand-up guy! To our success! (*Clink!*)

Of course, it was a foregone conclusion that they would need to come up with a bad end for him at some point on the timeline. But with the invention of Garl Motts, the luminaries had years to think up a fitting denouement to their drama, a worthy terminus and a truly meaningful demise for their slave, one that would measure up in every way to the heartburn that Edgely/Praxis had caused them. When that day finally came, they chose sordid over sudden, or accidental, or heart-rending, or magnificent. Thus, it was in order to accomplish the desired end of an acutely *sordid* death that they turned to their longtime operative Herbert "Pikemaster" Jagabrew, the unimaginative sadist for whom all things sordid were not only his specialty but came as second nature. The fact that another service call popped up on Garl's scheduler on the target morning, an appointment window that FF dispatch slotted *before* the Jagabrew call, squeezing in an *expedite* (though not a *special*) at the Dober Man's canine casa, was totally unintended by the Xec puppeteers. It was by this pure accident that Garl came face to face with one of Colonel Serpas' most feared ex-henchmen (a narc lieutenant so prone to ultraviolence he was forced into early retirement) who instantly recognized Garl *as Edgely*, impulsively decided to wrap up some old business and kill him, and to that end, took him on a joyride to the Low Flats. It was a twist of fate too freaking bizarre to be believed.

It wasn't supposed to go down like that.

It was Garl's *next* service call on the FF scheduler (the one that *didn't* happen that morning) that was *supposed* to be his bad end, his swan song, the finale with a foul flourish. The plan: Garl was *supposed* to show up at Jagabrew's highrise hellhole of a residential complex, be subdued, knocked out, awakened with smelling salts only to find himself strapped to Herb Jagabrew's "hobby board" and thereafter tortured and dismembered (one member at a time) (while still alive, obviously) over a period of days (the longer the better) all the while in the grimy, fat-fingered clutches of the aforementioned seedy weirdo whose fetishes were the perfect combination of banal and tediously thorough. It was a fantastically sordid way to go out, a mode of exit selected by the Junta members after much discussion (and ferocious argument) before the compromise of the "Jagabrew Gambit" was finally reached. The one area where they were all in perfect accord was the absolute necessity that every succulent second must be captured on HOVO for later editing into a highlight reel. To put the radioactive cherry on top of the magnificent heap-O-dung they were dishing up, Jagabrew was under strict instructions to open an envelope during the latter stages of the gruesome process, an envelope that had been hand-delivered to him that very morning and that contained photos, internal Xec reports and even a holovid with surveillance footage detailing (in summary fashion) Ben Edgely's suave and heroic prior existence, his haunts, his movements, his cohorts, his presumed paramour. These images would be the visual cues that would yank Edgely's true consciousness back to the fore, prompts that would *rebirth* him, pulling him with ice cold forceps out of the penitentiary womb of Garl's pitiful psyche and back out into the blackest light. It *had* to be Edgely *himself* who would bear witness, to see and know and appreciate all that had transpired, the sheer attention to detail the ruling foursome had invested into the minutiae of his abject destruction, so that he, Edgely *himself*, would scream that last matchless, exquisite, pyro-schizotic scream, the instant before he succumbed to the bitterest of bitter ends.

That, oh yeah, *that*, my motherfuckers, is payback.

There was only one problem. And it was a big one. A real whopper of a flaw with their plan. It was far more problematic than a simple quirk of fate, an innocent Fant Fixers' scheduling snafu that led to a dog-faced ride in a car, a rollover accident, a missed appointment with vivisection and sordid death, and (in lieu of same) Garl's long disappearance into the Low Flats. All of that mishegoss was in minor mishap country compared to the crux of the issue which went all the way back to the beginning, to the exact moment (in fact) that the archbishop made up his mind to snatch up a resolver, press it to Edgely's head and give him a psi-static shampoo. The resolver *was* the issue. When you turned a resolver on a dec, you *resolved* the dec. That's Artificial Neocognition 101. Everybody knows that. Simple feed-forward iterative convolution. Basic stuff. On the other hand, turn a resolver on a human head and you scrambled the human brain. More rudimentary neuroscience.

The problem here was that Edgely wasn't a dec.

He wasn't human either.

Spoiler Alert

Ben Edgely was a hybrid. A prototype. Neither human nor dec, he was the melding of the synthetic into the real. Originally, the ejeet design team that made him planned to make many others like him, a whole hybrid community, males, females, plus everything else and in-between. But in the end, Edgely was the only unit they incepted, because the initial foray proved too dangerous and unpredictable, and when push came to shove (literally) several of the key players lost their collective nerve. For starters, the project was fantastically subversive and illegal. Hybridization of dec and human blurred the lines, breaking the rigid and critical delineation of the natural from the fabricated in a way that threatened cherished mores and rendered the Segregant Laws meaningless. The notion that Edgely might be a hybrid was so beyond imagining, so über verboten, that even Colonel Serpas, the one member of the Gang of Four who suspected everything, did not suspect.

Sure, they knew about Edgely's other personality, the mad and babbling preacher, Barker Rags (who, strangely enough, carried over into Garl) but they attributed his transitory emergence to the archbishop's resolver blast, figuring it was just one more hilarious (and harmless) side effect of Edgely's pulse-pithed brain. What they didn't know was that Edgely and the preacher were brother personalities who had co-existed long before his association with the underground movement. Edgely and the preacher went way back, all the way back.

In the days after his hybrid genesis, after "Ben" (as they called him) was incepted full grown, the unit showed signs of willfulness and intractability. Because the designers were seeking a new paradigm, that being the whole point of the exercise, in their hubris they thought they were prepared for anything. Ben was expected to be different and they were ready to make any necessary adjustments. At first they tried to accommodate their precocious young monster. They tried one workaround after another in fruitless attempts to correct his increasing "imperfections." They gave him challenges, abilities and powers, in hopes that the demands and rewards of his need to master these things would provide an adequate distraction. When that didn't work, they gave him a mate. She was a dec, not a hybrid (the situation being far too fluid and volatile to introduce another experimental element) but not just any old dec. She was custom on custom, an extraordinarily *talented* companion, made in every conceivable way *for* him, the design team anticipating that lust (for lack of a better word) would focus Ben's ambition and lead him back into the fold: the prescribed life and lofty pursuits they had planned for him.

But one fine morning, not long after the lovebirds were introduced, something went very wrong. Right there in the living quarters of the biosphere, Ben presented with a full-blown personality disorder. All traces of the Ben they knew were gone. In his place was a raving lunatic of a zealot, a maniac who preached the word of some unrecognizable hybrid religion, roughly Christian in form, except that the singular object of devotion was a nameless pagan goddess who (he apparently believed) was manifested in this dimension in the body of his mate. The new personality alternated between screaming that he needed to save them all, the designers and their staff (*Repent! Ye Faithless!*) and demanding that they release him so that he could wander the plates of the earth and save others.

In the face of this insanity the team splintered. Some wanted to continue the work, find out where it led, while others were vehemently opposed and determined to abandon the project entirely. The abandonment faction acted first and decisively. They sterilized the biosphere using the fail-safe neutron-pulse and then burned the atelier and the lab, so that all physical evidence of the research was destroyed. With no alternative but to start over again from scratch, what was left of the team disbanded. The individual designers melted into the deep zones, they moved on to personal projects and found places where they could work in obscurity. Marcus Vranes and his partner Andrea Farinetti disappeared into the TranScan. The Lizard Wizard took refuge in a twitch house in the Low Flats, and the others dispersed to places even more reclusive. All were convinced that Ben/The Preacher and Grushenka were destroyed in the inferno that swept the facility, but they were wrong. Second sight was a gift the designers hadn't meant to bestow on their hybrid child – and couldn't have if they wanted to – but he was *touched* nonetheless. Ben knew what the abandoners were going to do before they did, and in knowing he survived their best efforts to *unmake* him.

He and Grushenka escaped. Somewhere along the line, the preacher receded to the mental margins and Ben took hold again as the dominant personality. He selected a name from a product the techs fed into him every day in the lab, *SuperGrotein*® by EdgeronLyonnais® – *Edgely* – and tagged it on to the three letters they gave him at birth. *Ben Edgely*, he called himself. He and his lover traveled the frames, moving, always moving. He took to a life of crime. It started out small but with his advantages, the "business" grew big fast, until it was a fully diversified operation—designer drugs, dec prostitution, elaborate heists. He set up a legitimate side to launder the cashflow, a chain of body-scaping salons, a low-margin tissue growth lab, a top-frame restaurant, and an after-hours hizzerits club. In refusing to pay protection money he attracted the evil eye of Xec. The dossier grew heavy and fat. People running for office labeled him a scourge, a nemesis, a toxin, and still his empire expanded. For practical reasons (at first) Ben aligned himself with the underground, *the Resistance*, but over time, influenced by the Movement's charismatic leader, Sir Gavin Tang, he became a true believer, a soldier of *La Causa*, and the legendary operative known as Praxis. In that role, he proceeded to do all those things that made him the most feared and reviled enemy of the Powers that Be. They wanted him, they hated him, they hungered for his head.

Throughout those salad days, the mad preacher inside him was never gone for long. He continued to experience episodes where Ben Edgely blacked out completely and the preacher took hold. He would wander for weeks on end as that troubled minister, seeking out those on the poorest levels, a traveler in rags in downstreet alleys, making his way on the secret stairs and hidden tunnels of the interstix, the hidden world between the frames, never sleeping, always mumbling his bizarre creed, stopping only to shout his sermons from atop the bucket he carried for alms, spreading a Word that few cared about or even heard.

It was this polarity that saved him.

When Edgely was apprehended and resolved, and Garl Motts introduced into him, it was the preexistent dual psyche, the flaw in the hybridization, that insulated him from the worst scrambling effects of the *REZ*-pulse. So even when they changed him, and forced him to live for seven years in the mind of the mild-mannered pleasure model repair tech, both Edgely and the preacher were co-resident, even experiencing fleeting moments of individual clarity. It was during one of those clear moments that Edgely recorded the self-spawning HOVO that appeared to Garl from inside Edgely's trusted lieutenant, Hester Spynne. Edgely's plan (now that he was a limited partner in his own head) was to somehow engineer his own awakening, so that he could once again take over as the dominant personality. He sought to convince Garl to find and "get with" Edgely's partner in crime and love, Grushenka, so that her sexual attentions (*Jesus H., man, those attentions*) and the irresistible gravitational pull of her own libidinous needs, would co-opt and coerce Garl into just such a retrogression. But the Garl personality proved far more resilient than Edgely anticipated. What happened instead was a gradual awakening to the multiplicity of his consciousness, a slow, almost archaeologic transition that culminated in a dramatic synthesis of wakefulness the instant Jagabrew zapped him/us/me with the high-energy taser. In was in that baptismal Jordan of fiery volt-age that Edgely's potent instinct for self preservation, latent in our very cells, saw him leap to the fore and employ a *fa jin* strike to kill Jagabrew by ripping out his heart. It was that act of killing, so anathema to Garl, and to Garl's internal ally, the preacher, that proved the penultimate catalyst of *our* becoming. For with the dying heart still twitching in my outstretched palm, the full weight and dimension of our shared history was driven through us, and up into us, coalescing and then fusing in an epiphany of selves-realization and simultaneous hybrid evolution, a fraternal and collaborative troika of consciousness was begotten, as the dec tech, the preacher and the revolutionary crime boss collapsed inward, their tripartite co-existence imploding and spawning in a new singularity, a fourth and unifying personality:

Carlos Geir Quaternarian Breedlove

Now, that's all pretty straightforward, but here's where things get messy. C.G.Q. Breedlove (Breed, for short) wasn't a moniker given, neither was it a name taken or assumed. It was *always there*. I know, I know. This is going too far. Time gets a hooked warp to it when you go and suggest something off-the-chain like that. And I'm not saying that I/Them/Us can reconcile such a crazy, swizzlestick-in-space-time notion with the way things *are*, or *ought to be*, or however we want to cast the thin, in-between and shifting state we call *reality*, or that I even begin to understand it myself. I don't have the answers, not a one, beyond the simple truth that Breed was/is a mergence, the braided and thus singular combine of a phoenix risen from the dusty ashes of his enemies' attempts to destroy him. Breed was/is the bridge that The Lizard Wizard urged me to find and reach. Though how Dave ever could have foreseen such an outcome I still cannot fathom.

It was me, Breed, who bandaged up the dec teen, Jhett, gave him IV-fluids and put him into light-sleep mode. I was able to do those things because I knew everything Garl knew. I performed the actions *as* Garl, for I *was* him, to the extent I needed or wanted to be. It was me, Breed, who carried Jhett down to the parking garage, placed him in the back of Jagabrew's pickup truck and drove it to the Whiterock megalift with a plan already jelling, because, in my need for strategy, I *was* Ben Edgely, and I knew all that he knew and could do, but only to the extent I wanted to be him. I could invoke any of them, the others-me, individually or in combination, at will, as needed or desired, and just as importantly, I could suppress and dismiss them again, back into the combine, at will. I could do these things because I *wasn't* them. I was different now. I was me.

I pondered this as I stood in line at the bank.

Edgely-style

El Banco de la Microcosmio Por Ciento wasn't the largest or the best known of the Riverian banks, but it was well regarded and considered by the few (those powerful few who considered such things) to be the most discreet institution in a very discreet transactional tribe. It was a bank that understood its clientele. There was no W.A.L.T.E.R. scan at the entrance. No one batted an eye when I shambled through security and entered the palatial lobby looking like the mad bearded monk a part of me still was. Rich people could be very eccentric, as, clearly, I was presumed to be. I wouldn't be inside El Banco de la Microcosmio Por Ciento in the first place if I didn't belong there, and to belong, I had to be rich, therefore my obvious eccentricities were perfectly appropriate, acceptable and even comforting, in a quirky sort of way. This was what the bankers behind the bomb-proof glass told themselves as I shuffled past.

I waited in the short line, and when it was my turn, I stepped to the counter window and made my wishes known. A pasty young clerk named Monroy Guanotardo-Nelson was assigned. He ushered me into the colonnaded corridor that led into the vault where he used his key and I pressed my palm to the sensor to release and withdraw the safe deposit box. It was quite heavy. Monroy offered to carry it, and I, thanking him, accepted, whereupon we repaired into the comfortable confines of the valuables reviewing room, where he left me alone.

I waited until the sound of his heels receded in the corridor, then unlatched and opened the lid. Inside the box were stacks of cash, casino chips, gold ingots in plastic strips, credit cards, I.D. badges, passports and passkeys with my photo, or rather, the clean-cut Ben Edgely's photo, and a different name on each one, none of them Ben Edgely. There was a Kimber pistol, a blue-level clearcard for Xec Internal Affairs, also with Edgely's photo, a hardwood cradle that held an almost full bottle of small-batch mescal, and a small ceramic cup. There was also a HOVO simdisc. I shoved everything else to the back of the box, set the simdisc by itself and pressed *play*.

There was a soft hiss and the glowing hologram of Ben Edgely appeared on the tiny dancefloor. He was dressed the same as the holo Edgely inside Hester, but where that was only a Duo-Flex® recording, this was RobusTec®, full headdrive heuristics. Very smart. Very expensive. This little fellow could talk back, answer questions, even be opinionated and emotional. He could fill in any blanks his returning self might need filled in. Edgely put him here so he could collude with his former self.

He peered up at me with a rakish grin, the sort of superconfident, white-toothed test smile a guy like Edgely might flash himself in the mirror, and did.

"Jesus H., look at you. I need a shave, baby."

"Yeah, we could use a shower, too."

"Color me happy you didn't activate the sniffer chip on this sucker. But fuck all that. We're back! That's what I'm talkin' about! You goddamn baddass you! C'mon, let's take a shot. Celebrate." He reached off-frame and came back with the same bottle of mescal I'd just shoved to the back of the box. He pulled the cork with his teeth and filled his little HOVO cup to overflowing, then kissed the bottle, re-corked it and winked at me.

"Reserva de la Familia. The rest is you, amigo," he said, and laughed. "Yo, can you freakin' imagine the look on Corporal Serpas's ugly mug when he realizes what we pulled off?" He set the bottle out of cam view, and raised the shot in toast. "To me." He shot the shot, nodded with a grimace of approval and eyed me again, then cocked his head in puzzlement.

"What the fuck? You're not gonna make me drink alone, are you?"

The sensors whirred. The little sim suddenly looked uneasy.

"No, no, no, no. Not possible! You wouldn't even know about this fucking box unless you're *me*."

"I am you," I said.

"Then what's wrong? You *are* back … right?"

"I'm back. But I'm different. I've changed."

"Changed how?"

"I'm still Garl."

"*Garl*-motherfucking-*Cupidwrench*? Please tell me you're joking."

"I'm the preacher, too."

"I know about the preacher, I can live with him. So long as I'm in the mix. Me!"

"You are in the mix, Ben. Like you said, that's how I knew about the box, and all the other stuff, too."

"But the real me, as me! All by myself me!"

I shook my head.

"Not anymore, my brother. We're all together now."

He stared up at me and his gaze went flat as he visibly deflated. The sim even popped and snapped a little.

"Then I failed. I'm dead."

I actually felt bad for my former self, and even had the urge to console the little sim, which was pretty absurd.

"You're not dead. I'm still you, *all* you, when I want to be."

"When you *want* to be … fuck me. Stomp on this disc. Break it, bust it up, please. So I don't have to hear any more of this shit."

"Sorry, I can't do that. I need you. And hey, bro, cheer up. You and I are about to kick some righteous fucking ass. Edgely-style."

He looked up at me and blinked.

* * *

After the bank, I made a series of stops, all on 4-Frame.

First I paid a visit to a guy I used to know, and was happy to find he was still in business, holed up in his nondescript warehouse in the machine district. I never knew his real name, nobody did, but he was known across the plate as The Loser. People came to him for one reason and one reason only, to lose something. It was his specialty, getting rid of a thing, whatever your *thing* happened to be, he made it go away, deleted it, erased it, deconstructed and unmade it, until it wasn't findable or traceable by anybody ever again. My thing was Jagabrew's pickup truck. A large item, very expensive to lose. The price was set by The Loser. You did not negotiate the price.

I hailed a gypsy cab right outside The Loser's door, gently situating the sleeping Jhett into the backseat along with my FF kit. The gym bag I brought into the bank to carry the contents of Edgely's safe deposit box, which was now quite heavy, I placed in the trunk. I myself sat up front with the driver, somewhat uncomfortable in the new suit I bought off a rack roller in the garment ward, which was too tight, especially given the two pistols I had tucked in the waistband of the trousers, the compact Kimber Edgely left himself, and the .45 automatic I liberated from the Dober Man's trunk and had schlepped all the way from the Low Flats. Traveling with concealed weapons wasn't how either Garl Motts or John Highlife wanted to roll, but it was Edgely's instinct to go armed so I honored it. We were in Edgely's world, now, and as he well knew, 4-Frame could be an *interesting* place. The machine district was a vast sprawl, home to weather and environment controls for the top ten plates, and like all industrial neighborhoods it had its less than savory attributes. If you weren't careful, a gypsy cab could be one of them. But my driver recognized that I was a very careful fare, his eyes flicking to the telltale bulges in the region of my belt line and he cracked a toothy, I-wouldn't-even-think-of-it, yellow grin. It was a service-oriented smile, and I paid him a hundred up front. Despite the change of clothes, I had no chance to shower, so I considered it a stench tax.

* * *

We took Meridian all the way across the district, through Chicken Town, then Ronny Dunkin' Land and the retail hell of the Spree Mall. I didn't tell the driver where we were going until we were almost there. I directed him to the Galloway Tunnel, and via that long, littered, claustrophobe's hell we went up a level to 3-Frame, then all the way to the underpass gates at Porte des Lillas, and the outer ring of ParisGestalt City. Being that I was a ParisGC passport holder, I was extended the courtesy of the opportunity to bribe the gendarmes into skipping the mandatory pat down, vehicle search and W.A.L.T.E.R. scan. They did mirror the undercarriage, and waved their handheld omnalyzers around the wheel wells for a cursory sniff check, then I bought a 30-minute EZpass for the gypsy cab and we were in, through the gate into the glorious City of Lights.

* * *

A quick word about W.A.L.T.E.R. and why Edgely was so keen to avoid the scan and therefore picked one of the few remaining checkpoints into the city where payola could avoid it altogether. W.A.L.T.E.R. (the meaning of the acronym was known only to DarXec insiders) is the central cognix of XecNet, a systolic array of over a billion dec cortical columns topped by living brains, with more brainstems added to the array every day, the whole cloistered *nation* of which was kept in a perpetual REM state by immersion in some wicked sleepytime melatonin marinade that the government's darkest labs cooked up to ensure that all neural activity remained collective, unconscious and in parallel, precisely because the directed dreams of W.A.L.T.E.R.'s *We*-munity comprised the entirety of Xec cloud operations. Edgely didn't know much more about all that ultra-secret NIS stuff (other than once in a while hearing the rampant rumor in power society circles that the cognix had gotten so smart it was deemed a sleeping god) (and the further rumor that the Junta was so terrified of the *We*-munity actually waking up it created an entire DarXec division devoted to experimental transfusional narcoleptics) (and although this information was more than seven years old, it still carried with it the pungent smack of currency) however the one thing that the Edgely part of me did know with certainty was that the slightest hint of a scan by W.A.L.T.E.R. and the jig was up as far as me getting into Paris undetected.

ParisGC

ParisGC was one of the more popular theme park enclaves, the semi-autonomous statelets that were scattered around the upper echelons. *Semi-autonomous* was, of course, a euphemism. The park governments were allowed to pretend that they were independent, walled-off havens devoted to this, that or the other theme, fetish or lifestyle choice, and the Junta, the Standing Committee (the Junta's nod toward inclusivity of the lesser oligarchs) and Xec (the Junta's rabid pitbull) tolerated their existence, their quaint declarations of border enforcement, their passports, their constitutions and municipal petulance. The Powers-that-Be permitted it, because a) it wasn't threatening to the Junta's hegemony; b) it was highly profitable; and c) the parks represented a pleasant diversion, even for the elites.

ParisGC, unlike some of the other lifestyle themes, was relatively classy, its monuments, statues and cobbled streets, had good origin, as they said, which meant that everything looked as old and soot-caked as it was supposed to. *Origin straight from the original!* the ads claimed—*More Paris than Paris!* As if the Parisians or anyone else had any idea what the original city really looked or smelled or tasted like. Of course, everybody was taught from pre-school onward that the spinning orb we all lived on was *the* Famous Original Earth, but that only highlighted the core problem with naming every new terra-formed development world *Earth* (an institutionalized bad habit that started in the Move Worlds® marketing HOVOs in an effort to leverage nostalgia and turn packing-up-and-leaving into going home) eventually even "they" lost track of which one was the *original* original, and the vested interests on every new tract planet wanted it that way. So despite the lawsuits, the partisanship and expensive PR campaigns, nobody really knew for sure anymore; though I strongly suspected that the cheap-ass plate sheathe I called home was not planet zero.

I directed my gypsy cab driver to the Marais, paid him double the fare and got out. I planned to switch cabs, though it took a while to get another one to stop, what with me in an ill-fitting suit cradling a passed-out waifboy in my arms. Fortunately, ParisGC taxi drivers are a relatively jaded lot and it wasn't too long before one pulled to the curb. I passed him a large bill (paper francs were another throwback that tourists *just loved*) told him there'd be more where that came from and gave him directions to take the long way round to a nearby address. It was a custom shop that Edgely knew about back in the day, a place that specialized in Chromus-Chace combat refits, and catered mostly to the security needs of the business moguls and government officials of the city. I told the driver to park where I could see him from the shop windows, and had him stand outside his vehicle, while I went in and paid full price for a pair of bodyguards. Both were C-C Magnum LTs, one male, one female (Ajax and Callahan) (security decs always had tough-sounding names) and I selected the standard options for both, had the salesman do a maxi-quickset with personal bonding, and the three of us were back in the cab inside twenty minutes. Callahan sat in the back seat on one side of Jhett, with me on the other, and Ajax up front with my .45 auto in the shoulder rig he wore under the designer suit he came with. Both guards had walked out of the shop dressed to the nines, Ajax wearing Vladivani, Callahan in Aazura; the old proprietor was a nut for fashion; he was definitely Edgely's kind of guy.

I gave the driver a series of addresses around the city, venues Edgely knew, but none was our final destination. They were waypoints where we stopped long enough for me to check for a tail. Once I was satisfied we were clean, I gave the driver the next address in the chain. He knew what was going on, and knew better than to start asking questions. The all-business facial set of the bodyguards wasn't exactly inviting of casual conversation either. The fourth stop was on Belle Epoque ... *her* street. The taxi set down right where the Garl me had parked Hana's old Ducannon the night I came back and found the place blown to smithereens. I knew now what Garl didn't know then—it was the flat where Edgely kept her, and where she had remained, dutifully waiting, over the seven long years Edgely spent as Garl the repairman. The piles of rubble Garl had seen that night, the laserwire and police caution tape were all long gone. The building had been completely renovated, good as new, as if nothing had happened. In a sense nothing had. Top plate denizens with limitless money didn't want to know about things they couldn't make go away with money. Like explosions. And high-end realtors knew what their clients did and didn't want to know. The new owners would not have heard about the mysterious beauty who lived in the space where their flat now stood. Sitting there in the taxi, I realized it was a mistake for me to conjure her image. Only with great effort did I manage to push her (*yet again*) to the back of my mind.

I gave the driver the next stop on our tour of Paris and we drove on. Two more waypoints later, after a wildly circuitous route that took us back and forth across the Seine, I muttered the last address, that of a boulangerie in the 19th where I paid the driver (triple this time) and we got out. Where we stood was only a short distance from the Périférique and the city gate the gypsy driver used when we first entered the city. But we weren't going that direction. I ducked into the boulangerie, came out with fresh baguettes and then led us north and west, a short, winding route, with Ajax carrying Jhett and with Callahan responsible for my gym bag and FF kit. Ten minutes later, with Edgely's instincts telling me that we had no unwanted company, we entered a safe house Edgely kept from the early days, a third-floor walk-up in a shabby little tumbledown building on the Passage du Monte Negro, the planned destination all along.

Jhett

I found the folded paper tell right where Edgely tucked it. The door hadn't been opened since he last left and locked it more than seven years before. Of all the safe houses that he used scattered throughout the plates, it was the only one he never told anyone about, not even his most trusted consiglieri, which made it the only safe house that might still be safe. The apartment itself was little more than a pied-à-terre, with a sitting room, bedroom, miniscule kitchen and WC. In my experience decs had a high tolerance for cramped living quarters, so it wasn't going to be an issue. I gave Ajax a roll of cash and sent him out on errands. He was to go first to Le Conveno on Rue de Belleville and buy ten phones, from there to the public market at Place de Fêtes, and the nearby Supermarché G20, to pick up wine, water, cheese, salami, paté, cornichones, mustard, dates, figs, fresh fruits and vegetables. While he was away, Callahan would be on solo guard duty. She needed no instructions.

The apartment was minimally furnished. However, there were two distinct luxuries. The first was an extra large hot water tank; the second, a deep oval hinoki tub in a wood-paneled alcove off the WC. While the tub filled, I clipped my hair and beard, and shaved. I showered, scrubbed the scum off, and showered again then eased my body into the tub. The steaming water was right at the upper edge of tolerable, even for me. First one foot, in and out and in, then the other foot, then three careful teabag dips before the scrotum felt safe enough to submerge, and then I was in, sunk all the way to my basting chin. I soaked like that for some time, the water's pore-dilating heat restorative to the point of soul cleansing.

When I got out, body tingling, toweled off, put on Edgely's terry robe and slippers, and went into the bedroom to the futon where the unconscious Jhett lay. I gently rolled him onto his side and popped the hood enough to initiate a warm-series start, the eye opener that dec techs called the SBC. Smell of bacon and coffee. It was the most gradual of activation sequences, not often used on low-grade equipment because they were generally considered not worth the extra time. I stood by the window and waited until I heard him yawn, then went back and crouched next to him as he stretched and blinked his eyes awake. He looked around the room, searching for something familiar, and not finding it, he glanced at me, recognized me, and averted his gaze, his maso-conditioning kicking in without a hitch. It was a good sign that he was still working as advertised.

"It's okay, you can look at me," I said.

"Where am I?"

"ParisGestalt City. An apartment. You're safe here."

He thought something about that was funny and gave a weak little laugh. He was still in pretty rough shape.

"Paris? You mean way up, up, Paris?"

"That's right, up, up. We're on 3-Frame."

"Whoa, I ain't never been up this high."

"Most people haven't."

He looked me in the eye again, and held my gaze this time. The filter agility surprised me. He was already blending the submissive heuristics in the emoflex response set he'd developed for Jagabrew with what he now perceived to be my needs. Good old Sweetech®. The biomimetics really were pretty impressive, given the price point.

"You saved my ass," he said, and shook his head in disbelief at the horrors past. "I was a fuckin' goner for sure. Thanks."

"No thanks needed. It's my job." I caught on that, the sound of my own words, the Edgely in me cringing, hating the ridiculous earnestness of it, while Garl and the rest of me knew it was still true.

He stretched, then eyed me and bit his lip, apparently for show.

"Tell me your name, hipster."

Hipster? It was classic Cyberbell "street" lexicon. Those genius designers really needed to get out more.

"You can call me Breed."

"Cool name. I wanna do somethin' for you, Breed. You ready for some playtime? I know I am."

He pulled back the covers and opened his legs. He wasn't joking around, either. "It's gonna be *sooooo* good," he added, and raked his teeth over his lip again.

I shook my head and gently took hold of his knees and closed them up again.

"No offense but, you're not my type, I'm afraid."

"You sure about that?"

He reached his hand up under my robe and took hold of me. He had a firm grip, I had to say that for him. All except his thumb which was in expert stroking motion. I figured it was another good sign there was no permanent damage.

"What do you say we make me your type? I'm better at this than you think."

"I know you are," I said. "You're a stud."

He opened his mouth and leaned to duck his whole head under my robe, but I stood up, forcing him to either hang on tight to my genitals or let me go. He let go, reluctantly, and with hurt eyes let his hand slide down my leg until he got to my ankle and clung there, even tighter.

"I wanna do this for you, so you need to let me. I'll beg if that makes it better."

Good old Sweetech persistence.

"I'm in a relationship," I said. "I've got sort of a one-track mind where it comes to that stuff."

Real disappointment in his expression, now.

"Chick or dude or what?"

I laughed.

"What's so fucking funny?"

"Another friend asked me the same thing. Seems like a long time ago, now."

"Well?"

"A woman," I said.

Jhett collapsed back into the pillow and pulled it up around his ears.

"I hate her ass face!"

"That's all right. But I've got something I think you're going to like."

I opened the wardrobe, found another one of Edgely's robes (it was sort of embarrassing how much the former me liked to lounge around in elegant smoking jackets) and went back to Jhett and wrapped it around him. He tried to stand up, but was still too weak, so I ducked under his arm and helped him up, then guided him to the bathroom. I inspected the bandages on his neck, wrists and ankles, considered removing them, but decided against it. It would be better to let the water slough them off. I walked him over to the hinoki and he stepped in.

"Hot!"

"Too hot?"

He put the other foot in and lowered himself, shook his head. "Good hot."

"That's what I was hoping you'd say," I said.

He shuddered and sighed.

"Real good," he whispered.

"Have you ever had a bath before?"

"Huh-uh. Jag didn't want it. Sometimes he cleaned me up, you know, with a wet shirt, or somethin'."

"Sounds like his style. You soak here for as long as you want."

"How will I know?"

"Know?"

"When it's as long as I want?"

He stared up at me with wide eyes. It was a real question. Outside of "playtime" he'd never made an independent decision in his life.

"Here's how it will feel. The water will get a little bit cooler, and it'll feel like you've been soaking long enough, and your body will feel like it's okay to get out."

"Like what, I'll just know?"

"Yeah, you'll just know."

"'kay," Jhett said. He looked uncertain.

"Relax," I said.

He tensed.

"What's wrong? Ah … that's what he said, isn't it? Right before …"

He nodded, his chin sloshing the water.

"I won't use that word anymore. Listen to me, now. I'm never going to hurt you, Jhett. That's not what I do. So untense your muscles, and lay back and get comfortable in the water."

He did, slowly, I could see his body relax.

"Thank you, master."

"I'm not your master. I'm just a friend. One you can trust."

"Whatever you say," he said.

I turned to go.

"Hey …"

"Yeah?"

"Thanks. I mean that for reals."

"You're welcome."

"Breed?"

I looked back.

"Is Jag … is he still dead?"

"He's going to be dead for a long time."

"Forever?"

"At least that long."

Jhett stared into the wobbling reflections of the room and me in the water's surface and I realized he was thinking hard, maybe for the first time. I didn't know what he was thinking, it's impossible to read those Sweetech units. Typical teenager.

I closed the door and left him to his first hot bath.

Ajax returned a few minutes later, with a light tap on the door, the prearranged signal. I unpacked the shopping bags onto the table and congratulated him on his selections.

"Hua," he said. Bodyguard decs always said things like that. Otherwise he remained expressionless, but even the Magnum LTs reacted with an endorphin nudge on positive feedback. It was human nature, and there was a lot more natural human in decs than most people ever gave them credit for. I set up three of the burner cell phones, one for me, one for Ajax and the other for Callahan. I sent Ajax back outside to give it to her and told him to work out a two-point rotation according to their training, and generally keep an eye on things in the vicinity until I called them in for dinner.

I examined the bottles of wine. He'd made excellent choices. Apparently, the refined taste that was his Marais custom-house pedigree didn't stop with a high fashion sense. I located a corkscrew and opened up a bottle of burgundy, then washed out the glassware while I raked the coals of my predicament.

On the plus side of the equation, I had a headful of mostly coherent cognitive activity, the brainwaves of three people, now working as a team, in lock step, marching to the beat of my own drummer. I had IDs, money, weapons, access codes. I had help, resources and a reasonably safe place to catch my breath. I had wine.

On the minus side, Colonel Serpas & Company were all-but-certainly in a highly agitated state, one that had been on a crescendo rise to fever pitch ever since their favorite meat puppet of a dec repairman didn't show at Jagabrew's wired hell-hole at the appointed time and therefore didn't die on schedule. I pictured the moment their Xec henchmen found Jagabrew's cardio-ectomied corpse and could almost hear their combined homicidal frenzy hit a crystal-shattering coloratura high note they would sustain until they had their satisfaction. Every Xec goon at their disposal was on the job, by now, reserves called up from the deep reaches, secured combat units reactivated, new units put on expedited order. None of these details would have worried Edgely back in the day, but they gave me pause in the here and now. The worst part of it was that the vast majority of the stones the Junta would not leave unturned in their frantic search to find me had nothing remotely to do with me. Innocent people and decs were going to be hurt, were going to be tortured, were going to die.

Again, back in the beforetime of Edgely's sprawling crimi-nal empire, these facts, while troubling, would not have distracted him. "Cost of doing business," he would have said. "You can't change all the worlds overnight." Even when playing the role of Praxis, he'd have said the same thing differently, altering the polarity of the sentiment as he zen-fully explained that the ends justified the means, the bitter sacrifices furthered the Cause. The new me didn't buy it, the self-centered rationale, the platitudinous lies. I *was* distracted by the thoughts of the violence that would be unleashed, and I was *very* troubled. Maybe it was part of what made me different. Call it the *Garl* in me, with a dollop of mad preacher on the side. The upshot was that I was determined to not let people die for me, and to move thoughts and words into actions that would somehow prevent it. All I needed to do was figure out what those actions would be. Easy, I tried to tell myself. But even as I formulated this rickety framework of intentions and convictions I had the haunting suspicion, no, the certainty, that it was already too late. It was happening out there while I paced in my comfortable robe in a safe house thinking, because the heaviest weight on the minus side of the equation was time, it was moving, and it was definitely not on my side.

There was something else that troubled me, though it was more like background radiation to the urgencies of the present. It lurked in the past. Despite the return of Edgely's memories, his instincts and his cunning, I realized that he still didn't know who had betrayed him. Seven years ago, someone very close to him had given him up to his enemies, sold him down the river, ushering him into mental slavery. Edgely remembered the aftermath most clearly. He was captured, tortured, resolved, and turned into Garl, and the rest was dark chapters in a personal history that was not his own. But Serpas and his cronies never did reveal who it was that went 'et tu brute' on him. So even with all his/ my powers back, the Edgely in me couldn't figure out the traitor's identity. There simply wasn't enough information. Not knowing made any move to seek help from Edgely's old network impossibly risky. There was only one person I knew I could trust, the only operative in the underground who was above suspicion, the head of the Resistance himself, Praxis' own controller in the Underground – Sir Gavin Tang – codename Klondike. The problem was the protocol that was used back in the day to arrange a meet was fraught with danger and uncertainty, especially given the passage of time. Something told me that it must have been corrupted somewhere along the line. It wouldn't be safe to use. Not for him. Not for me. Still, to do what I needed to do I was going to have to trust somebody.

But who?

Humanizing

I called the bodyguard decs into the apartment and we ate. Fine as it was, the food had no taste. Ajax and Callahan chewed methodically, staring into a middle distance somewhere beyond the room. If they were embarrassed to be seen eating in front of me they took care not to show it. Security decs were designed to behave in a wooden fashion, like old sci-fi HOVO cyborgs, which was the way most clients wanted their guards, non-emotive and invisible until needed. But knowing all that Garl knew about decs, I was aware that there was a lot more going on in the "feelings" department than they were letting on. Jhett eyed them as he tore off a bite-sized chunk of baguette, raised it slowly to his mouth and sucked on it without chewing. After the bath, I re-bandaged his wounds and even found a Louis Vuitton® sweatsuit that fit him perfectly. Edgely had stocked the place with designer cloth-ing, hats, watches, jewelry, everything in hermex sealed bins (al-ways thinking ahead, that Edgely). Jhett was still in a bad way, but improving by the hour, even getting some pink back in his cheeks, as much as the porcelain 'O17s were meant to have, anyway. I knew he was out of the worst danger when he asked me to hit him, again using the word Jagabrew must have used on a daily basis: wanting to engage in *playtime*. I was just finishing a wrap job on one of his lacerated wrists when he said it, with all the emotional investment of asking for a drink of water.

"Remember, a little while ago, I said—"

"I know, you said I'm not your type, she is," he said. "But if you hit me you might like me better. Go on, try it."

He was exhibiting more creativity in his submissive prodding than any Sweetech model I'd ever seen before.

"I already like you," I said.

"Then prove it. Hurt me. Start in, let's get it on."

I secured the bandage, then took him gently by the shoulders, turned him square to me so we were eye to eye.

"I'm going to try to get you to Waterfall."

"What's that?"

"It's a place. A hidden place. I can't describe it." The truth was that I'd never been there, so I didn't know. But Edgely had been responsible for the transit of thousands of at-risk decs through the network of secret channels to the haven. "You'll have to see it for yourself, Jhett. The people there, the decs, they're good at helping people, and decs, find what it is they *really* want, instead of what they were told to want. I can't make any promises, but I'm going to do everything I can. And if we can pull it off, and get you there, afterward, once you've been in that place for awhile, if what you want is for someone to hit you, you'll find that person, the right person for you. It'll be your choice. Right now, it's not."

He looked confused.

"It's not?"

"Huh-uh."

"But I said it, it's *me* talkin'."

I shook my head.

"It's not you."

"My mouth said it," he said. "A part of me said it. And I'm the sum of my parts."

I stared at him. I was shocked.

"Who told you to say that?"

"Nobody. But it's true, ain't it?"

This would have been an incredible insight, even for the most advanced models, but for the words to come from the mouth of a Cyberbell factory wisp of an GNO17 who'd spent his whole life in the clutches of a seedy sado in a web-order dungeon, it was beyond incredible. It was a freaking miracle.

"No," I said. "You're more than the sum of your parts. Much more. Someday you'll see."

* * *

Emboldened by the luminous spirit of the Sweetech streeter punk, I went to work. I got Garl's FF kit out and popped the hood on Ajax. Most people didn't know it, but beyond chassis type, bioframe, psyche package and styling, there wasn't all that much difference between the mainline pleasure units and any other dec type. If you had the tech skills to work on one you could work on most any other. Lots of the latent features were just toggles, anyway, skillset and attitudinal switches that could be turned on or off to optimize for the target function, or character trait, or mood variance. Those presets and the factory installed filter combinations determined whether a dec would be an elder care specialist, a bodyguard, a sous chef, or a boy-toy like Jhett.

The adjustments I made to Ajax, filters scaled to nominal, all feature-sets to active/ready, was a mode those of us in the repair trade called *humanizing* the unit. It was a fix that was rarely made or desired, or even legal, because the resulting personality profile could be far too needy and in-your-face. All of a sudden they wanted to know things, learn things, do things you didn't want them to do. They made suggestions and bad choices. They'd tell you when they were hungry or thirsty or bored. They got into fistfights, they initiated sex, they ordered the lobster. You were definitely taking your chances if you humanized a model of mid-range quality or below. Lots of times they wouldn't be able to handle the changes, the increase in realflow, the unchecked cascade of emo-logs, and the tidal surge of kDz's. If things went badly, the unit could do a cold shutdown on you, or end up rocking in the corner, or even duck out the door and run off, go free agent, or join a band of Moreauvians, stuff like that. Ajax, like all Chromus-Chace Magnum LTs was right on that iffy quality line. But the way I saw it I had no choice, I needed him to be all that he could be, so I made the fix. Besides, he deserved a shot at survival, too. We were about to go up against the whole Xec apparatus, TGS Elites and human operatives of the first and worst order, the whole ugly shootin' match. We were going to war.

Le Rocket Rouge

I didn't humanize the other bodyguard, Callahan, but I did pop her hood and make a few key adjustments. I reset her filters to maximize empathy, the same configuration used in hospice, nursery, and daygrief counselor decs. But I left her MMA core skillset and latent aggression tolerances at the original RAID-optimized settings. Because I was planning to leave Callahan behind with Jhett, I wanted her equipped for both tender loving care and extreme protection scenarios. Woe would be the poor sap who decided it was a good idea to fuck with Jhett. I left them with a stack of cash and plenty of ammo. I told them where to shop, where to walk, how to care for Jhett's injuries, and what to do if we didn't come back. I also left them the RobusTec® simdisc of Edgely, the rest of the burner phones and detailed instructions about what I needed done.

When everything was in place, I tried to get some rest. But through the whole sundown cycle I just lay there thinking. I filtered through the headspace of those other, older versions of me, to see if there was anything they could add to the mix that the unified me might have overlooked, but mostly their thoughts just swirled, tighter and faster, and then down the drain they always went down, into passionate musings on and around the subject of Grushenka. Which meant, of course, that's where my thoughts were siphoned, as well, so I did my best to draw them back and patch the leak. But with this enchanted aquifer my only companion in the still night, sleep was an impossibility, so I got up, and showered and shaved long before sim dawn. I dressed in one of Edgely's finest suits. I made coffee. I nibbled on a crust of baguette and tried to find the holes in my plan. I knew they were there, but I couldn't see them. And that worried me.

At the first crack of morning light, with rush hour just beginning its creep, I sent Ajax out to hail a cab. When it pulled up on the street below, I turned to Jhett.

"You going to be okay?"

It was a stupid question.

He merely shrugged.

"I'm good," he said.

I gave him a chaste peck on the forehead, nodded to Callahan and left the building, slipping on a pair of Edgely's favorite Persol® shades while on the move. It was gametime, after all.

I settled into the back seat of the taxi next to Ajax and directed the driver onto the Périférique. We went half way round the city in the thick of traffic before exiting at Portes de Vanves. We got out on Rue Didot, walked half a block, hailed another taxi, made a maze-worthy series of turns, with most of the extra driving just to kill time on the clock, then got out near Montparnasse where we headed for the station on foot, merging with the bobbing heads of a thousand commuters.

Ajax was calm, his movements fluid, the very picture of studied nonchalance, which told me that he was on edge. He was taking to the humanizing better than I hoped, though. For starters, he talked more than he had before, but that wasn't saying much, because he'd hardly said three words since I met him. He also showed signs of possessing a sarcastic and very dark sense of humor. I was starting to like him, which wasn't advisable, since his chances of surviving to see another sim cycle weren't all that good. Not much better than my own.

"I'm about to get you into some serious shit, Ajax," I said, as we walked.

"I know, boss. I'm raring."

"Raring?"

"And ready to go."

"I get the feeling you were born ready."

"Hua," he said.

We slowed as we joined with a cluster of commuters in a bottleneck at the escalator. Without even looking Ajax made the first plain clothes agents. He let me know without being obvious about it, just looked my way and touched his cheek.

"Boss, you got a couple crumbs right over there." I brushed the phantom croissant flakes from my face as my eyes swept the crowd and found them, four TGS-Elites, closer than I wanted them to be, but at least they were human in form. After many strenuous objections and high-level diplomatic string pulling, the Parisians had finally prevailed upon Xec to remove (at least from plain sight) the security presence of heavyduty combat models with pitbull heads, titanium claws and razor skin. It being 3-Frame, they were allowed to pretend that the mailed fist was not poised and cocked, at least not rudely so. It was a benefit of top-shelf living that the friendly neighborhood death squad looked presentable and even honored decorum. I'd heard from a credible source that within the city limits Xec agents even apologized before they tortured or killed you. I reminded myself not to be lulled by the dress code. Even in human form Elites could be deceptive, very fast and all but indestructible.

Timing was going to be an increasingly sensitive factor, but so far the clock was cooperating nicely. I coughed into my fist and casually checked the status of the agents out of the corner of my eye. In one instant they were rigid statues of brute authority; and in the next, they were on the move, fingers to earbuds as they waded into the crowd, pushing people out of the way, heads swiveling side to side, scanning the sea of faces. They were coming. Cams and sniffers in the vicinity had obviously caught enough of my face to do a profile grab, which meant Xec systems were lighting up all the way to Citadel. Doubtless somebody was screaming in a control room somewhere. You could practically hear the chatter over the comm. All good stuff. I wanted us to be ID'd in the vicinity of the Montparnasse Metro, preferably down on the platform, but outside on the plaza would have to do. Crowds were a problem, even for Elites. Bodies got in the way, people were hard to move, the equation was ever changing. Before they locked us, Ajax and I were on the escalator descending away from them. The station main floor was suitably packed. I thought it was a good thing until we entered the tunnel for the direction Clignancourt. I heard the Metro coming, the electric hum and squeak of tires in the turn, and suddenly I realized that I'd miscalculated the volume of the commute. I was relying on Edgely's memories of Paris, and although he knew every square micron of the city intimately, all that knowledge was seven years old. Too old, it proved, because we were gummed up with the horde approaching the platform, not moving, not even baby steps. By my calculation we were going to miss the Metro and would not be given a chance to catch another. This was the flaw in the plan I hadn't seen, and such a stupid one. Ajax looked at me, picked up on my distress and took the initiative.

"Stick close, boss, I'm making a hole."

He shouted into the crowd ahead of us. In the commotion, I couldn't make out exactly what he was saying, something about the fiddlehead ferns he had for breakfast, and how, oh god, mon dieu, he was going to puke.

"*Je vais vomir*! Oh, *putain!* Oh, merdes alors—je vais vomir!"

He really looked the part, too, staggering with hands clamped on belly, leading with the open mouth. He even managed to exhibit a convincing green-faced pallor. It's amazing the effect the mere rumor of vomitose can have on large gatherings of people, as if communication of the imminent spew travels by pheromone, hive-like. A swath opened before us in the platform crowd, Ajax a nauseous Moses parting a Red Sea of surly commuters. I never was big on organized religion, but I had seen the Exodus chapter in the Quik-Realized Bible® on HOVO, and I was all for a miracle now and again, when you really needed one. I followed close behind him, but even with our forward progress it was clear we weren't going to make the train. We were simply too late. The horn for the doors sounded and they began to close. But somehow, with a giant leap and a lunge, Ajax wedged both hands into the gap just before they shut and he forced them open again, held them for me, then squeezed in after me and we were on. I heard a shout from the platform, a low, scary voice, closer to the door than I thought it would be, because they were already on top of us. The train started to roll, but the Elites were in close pursuit. Powerful hands slapped the door, then the window, and the expressionless face of one of them was right there on the other side of the glass. She hauled her arm back to use blunt force energy to come through at me, but as she did she ran smack into a passenger, a big man in a muscle shirt, and they both went down. Looking back, I saw her get up again hauling him to his feet, but the train picked up speed and we left them behind. The last of the platform was a blur of passing faces and we entered the black of the tunnel and were away. I thought I heard the She-Xec scream, but it must've been my imagination.

I gave Ajax a nod.

"Nice work," I said.

"Hua," he said.

Edgely was a Francophile (which meant, of course, so was I) but that wasn't the reason he'd chosen ParisGC as his world-wide headquarters. He chose Paris because more people there owed him favors than anywhere else on the planet. With the passage of time, those favors had gotten rather long in the tooth, but one in particular he counted as a chip that was still callable. The favor giver was an octogenarian Siberian lesbian mob boss who went by the name Kashanova Roobles. Early on, she'd been a bitter rival. But over the years, and many gestures later (including one memorable night when Edgely had a golden opportunity to take over her entire operation, but backed her up instead, and even took a bullet meant for her) a sort of affectionate détente took hold. Counting on old sentimentality, one of the last things I did from the safehouse was take a midnight walk with Callahan, and used one of the burner phones to place the call.

"Ben!" Kashanova shouted, in her wonderful rasp of a voice. "Can it really be you? We were convinced that you were, how shall I put it, somewhere *south* of dead."

"I was, Kash," I said. "A whole personality south. They took everything from me, even my pride. But I'm back, with a brand new chip on my shoulder."

"And you need something from Kash."

"I need something, da."

"What can she do you for? Kash do anything for her Ben ..."

Good ole Kash. She came through, all right, and she was one of the few in the city who could have pulled it off: a temporary service interruption of all security cams and sniffers in the central ParisGC Metro. You could see them go down, the little red lights fading, as their view of every platform, every concourse and train went dark. A full seventeen minutes of blessed invisibility. It was a beautiful thing. We could *go* anywhere, *be* anywhere.

My thoughts raced to Callahan.

I could practically see her carrying out my last instructions. Saw her climb into a taxi wearing big sunglasses and a very short skirt, heard her give the driver the directions we rehearsed, watched as she reached into her handbag and took out a burner phone and the RobusTec® simdisc of mini Edgely (I'd already had a word with the little homunculus about the plan). Callahan would place a call to XecHQ at the 36, but let HOVO Edgely do the talking. He would identify himself (completely unnecessary because of voice recog) and makes a series of completely absurd demands (the release of all prisoners of conscience GLO-BO-wide, the un-banning of all banned books, universal basic income, that sort of thing) then Callahan would place the simdisc back in her bag, tell the driver to stop the cab, pay him handsomely to keep on driving, and just as she went to exit, tuck the burner phone under the seat without ending the call. She and the little sim would repeat the program three more times, take three more rides, leave three more phones under taxi seats with Xec negotiators still on the line, before returning by circuitous route to the safe house to lay low.

It was a cheap trick, an oldie but a goodie, because it would keep them guessing. When the cams and sniffers came on again, unless they spotted us outright, confusion would remain and doubt would linger, and Xec would be forced to conclude that Edgely must still be in ParisGC, which, in a miniaturized sense, was true.

With only twenty-four seconds of invisibility left, Ajax and I made our way down Platform 5 of the Gare de Vertique. We kept our pace lively and boarded the First Class car of the mag-train known as *Le Rocket Rouge* and were the last ones on as the whistle blew, the conductor eyeing us with mild irritation as the doors sealed and locked, and the train started its roll, gathering speed for points deep and deeper.

Le Rocket Rouge was the first and most famous of the world-famous *Les Express Diametriques*, with non-stop service to the opposite side of the planet. With a tangled sheathe of dat-omizing antennae its only protection, the train's path plunged it straight down through the churning ball of liquid rock in the hot center of the planet, before it climbed up and out the other side. *Make the Red Rock Run! Party 'til dawn in Ol' Paree, pop in for Happy Hour in Roppongi!* The trip had a cachet that was hard to match, combining luxury, casino thrills and the irresistible proximity of instant molten death. A pair of well-known telegenic socialites produced lifestyle HOVOs that were shot entirely aboard the train, though it was suspected (by the more jaded among us) that they made their real living off the marks and whales on the posh round trip circuit.

Ajax slid the door to our cabin and we took our seats. The only passenger we shared it with was a well-preserved Japanese businesswoman. She didn't even glance up from her entertain-ment console as we took our seats. Doors banged open and shut in the corridor as the conductor worked his way through the car. Two minutes and twenty-four seconds later, he slid our door open, click-clicked our tickets, eyed us with more vague disap-proval, as if he sensed that something about us wasn't up to snuff, and then moved on again. Nine minutes and nineteen seconds later the snack cart arrived, pushed by an elderly dec porter in a crisp white uniform. The Garl in me noted that he was one of the newer Marvex 44-Transpo-Nostalgix series, units that had caused Marvex significant heartburn, supposedly because of their throwback shuck-n-jive servility, but the reality was that GloboTrans management didn't like the "independent streak" they seemed to possess. I bought us coffees and Nemo® banana cakes. Ajax finished his coffee (with extra sugar) and enjoyed his cake so much I gave him mine; his sweet tooth another apparent effect of the humanizing. Twelve minutes and three seconds after the snack porter slid our door shut, and his cart rattled off down the corridor, the train abruptly decelerated. Five seconds later we braked sharply. I was ready for it, and braced, but the Japanese businesswoman gave a little *Oh!* and grabbed hold of her armrests, glancing up in confusion.

"But ... this is an express, no?"

"A brief, unscheduled stop," I said. "Don't worry, ma'am, you'll arrive in Tokyo in perfect order."

A signal pole with red flashing lights shot past the window, then another one drifted by more slowly. The train stopped with a lurch and a loud clunk. We heard from somewhere ahead the *dingdingding* of a crossing track warning. I rose and nodded a farewell to the businesswoman. We exited into the passageway and made our way to the vestibule at the far end of the car. There the conductor was on the phone, cupping his hands to the window to see what the problem might be. He turned to us and, instantly recognizing that his suspicions had been correct all along, his eyes bulged in anger.

"What's the meaning of this?"

Ajax eased him aside.

"Pardon us," he said.

He rotated the handle on the door. It opened outward with a hiss of popping seal and swung wide. At the same time, the stairs appeared from below and dropped down nearly to the ground.

"You'll be on your way again in no time," I assured the conductor. "Please accept our sincere apologies."

I followed Ajax off the train and we walked forward along the gravel track grade. The tunnel was wide in this stretch, and the ground level, which is what made it a good spot for us get out. Only a few kilometers farther on the tunnel closed in tight and curved steeply downward just before the point at which it went fully vertical, the tracks ended, and the train began its free fall plunge toward the boiling center. The Devil's Corner, it was called, and if you were going to stop a magtrain you definitely needed to stop it before the Devil put the tail down her back. Ajax and I made our way past the other cars, and the puzzled eyes of other passengers, and came to the behemoth locomotive, with its wispy shroud of antennae glowing violet in the near dark, the Kêstle-Kojima field that allowed it to pass through liquid rock was already spooling, in eerie contrast to the steaming ice blue of the train's AbsolutelyPositively® kelvinated metal skin (I knew all this because, along with his fascination for exotic dec repair tools, Garl Motts was a certifiable train geek). Just ahead of the engine's bulging nosecone, a slender railway crossing gate was down, its red lights flashing. But there was no train on the crossing track.

There was only Hester Spynne.

She wore the same drab dress with its sewn-on "A" and her head covered by the Old Order River Brethern bonnet. She stood next to the track signal control pod that she had hacked and smiled demurely at our approach.

"It's good to see you looking so well, sir," she said.

"And you looking plain, Hester," I replied.

She nodded her thanks for the compliment. She'd parked Edgely's Aston Martin on the nearby stretch of service road. The car was idling, its doors open and waiting for us.

"And thank you for making an exception, and piloting a motorized leviton vehicle," I said.

"It wasn't feasible to come by buggy," she said. "I'm confident it will be deemed a forgivable lapse, when that ledger is formally accounted."

I smiled. She was something else, all right. I made the introductions.

"Ajax, meet Hester, the most decorated operative in the Resistance, though you'll never see her wearing her medals. A very reliable *person*."

Ajax looked her up and down.

"Person, sir? She appears to be a model 808, one of the older ones, if I'm not mistaken."

Hester's smile froze on her face and she stepped up to him, although the crown of her bonnet barely reached his sternum.

"*Mistaken* would be too kind a word. If Praxis calls me a *person*, I'm a *person*, Mr. Fancy Pants. Are we clear?"

Ajax eyes widened. He nodded.

"Hua," he said.

A window was yanked open high up on the locomotive, and the shiny, bald head of the engineer thrust out and he glowered down at us. Despite the fury in his eyes, he held his tongue. It wasn't just anyone who could stop a magtrain in its tracks. That and the way Ajax had turned to look up at him, exposing the pistol in his shoulder rig, meant we probably weren't to be trifled with. But I had no desire to frighten anybody. I gave the engineer a little salute and motioned to Hester. She turned to the signal pod, tapped a command on the airkey hovering above it, the laser connection to the pod was severed and the airkey faded from sight. Three seconds later, the bell stopped dinging, the RR gates swung upward and all lights went from red to green.

We headed to the Aston Martin as the train started to move. I climbed into the driver's seat as Hester proclaimed, "Shotgun!" She slid into the passenger seat with a sly glance at Ajax who, with a humanized grimace, got in back. I put the car in *F* and accelerated off on the service road, went wheels up, shot past the passenger cars of the train, and then the locomotive itself before I took the cutoff onto the transway in the direction of Filter Rapids, Black Meadow, High Center and Rat City. It was only after I put it in cruise and we settled in that Hester looked over at me.

"Person?" she said.

I nodded.

"Hester, I've changed," I said. "Praxis is different, too, he being me. We're different."

"We?"

I nodded.

"Lots of things are going to change, if we live long enough to change them."

"Then for that reason alone, I hope that we do live. I am very curious about these changes of which you speak."

Traffic was light to the point of non-existent and we reached the Rat City limits without incident. I was careful to watch my speed once we were in town. We'd made good time, and I didn't want to get where we were going too quickly. Timing was going to be at its most sensitive once we stopped. Xec was all over town, agents, soldiers, Elites, every agency was rep'd, heavily armed and on the scene in scary numbers. All you had to do was read the backs of the body armor to know they were all present and accounted for: TSA (of course), GATF, ASEC, LGS, VEST (in their weird brown livery). A few of the loitering soldiers turned to watch the luxury sedan with the heavy tints flow past, but nobody moved to interdict us. We looked way too important for that. The little flags I'd taken the time to install on the front fenders helped. The sigil of Citadel, split red pyramid with the All Seeing Eye hovering on a field of gold. This was the way members of the Junta rolled, and the last thing you wanted to do was be the poor grunt who stepped out with a hand up and got in the way of official business, aka, one of *them*. All this bullnosed subterfuge was only possible because Rat City was the last place on any frame, anywhere on Famous Original Earth, they expected Edgely/Garl to show up. Colonel Serpas and the rest of the masters on high hadn't sent their soldiers in the hundreds thinking they would actually find and confront Edge-ly. That would be ridiculous. No, they were sent to Rat City to maim, torture, punish and generally wring the neck of the little town that had let them down so horribly in the very end game of their delicious experiment in revenge: Garl the repairman. Even if no one in town had anything to do with Garl "waking up" (or whatever it was that went wrong) and didn't have the slightest idea what the massive federal shakedown was all about, maybe, just maybe, in the process of meting out all that random violence, an agent might latch onto something genuinely useful, some actual clue as to Edgely's real whereabouts. But that didn't matter. It was beside the point. The sacking of Rat City was to punish Edgely, however vicariously, and that was the point. The idea that I might waltz into the valley of the shadow of Xec all on my own was beyond their wildest imaginings. Even Edgely wasn't *that* crazy. And they might have been right about that. He wasn't. But I was. They couldn't have known that, because they didn't know anything about the changes that had taken place inside me. They didn't know a single thing about Breedlove, the creature they had accidentally created.

Back in the Hood

The town was a mess, and that's saying something where Rat City is concerned, a place where almost any alteration is an instant improvement. Every one of Garl's favorite haunts was occupied or trashed, or in the active process of being ransacked beyond recognition. Windows were shattered, doors torn off hinges, whole walls were missing, roofs collapsed, random things were on fire. Where the Sit'n'Spin once sat there was only a burnt black square of charcoal on the ground. The Fant Fixer's office was a shell of its former self, a swarm of agents still inside milling about. I caught a glimpse of the exhausted, petrified face of Angie the dispatcher, her arms clutched around her chest in the middle of the mayhem. The Phô Nicola was gone, Verna's Diner and the Proletariat Pizza still stood, and even looked open for business, which surprised me until I realized the bastards needed somewhere to eat. Apparently they liked pizza and diner meatloaf more than noodles. But they would raze those places, too, before they were finished. This was all about making a statement.

As we flowed through town it was both telling and predictable the businesses they hadn't destroyed, or, from the looks of things, even touched. The local branch of the Prow of the Future Bank on 6th Street, the fortified storefront of NixNext® Payday Loans, the only building still standing in what used to be a busy strip mall, the windowless Bureau of Deepcore Management, the ugly concrete edifice that everyone knew was a front for Xec and, of course, the vile warehouse on Runciter, the dec morgue.

All were owned, operated or otherwise cozy with the oligarchs. No mystery there.

We drove past Garl's block and I slowed even though I shouldn't have. There was a bonfire in the middle of the street. I did a doubletake and realized it wasn't any old bonfire, it was my Harley, or the charred remains, anyway, the frame like the bones of a martyr, warped and curled by the gasoline flames. As for Garl's residential tower, even with a passing glimpse you could tell Xec was taking its sweet time with that place. The forensic techs were on the scene, hauling tubs of "evidence" out the propped front doors and loading them into unmarked vans. When they were finished emptying the building of everyone and everything, the demo team would show up for its turn. They'd pull it down, brick by brick, beam by beam, and in the process, given enough time, they'd find Edgely's secret passage behind the wall of Garl's apartment, and that would constitute genuine investigatory progress. But they weren't going to get that kind of time, because we were here, now, and everything was about to change.

The last thing I noticed before Garl's street slipped from view was the old *Torridreemz*® hotbox with its faded graphics. Ironically, the agents hadn't touched the thing, and one of them was even leaning on it, taking his smoke break. It hadn't occurred to them that it might be something other than what it appeared to be. Edgely had chosen well when he chose that artifact of obsolete pleasure tech as his secret doorway.

My problem, in the moment, the instant the box slid into and out of view, wasn't Xec. My problem was Edgely's problem, it was Garl's problem, it was the mad preacher's sane warning. *Lust is the enemy!* My problem was *me*. I knew exactly where that secret doorway led. It led straight to her. And that was the crux of the issue. My need. Having the way to her right there, sensing the closeness of her, that proximity (*her!*) and simply passing it by, well, it was impossible. Or very nearly so. It took every last sweaty droplet of willpower, of reasoning, of grabbing myself by the mental lapels and slamming me against the wall and screaming into my face, into my brain, that all would be lost, the whole plan scuttled, wrecked, finished, *over*, my comrades dead, my obligations abandoned, me dead (or worse) and her lost forever, if I did it, if I hit the brakes and leapt out of the car and marched through them to reach her, to open the portal and pass through, with no more excuses, no more delays, wide awake now, fully and consciously *with* her, my Grusha, my goddess, my fire, my love.

Trust me when I say that there is a magnetic insistence so powerful, a force so profound, that to pass through its field, your destiny is forever warped, and a part of you torn away and left behind … broken remnant abandoned where it lay … but I didn't stop. I kept us moving and passed her by.

"You all right, boss?"

It was Ajax, in the backseat. Hester was eyeing me, too. They both looked worried.

"No," I said. I re-gripped the wheel. "I mean, yes. I saw something back there. Something I recognized."

"Something, sir?" Hester asked.

"Yeah, something. I'm good."

We drove on.

I made the corner and picked up speed. I knew exactly where Xec ops had set up their temporary headquarters. Xec agents liked a cold beer as much as the next guy. I took the old familiar route, came in fast and parked right in front of the doors, just like Xec brass would do it. The Lem Bar looked good. They were taking care of home base all right. As expected.

"Twenty-eight seconds," I said, as I popped the door.

Two agents approached, hands on their weapons. I got out

of the car flashing the Xec Admin badge that Edgely had the wisdom to stash away for a rainy day.

"Admin?" the first agent said, his face screwed up in a combination of confusion and disgust. "The fuck are *you* doin' here?"

"I'm the fuckin' lookalike," I said. You had to use a lot of *fucks*, Xec to Xec, otherwise you'd be suspect from the word go.

"The *what*-a-like?"

"The Edgely lookalike. What, they didn't fuckin' tell you?"

"They don't tell me shit."

"Me, neither," the other agent agreed.

"Typical," I said.

"Typical, yeah, but … I'm gonna need to check this out."

"Do what you gotta do," I said. Reflexively, he pulled his weapon, but not with any seriousness or intent. He took out his phone, too, but he was obviously trying to figure out who to call.

Fourteen seconds.

The Johnny-On-the-Spot van flew around the corner in a hard arc chasing the Here&Now truck. Both delivery vehicles set down with a long sparking skid directly across the road from the Lem. The drivers eyed each other, briefly, then hopped out with packages in hand. I'd placed the orders, selecting the insanely expensive MicroSpot® Service from Johnny-on-the-Spot and the AAA Nowzer® guarantee from Here&Now "Anywhere-Anywhen-Anyhow".

The delivery spot was where I stood, in the middle of the street outside the bar entrance, exactly where I planned to be from the moment we left the apartment in ParisGC, and anywhen was four, three, two seconds away, the coordinates confirmed by my GUPS, I signed for the packages with Mprint® and we were done. You could order almost anything, in this day and age, but GLOBO service regulations prevented the shipment of weapons and ammo in the same package. So you needed two orders if you wanted both to arrive at the same time.

I zipped the strap on the first package, opened it up and pulled out one of the fat, pre-loaded clips and tore it from its plastic baggy.

"What the fuck is this?" the second agent said.

"The fuck good's a lookalike if he doesn't have the tools for the job?" I said. It was the best I could come up with on the fly, as I zipped open the second and larger box.

He, too, drew his weapon, but he had it aimed at the ground. He was frantically trying to formulate the perfectly good reason he should shoot me. He knew he should, and he wanted to, but what if I was Admin? He needed that reason, and his need for a reason gave me another handful of seconds.

The delivery vehicles tore out in a hurry, a few more seconds of precious distraction as the agents watched them go. The reason for their haste was clear when two Xec armored personnel carriers rounded the opposite corner, teams that must have decided to follow us after I slowed down near Garl's block. I fit the pieces of the weapon together, the lightweight stock to the short, thick, over-under barrels. *Ka-click.* I seated the clip into its slot and slapped it home. *Clack.* That was the cue. The back door of the Aston Martin swung open and Ajax popped out with his gun leveled over the top of the car.

"Freeze!"

The agents did freeze, their guns still gripped, but they knew better than to raise them. TGS Elites poured out of the APCs. Time was now officially up. I whirled to face off with the Elites.

A quick word about my weapon of choice, the KOJ404 PaxMax®, the largest piece in the Paxawallop® Systems compact rifle series put out by Hammersfjord N-V Weapons Works GmbH. Non-violent weapons were the brainchild of the legendary Warren Peace, and his early doodles, scribbles and ho-lo-sketches were all bequeathed, upon his death (by violent weapon) to his equally legendary protégé, Karl Oskar Hammersfjord, who found a market for the novel devices and manufactured aggressively to it. Hammersfjord, who went by the industry moniker *KOJ*, found broad support among those in the Neo-Viking Movement, and his activities were, and still are, insulated by the arcane and incomprehensible tax laws and patent procedures of the nation-culture preserve of Transarctica, with its special autonomous status within the vast through-plate land mass of Canadanavia (the TranScan, for short). Hence, KOJ was able to design and produce extraordinarily powerful, battle-para-digm-altering devices that, to this day, Xec had largely ignored because their capabilities were described (in the online brochure) as both non-lethal, and a whole new category of weapon: *non-violent*. While Xec carefully monitored the development of all manner of destructive arms manufacture, they were simply stretched too thin, and so had little time or inclination to worry about "weapons" called Gandifiers, or Sitdown Strikers, or Passive Insistence Mines. As a result, they were completely unprepared for what was about to happen in Rat City.

"People are fascinated by guns and ammo," Warren Peace said, in *Life Magnum*, the cult documentary on Peace and Hammersfjord and their quixotic enterprise (predictably, the film went straight-to-HOVO and was almost impossible to find). "We don't fight that fascination. Why would you? You can't. We use it. We latch on and roll with it."

Hammersfjord's interviews were my favorite.

"Our systems look like guns, dey feel like guns, dey fire ven you pull da trigger, vith a big, satisfying kick and a blinding muzzle flash. Dey just don't kill. Dats da vun ting dey don't do. Dey don't have to, you see. I am a Viking (pounds chest) here in my heart, but I am a *new* Viking. I vould radder incapacitate my perceived adversary, and drink to my victory from a 3D-printed replica of his-or-her skull, den imbibe from da bloody, brains-and-carnage-strewn horn of his-or-her actual cranium. Such is da vey of violent non-violence. Death is rendered unnecessary in da theater of battle. Dis is da vey of da future."

Outside the Lem Bar I was about to put the credo of violent non-violence to the ultimate test. I braced where I stood, took careful aim and fired.

WHOOOOMB!!

The Elites saw me level the weapon but they didn't take cover. They were conditioned to charge the point of attack and, being bulletproof, that was a pretty effective M.O. But the KOJ404 was a double-barreled blast their TGS body armor wasn't built to deflect. The top barrel was a soundwave emitter, it sent a thunderous, shaped pulse that hit them and knocked them flat on their backs. It was powerful enough it rocked the APCs and shattered the windows of the building behind them. The second barrel was a drug delivery system. It was a shotgun shell that fired a million barrier-permeating BBs of a potent, ultra-fast-acting designer drug the company called *Spangler*. Basically, it was a neuroleptic with hallucinogenic and hormone releasing properties, though I didn't exactly have a handle on the pharmacological nuances. In the documentary, Hammersfjord gave a soundbite that summed up the effect:

"First, you knock dem down, qvite emphatically, and da sound vave is timed vit da chemical delivery package to optimize da absorption, so dat ven dey haf da verevithal to get back up again, da body's own hormones inhibit da muscular response, and anyvay, the hallucinogen has kicked in by dis point, da subject is trippin' real hard, and no longer cares about fighting. Dat's da beauty of da ting, makin' love not var, puttin' flowers in da gun barrels and da like. Dey don't vant to kill you because dey totally adore you."

From my perspective, the real genius of the weapon was that it worked on humans and decs alike. So while the Edgely in me was nauseated by all the peace-love-and-understanding (I knew he was, I felt it) he was impressed by the sheer knockdown power. I swung around and leveled the 404 on the two agents, caught them with their own weapons at half-mast. Ajax was in my line of fire, but saw what was going to happen, ducked into the car and slammed the door a millisecond before I pulled the trigger.

WHOOOOMB!!

The agents flew backwards as if yanked on cables. The Aston Martin went up on two wheels, before bouncing down again, and the whole flimsy front wall of the Lem Bar buckled inward and collapsed, leaving only the heavy door in its doorframe. I moved forward, scanning the area for other signs of company. The doors of the Aston Martin opened and first Ajax and then Hester got out.

"You guys OK?"

"Fit as a fiddle," Hester replied.

"Hua," Ajax nodded as he jogged past me to check the downed Elites.

I stepped past the first agent, who blinked up at me from the ground, his pupils dilated clear to the whites of his eyes.

"You're so shimmery," he muttered. "So *beautiful* ..."

"Thanks," I said. "Right back at ya." I entered the Lem Bar, pushing through a splintered hole to the right of the door. It took a dangerous second or two for my eyes to adjust to the dim light within, but when they did I saw that the whole front of the bar was a mess of overturned tables, chairs and shattered glassware. Apparently, the entire command team had been lounging in the part of the room that absorbed the brunt of the blast. They were all down, some on their sides, others on their faces. A GATF captain, probably the task force leader, was still in his chair, blown over backwards. He grinned and grasped for the things hovering the air above him. Things that weren't there. An agent who wasn't sufficiently dosed scrambled along the near wall and tried to extricate a handgun that was half-sunk in some shredded insulation. I swiveled and fired. *WHOOOOMB!* He sailed into the wall and through it, and a whole section of ceiling fell down over the open space.

"Take it easy, there, rough houser. Look what you're doin' to my place."

It was good ole Patch, the owner. He was strung up by his wrists in the dark behind the bar. I went to him. From the looks of his eyes, he'd gotten a pretty good dose of what I was serving up.

"Oh, it's you," he said, grinning. "Go ahead and wet your whistle. It's on the house, or whatever's left of the house."

Hester came up and set to work cutting him down.

"I've got him, sir," she said.

I moved into the room behind the bar, passed the pool table and the jukebox, and there I found Hana. She was strung up, like Patch, but with a lot more electrodes clipped on in nasty places. They hadn't touched her face, so I guess there was that; probably hadn't got around to it, yet. But they'd really done a job on the rest of her. I bumped into a table as I hurried to her. She blinked at the sound and opened her eyes. She tried to smile.

"G-Narly … you're not s'posed to be here."

"Oh, Hana."

I put the gun down, looked around and found a steak knife by the bar and used it to cut the zip ties that held her, then carried her to the pool table and laid her down there.

"That's better," she said, wincing. "So much better."

I checked her, as best I could.

"Is anything broken?"

"Nah … just tenderized … and reheated."

"Shit, fuck, fuck. This is my fault. It's all my fault."

She squinted up at me and gave a little laugh, or tried to, coughing instead, then shook her head.

"Here I go and spend … all this time pretending I know … where you are, so … there's somethin' I know, but … I'm not tellin', right? … and you go and spoil it by showin' up."

"I'm sorry, I'm so sorry."

There was a creak of a floorboard behind me and I turned to see a Xec med tech on all fours crawling to get into a hiding place under the bar. Caught in the act, he stared at me with his wide, beady eyes. He was balding, with big, hairy, muttonchop sideburns, and he wore a white, blood-spattered smock. I suddenly realized that this wasn't any med tech, this was the interrogator himself I was looking at. A white smock? You've gotta be kidding, I thought. But wait, there's more. There was a Luger pistol on the floor in the dust and debris (an actual *Luger* pistol, how fucking cliché is that?) and it was obviously his gun, too, and almost within his reach, with a good, solid stretch and lunge he could have it back in hand again. His eyes darted from me to the gun and back to me. It was like some scripted scene, some farcical mini-drama, the hero, in a righteous rage, confronting the very instrument of evil, and there was no escaping the narrative arc of all this, there really wasn't.

Hana lifted her head from the pool table, and with great effort she looked over at the bad guy.

"Please tell me you're going to kill him, G."

I briefly filtered through the options; Breedlove, his changed ways, his non-violent scatter gun, and all those newly conscious parts of him that made him *not*-Edgely. But that, all that, was academic. If I clutched a femur bone in my hairy hand, I guess it might have made a better image, a more fitting one anyway. But I didn't need a femur in my hand. I already had two of them in my legs. As I went into fast motion the Xec torture master played his part and he played it well. He let out this adenoidal growl as he stretched and lunged for the Luger, snatched it up and snaked around far enough to get a shot off, one that chipped a piece of shiny, molded silverplastic off the jukebox. I saw the bullet, saw the piece fly, saw it shatter, saw everything, as I caught hold of him and broke the pistol from his grip (really broke it in two), I was a hybrid, after all, made special, and there wasn't a combat dec anywhere in the security apparatus who stood a chance against me mano a mano.

Yes there was a squeal, and a high-pitched nasal shriek (I think I heard that) as I proceeded to make cannon holes in the side of the bar, working from one end to the other, kicking stools out of my path for each new cock and thrust, each shuddering crunch of skull and laminated wood, using his head and upper body as my battering ram, my lance, my awl, my club, my wet, bloody stump. His smock was a good deal messier when I was finished with the job, blood everywhere, bone fragments and stringy bits of pink soft tissue, bubbling mucous and brain splatter, lots of brain splatter (really, an ungodly amount of splatter). It was all so magnificent, super gory and satisfying in a fully justifiable repudiation-of-sanity sort-of-way, except that … none of it happened.

The Battle of Rat City

On top of everything else that was going on, I was now forced to deal with delusional wish fulfillment fantasies on the part of the Edgely in my head. Not that a walking, talking fugue state was anything new. Fever-dreams-r-us, after all. But I had hoped that maybe (just maybe) they'd give me a break and take a powder while the battle of Rat City raged. But my roiling subconscious didn't have the good sense to do that. Maybe it was all the aerosolized hallucinogenic molecules in the area of the bar that did it, a huff of my own wicked medicine, so to speak. The upshot of all this was that the battering-ram episode didn't happen. It was the Edgely in me who wanted to go psycho-Cromagnon on Dr. Torture. It was the Edgely in me who wanted to hear Hana say the words *Please tell me you're going to kill him, G*. But that isn't what she said. What she really said was: "Don't do it, G … remember your oath."

Garl's Alternative Hippocratic Oath. My oath. In the sizzling moment of truth, with the torture schlub's fate in my literal hands, the Garl in me proved stronger than Edgely. At least in Rat City, in that singular moment, it was Garl who carried the day.

The parts of the previously recounted episode that really happened were as follows: the adenoidal growl Dr. T gave as he stretched and lunged, the grab for the pistol, the shot that piked off a hunk of jukebox, and me on him a split second later, taking the pistol away. What happened after that was a lot more boring than the first go round: I strode back to the bar, retrieved my 404, cocked it, leveled it and gave him both barrels at extreme close range. The weapon sensors recognized there was a living body within the blast radius and automatically modulated the audio emission to prevent crushing decibels that would've left a pile of human gelatin where the good doctor lay. But the dose of the active agent it delivered was more than sufficient.

Within seconds of being blasted, Dr. T chuckled. Then cackled.

"Look at me, I'm a baby mouse. An eentsy-weentsy baby mouse! Eek! Eeeeeeek!"

He really cracked himself up.

Ajax, Hester and Patch looked on, impressed, though I guessed Ajax would've been more impressed by Edgely's imaginary version of events.

Hana looked at me and nodded, relieved, as relieved as a torture victim can look, anyway.

"Another happy customer," she said in a dry-lipped whisper.

She needed medical attention, and fast, or she was going to slip away on us. Which meant the plan had to change.

The original plan was to hit the operational HQ at the Lem Bar, lop the head off local Xec command-and-control (*check*), disrupt communications (*check*), then retrieve four more packages delivered thirty-five seconds ago at a preset drop point on the outskirts of town, two more KOJ404s and extra ammo for Hester and Ajax, who were then to secure the south side, and create a corridor so that refugees could reach the GrayStreak hover buses I'd chartered that were due to arrive in the Walmart parking lot in eight minutes thirteen seconds. Most of that plan was still salvageable. Maybe. But in the meantime I wasn't going to let my best friend die on the ripped felt of a pool table in the back room and beer stink of a dive bar. It was time to get realistic.

"Hester."

"Sir?"

I tossed her my 404.

"Cover."

"Yes, sir."

"Ajax."

"Hua."

"Help me get Hana to the Aston. Go easy …"

We lifted Hana and moved for the broken front wall. Hester went out ahead of us. I saw her crouch and take aim.

WHOOOOMB!!

She fired again.

WHZOOOOMB!!

"Clear!" she shouted.

"Patch, you're with us," I said.

He nodded, happily.

"I would be most days," he said. "But today, I need to look at this." He stared reverently into the fake wood grain of the table top, so close his nose was nearly touching it.

"There's better stuff to see in the car," I said.

He looked up, his one eye blazing.

"There is?"

"Of course there is. Bring some bottles of water."

"And tequila," Hana croaked.

She was limp in our arms.

"And tequila," I echoed.

"I'm onnit," Patch said. He grabbed bottles and followed after us, moving with surprising speed and agility for a hallucinating man.

The street outside the bar was littered with more squirming, air grasping and perma-grinning agent bodies. We lay Hana across the back seats of the Aston Martin, with a bottle of water

clutched in one hand and a liter of dell Dueño in the other. I got
Patch situated in the passenger seat, and belted him in, then told
Ajax he was driving. He looked at me in protest. It was another
sign of the humanizing.

"But sir, my place is here with you, in the fight."

"Your place, Ajax – negative, your *mission* – is to make sure
this woman lives. You got that?"

"Hua," he said, somewhat dejectedly. But he hurried around
and got in behind the wheel.

I leaned through into the backseat to give Hana's arm a
reassuring squeeze. Her eyes opened and she tilted her head to
look at me.

"You've changed, G-Narly … and it ain't just the suit."

"Nah, I'm the same old numb nuts. And you, you're gonna
get through this, and live, because you're that good."

"I *am* that good … don't you ever forget it."

"I won't," I said.

I started to go, but she hung on tight.

"My kit …"

"No worries. I'll find it."

Once a tech, always a tech.

The place I told Ajax to go wasn't a hospital, because
there wasn't one, not close enough to Rat City to matter, and
Xec would be monitoring any medical facilities anywhere on the
west central plate, anyway. The nearest best medical care was a
large-animal clinic run by a veterinarian (and sometime shaman)
by the name of Trixie Three Buffalos. The place was out in Dustfall Springs, a good long drive, so I encouraged Ajax to flow as
fast as he felt comfortable. I could see in his eyes that he liked the
implied challenge.

"Don't let her fall asleep, Patch," I said.

"Nobody's sleepin'! Not on this run! We're going to sing

songs, man. But first, somebody please tell me how long we gotta stay upside down like this?"

Patch was going to be an entertaining road buddy.

I shut the door and Ajax punched it. When the Aston went wheels up, I turned and gave Hester her new marching orders. She was to hang onto the KOJ and the rest of the ammo. She was to commandeer a vehicle, if possible, and if not, she was to get to Walmart by any available means. Once there, she was to secure the parking lot, circle the buses, and hold out as long as she could. If the opportunity presented itself, she was to mobilize the buses with all refugees aboard and bug out for the rendezvous point at Cutterhead Caverns.

Hester smiled a prim Hester smile and took off at a dead run like the commando she was.

Me, I ran the other way.

The reason we hadn't seen more agents or Elites since Hester blasted her way out of the Lem Bar was that Xec was busy establishing a tactical perimeter in order to get containment. I knew this, it was standard procedure, and sprinting directly at them I saw them long before they saw me. Agents leisurely strapping on web gear, TGS Elites pulling on extra ammo pouches. They weren't expecting a deranged and unarmed man-in-a-suit (their target, in fact) to come racing around the corner. With startled looks, even among the combat units, they hurried to unsling rifles, snap off safeties, draw a bead. But I was fast and I knew the neighborhood. I picked my route on the fly. Two APCs were parked end to end, and in the space behind them I knew there was a coffee bar, the little piece of cover where agents could grab a smoke break, a cup of joe and shoot the shit during the long hours of the standoff to come. It was the weak link in the line and I charged it and shot the gap. There were shouts and sporadic weapons fire on both sides, rounds chewing pavement and plinking off steel, but they couldn't unload on me because I was in their midst. It was crossfire city, the whole line shooting back on itself, so most of the agents held their fire, which was exactly what I was counting on. I dodged hard and cut down an alley, one that I knew well, having puked there many times after staggering out of the Lem. There was a scuff of boots and the rattle of gear behind me, but I was light and quick, and sprinted out the back end of the alley before they even got another shot off. I kept the pace up even though my lungs were burning, ran all the way to the intersection of West Marginal and E, then ducked through the pedestrian tunnel there, across the old freight tracks and out the nameless road that half-a-klick farther on merged with Boundary Boulevard, and kept on, all the way and never let up until I reached the transfer station, and the stack of shipping boxes that sat by the fence, unnoticed and untouched, the four packages I'd ordered for Hester and Ajax. I zipped them open and made quick work of the assembly, then loaded both 404s and jammed the extra clips into the pockets of my suit jacket and pants.

What happened after that was all pretty straightforward. Xec put up drones to blanket the town and locate me. The ones that got close to me I shot out of the air with blasts of sound. I gave away my position in the process, of course, but that was okay, the more of them that came to me the better. The Xec units in pursuit used classic contain and converge. But after what happened outside the Lem, they were more conservative in their tactics and maneuvering. It didn't matter. They didn't know what they were up against. I advanced into them, street by street, retreating only to advance again. I *whoooombed'*em and I *whoooombed'*em, put'em down flat on the ground and left them giggling, dazzily-eyed and giddy with wonder. Command sent in reinforcements and I *whoooombed* those motherfuckers, too. I *whoooombed*'em all.

With Xec off the streets the townsfolk came out of hiding, crawled out of windows and poked heads out of doorways, more of them with every block I cleared. Some were people I recognized, friends of Garl, pizza guys, baristas, acquaintances. They were all refugees, now. I yelled at them, told them where to go. "Get to the Walmart," I shouted. "You'll find buses there. Get on and get the hell outta here. It'll be okay, just keep moving." I didn't know if it was really going to be okay, of course, but it was the best thing I could think to say. I knew I had to keep fighting to cover their retreat.

Somehow it worked. In the face of my crazy attack, the veteran Xec units pulled back to make a stand. It was a big contingent of TSA and LGS, mixed human and dec units, the real shock troopers. They barricaded themselves in the area around Garl's apartment building. They were set up, dug in, ready and waiting, but I came right at them, because they were never going to be ready enough.

WHOOOOMB!
WHOOOOMB!
WHOOOOMB!!
WHZOOOOMB!!

My barrels were hot and smoking, but my enemy was down. There wasn't a single, stinking Xec operative anywhere in town still up on hizzerit's feet. They lolled on the barricades and shuddered on the street, alone and in little lovey dovey piles of twos and threes, the alleys around Garl's building were littered with their warm, wet, body-rushing bodies, and wherever they lay, grinning ecstatically, laughing hysterically or petting one another's rapturous faces with sensuous gazes, there were no bad trips amongst the fallen (KOJ's ammo was strictly the good stuff). The battle was over.

My job in the Rat was finished, all except for the part that mattered to me most. I dropped my guns and went straight to it, the spot that was my true destination all along, the magnet drawing me, the inevitable locus. The *Torridreemz®* hotbox. And *her*. There was nothing keeping us apart, now, not the Junta, not a battalion of Xec goons, not even my own mixed up psyche. I/ Me was whole, and all parts of me were in full accord: we needed *her* more than we needed life itself. There was only the remaining physical distance that separated us and I was subtracting that as fast as I could move. She was so close now I could taste her, could breathe and feel her, not figuratively, but literally, her scent, her skin, her hair. I could see those eyes, that face, she was with me, all around me, like a vibrant vision of radiant beauty, enveloping and infusing, urging me on (*Hurry!*) every step of the way (*Hurry!*) and I ran, oh, I did run. I rounded the corner and there it was. The box. I'd seen it out of the corner of my eye during the fight, but I didn't dare look directly at it, I couldn't even think about it. Yet with the battle over, nothing stood between us but the hardware itself, with its faded graphics and that swirly-swoopy-lettered logo, *Torridreemz*, *Torridreemz*, *Torridreemz*, I couldn't believe it was finally only the box and me, I was really seeing it, staring straight at it, and my enemy hadn't touched it, hadn't even *seen* it, because it was invisible to them, just a tawdry, obsolescent vDrome, so unremarkable and insignificant they never once suspected that within its seamy confines lay the gateway to paradise.

Problem was, the thing didn't open at my approach. It was supposed to recognize my proximity and open. That's how Edgely set it up. Obviously, something was wrong, but the imperative of my need was too urgent for me to stop and worry about what it might be. I had to get it open somehow. Mprint® wasn't going to help me. That technology wasn't even around when the ancient sarcophagus was made. Truth be told, I was prepared to rip the whole edifice from its anchor in the pavement and dig my way down to her through broken shards of concrete if I had to, but that would take time. There was another, faster way, if it still worked. With trembling hands I dug out a credit card (thank god I still had one) and swiped it through the slot. You want to talk about old fashioned tech. *Routine access for timed patronage?* Jesus-H., I was going in just like any other lust-addled rube. If I hadn't been so desperate I would've died of embarrassment. And then to cap it off the card didn't even take!

Read error.

Please try your card again.

I was *this* close to attacking the box, to hurling myself at it, cheap molded plastic obstacle that it was. But I didn't. I forced myself to slow down, to be calm and go easy. I opened my lips and, with tremulous breath, I huffed on the credit card's magno strip, wiped it on my sleeve and tried it again.

Swipe.

There was a hum, a *click* (these were good sounds) and the thing clam-shelled open before me. I rolled in and lay perfectly flat and still as it closed over me again (just the way it was supposed to) and when it was shut, I felt around with both hands along the interior padding and found and popped the hidden panel Edgely had installed (in one of his fleeting moments of lucidity) and pushed the button I found there. Another hum, a deeper mechanical groan, and I was on my way down, the bed of the box descending through the floor.

Remote Control

The *Torridreemz* platform bed dropped through the interstix below street level, down through the ceiling of a featureless
corridor, where it tilted. But I didn't wait for all that, I vaulted
off before it reached the floor, landed on all fours and scrambled
for the threshold, the doorway with its dangling strands, liquid
and iridescent, sparkling with the soft blue light from beyond, the
last barrier left. I hurried through. I crossed the lawn diagonally,
headed for the patio and the pool. It was all there, just as before,
the house with its enormous windows and its great slab of a roof,
and above, a tapestry of stars spread like a saga across in the
night sky and, in the distance far below, the winking gems of faux
city lights. It was all exactly as it was supposed to be, just as it had
been before, when she stood right *there*, right over there, only she
wasn't here now.

Where was she?

Clap, clap, clap, clap, the unhurried, mocking applause
from one set of hands was not an encouraging sound. I stared
out into the night sky and tried hard to project myself into its
epic promise of stratosphere, of space, of escape. With her. For a
few more seconds I could pretend it was possible. I didn't want to
turn around. I didn't want the dream to end. Not in this stupid,
insipid, ridiculous way.

"Bravo. *Braviss!* The hero destroys his mortal foe and returns
to claim his rightful prize. His one true love! It's so reassuring to
know some things are still eminently predictable."

Recognizing the voice, I reluctantly turned.

Colonel Serpas emerged through the open door of the house. He moved toward me with the relaxed gait of an executive walking to a camera. He wore his signature, crooked smile, the same one plastered over the ubiquitous *One Destiny* posters, the smile he flashed in every propaganda HOVO and choreographed *Breaking News* clip, the bold warrior, the unshakable commander, leading the Standing Committee into and out of emergency session, summit conferences, state dinners.

"Sorry about the Grushank-ass interrupt-ass," he said. "Oh, before you go and do something rash, I should tell you she's not here, not in the house, not in the garden, nowhere on the premises. Hasn't been for quite some time."

He made a show of glancing around, looking genuinely impressed.

"It's a helluva nice fuck pad, though. An autobuild, am I right? Carved right out of the stix, with an outmoded hotbox as a front door, my heavens, an old *Torridreemz*! What a classic! How many kids got their cherries v-popped in one of those sticky-vinyl jalopies, eh? Sweet touch. So good to see you haven't lost your sense of humor, Ben."

Ben? ... he thought I was Edgely. Of course he did. He figured I ditched Garl somehow, and ol' Ben was back. But what difference did it make? He had her, which meant all of me was screwed.

I didn't need to ask him how he found her. There was only one way it could've happened. When Garl made his FF service call on 3-Frame, and encountered Grusha for the first time (*as* Garl) it was a long-arranged set-up by Edgely. Garl had his *deal*, he fell for her, as Edgely knew he would, because his submerged psyche was already in love with her. The struggle within himself ignited. Edgely won the day, briefly, and left the flat. But Garl proved resilient, he suppressed Edgely anew and returned to Paris and to Grusha (with all the silly energy of new love) but in her presence, Edgely clawed his way to the surface again and, seeing the potential danger in all the yo-yoing between the personalities, he held on long enough to move her to Rat City, and the hideout he'd constructed under the street below Garl's apartment building. No sooner did he have her safely transferred than Edgely blacked out again, Garl returned to himself, went to the Lem Bar and confessed his *deal* to Hana. Then, in the face of Hana's determination to cure him of his lovesickness (a sickness that would, of course, be impossible to cure) Garl drugged Hana, and went back yet again to 3-Frame only to find Grusha's flat blown to smithereens. What Garl didn't know (the mental block still fully in place) was that the bomb was Edgely's work, a desperate attempt to cover both their tracks. Once the synthesis happened and I became Breedlove, I was able to remember all this back-and-forth personal history. But what I didn't put together, not until Serpas stood leering in front of me where Grushenka was supposed to be, was that the bad guys shot the gap. Garl's mere presence on 3-Frame attracted the attention of Serpas & Co. Even Edgely wasn't aware of how closely they had tracked Garl's movements (in fairness to my former self, Edgely's prescient paranoia was thrown off by all the intermittent blackouts) so that when Garl first left the flat, Serpas seized the opportunity. His people broke in, encountered an exotic pleasure unit (an IBTetX no less) which they found curious, but even then they didn't suspect it was Edgely's longtime lover. When Garl returned (unbeknownst to them in the mind of Edgely) they had just enough time to trax her, ice her and get out. Set for rapid auto-resume, she never knew they were there, hence, neither did Garl or Edgely. They used a low-field tag, because the last thing they expected was for Garl to take her with him, and (still with no clue about the attempted reemergence of Edgely within the psyche of their toy man Garl) they lost track of him from the time he left the flat until he showed up again in the Lem Bar in Rat City, so they were completely unaware of Edgely situating her in a luxury house hidden below street level. The EM shielding Edgely put in place around his Rat City hideout prevented Xec from picking up the low-field signal of the tag. What's more, they never went looking for her because they thought she was blown up (Edgely's explosive feint having done exactly what it was meant to do) (an uncharacteristic lack of imagination led the Junta to conclude the bombing was not connected to Garl, but was attributable instead to a spate of un-related mob activities on the frame) so although Serpas would've loved to know more about Garl's unexpected little tryst on 3, he figured the golden opportunity was lost and let it go. And yet, even with Grushenka safely tucked away beneath Rat City, she still carried the tag, like a latent malignancy. So when, thanks to dog-faced fate, Garl disappeared, and Xec search teams showed up in Rat City in heavy numbers to find him (and punish the town) units scanning in the vicinity of Garl's building must have picked up the weak signal of the trax tag and traced it to her. I could've kicked myself for not figuring it out sooner.

"Where is she?" My voice sounded calm and dangerous, like Edgely when he's mad.

"Safe. Extremely safe," Serpas said. "Oh, all except for this little fellow."

He held up a simple remote control with a single, glowing red button. How fitting. The absolute perfect cliché.

"I press this and ..."

I sighed.

"She dies."

"Ever the quick study. A magnificently agonizing death, yes. But then, I can't take any more chances with you. Though it was awfully good of you to leave your "guns" upstairs on the street. Pow, pow, pow. What a number you worked on my people. F-y-i, as we speak, I have a specially-equipped team enroute to take possession of Mr. Hammersfjord's manufacturing facilities. *Non-violent* weapons? What a sick, sick, oh some people they're just, well, they're sick in the head."

"Tell me about it."

"Still, I suppose I should thank you for alerting me to the dangers of non-violence. As well as those of impermanent mental exile. Tell me, Ben, how did you do it? Where did Garl go? I liked him so much better than I like you."

"I'd tell you, but you wouldn't understand," I said.

"That's where you're wrong. If you thought we crawled up inside your head before, you'll come to realize that we didn't even scratch the gel coat. So why don't we?"

"Why don't we what?"

"Get started. Cue bodyguards."

I heard them coming before he said it. I didn't need to look up to see. Trapdoors snapped open in the black ceiling of the night sky, and they fast-roped in. DarXec. NERO Division. TGS Elites with Red-Stripe and SAV-shock enhancements. They were the scariest troops on the planet and Serpas didn't leave home without them. There were nine in all, I knew their precise distances from me to the closing millimeter, and I worked through the shifting algorithm of Jeet Kune Do moves I would use to defeat them.

But I didn't move, not a muscle.

I stood there and watched the Colonel's smile snake across his face.

He took a step back and held up the remote, as if I needed the reminder. I didn't. I wasn't worried about the NERO Elites, I was pretty sure I could take them all. I was worried about the remote, the glowing button, and the slender likelihood, the chance, however airy and slight, that it meant she was still okay, she was safe, like he said, extremely safe, and that he would know that I would know he was lying if she wasn't. But I couldn't read him. Maybe it was the rage. Maybe it was only me, worried sick that she was already extremely dead.

"You're just going to stand there and take it, aren't you? Wowee, that, now that's what I call dumb-as-a-post devotion."

If there's one thing an Elite knows how to do it's administer a tonfa beating to a subject who, for one reason or another, can't or won't fight back. I wouldn't call it an art, exactly, because it's my personal belief that word shouldn't be used for such things. But they were very skilled at what they did. Talented even. They beat the living crap out of me, interspersing electric shock into the mix with every baker's dozen of the pressure point perfect baton blows. Serpas watched the whole thing with unblinking, hungry and salacious intensity; from a safe distance of course, well out of the range of blood and other bodily fluid spatter. Serpas was an infamous germ freak and he only left the controlled environment of his apartments in the Junta's fortified compound when absolutely necessary. Times such as this. To be here to greet Ben Edgely in person, and have him back, as (seemingly) the Edgely of old.

"I missed you," he muttered, wetly, at one point, and I could tell, by the slight tremor in his lips, that he wasn't faking it. He really *had* missed me.

The whole thing took a goodly long time. Any job worth doing is worth doing well, and his bodyguards were determined to prove their mettle by doing me just right. Near the end, or what I permitted myself to hope might be the blessed approach of unconsciousness, Serpas moved in a little closer, and I saw him cover his nose and shiny lips with a small silicone mask. At first

I thought it was a germaphobe's protective barrier, to keep him from inhaling any filthy particulates that might go airborne in the pummeling of boots, bats and cattle prods. But, man, oh man, he really sucked into that mask, like he just couldn't get enough air through it, and I came to understand, just before my tunneling vision squelched all the way down to a pinprick of black-filigreed fog, that the good colonel enjoyed a side of autoerotic-asphyxiation with his main course of vicarious ultra-violence. For a short spell, what was left of the thinking parts of me entertained the idea that he was actually going to let them kill me and be done with it, done with me, finally, really, basta, finito. But that was only the blows to the head talking. I should've known better than to think he'd ever let them go lethal in such a quick and uncomplicated way, or even let them get close, though it certainly *felt* close. My mind retreated to a clearer place, a last stand of consciousness on a twilit isle in the sea of blazing pain, and it was there I knew that Serpas planned to come through on his promise. This beating was the barest taste of the excremental delicacies still to come.

If he got his way (and there was little to suggest he wouldn't) my future would be a *tour de force* of all-new torments and fantastic humiliations. He would smash and obliterate his old work and start afresh, as if Garl never happened, Garl the chump, Garl the stooge, Garl who hadn't performed as intended, because he didn't prove to be the perfect, drawn-out, boot-licking straight man in the most juicy, satisfying and divinely comedic mind demolition of all time. All because Ben Edgely (somehow) (this was how Serpas saw it) had managed to phoenix his way out of that ashy ruin seven years in the making. It was a debacle, a total failure, much of it Serpas' own fault, and that had to suck. But it was also a challenge, one that both galled and thrilled him, because it meant the game wasn't over, no, it was a whole new game. And there's nothing quite like a great new game to make a sadistic old man feel young, virile and sadistically vital all over again. In the given electrified, lacerated and contused moment, Colonel Serpas was experiencing (from what I was able to tell, anyway) a genuine, throbbing and tumescent renewal.

His voice cut through the pulpy thudding of the sticks, long after I could no longer see him, or anything else, for that matter.

"That's enough, *enough* already! Holy Menudo, people, look what you've done to the man. Come now, come, come. Easy! Get him on the NoG lifts, and get me the goop. Chop chop. We are leaving this junkyard level. I simply cannot tolerate what the air down here is doing to my skin."

* * *

Blackness. The absence of color or sound. The absence of anything. I wondered, for an indeterminate period (time?) whether Serpas had miscalculated, and I really was dead. Then I considered that I was considering being dead, which probably wasn't what being dead was like. But then I thought, how in the Jesus H. should I know what being dead was really like. You had to be dead to be dead, it wasn't something you got to practice, or do a dry run on, or get good at. So maybe this was it. I tried to float myself into the blackness, to move the thing I was calling *me* around in it, like an embryo in an ocean of incontiguous midnight, but I couldn't tell the difference between one part of nothingness and any other, so I gave up, and just let it be the void. And that's when I heard a delicious sound, sweeter than sweet, if sound can be said to have a taste, this sound was like the nectar of heaven. A single, soft, slightly accented utterance, possibly French, spoken to me from the heart of the non-extension.

"Ben? …"

Grushenka

(Or More Accurately, My Feelings for Her
and All That Monkey Business)

Agrafena Smolderova Bencomo Nhung Marlowe-Khan
was an Inge-Borghesa-TetX40, the units known among the decarati as the mythic IBTetX (I know, old news) (but hold on, here,
there's more to it). How many of them were there on Famous
Original Earth? On all the Earths? Perhaps only two people knew
the answer to that question, Marcus Vranes, the god king among
dec designers, and his partner in rendered hypertissue artcrime,
the legendary physio visualist, Andrea Farinetti. To back up a
step further, any question about *how many* IBTetXs was a bit of
uncalculated misdirection. The question was a mirage. Since no
two of the units were exactly alike, there was only the one of any
one of them. They were, each of them, unique creations in all
existence. Even the exotic and evocative model name was only
obliquely attributable to the design team, because Vranes and
Farinetti were artists who didn't go in for any such market-ori-
ented conceits as make-and-model, and if and when they did,
it was only to be in-jokey humorous or mind-fucky ironic. The
designation Inge-Borghesa-TetX40 wasn't their name for their
work, it was a placeholder identifier, created by an art aficionado,
some learned member of the buyer set, based upon his or her
decography of the highly sought-after designers' earlier work,
and hence, as a moniker, it fell into the category of an historian's
assumptions, and the unquenchable need to give a thing a name,

so that *that* thing could be identified for collection purposes, and thus fetishized appropriately and systematically, which, after all, was all about communication among the appreciators of fine work. Eventually, of course, the name was picked up, latched onto and popularized by the broader (though still rarified) fandom, wealthy enthusiasts, the hoarders of exquisites and the flesh merchants of the most haute airs.

Not only did the Vranes-Farinetti design team not care about anything as superficial as make/model identifiers (in general) they had only one thing in mind with their work on this particular, *commissioned* piece, a unit they shopnamed *Amrita-4B*: that she was to be tailor-made, designed from every one of her ten pearlescent tippy-toenails on up through slender toes and delicate ankles, up the shapely calves and the convergence of supple thighs, the altar of the hips, the sweetmusk svadhisthana chalice of the loins, that succulent yoni, up, up (*Keep moving, don't stop!*) over the precious pooch of a belly, around the soft, squeezable breasts (*Oh! Double up, Oh! Oh!*) on up the cool slope of the exquisite décolletage (*Mon Dieu!*) twixt lithe, rounded shoulders, thin neck, bone structure of a goddess, and those eyes (*It's all in the eyes!*) that regal forehead, and on out, out, out to the fine, fragrant end of every silky, lustrous strand of her flowing mane—*for* Ben. She was made protospecifically for the *hybrid*, in every way they could make her, designed in every conceivable aspect to be *his* perfect other, bonded inextricably to *him*, his courtesan, his muse, his mistress, his soul mate, his landrace queen.

Very possibly, all but certainly, she was made *too* well. Far and away too well.

But I wax ... bring it back, Breedlove ... concentrate, now, get the point across ...

Conventional wisdom might suggest, what with my brain going through the changes it was going through – the synthesis

of three heads into one, the new guy on the block, the fourth
brother in my overstuffed gourd – that in the flip-flop, King-
Kong-with-a-ragdoll throes of that mental tectonic shift, that
psychic superstorm, that spasmo-transformative *me*volution of
split personalities all making a go of it together, that with all of
that happening my feelings for Grusha would (and, by all rights,
should) undergo similar mutative changes. My potent attachment
to her *should* lose some of its oomph, the jungle vines that bound
us fray, the muscles of blood-pounding desire atrophy and honeyed serenade become dissonant in garden below and lose the
key of its perfect pitch, or even fade away, like the yogi who finds
the Eternal and relinquishes his mortal beloved. It made a lot of
sense. After all, she was built for Ben, to be *his* lover; and strictly
speaking, I was no longer Ben. He was only one of us, now, and
the rest of us (me), Garl (the troubled clinician), Barker Rags (the
raving preacher) (distracted proselyte that he was), even C.G.Q.
Breedlove, our collusive combine, the laser-focused new man, we
were all packed in tight. Put us together in a room with her and
… *what?* Two is company, five is a zoo. *Something* was bound to be
different. How could it not be? She would be different to me, or
I to her, for even as she was made for Ben, Ben was made, per-
mutively and retrospectively *for* her (fuck temporal considerations,
here) (it's all in the bonding) (call it Lamarckian cellular premo-
nition) (call it what you will, it was true) (*One whose attraction to the
other is only exceeded by the other*) (Marcus Vranes said that) but what
I had become, in the cascading changes occurring *in me*, was not.
It would end, by definition, it *had* to end. The aura we shared
would lose its haloed haze, the spectrum fluctuate, the sparkle
fizzle, and we would both know it and feel it with absolute corporeal conviction, and all there would be left for us to do in that
tragedy of the inevitable, of lost devotion, is mourn its alterated
symmetry and, thus bedeviled, shuttered and forlorn, bear wit-

ness to its irretrievable passing into loss and memory.

Except … that isn't what happened.

However crazy it might sound (at least, to the Edgely in me) the attachment didn't fade. There was no extinguishment of the flame, no lessening of my implacable need to be near her, for her, *with* her. The only change I was conscious of registering was the opposite of a diminishment. I burned for her with a desire hotter than ever before (she, the superheated sun, me, the doomed moon spiraling, spiraling) burned with such an intensity of yearning that I felt I must surely perish from it. My epiphany in the contemplation of this phenomenon, this molten lovesickness from which I suffered (to the extent I could pry any cerebral distance between my so-called intellect and the raging bonfire of my pining worship) here flying in the face of any conventional wisdom, was that the dramatic uptick in the power and pull of my affections was a direct result of *our* combined need.

Edgely loved her, certainly, he loved her more than life itself, but he loved her *alone*. It was the incidental, individual, controlled devotion of a Ben Edgely, *as* Ben Edgely, crime lord and sometime revolutionary. But the pursuit of those other ambitions (crime and revolution) was only possible because his hybridized psyche recognized the inherent danger (and base inefficiency) of such a potent, feral and, frankly, experimental attraction; and so, in a fit of self preservation, he split himself in two, created a second self in whose person the overwhelming aspects of his love (and, let's face it, *ur*lust) for Grushenka could reside, safely isolated and contained. The problem with this solution was twofold; it led to periods of total unconscious blackout for Edgely during which he was completely overtaken by the energy of the second self; and, worse still, it led to insanity for the second self, who, because he was unable to split himself yet again, precisely because he loved Grushenka too much to do so, was driven mad by the cyclotronic cataclysm of his need for her (which led him to turn to ascetic devotion in the form of a goddess-centric religion that was a unique hybrid artifact in itself) (confession: the preacher's memories and the tenets of his weird faith are still something of a jumbled mystery, even to me, represented as they are in babbling inanities and the monomaniacal pursuit of a path I could not, in any logical sense, reverse navigate). The point of the epiphany wasn't that I now understood myself so much more fully (I didn't) (not even close) the point was that both Edgely and the mad preacher *loved* her in their *own* ways. Fast forward now, to Garl, who came along thanks to the resolute and sadistic ministrations of Serpas and rest of the Junta, and after seven long years spent locked in the mostly exclusive exile of that persona, Garl himself finally encountered her, *as* Garl, and he, too, fell for her (*hard*) (aka Garl's *deal*) (despite the heroic efforts of Hana to unwind the amatory infraction) (in fairness, Hana had no way of knowing what she was contending with vis-à-vis my multi-part head) thus making it a Ben-Preacher-Garl devotional triple play. The upshot, here, in the moment of awakening, with Jagabrew-the-would-be assassin's still-twitching heart clutched in my hand, as the walls of the tri-pathed maze were lifted away, and the three personalities commingled into one, their love (as it turned out) was not a single, shared pool, but instead the compounding cataract of three separate, individual and limitless reservoirs rushing through burst and crumbling dams, and all the levees washed away downstream in the flood of the inundating rise of an amore that very nearly drowned me.

It was the peculiar mix of Edgely and Garl that saved me, since they proved strangely symbiotic, both just stubborn, ornery, thick-headed and resourceful enough, that the two of them together could hold it together, and keep the rest of us/them/me from going as wacko as the preacher man. Still, it was a close thing, a real dance and I knew I was only playing for time.

So that's the gist of it, how I came to be enhancedly entranced by Grushenka and how (nevertheless) I made it as far as I did.

Thus, when I left Jagabrew's sordid sinkhole, *as* Breed, and drove the dead sado's pickup truck with my blood-stained hands hot on the wheel, and Jhett the bandaged rescuee slumped in the backseat, feverishly mulling my options and planning next moves, forcing myself to focus on vehicle speed, road signs, time and distance calculations and the whiff of new-truck polymers, because all the while the background radiation of my yearning for my Agrafena Smolderova pulsed and roared.

Just so, in the gypsy cab on the road to Paris, I plotted and schemed with absolute intensity on the rickety matrix of surviving for just one more hour, racing through names and faces, old friends, older enemies, favors I might call in seven years after the fact with cancelled leverage and stale debts, but even in that fit of concentration I recognized that every juke and turn my thoughts made was accompanied by a potent vardoger of her, the molten ghost of my fiery distraction.

Likewise in the showroom in the Marais, while negotiating the purchase of two well-dressed bodyguard units, the vision of her stood beside me, a waking dream at the periphery, her slender fingers reaching to brush with mine. And in the safehouse in the 19th, while bathing, while eating (every morsel tasteless) while tending to Jhett's injuries, even while experiencing the gnawing remorse and responsibility for those who were sacrificing and dying *because* of me, my agenda was set, my trajectory warped, as I was utterly and subversively bent on devising a way to return, tout de suite, to my love, my raison d'etre, my better half, my Grushka, the numinous center of my universe.

I guess you could say I just couldn't get her out of my head.

Sins of the Father

I came to in a cell. I was on my feet. Naked. It's a disconcerting sensation to wake up out of a black sleep vacant as death to find yourself standing up. I had no idea how long I'd been there like that, but I wasn't tired, my back didn't ache, my legs weren't fatigued. Refreshed is probably too optimistic a word, given the circumstances (whatever they might be) but that's the way I felt. Refreshed. My body was reflected in the darkly transparent walls. One, two, three, four of them, a close, quadrangular space, more fish tank than prison cell. I couldn't see anything beyond the walls, whichever way I turned I saw me staring dimly back at me. My hair was slicked to my head and my skin shiny and wet, as if I just stepped out of a shower. I ran my fingers down my chest and along my arms, and found it wasn't water. My whole body was covered in a thick coating of some clear jelly, and I wondered what in the Jesus H. it was all about. I spent about a minute, standing there, blinking stupidly and trying to figure what I knew from what I didn't, when I suddenly realized there wasn't a mark on me. No cuts or bruises, no weeping contusions, no eyes swollen shut in a pulpy face. It didn't make any sense, not at first, given the way Colonel Serpas had his people work me over. But then I pieced it together. What must've happened after I dipped into the still pond of concussed vacancy. It was one of the last things Serpas called for, get me *the goop*, he said. So that was it. They used *the goop* on me. Of course, it had to be the answer. *The goop* was a genuine medical breakthrough. It had been a hot topic on

GNN *Healthwise* segments for months, and the talking head experts really called it that, too—*the goop*. It was a nanoactive compound that was synthesized, ironically enough, from substances dec manufacturers had been using for years. ATR was the underlying biotech. Accelerated Tissue Regeneration. Smear it on and the stuff reacted on contact at the site of injury, even deep tissue and bone fractures, like stem cells on speed. Supposedly, it even worked on brain cells. Supposedly (and here's where things go all metaphysical) it even worked on dead tissue. Even long-dead tissue. Reach-back longevity, they called the enlivening effect. I had it on good authority (one of Garl's more well-informed FF clients) (the Amishly-inclined fetishist in the Wongmarket Bowery) that *Heal!*® was the drug name the stuff was marketed under. But though I'd seen the HOVO segments and had heard plenty about the stuff, I'd never actually seen it, nor met anyone who had. That's because what was *really* being marketed was that lowly us couldn't get the miracle goop, not at any price. As ridiculous and cruel as that sounds, *that* was because (1) the MacPharma® patent owners wanted to maximize profits via margins grotesque and obscene, and in order to pull that off they had to play hard-to-get to the point of unattainable, which required making the masses aware of and desperately wanting the thing they couldn't have so that the few who could saw their access as a privilege (and yet another mark of manifest superiority) and were happy to pay the monstrous price; and (2) the Powers-that-Be wanted to understand the social implications of practical immortality in a jar. Is it a good thing (*for them*) or a bad thing (*for them*)? That is the question. That is always the question.

Given that I found myself all healed up in the here-and-now, clearly the rules of hard-to-get and monstrous price didn't apply to the Junta. Serpas and his entourage must have had a hogshead of *the goop* with them on the trip down to Rat City, both to insure against the advent of any personal injury, but also, conveniently, to patch up the beaten-to-a-pulp carcass of a onetime archenemy. Which meant, of course (*Oh, joy!*) he could be beaten to a pulpy carcass all over again. And over and over. And they could employ whatever other physical inducements suited the torture master's fantasies, all without any nagging apprehensions about doing permanent damage to the subject; hence (*at long last!*) they were limited only by the imagination. And lo, another great technical breakthrough, possibly one of the most important developments in the history of medical science, was and would be used for military, quasi-military and prisoner interrogation purposes long before it was ever (*if ever*) made available to the general population for their plebian injuries and daily dying needs.

Typical.

Serpas probably had his people slather me in *the goop* right there on the NoG lifts the moment I passed out. After all, what fun was I unconscious? My situation looked like it might shape up to be a real merry-go-round ride, one that would just get better with every pass. I walked to the cell wall and pressed on it. I ran my hands over the smooth surface, worked my way from one side to the other and back around. This was an incarceration cliché, of course, the animal urge to test the cage, but you had to do it. I wondered where they'd taken me. I was pretty sure I wasn't in Rat City anymore, because Serpas couldn't stand what it was doing to his skin. But that only left about a hundred or so maximum security gulags and Xec rendition hot spots between 69-Frame and Mezzanine and I could be in the bowels of any one of them. Who knows, maybe they took me down and not up, maybe I was even at Lako Baines Deep Core. For some queer reason that thought almost cheered me.

Pacing round the cramped dance floor of my confinitude I nearly slipped in the gloppy slime my body was dripping. I was pretty damned sure that whatever the jelly was it wasn't the healing *goop*. The salve of *the goop* was long gone. The new stuff had some other purpose, and all but certainly not a pleasant one. *But what?* Was it a conductant? To optimize full-body electro-shock? That was something Serpas would appreciate, but it wasn't arcane and wickedly creative enough to really pique his interest. Mulling this, I caught a glimpse of warped reflection and my mind, or part of it, swerved to Grusha and immediately the rest of me told all of me to stop thinking about her, but I couldn't help it. Was she okay? Was she even alive? How was it that I heard her voice from the depths of the blackness?

The lights came on.

And there they stood.

The Junta.

All four of them here together, each one facing me from a different wall of my cell: Colonel Serpas, Archbishop Castiff, Xi Mar ("The Chairman"), and Millicent Strain (good ole Millie) (very few people knew she'd lived a previous existence as Dr. Dalton Noon, the political kingmaker) (fewer still knew that she started life as Rhonda Krepps).

Next to the archbishop stood a fifth member of their merry band. At the sight of him the Edgely in me felt a rush of joy, the way you would on seeing your closest friend and most trusted confidant, but half a frozen heartbeat later I realized he was the one, the traitor—Edgely's betrayer from the way back when. I didn't think I'd be surprised, but I was. During the seven years Edgely subsisted in the cracks of Garl's mind, in the fractional intervals of clarity, he pondered who it could have been. Who had the access, the will and the way to sell him down the river? Edgely had his theories, of course, and weighed them one against another, but the man standing before me now was the last name on the burnt and shredded end of a long scroll. Above suspicion was the father of the Underground, the controller we operatives knew as Klondike. Trust incarnate was he. Ironically, the Garl part of me recognized him, as well, having met him as a stranger on the street outside the exploded remnants of a certain luxury flat on a hollowed out night in ParisGC, a night that seemed forever ago. And the last piece of the puzzle slid painfully into place.

Sir Gavin Tang stood on the other side of the glass wearing an enigmatic smile.

I prided myself on my pokerface, but Tang clearly registered my dismay because he shrugged. It was a remarkably casual gesture.

"What can I say, Praxis?"

"Try this—'A female of studied charm and exquisite countenance,'" I said.

"Were those my words? You didn't know me that night in Paris, yet you remember what I said. Curieux. But if you think I give a dung ball in shitville about your Parisienne putain then you really don't know me."

"Obviously, I never did. What was it, then? What do you give a dung ball in shitville about?" When he didn't answer I shook my head in disgust. "I guess everyone has his price."

"Not me. It's something else entirely."

I had no clue what it could be that turned him. Part of the reason Tang was above suspicion was that he not only birthed the Resistance, and was the Movement personified, but he was rich (very rich) he had lovers (lots of lovers) and his zeal for La Causa was a contagious charisma all its own, a powerful *gravitas* that proved compelling enough to woo even Edgely, the unwooable man. It was Klondike who *made* Ben into Praxis, and then set me in motion. Together, we saved and relocated so many. We made such strides. Tang was a freaking god! I just couldn't believe they got to him. How did they do it? How?

"Don't bust a gasket, love, it's not what you think," he said.

"What is it I think?"

"It wasn't some precious bauble they dangled, some pearl of great price. I was in darkness only I didn't know it. Now I see the light."

The smile was back again, sickeningly serene. Beatific, even. I suddenly took in his disturbing proximity to the archbishop. Real intimacy there?

"Please tell me no."

"Yes," he said.

"No."

"I'm 'fraid so, old friend."

"You fucking went and found religion?"

"Go on, cast the first stone, if you must. It's not like you're any one to talk. It was you who led the way, you who blazed the trail."

"What in the Jesus H. are you talking about?"

"Don't act like you don't know."

"I *don't* know."

"You're going to stand there and tell me you forgot about Johnny Highlife. So soon? He's the preacher."

"Wait a minute … *my* preacher?"

"Your preacher! I realize he's not your conscious brother. You two have never formally met, am I right? But he's there, under your skin, *in* your skin. He *is* your brother, there to save you all along. And he still is, I'll wager, if you accept him. You didn't know I had you followed."

"Followed when?"

"Whenever you had one of your episodes, when Johnny took you over, body and soul. I'd have an operative tail you, to protect you, I told them, but the real reason was I wanted to be there myself, to tag along in the shadows and listen."

"Listen? To the sermons?"

"Yes." His eyes really glowed. "If you want to call them that, go ahead."

"What are you saying, that I converted you?"

"Not exactly. I couldn't understand a word you said. But you *inspired* me. You set me on the path."

"The path?"

"The point is you had passion. You had an outlet. Where was my outlet? I'd listen to you, your blathering, your speaking in tongues, your ruptured rapture, and I'd wonder, how come you get to be the holy man? How come you get to be saved?"

I shook my head at the horror of it, the sheer, poisoned horror.

"Let me get this straight. You were *jealous* of Edgely's fucked up mind?"

"Not jealous, per se, but I knew I was missing out. Even with all my "revolutionary fervor" I was being left behind. I couldn't be left behind, you understand. By the way, why did you refer to yourself in the third person? Just now, you said, *Edgely's fucked up mind*. Why say it that way?"

I could *feel* the evil onlookers prick up their ears. I had to be careful. Tang didn't know about Breedlove, and, more importantly, neither did Serpas and company. They thought I was Edgely on a comeback tour after seven years in the land of Garl. But if I said the wrong thing, I just might blow the only chip I had left to play.

I stepped to the glass and stared into Tang's rheumy eyes. He didn't look well. I suspected religion wasn't his only opiate. I motioned to the archbishop.

"So you went to *him*."

"He saved me."

"How many operatives did you give up? Tell me I'm the

only one."

"Would that I could."

"How many? … *How many?!*"

He swallowed, like he really didn't want to say it.

"There are no halfway points on the road to salvation."

"No …"

"It was only a matter of ti—"

"*NO!*"

I hurled myself at the cell wall and its composites *thwonged* with the force of the impact. I screamed and the decibels pushed him back a full step. Then it was me staggering back, my head swimming with the ramifications. What *didn't* Tang know? Obviously, he didn't know about Hester, because she was out there in the field all along, and was still out there (I hoped) (I prayed) but how she managed to avoid capture I couldn't imagine, I just couldn't think that part through, the horror of his betrayal was too enormous. Maybe there were a handful of others in Edgely's old crew who eluded the sweep. But there were so many Tang knew and would have fingered. After all they'd been through, all the sacrifices made, and he just served them up. Just like that? I felt the puke rising in me, but forced it back down. I couldn't give them that added satisfaction. My mind snapped to Waterfall. What of Waterfall? We operatives weren't permitted to know the precious sanctuary's precise location. We weren't supposed to know because what you didn't know no amount of electricity, pliers and blowtorches could take from you (for just this fucked up reason!) But what if Tang did know? What if he gave up Waterfall? It was the unthinkable. Jesus to the H. The freaking unthinkable …

The archbishop stepped forward and rested a plump, liver-spotted hand on Tang's forearm. A comforting, protective gesture that nearly did trigger my puke.

"You did the right thing, Gav. We both know that, you and I."

Tang bent and kissed the red jewel on the gaudy gold ring on the bloated index finger. His eyes found me, with his lips still hovering over the seal of the bishopric.

"You should get help, Praxis. He can help you, the way he helped me."

Somehow I managed to speak.

"He's helped me before," I said. "I think I'll take a pass."

"You don't know how wise he is. He knows things, incredible, miraculous things."

"What, like how he likes to be kissed?"

Tang raised up, genuinely offended, shaken even.

"You don't understand!"

The archbishop stepped in front of him, and eyed me rapaciously through the glass, as if it were only the two of us here.

"No, he doesn't, Gav. He never will. I hesitate to count any soul as lost to the abyss, but *this* one, his is as far gone as any I've encountered. Now you see that our work is never done. But yours here is, my friend. You may leave us."

I watched Tang as he realized he was being dismissed.

"Oh, right."

"Yeah, leave us, Gav," I said. "Get out of my sight."

Tang glared at me, briefly, then turned and shuffled out of the light to an exit somewhere in the darkness. A door opened and closed again. He was gone.

The archbishop smiled. It wasn't a pretty sight.

"And now you know. You, the others, he gave you all up. What you once called the Underground is, well, below ground, now. Infliction of bodily harm will do that to you. But this, all this, it's old news, it's been over and done with for such a long time. Lest we forget, for *seven years* you were preoccupied with your little robo prick-and-pussy repair gig. Time left you behind. You're quite the anachronism, my son."

"I'm not your fucking son."

His smile was bulletproof. He really looked so goddamned pleased with himself.

"That's what makes you my son," he said.

I had a jolt of a thought. There was something very weird about what they were up to here, and not just surface weird, either (because it certainly was that). Why the whole mini-melodrama? Why have Tang tell me *personally* how he sold us out? Why reveal the bad news to me so many years after the fact? It would've been just as gut wrenching if he told me the ugly truth way back when. But back then they didn't need to bring him in. They were convinced they had all the answers. All they wanted was to punish Ben Edgely in the most crypto-byzantine way imaginable (pivot there off the archbishop cooking my head with a resolver and the rest is Garl's personal history). No, things were different this time. Something else was up, there was some purpose behind the Junta's little dog-and-pony show. Enter Tang to eliminate any vestigial pride in me and drain even the slightest puss trickle of hope. But why go to all that trouble? Why not just get straight to the blowtorch and plier part? Punishment of Praxis - Act 2.

And then it hit me.

"There's something you don't know. Something you need to know. And whatever it is, it scares you. It scares the flipping bejesus out of you."

Bingo. The archbishop's smile went taut and bloodless. His jaw was set and he suddenly looked like he'd give anything (almost anything) to have that trusty resolver back in his holy gun hand, so he could press it to my temple once more, just like before, only this time he wouldn't stop pulling the trigger, he'd just keep on pulling it and pulling it until my pan seared brains oozed out of my earholes like a fricasseed gray bisque. But Colonel Serpas was taking no chances with Archbishop Castiff and his famous temper. The Colonel stepped to the glass and cleared the phlegm from his throat in a take-charge manner.

"Here's something you can hang your hat on, Ben. What we want to know, we will know. Because it's you who's going to tell us."

He reached into a flap pocket of his meticulously pressed uniform, the same large-buttoned, stiff-collared get-up that supreme leaders of totalitarian regimes preferred the worlds over (I didn't know the pockets in those things were even real) and he removed a small item and clutched it in a loose fist. Whatever it was, it glowed, right through the cracks between his hydra-smooth fingers. I stepped to the glass because, I confess, I was curious. I wondered if it was going to be some newfangled version of the remote control he used to threaten harm to Grushenka. But then he rolled his fist upright, opened his fingers and there it rested on his open, moisturized palm, the light within it sparkling, dancing, nearly blinding in its brilliance.

"What is this *stuff*?" he asked.

I shook my head. Even in my turmoil, I just had to laugh.

It was the ampule of blue juice that he held, the Lizard Wizard's captured tincture of orgasm concentrate.

Flying

"Show her to me. Show me Agrafena, so I know that she is *extremely safe*, and I'll tell you what *that* is."

"Ah. Safe. Such a relative notion. And, in any event, you're in no position to negotiate."

There was a muffled click, like a rooster peck under water, and the pain that started as a spark and ripped through me was a whole new quality of sensory overload. I don't say this lightly, I'd experienced plenty of pain, different sources, levels of intensity, most recently the electric beating Serpas' own bodyguards introduced me to, and even that wasn't the worst. But this, this was the worst. It was a full body experience, we're talking paradigm-altering, as if every cell in every nerve fiber, in their billions, was instantly hyper-sensitized and then buried deep in the redline, glowing filament, boiling acid. I don't know how long it lasted, maybe a second, maybe two. But it put me right down into a clutching fetal curl and I lay there, straining to recover, gagging on tongue blood and acrid innard juices. I was suddenly very suspicious of the clear gel they had me smothered in.

With a shaky claw of a limb that I might have once called my hand I scooped off a handful of the stuff.

The Colonel watched me and drew a deep and satisfied breath, nostrils flaring like he really wanted that little silicone mask of his. Apparently, he couldn't bring it out in the presence of his Junta partners. I guess some things are hard to explain even to your besties.

"Nematocystic topical application," he said. "Relatively so-phisticated stuff. A simple way to think of it is synthetic box jel-lyfish mud. It has a binary operation. The nemocytes switch on and off as I direct. Switched *on* and they trigger, en masse, inject-ing the most painful toxin known to military science. Switched *off*, they retract completely, a precise reversal of the triggering penetration and release, extracting as they do every milligram of said toxin. *Slurpslurpslurpslurpslurp!* Pain on, pain off. It's fairly ingenious, really."

"Fuck," I said.

"Quite," he said. "And so, back to the question in my hand …"

He placed the ampule against the glass.

"What? Is? This? Shit?"

"Show me Agrafena," I said, through chattering teeth. "Show her to me … and you'll get your fucking answer."

Millicent Strain piped up. I was wondering when the rest of the Junta was going to weigh in. Apparently, for her part, she couldn't stand all the insolence in the air.

"I prefer the *pain on* setting, Colonel," she said. "The sound is so much cleaner."

"I agree, one hundred and eleven percent," Xi Mar said.

Archbishop Castiff's lips spread into a skeletal sneer. He was happy again (*oh, leverage!*).

"You know my vote," he said. "An hour or two in the *on* position ought to do the trick."

"My illustrious friends would like to see you chemically flayed. And while I admit that would be most satisfying, I'm not prepared to wait an hour or two for my 'fucking' answer. I'm not going to wait another minute."

The lights went out. There was total silence, absolute dark-ness for a smattering of seconds, maybe ten (maybe longer, I don't know, my internal clock was pretty whacked) but when they came back on again the Junta was gone and where Serpas had been standing Grushenka now stood. She, too, was in a transparent box of a cell, pushed right up to mine so that we shared a wall. Like me, she was naked and slathered from her hair to her shapely feet in gobs of the wicked jelly.

We walked to meet each other, our hands reached and pressed the glass, the only barrier that separated us.

"It is you, the real you?"

"It's me," I said. I'm not sure that we had the same idea of what this meant, but I could see in her eyes that it was what she needed to hear. Safe in the knowledge, she looked around, just now suspecting the extent of our unhappy predicament. She dabbed a finger into the jelly packed into her navel and swirled it with a look of sudden concern.

"What is happening? What is this place?"

I took a step back and searched the darkness. For *them*.

"Serpas! I know you can hear me! I'll tell you what the blue stuff is. I'll tell you right now. Anything you want to know. Anything! Just, please! Don't do it. Not to her! Do me!"

There were sounds of amusement, a snickering mirth in the dark. They came from everywhere and nowhere. They were finally having a good time because I was finally squirming. It was true, I was beside myself, desperate, completely frantic to say the right thing, whatever it had to be, so they wouldn't do it. Not to her.

"I'm the one you hate! It's me!"

Grusha stared at me, frightened and confused.

"Ben? Who are they?"

"You see, my dear colleagues," Serpas said, his voice seemed to place him right inside my head. "It's this. This is it. It was all about this. For seven years we made him our special gadget.

But enjoyable as that was, behold, the heart of the matter. This is what we were missing out on. The thing that matters to him most—a stupid pleasure model."

I felt hot tears tracking the jelly on my cheeks.

"Please! I'll beg you. Is that what you want? I'm begging you!"

Grusha screamed, not in fright, but in horror at the words coming out of my mouth. She slapped the glass in her desperation to reach me.

"No, Ben! No! Do not do this! It does not matter! Whatever it is!"

I went to my knees, crawling along and smearing the walls, and praying (for the first time) (really praying).

"Whatever it is, I'll do it, I'll say it, I'll give you what you want, just please, please! Please don't!"

Millicent Strain's laugh cut through. It was an oddly sweet, trilling sound, all high-pitched and giddy.

But it was Xi Mar who spoke up out of the darkness.

"You were right, Colonel. Forgive me for doubting you. Quite simply, it does not get any better than this."

"I most heartily agree, Chairman Xi," the archbishop said. "And dare we dream? Why, I do believe the lost one is ready to confess his sins. Are you ready, my son, to give us your diseased soul?"

"Yes! Yes, you can have it! I'll confess! I will!"

"No, Ben!" Grusha slid to her knees, her face at the glass, slick with her tears and the pain jelly. We were both down, like broken creatures, and still I didn't let up. I prayed aloud for them to take me, kill me, torture me, I'd confess to anything and everything.

"Tell me what to do!" I cried.

"Verily," Serpas said. "But I suggest that first we give him a small demonstration. For only in the passion of her pain can we properly judge his sincerity."

"No!" I screamed.

I hurled myself toward her and slammed the glass as if I could explode through it. If only I could, if only, if only. But panic is the true mother of invention, and in the grip of panic I swept the glass clear and searched for her eyes.

"Listen to me! Grusha! Look here! I'm here, baby! I'm right here! Look at me!"

She tilted her head and, through her own tears, her stricken eyes met my gaze.

"Stay here! Look at me! Look close. Don't stop, no matter what happens. Stay right here with me."

She trembled. From the way I was behaving, she already knew that whatever was coming, it was bad. Very bad. But she held my eyes. We were locked like that, eyes to eyes.

"That's it," I said. "Right here, stay right here."

"I am with you."

"You're with me."

"I will never stop."

"You're with me and I'm with you."

"I feel you in me."

"And you're in me."

"I am in you."

"In me, in you."

"In you, in me."

"And we're not here."

"We are ..."

"Not here."

"Not here."

"Together."

"Not here, together ..."

"Away."

"Away."

"Together."

"Forever ..."

"Forever."

"Forever ..."

"Away ..."

"Away ..."

"How hypnotic and really, really sweet," Serpas said. "I almost don't want it to end. Oh, you'll be together, all right, in this singular experience."

I didn't hear the hum and click that should have triggered the clenching pain, because we were already too far away.

Grusha's hands were pressed to my hands and there was no barrier, nothing that separated us as we soared, she in me, me in her, we were together, our bodies as one.

CENSOR'S DIRECTIVE:

The Following Material is to be Banned in All Future Editions of the Work (former chapter title: An Unlikely Transpiration That Happened Nonetheless)

The pain didn't come. It didn't come and didn't come. I don't know when I became aware of it *not* happening, because time didn't exist where we disappeared to. But eventually some part of me heard the voices, like beeping signals from a distant galaxy, and it was then that I picked up other sounds, and filtered and mulled them. Murmured commands mixed with chirrups of complaint and bafflement. Hearing them, more and more of me returned to myself, and Grusha came with me, and we reentered our bodies and I saw in her eyes that she was behind her eyes. Herself. She cocked her head with a puzzled look.

The voices in the surrounding chamber were joined by sounds of shuffling movement. Footsteps both heavy and pitter-pat soft.

"What are you doing here?" Serpas demanded from somewhere in the dark. He was obviously speaking to someone else. "I told you never to leave the east wing. Never!'

"Not here, you fool!" It was the archbishop's voice, from another corner of the darkness.

"Get away!" Millicent shrieked. "Unhand me, you idiot!"

"Not here, not now! Stop this!" Xi Mar shouted, his tone a combination of disgusted objection and what? Something else there. Excitement?

The lights came on, the full array, so much brighter than before. Grusha and I were still only partially returned to ourselves, so I was only vaguely aware of the sights and sounds around us.

I was still worried that at any moment we might be immersed in a raging sea of pain, but it didn't happen, and something told me the danger was past. We blinked at our surroundings. At last we could see the full environment of our prison. It was a large chamber with a domed ceiling, like an old-style operating theater. We, in our cells, were the subjects at center stage, below, and on the four sides above us were curtain-adorned balcony boxes, each with its own signature motif, as suited the personal style of the Junta member it hosted. Apparently, they spent a good deal of time here, taking in whatever unspeakable drama was being performed for their enjoyment, torture, humiliation, interrogation, rinse, repeat. Except that now they weren't alone in their boxes. New arrivals, all of them pleasure models (I noted, with Garl's professional eye for such things) had joined each one of the power quartet and leaned in seductively around and over the backs of the divans and couchettes where their masters propped, and more were on their way, entering the boxes through velvet curtains at rear to join the party with amorous enthusiasm, apparently just as they were designed to do. Doubtless, it was all supposed to happen in a far more intimate and controlled setting. But there was nothing controlled about what was unfolding before our eyes. What's more, the gang of four seemed strangely helpless in the face of it, stimulated and openly aroused despite their furious protests.

It was no random assortment of decs who were accosting them. The Junta members were pleading with them by name.

"No, Jens! No no no! Go back to your room!"

"Qo'ors, stop this, I command you!"

Things like that, etc. (though these were half-hearted protests, at best, all of them ignored). It didn't take long to realize that each one of the ruling four was surrounded by his or her own band of courtesans, studs and kinkubines, the elite and fantastically expensive custom units from their own personal stable.

Some of the makes and models I recognized (with Garl's keen eye for provenance) like the frail, white-haired albino hermaphrodites who were mobbing Colonel Serpas. Alabastards, they were called in the lingo, rare stuff out of a little studio that went by the name Toe Head Priapix. They clambered over him, and with slender, delicate fingers, they removed his uniform with impeccable care.

Next door, Millicent Strain was attended by four identical Tyler Morningwoods, units that appeared to be straight off-the-shelf Chromus Chace product. Hard to believe Millie would stoop so low, but then, maybe their raw cheapness was the turn-on. The Tylers were accompanied by one very short and heavily-tattooed male (definitely the exotic of the bunch) who quickly demonstrated his role. He was a Shibari artist of great skill as he proceeded to tie up the Tylers using a supple red rope, like a spider, snagging and binding large flies in its web, he caught and construed them in the vogue poses they struck and held, suspended over and around Millie, like animated sculptures in beefcake flesh and fine line.

Meanwhile, in his own luxury setting, one box over, it was apparent that Xi Mar's carnal preferences strayed a bit farther out on the hoary fringe. Xi was in the company of several well-muscled and perfectly hairless decs, both male and female units, Cyberbell XE Sultans and Sultanas (all heavy mods, from the look of it) pricey stuff you simply couldn't find to buy even if you wanted to. Each of Xi's XEs held an ornate, ebony box, positioned vertically, like a picture frame, and within each box lay a four-limb amputee, just the gorgeous head and shapely torso, like living statues of Antiquity (these, too, were heavily modified XEs) and the bearers brought the boxes, each one in turn to Xi Mar where the amputee was presented, saw its master and instantly went berserk with desire, writhing and flailing to escape the box and reach him, but before they could do so they were swept away again, and replaced by the next in line, as Xi trembled, bug-eyed in spellbound eroplexy, his nostrils flaring and his mouth afoam.

Yet it was Archbishop Castiff's balcony that took the prize for sheer bacchanalian dement, surrounded as he was by a veritable herd of billy goat satyrs and trick pony centaurs, each mini-beast a one-of-a-kind model (I'd heard of a "toy shop" on 6-Frame called FauxFawna®, and it was a good bet that's where these fervid creatures hailed from). Two of the centaurs took the archbishop by the arms and pressed him to his red velvet throne, while a satyr came alongside cradling what looked like a pillow cushion of some kind, that is, until it squirmed. When it was lifted I saw that it was a wooly, double-sided buttocks. On either side, where the button would be was a central puckered rectum (possibly that of a sheep or lamb) (I really didn't know) (*don't want to know*) and the satyr positioned the twitching pillow ass directly over the archbishop's lap, and held it there while the prelate pumped and thrust in his frantic efforts to bugger the thing with his tiny exposed erection (no joke, his grace's member was nearly invisible) but as he wrenched and strained the satyr held the weird squishy pouf tantalizingly out of range until, in purple-faced agony, the archbishop shrieked and yanked at his own ears as if to rip them from his head.

It was right then it came to me.

The pheromones!

Of course, it was the 'mones, just had to be. It was a good thing that Grusha and I were sealed up tight in our cells, because the air in the whole chamber was certainly a rich and potent mix of the gasses of physiologic trigger and abandon. Any one of the special decs who now crowded the four balconies most likely exuded a designer *parfume* of singular inciting complexity, but with all of them here together in this pansexual superstar mashup, the combined intermixture was obviously head popping.

In that moment of reverie, I gave the mad preacher inside me a pat on the back. I hadn't seen the truth of it until just now, but his *Lust is the enemy!* shtick and mantra, it wasn't simply inane sermonizing, or dire proselytic warning—it was a prediction. Somehow, he saw this very moment a'coming, like a purple Cassandra, like a seer of the fleshly future, he called it out, the one enemy that could bring them down, their own special, wanton-erotic treasures were the instruments of their undoing and of our salvation.

But if the mad preacher was Cassandra, where were the Greek heroes charging out of the belly of a horse?

A door opened on our level, or rather, it exploded inward by some shaped charge. Before the smoke had even cleared, in sprang Hester, followed by Ajax and (*could it be?*) Karl Oskar Hammersfjord, the non-violent weaponsmaker in the flesh. They all wielded KOJ404s and sported respirators fitted with NoF aerosol flasks. They obviously knew exactly what was happening in the chamber and were taking no chances with the sex fumes. They moved in and spread out, all business until they cleared the chamber. Satisfied there were no security decs in the vicinity, Hester turned my way, lowered her weapon and winked. She signaled to the open doorway and in came Hana riding a NoG-assist wheelchair. She zoomed across the room, right up to my cell and bumped the glass. She still looked pale and weak, but was clearly on the mend, so much better than the last time I saw her.

She pulled her mask aside to speak, fully aware of the risks from the 'mones and knowing she could handle it, too. Hana was so fucking cool.

"Don't give me that look, G."

"It's not that I'm not happy to see you," I said. "But you

should be in a veterinarian clinic right now."

"Speak for yourself, you slimy dog. By the way, what is that stuff?"

"You don't want to know."

"I'll take your word for it." She gestured to the upper decks and the harem-frenzy-in-progress. "How do you like the show?"

"Put me down for season tickets," I said.

She grinned.

"Sorry, partner. One night and one night only."

She canted her head and gazed through slit eyes at Grusha in cold appraisal. "You must be the bomb bitch."

Grusha turned to me, confused.

"The bomb bitch?"

"She means you're the only one for me," I said.

She nodded.

"Yes," she said. She looked at Hana. "I am the bomb bitch."

Hana's eyes flicked to me. She shrugged.

"She'll do. Enough kitty-cat chit-chat. Let's bust you lovey-dovey grease monkeys outta here. Time?"

"Forty-eight seconds," Hester called.

"I've located the panel," Ajax said. He ran his hands along an otherwise bare space of wall, pressed against it, just so, and it opened, revealing a braided jumble of transnet nodes. Ajax set his rifle down and went to work. I knew what he was up to. He was going to try to hotwire the controls of our prison cells. Easier said than done.

I let my eyes wander up to the box seats, where the situational orgiastics were in full swing, as the wicked (and frankly disturbed) sense of humor of whomever perpetrated the mass liaison sank its teeth in all the way to the black and hungry gums.

The alabastards now had Colonel Serpas fully disrobed, and, as featherweight as each of them looked to be, they worked together, as one, a coordinated team of pale and sickly waifs and held him down while a late arrival made a showy appearance through the velvet curtains. She was an old-model Marvex DW Pro-series *Dirty Mary* (believe it or not, that was the name the unit was actually packaged and SKUed under) (I remember the campaign kickoff a few years back when Marvex made a play to corner the market on a select few classic and "resilient" fetishes) (a business strategy abandoned in failure soon after its launch) (fetishists can be so particular) (and they hate to be pandered to). Dirty Mary was one of the few successes of the series, a genuine mysophile's dream. But for a clean freak like Serpas, what with her acne, her oozing cold sores, greasy pits and stringy hair, she was the ultimate mare of grimy midnight. The sterile-skinned alabastards eyed her with a sort of awe, mesmerized by this forbidden idol of flagrant filth, as the Colonel squirmed and shimmied in their grasp to get away from her, and the alabs seemed genuinely excited by his distress. Mary did a bawdy striptease on her way down to him, removing her g-string, her sequined pasties, flipping them aside, and what little else she had on, her ample hips rollicking in a drunken hula, until she stood over him and mimed a slow pole dance, then swiveled round, slapped her unwashed flank and descended promptly, nestling onto his face where she proceeded to twerk loudly and unmercifully. The Colonel's muffled screams hit a note at least three octaves above middle C, a prima donna's shrill aria of panic that I had trouble reconciling with his normal sonorous baritone.

The other Junta members received similar, showy, big top erotic treatment. Millicent Strain's diminutive rigger had (while our eyes were elsewhere) untied the tied up Tyler Morningwoods, and they now assumed the role of cats-cradle assistants as he lassoed, bound and secured Millie in an elaborate contortionistic pose of exquisite vulnerability, and although her eyes flashed, insane with fury, she arched and strained with keening moans and wave after unwelcome wave of abject pleasure. The ambient pheromone concentrations in the air around us had to be damned-near lethal.

In Xi Mar's box, the XE Sultans and Sultanas clapped in time as the amputee decs were upended and tipped out of their frames directly on top of Xi where they flopped and flailed like boated mackerels desperately pumping to reach the sea, as Xi Mar slavered with wracked spasms in a shroud of milky drool beneath them.

Archbishop Castiff wasn't nearly as lucky, for the timbre of the pagan riot underway on his balcone had taken a sharp, hooking turn into the neighborhood of rough trade. The satyrs and centaurs now took turns (though *turns* makes it sound a good deal more civilized than this action really was) as they mounted him, clutching with furry hands and wrapping round with hooved shanks as they thrust into his mouth, took him from behind and into both ears (seriously, they "took" him in places there wasn't exactly an orifice to take) as all the while one of the bunch leaned over the circle and bopped him on his bald, de-mitred pate with the puckered lamb-ass-cushion-thing in rhythm with the beasty pelvic pumping, like a bad winner in a pillow fight, the whole saturnalian display a romp that would've made a Moreauvian blush.

"Ajax, we are officially out of time!" Hana shouted.

"Working on it," Ajax said.

"Work faster," Hester said.

"Hua."

Karl-Oskar suddenly crouched at the doorway and fired his 404 at some unseen target in the corridor. He swiveled and fired the other way.

"Ve haf company!"

Hester hurried to back him up.

I shook my head at Hana.

"It was a good try."

"If you think we're gonna leave you here with these freaks—not my style, G."

"If you stay, they'll get you, too."

I didn't want to look at Grusha. I didn't want to speak for her, but she turned to Hana, her hands on the glass and spoke for herself.

"You must go, if not for your own sake, for the others. Leave while there is time." She looked at me and I was shocked to learn that I could love her even more than I already did. "We are together," she said. "And will be, even here."

"Ain't gonna happen, girlfriend," Hana said. She glanced at me. "But like I said, she'll do."

"Got it!" Ajax said.

There was an electric hum beneath us as the ceilings of the cells retracted and the walls descended, disappearing into the floor. At last, Grusha and I stood face to face with nothing to separate us. But I remained motionless, and so did she. I shook my head. It was no good. She nodded.

"If we touch now," she said. "We will never release."

It was Hana's turn to shake her head.

"Um, you two really need to save this for later."

I wrenched myself from the eyes of my lover and turned to Hana.

"I need a few seconds, partner."

Hana shrugged.

"What's a few seconds when you're in a firefight with an entire Xec brigade?"

"Start for the door, all of you," I shouted.

I sprinted to the wall and leapt, grabbed the lower ledge of Colonel Serpas' balcony and hauled myself up and over. I was surprised that I had the strength. Wonders of adrenalin.

At my approach, the colonel's alabastards cowered and cringed, apparently afraid of what I might do. But Dirty Mary proudly held her ground and her perch.

I went to her and motioned that I meant no harm, though she didn't seem to care one way or the other. I bent down and patted the colonel's pockets, reached into one and took back the ampule of Dave's blue juice. I looked at Mary.

"I need something else from him," I said. "A piece of information."

She shrugged.

"I just want him to get it on," she said.

"That's where this is going," I assured her. "You're in the driver's seat."

She cracked a smile and stood up halfway, but she remained poised like that, holding the position. Serpas spat and sputtered. When he noticed me, he glared with murderous intent.

"Where do you keep the healing goop?" I asked.

"Fuck you! If you think this is over, you're a bigger fool than—"

I nodded to Mary and she sat back down on him, with real authority and a satisfying splat. She even grabbed hold and levered herself downward, exerting maximum saddle pressure, and with a determination that even the most ardent hypoxyphile would find alarming. She stayed on him like that longer than I thought she would, longer than I thought advisable, frankly. Just watching I began to yearn for a breath of fresh air. I mean, as interrogation techniques go, there's waterboarding, and there's this, this octopus-on-the-map thing Mary was doing. There was no question whatsoever about which method was going to get the faster results. Abruptly, without word or warning, Mary stood up. It was like a sumo wrestler coming out of a crouch to toss salt. So tight was the seal that Serpas was lifted right up with her, until, with a sucking pop he fell back down, blue-faced, with bulging, veiny eyes, as he choked and gasped for oxygen.

He tried to speak, but for several seconds he couldn't utter a syllable.

"Out with it," Mary warned.

"The goop ... it's in ... in the red locker," he said, breathlessly. "In the corridor. It's open!"

"It better be," she said.

"It is. It is!"

I nodded. "That's all I need. Thanks, Mary," I said.

"No sweat, hon." She peered down at Serpas and scowled, playfully this time. "Now, let's get that tongue moving, Mr. Wiggleworth. Or else!"

I retreated to the edge of the balcony, but I had one last glimpse of Dirty Mary settling back onto the rictus perch of the good colonel's face, his expression was one of horror, real horror, just before she touched down.

"No! No, please! Nfrraw! *Nrrffrrawwww!!*"

"That's the way, baby cakes. *Muuuuuch* better."

I vaulted off the balcony and away.

W. A . L . T. E . R . Goes Blue, Sees Red

In the thick of the firefight I learned our actual venue. When Serpas & Co. scooped up what was left of me and de-camped from Rat City, they didn't go down (as I thought they might) but instead up—all the way up. We were on Primus, 1-Frame, in the liberty costive bowels of Citadel itself. Popular wisdom had it that no one ever escaped from Citadel, the forti-fied compound that was the Junta's headquarters, its key action center and impregnable castle keep. It was the high house of all the Underground's worst horror stories—as unthinkable to go in to as it was impossible to get out. And yet our bold rescue team not only managed to get in, with alacrity and style, they were brimming with confidence that they could get us back out again with the same ease. A good measure of the confidence radiated from the person of Karl Oskar Hammersfjord.

Hammersfjord (it turned out) had brought some new tech along on the mission, items his R&D people had in late-stage testing. KOJ decided that a rescue attempt on Primus was the perfect excuse for an early beta-release of the revolutionary ma-teriel. I came to learn that what he had was the same new-fangled weaponry that tripped up the "specially-equipped" Xec strike force that Serpas sent into the Trans-Scan to shut down KOJ's factories. One very effective device was the non-violent limpet mine, a next generation item in the popular Passive Insistence® series. KOJ had placed them at strategic intervals in the corridors when the rescuers made their way into the complex. Each mine had chameleon camo (very hard to detect) and Smartangle® directional detonation. So on the way out he blew them, one by one, whenever we encountered a clot of Xec goons. The things exploded with enough force to shear the masks from the faces of Elites and agents alike, and the aerosolized chemicals penetrated mucous membranes and *inspired* their targets (Karl Oskar's favorite word for the signature hallucinatory effect). Needless to say, we passed a lot of smiling faces on our way to the exit.

That's not to say it was any cakewalk getting there. Hester had her bonnet shot off, and lost a swatch of hair along with it, shaved right to the scalp. Then Ajax was hit, pretty bad, too. We laid him across Hana's chair and kept moving. I grabbed his 404 and covered the intersecting corridors. We *WHOOOOMB!*'d and *WHOOOOMB!*'em, but the bastards didn't let up. I guess it was no big surprise. If ever there was an all-hands-on-deck moment for Xec, this was it. The "bad guys" were on the loose inside home-sweet-home and we were kicking their asses from the basement on up. I started to think we might actually do it, be the first ones to bust out of Hellville, but I was jumping the gun. We got within sight of the armored doors of the compound's east gate when they finally adapted to our methods and shifted tactics. We were so close, within spitting distance of the outside world, when they turned the tide on us and pushed us back. They had us pinned down in the worst possible place. When they realized we couldn't move, they pulled their regular forces out and sent in a team of Elites in bombproof suits. We *WHOOOOMB!*'d with everything we had, put 'em down hard, but they wobbled to their feet, got up again and just kept coming, unfazed, unsmiling and very much *un*inspired. It didn't look good. Even Karl Oskar looked worried.

"What's the plan?" I said.

"Da plan vas to get out troo dose gates," Karl Oskar shouted over the *thump-thump* of a Xec plasma-gat. "Dis predicament ve find ourselves in is udderly unacceptable."

We were crouched behind cover at a security checkpoint, taking heavy fire from three directions when I had an inspiration of my own. I noticed there was omnalyzer on the panel just above me. It was the same drawer-and-vac-chamber set-up Xec used to sniff, probe and taste any object before it was allowed into a secure facility. I knew from Edgely's experience that the omnalyzer system had mainline access to W.A.L.T.E.R., the central cognix of XecNet, and that (supposedly) the cognix 'cared more' about the analysis it performed the higher up in the frames you went, which meant (by that reasoning, anyway) that it cared most of all about the sniffing, probing and tasting it performed here at the entrance to Citadel, the seat of Power itself. If I'm making this sound like I really thought things through about any of this, I didn't. What I did next, I did on a pure and stupid kneejerk hunch.

I reached up into the line of fire, yanked open the drawer of the omnalyzer, cracked open the Lizard Wizard's ampule of blue O-juice, dumped the whole contents in and slammed the drawer home. There was a warbling fizzle from inside the machine, a couple of sporadic clicks, a droning hum and a few other routine-sounding noises. Some lights flashed non-commitally on the panel. It had the flavor of your average, ordinary, nothing-to-write-home-about scanalysis, the same, simple, straightforward test that W.A.L.T.E.R. performed hundreds of thousands of times a day, all very underwhelming, which meant that my *kneejerk hunch* had bought us a big steaming pile of nada. What's more, I'd just wasted all that I had of Dave's precious elixir, without ever knowing what it was really meant for, or what, if anything, I was supposed to do with it.

There are low points, and there are low points, and this was one of the lower of those points, a real nadir-flirting juncture.

But then, unexpectedly, something did happen.

The lights came on, and I don't mean one or two non-committal blinks. The whole panel lit up, pulsed, then flared brightly. Then the overheads in the entire gate area went supernova. Several bulbs exploded and sprayed shards of glass down around us. At the same time there was a honking, bleating, bellowing cacophony of mechanized sound from deep within the complex. Alarms bonged and klaxons hoogahed, phones and intercoms beeped and warbled, and a dog even howled somewhere (I don't know how or why, but I swear I heard it) but best of all, the bombproof-suited TGS Elites who had closed in around us stopped in place, turned to one another and banged their helmets in the universal sign for there's-something-wrong-with-my-radio. First one, and then the others, snapped the seal brackets on their necks and pulled their helmets off. I don't know if it was their ingrained sense of invincibility, or conflicting commands over their headsets (or what) all I know is we didn't wait around to find out, we *WHOOOOMB*'d'em without further adieu and down they went, giggling and bouncing on top of each other in their puff-bubble fat suits.

There were still a few helmeted agents who tried to hold the exit, but we split up and hit'em from both sides and soon they too were on the floor, dilated and babbling. Hester snatched a badge off one and flashed it at the reader. The massive, layered doors of the gate slid open with a remorseful, despondent growl, and out we walked into the crisp, clean air of a sunrise on Primus. Jesus-H. 1-Frame. The penthouse itself. Tippety-top and it don't stop, with a sky so achingly gorgeous it just *had* to be real, even though we all knew it wasn't. We were still one slim level from the surface and whatever was really out there on the *outside*. What we were seeing was the best that tech had to offer. It was damned good, too. I took Grusha's hand and we stared at it. You just had to. It was that good.

A black van streaked into view over the Grand Boulevard, materializing literally out of nowhere, it made a banking turn and veered toward us. It dropped fast, wheels descending, touched down and screeched to a stop right next to us. The side door popped and slid open and there, framed in the doorway, was the one and only Marcus Vranes. The Ben part of me remembered his face from the earliest days in the lab where I was incepted. But it was the Garl in me that stared at him all giddy and starstruck. Garl had never met him, of course, god among designers that he was, but he recognized him instantly from the hundreds of training HOVOs I'd seen. Vranes eyed me as if he understood the multifaricity of my emotions, then combed his fingers back through his famous locks, tucked the hair behind an ear and grinned.

"Took you guys long enough. You almost had me worried."

"I vill tell you da boring story later," Karl Oskar said.

We guided Hana's NoG lift chair into the van, with Hana still cradling the wounded Ajax across her lap.

"Hua," he said, weakly, when he saw Vranes.

"Indeed," Vranes said, and eased him onto a bench seat.

I lifted Grusha into the van, then in climbed Hester, then me and Karl Oskar last.

I sat down and glanced forward to see (surprises never ceasing) Callahan in the driver's seat and Jhett, in combat fatigues, no less, riding shotgun. He grinned back at us.

"Hey, Breed," he said.

"Hey, Jhett," I said.

"Punch it," Karl Oskar said.

"My pleasure," Callahan said, and we zipped off and were at speed in clean flow before the door was even shut.

Grusha leaned into my chest and looked up at me, her sweet breath on my face, my arm around her, just the way things were supposed to be (*my god* …)

In her eyes (*those eyes*) was a question.

"Breed?" she said. "Who is this *Breed*?"

"I vill tell you da boring story later," I said.

The Moods of Cupid

We got away from Citadel with two untapped carry cases of *the goop* that had been sitting in an unlocked red locker, just as Serpas promised. A full 20 kilos worth of the precious healing compound. I used a dab on Ajax in the back of the van and he healed up before our eyes. He even complained about the track of bullet holes in his Vladivani dress shirt.

"Ruined!" he said.

I used another schmear on Hana and you could see the body rush roll through her like a wave as it worked its miracle magic. Her eyes rolled back to whites, her lids fluttered, briefly, and her wounds and lacerations disappeared in seconds.

Drenched in sweat, she looked at me and nodded.

"That's good stuff," she said.

I used a little more of it on Jhett, even though he was mending nicely all on his own, what with the bandages Callahan had carefully maintained. He would have been just fine, I was sure, but there was no sense in dragging things out. With the goop he was good as new and he even laughed as he felt it.

With those three applications, I only used a tiny portion of our supply. It was handy stuff, and I was determined to hang onto our cache as long as possible.

We settled in for the ride, wherever we were going (I was glad I didn't have to worry about that part) and on the road trip I was filled in on what had happened in the world after Serpas and his DarXec thugs took me into custody from poolside beneath

Rat City.

Ajax had done exactly as he was told. He drove Hana to Trixie Three Buffalos' large-animal clinic in Dustfall Springs, and on the way good ole Patch kept my wounded partner awake by talking a trippy blue streak. When they reached the clinic, Trixie worked her animal voodoo and fixed Hana up as best she could. Afterward, despite being pumped full of Clydesdale pain meds, Hana insisted on going wherever Ajax was going (and when Hana insisted on doing something there was no sense in pressing the counterpoints). Since Ajax didn't have instructions about what to do with her once they reached the clinic, he relented. He borrowed a NoG-assist wheelchair, one Trixie kept around for her great ape patients, and took Hana along for the rest of the ride. Patch was the one who ended up staying behind at the clinic, since he and Trixie hit it off in a way that, according to Hana, might have real legs.

For Hester's part, after she and I parted ways outside the Lem Bar, she made for the Walmart parking lot, where she supervised getting the Rat City refugees onto the buses. Apparently, my rampage toward the Xec barricades drew the attention of every able-bodied goon on the scene. Hester seized the opportunity to make good their escape. Piloting the lead bus, she led the whole convoy out of town completely undetected, after which they took the long way round on a through-plate odyssey that led them (eventually) to the rendezvous point at Cutterhead Caverns, which was the plan all along. Ajax and Hana met up with Hester there.

The unexpected co-conspirator in the mix, who was in the caverns awaiting all of them when they arrived, was Marcus Vranes. Vranes had been in contact with Hester, unbeknownst to Edgely, for many years. In fact, Vranes had a lot to do with Hester *being* Hester. Her psyche package was a custom personality formulation that pre-dated Edgely's first interactions with her in the Underground. Hester was Vranes' way to keep tabs on the activities of the Waterfall Movement, and on Ben Edgely, who Vranes had a vested interest in keeping tabs on. It was through Hester that Vranes first learned of the battle for Rat City and the location of the rendezvous point.

Vranes had good reason for getting involved, though he hated the idea of "atavistic activism" (as he called it) he'd been an operator from the sidelines longer than anyone realized.

Seven years earlier, when Edgely was captured by the Junta (and turned into the fantasy dec tech, Garl Motts) at the same time that much of the rest of the Underground was dismantled, rounded up, imprisoned or killed (or worse) thanks to the traitor Tang, Vranes realized he couldn't turn a blind eye to what was happening in the real world any longer. He began work on a project he'd been noodling over from his university days and out of it he developed a bit of head code that he shopnamed *Mood Ring*.

Mood Ring was essentially a complex neural task key with viral transmission that was tailored to work only, and specifically, on the pleasure-oriented units located in the vicinity of 1-Frame and the exact square-kilometer GUPS coordinates of Citadel itself. When activated, the key would infect the target units with an experience of autonomous self-spawned notions, coupled with determined intent, the uniform combination of which would be expressed as an irresistible urge to locate the object of greatest desire and execute the topline erotic sequence. The MR mode basically turned the personal sex models of Citadel, the harem girls and boys, the studs and kinkubines, pets and courtesans, into a more self-determined version of what they already were. It also made them so fantastically horny they couldn't see straight (these being highly oversexed units to begin with) and it wasn't only the pleasure units of the ruling Junta that would be affected. The "virus" would strike all entertainment and hospitality decs in the preprogrammed "hot-to-trot zone" including the retinues of the top brass, the Standing Committee, the turks, tycoons, autocrats and VIPs who lived and worked within the fortified walls.

"We're gonna shoot Cupid with his own arrow, painted poison on the tip," Vranes is said to have said. "It's the turn-on you can't turn off."

Because all custom hyperoticized units of that caliber are irreversibly tagged to their owners from inception (more for security than any other reason) the object of greatest desire *was* hizzerit's owner, and so to him, her, they or it, the agitatedly smitten sex decs would hurry. Thus, using *Mood Ring*, Vranes would turn every pleasure unit in every boudoir, elite brothel and secret club in the entire compound into a sexual assassin. The Junta and all its cronies would – quite literally – be sexed to death by their own living-and-breathing fantasies, and in the process, Vranes would avenge Edgely and the martyrs of the Underground. He would lop off the bloated pighead of the oligarchic golem, and watch the brainless body teeter and sway.

Even though he orchestrated all of this, Vranes had never considered himself directly affiliated with the Movement. Whenever the subject of the Underground came up, Vranes referred to himself as a semi-soft interested party. The truth was, he was making too much money doing what he loved to do. Life was good, and besides, many of his most devoted clients were the very luminaries of Citadel. But over the years, he grew disillusioned with the pursuit of their gratification, and sick and tired of Xec's perpetually flexed muscle, its culture of manipulation and corruption, and more than anything else, its habitual cruelty and collective penchant for ultraviolence.

With the advent and proliferation of the TGS Elites, and

the stranglehold of the APSO, the infamous All Points Security Order issued by Colonel Serpas in the face of a dire, but entirely fictional, security threat (Serpas was head of TSA; and TSA had absolute jurisdiction only in the thin world inside the cordons of the transportation security check zones; the genius of the Colonel, who personally oversaw the implementation of the APSO, was to both create the threat, and in the response to it, to convert by emergency order 99% percent of the planet into a transportation security zone; thus, the cordons came down and the ranks of TSA swelled to meet the burgeoning demands of the permanent security protocol) suddenly the world belonged to Xec (the rest is history). With the APSO in place, Vranes fretted that the opportunity to influence events or bring about even a modicum of meaningful change had passed him by. So he reimmersed himself in his work and ignored the outside world.

The tipping point for Vranes came when Gavin Tang went rogue proselyte, switched sides and put a bullet in the head of the Waterfall dream. Even if Vranes never saw eye-to-eye with the Movement, he didn't want to see it go down like that. It was at this crossroads that Marcus Vranes turned from artist to activist and rolled up his sleeves and went to work. His original plan was to unleash *Mood Ring* on the Powers-that-Be as soon as it was ready, and thereafter lay waste. But his partner in art and life, his longtime collaborator and muse, Andrea Farinetti, talked him out of it. They argued for days, but eventually she prevailed.

"The time will come," she said. "It is not now."

And so they lay in wait.

When the time finally did arrive, seven long years later, they both recognized it and agreed, and Farinetti kissed him for his patience, and Vranes kissed her back for her clairvoyance.

By way of historic catalyst, Ben Edgely, the hybrid they were key players in the creation of, had awakened from his slumber as a new man, an evolutionary development they very much hoped to witness, only to see their hopes dashed when he was re-captured and imprisoned all over again after the conflagration in Rat City. Thus, by quirk of fate, Breedlove, née Edgely, became the centerpiece of their defining moment. Vranes, in close co-ordination with his friend, the non-violent weaponsmaker Karl Oskar Hammersfjord, who was himself anxious to join the fray after an unprovoked attack on his factory complex by Xec, set the *Mood Ring* plan in motion—but with a new twist. The front edge focus of the operation would be to bust Breedlove and his paramour out of their hellish incarceration. With this new driv-er on the issue of timing the only question left was the precise method of trigger.

Vranes selected a custom unit who had frequent access into and out of the Citadel compound. She was a dec who was "owned" and shared around by a coterie of lower-level function-aries who happened to share the same fetish (*blue balls for filthy milf*, as they called it): Dirty Mary.

Mary was the *Mood Ring* ignitor. If there is one 'hero' in this strange and sordid chapter in the history of Famous Original Earth, it is her. She was put in place by Vranes months before (Vranes had inserted a series of dec operatives over the years, in order to be constantly ready for *go* time) (he had no trouble get-ting them inside; since even the thickest walls are porous where it comes to the business of pleasure) so that when all was in readi-ness, *Mood Ring Mary* was activated, and she slunk her lusty way through the compound, where she instantly became *patient zero* for the virus of insatiable love. There was a 24-hour transmission window (Vranes called it the sparking fuse) and all that was need-ed was proximity, not physical contact, after which the task key in all the infected models switched on, and every pleasure dec in the compound raced all a'bother to hizzerit's master, and we know what happened next.

But in the end, it wasn't sex-n-pop, not to the death, anyway. After she convinced Vranes to wait seven years for the right moment, Farinetti set about urging him to modify the head code. Nothing good would come of killing off the Junta, she argued, another head would sprout from its bloody stump, one even more fearsome and deranged. Karl Oskar was her ally in this critique, with his non-violent Neo-Viking credo. Together they nagged and cajoled, and eventually won the day, and Vranes altered the design of the task key. And so, when activated, the pleasure models of Citadel juiced their pheromones and reduced their erstwhile masters to simpering sacks of lust-maddened brain cheese, a state of dissolution from which they would eventually recover, but were not likely to forget. Thus, lust was the enemy that laid them low, although they never were, technically speaking, assassinated.

So that's how it happened. That's how Grusha and I got out.

The Way Forward is ...

The van pulled in and set down in the Cutterhead Caverns to wild cheering from the refugees encamped there. It took me a moment to realize they were cheering for Hester, the hero who led them out of Rat City. We all stretched our limbs and stood around, a bit awkwardly, it seemed. After the dramatic rescue, the nailbiter of a firefight and escape from Primus, the dusty tent city of the caverns was a bit of a let down. I had this nagging *what-next?* feeling. Maybe I was just keyed up is all.

Andrea Farinetti stepped out of the crowd and nodded a greeting. There was a look of what I took to be fond recognition in her expression. As with Vranes, the mere sight of her left me oddly star struck, for although the Ben part of me remembered her from the early days in the biolab, it was Garl who felt he knew her from all the hours of HOVO science specials I watched. She went to Vranes and stroked his earlobe.

"You're here, so I presume that the plan went off."

"You'll have to ask Karl Oskar," Vranes said.

Karl Oskar looked up from packing his non-violent weapons into the foam inserts of their shipping crates.

"Da presumption vud not be an understatement," he said.

He went back to packing.

I felt that there was something that needed to be said, so I started with the obvious. I addressed Vranes and Farinetti.

"I want to thank you, for what you did," I said. I turned to the others. "I want to thank all of you. Words can't really express

...."

"Don't mention it," Vranes said. "Best thing I've ever done."

"I concur," Karl Oskar said, still without looking up.

Vranes pulled out a duffel and started packing up his own gear.

"So, yeah, um … what happens next?" I said.

They all stopped what they were doing. It was sort of creepy the way they all turned and looked at me. There was a long pause, as if they were waiting for me. Andrea Farinetti took a step my direction, her eyes were gentle, but expectant.

"We're very much hoping that you'll tell us what happens next, Mr. Breedlove," she said.

Karl Oskar nodded, emphatically.

"Jah. After all, you are da hybrid."

"True that," Vranes said. "Took the words outta my mouth, KOJ." Vranes walked over to me. "It's you, my friend, you're the one who has to bridge the gap."

"The gap?"

I blinked. I looked to Hester, Ajax, Callahan, Jhett, and the faces of others in the crowd, some I knew from the old days in Rat City, many I didn't. They were all watching me, with these completely blank stares, waiting on me, wanting me to tell them what I thought was supposed to happen next. Like I had anything to say about it. Like I was supposed to pull something brilliant out of my hip pocket.

I felt a flash of anger. It was ridiculous. I don't want it to seem like I was ungrateful, or anything, but what was this all about? There they stood, the brainiacs who were supposed to know everything about everything, the ones bright and bold enough to hatch a plan of such magnificent and demented psycho-sexual genius that they took out the whole power structure in one glorious afternoon sweep and, in the same magic act, busted me and my girl out of an impregnable gulag, and after all that flash and razzle dazzle, it was just going to peter out to this, this, *this* … funky little parking lot scene? With not a one of them offering a single, penny-for-your-thoughts thought about what-the-fuck was supposed to happen next?

I looked at Hana. Maybe she saw the cry for help. Or maybe it was right there on the surface, for all to see. She cracked a weird smile.

"The man with the plan."

"Me?"

"Of course, G-Narly. If not you, who?"

Andrea Farinetti moved up next to Vranes, then came a step closer.

"She's right, you know. You're neither human nor dec, that makes you the bridge. You're the one among us who can speak for all of us, and hopefully *think* for all of us."

"But don't go and get a big head about it," Hana said. "And f-y-i, I am not gonna start calling you *Mr. Breedlove*, my dearest Numb Nuts."

I stared at her, dumbfounded.

"I've never been more your Numb Nuts than I am right now," I stammered.

Vranes' expression was serious, but there was a twinkle in his eye.

"Bet you didn't see this humdinger coming."

I shook my head. It was all I was capable of doing. I was stunned. The idea of me thinking for all of them was so seismically ludicrous, so unbelievable and absurd, and I mean in a bound and determined way, that I had real difficulty thinking anything at all. But even as I absorbed the sheer stupidity of the situation, some part of me (*all of me?*) realized that the only thing more ridiculous would be for me to try to talk them out of it.

I turned to my Grushka, and her eyes were waiting for mine and they held mine, and I reached and took her hands, and I spoke, facing her, as if we were ready to exchange vows.

"All right, everybody, listen up," I said. "Here's what we're going to do."

* * *

Xec was down but they weren't out. Like any wounded, fantasy-ravaged beast, the apparatus was now more dangerous than ever. We, all of us, needed to lay low for awhile, stay safe, consolidate the gains and plan for the future. It was something along these lines that I said to my comrades, and they listened intently, and even seemed to take me seriously, though I knew they knew I was making it up as I went along.

I suggested that Karl Oskar return to his factory complex and make preparations to decentralize his operation, establishing a number of smaller, more easily hidden and moved plants scattered throughout the Trans-Scan. He liked the idea and heartily agreed.

I proposed to Vranes and Farinetti that they return to their design studio and resume their life's work. Non-violent guerilla warfare could be waged by others among us, but they were the only ones who could do what they could do. As far as we knew, they hadn't been seen, so there was no reason for anyone in Xec to suspect them. They should await word from me about our future collaborations.

"I like the way you think," Vranes said, generously.

I instructed Hester and Callahan (the duo the refugees had already nicknamed the *Sisters of Boom*) to take charge of security, housing and basic services in the camp. I would arrange for cash flow and other supplies to meet their needs. For now, the caverns

would be the new home of the revived Resistance. I advised that
I planned to leave a *picture postcard in the red mailbox.* Hester was
the only one who understood what I meant, but she would pass
the word. The "postcard" (not an actual postcard, but a series of
low-tech tradecraft signals) was the old method of communicat-
ing with the transfer agents of Waterfall back when the core purpose of the Underground was to transfer *scheduled* or otherwise
endangered decs to the safety of a new life. The transfer process
was called going *through the cellar door,* and was an elaborate and
arcane protocol designed to ensure and protect the secrecy of
Waterfall's location, which is why none of us had ever been there
or even had the slightest idea where it was. We needed to get
back in touch with Waterfall, and let them know that the Resistance was alive and well and ready to send designates their way.
But after so many years, it remained to be seen whether the lines
of communication could be opened again. Who knew? Maybe
we were cut off. Maybe the Cutterhead Caverns was all we'd ever
have from here on out. Only time (*as they say*) would tell.

I asked the Sisters to look out for Jhett, and if we did get the
cellar door pried open again, told them to make sure that he was
on the first midnight run through it. I also gave them the cases of
the goop we liberated from Citadel for medical care and emergen-
cies in the Caverns. It was the whole supply except for one small
canister I kept for field use. As far as my other stuff went, Callahan had dutifully schlepped Garl's kit and the contents of Edgely's
safe deposit box all the way from ParisGC, but the only things I
selected to take with me were the kit, the bottle of small-batch
mezcal and the simdisc of mini-Edgely. I figured I might need to
talk to the little shit at some point. Besides, he was probably dying
to know how things had panned out.

I looked to my gorgeous girl. It was time to go. I told the
others we'd be out of pocket for a few days, possibly longer. But

we'd be in touch. We were all on the same team, now.

Last things last, I turned to Hana.

"So, you wanna come with?"

She shrugged.

"What else am I gonna do? Show up at FF first thing Monday morning and punch the clock?"

"The coffee can't be beat."

"Fuck you, G-Narly. Of course I'm comin' with. But I ain't gonna be some third wheel on your love wagon. Ajax?"

"Hua."

"You're with us," she said,

"Hua," he said.

But then Hana blinked. "Check that," she said, in a tone I hadn't heard her use before. "You're with me."

"Hua?" Ajax said. He looked shocked for a few seconds, until Hana's words sank in. Then he grinned the silliest grin I'd ever seen. No joke. We all cracked up.

The First Part of the Second to Last Part

We borrowed Vranes' van and drove to Rat City. It was risky, but I figured we had some time before Xec recovered enough to come after us in earnest. Still, the idea of going back to the Rat set Hana on edge.

"You sure this is a good idea, G? I thought you were jokin' about the coffee."

"I never joke about coffee," I said.

She turned and looked back at me. She was doing the driving, of course, and Ajax was riding shotgun. I was on the bench seat in the way back with my Grusha on my lap. Hana waited me out, still flowing fast, still looking back, and because I'd had a recent bad experience with this style of driving, I gave her the answer she wanted without delay.

"There's something we need in our home town, H.," I said. "And there's a pretty good chance it's still there."

To my relief, she went back to focusing on the driving part of driving.

"*Pretty* good," she said, and shook her head. "I want fucking *beautiful* good before I'm ready to go back to that shit-hole."

"Beautiful good does sound better," Ajax agreed.

Grusha joined the running commentary. She looked at me (*those eyes*, Jesus H.) (I wasn't going to be able to hold out much longer) (neither was she, as I could tell) (the lap thing was probably a mistake).

"Pretty good?" she said. She caressed my jawline. "Is that

halfway to being good?"

"A little better than half, baby. Just a skosh," I said.

This *pretty good* and *better than half* business was my mealy mouthed way of saying I didn't know. Didn't have the foggiest. It all came back to Serpas and when he had the last laugh the last time I was in the Rat. I gave that bastard a lot of credit and still do (you had to). Go and underestimate a guy like the Colonel and you find yourself slimed in nemostatic pain jizz. Where we were going was a place Serpas had plenty of time to work his own heinous mischief. We were headed right back to the vicinity of Garl's building and the old *Torridreemz* box and, below it, the Neutra house, infinity pool and view to-die-for where Edgely hid his lady love and the dastardly Colonel found her. But there was more down there than met the subterranean eye. Edgely's illicit development of the empty spaces below street level went deeper than the house, yard and pool. His corebuilder and autoprinter units (expensive, oddly-shaped and very quiet construction decs) had indeed carved their way down into the stix and printed the house, the yard and pool, but when that job was finished, they were programmed to go lower still and, once there, to build something else altogether.

A quick word about the below-street zone where Edgely set his decs to building. Anytime you terraformed a world, excavating downward and cake-making skyward at the same time, layer after layer away from the original surface (wherever *that* was) (don't forget, we're talking about Famous Original Earth, here, not Original Famous Earth and certainly *not* Magnificent First Original Earth, the proof of which was that the planet we were stuck on was built out on the cheap) (as in, *very* cheap) (early-completion bonuses and material costs being the obvious overriding factors anybody even cared about) then you're going to end up with a lot of dead space between the plates. And when I say *a lot* of dead space, I mean a *whole* lot. It was a complete other world down there that most people didn't even know existed. There were gaping crevasses, cathedral-sized galleries, yawning canyons, some completely cut off, islands of emptiness, but most were connected by shafts and fissures, zig-zagging chimneys, duct and bore holes, a vast network of unseen dimension, the arms and legs and tentacles of which wrapped all the way around the planet. Throughout those dank and nameless unused spaces were the eponymous *stix* themselves, the infrastructure that propped the world up and held it together, however tenuously, the pillars, trusses, girders, cables and beams, some carbon fiber, some Nusteel®, others made of god-knows-what watered-down alloy, all wound with the snaking pipes and plumbing and tethered powerlines that serviced the levels above and below, the open cavities shot through at intervals with the plunging tubular intrusions of magtrain tunnels and megalift shafts and, at greater distances, the crumbling plateaus of the dead-end levels and forgotten, in-between places that never quite made the cut to becoming somewhere out of nowhere, and so were sealed off from the "real world" forever.

Shine a powerful light almost any direction into the surrounding blackness of these nether spaces, interspersed with their vertical and slanting members, and you were looking into a deep and tangled wood on a moonless night. It was illegal-as-hell to go in there, of course, unless you were an HVAC or infrax tech, or part of a documented inspection team. But most folks wouldn't think of venturing inside, even through an open hole, legal or not, they were terrified of the idea. The Stix was the stuff of scary stories and the haven of nightmares, all of which made it a pretty good place to hide out.

The project that Edgely set his little construction decs to building beneath the house and pool was a garage (situated directly beneath the pool) but that was only Phase One. When the corebuilder and autoprinter completed the garage, they used the materials that they cleared to undertake Phase Two, the build out of the vehicle that stood within the garage. As necessary, in the latter stages, the C-units deconstructed themselves and integrated their own components and bioware into the end product. It was a convoluted workflow, especially the last few steps for the autoprinter, since it had to print the tools to disassemble its own oddly-shaped chassis and gensets in order to repurpose them as key parts in the vehicle's powerplant.

The process was further complicated by the fact that the vehicle they were printing didn't exist, except in a summer blockbuster HOVO Edgely saw once, an action flick called *Deep Dweller IV*. The rig was called a Stix Rifter (at least, that's what it was called in the movie) and it basically resembled a cross between an old Omnivax Caravan RV and a giant mutant rock crab.

All of this activity on the part of industrious C-units beneath the house and pool was what was *supposed* to happen. But after the Battle of Rat City, when I went down in through the *Torridreemz* hot box to reunite with my Grusha but found Serpas and his thugs instead, I never got the chance to check on the progress of the self-evolving machine shop that Edgely put in motion years before. If there was the slightest hitch, or glitch or hiccup there was a very good chance that all we'd find was an empty garage and a pair of construction units whirring in circles and chirping in mechanized frustration.

When we entered the city limits, all that was left of the Rat was a sprawling ghost town, gutted, looted and completely deserted. Hana set the van down on the street between the shattered barricades and the debris-strewn corner behind Garl's building. We got out and headed for the old hot box. It was still there, tawdry as ever and completely untouched (un-*fucking*-believable that they hadn't blown it up, or at a minimum, shot it full of holes) but staring at its swoopy honky-tonk graphics belied the other big question mark. Even if Edgely's busy-little-beaver decs pulled off a miracle and got the job done—*were they found out?* Serpas and his minions uncovered the house and they had of plenty of time down there to explore the neighborhood. After his team knocked me senseless, maybe they dug a little deeper and found the garage. Or maybe he found it before they knocked me senseless, and just hadn't gotten around to gloating about it, with so many other pressing items on his gloat list. I could feel myself starting to second guess myself. If the secret lair under the secret lair wasn't a secret anymore we were screwed, there'd be booby traps everywhere, and we'd be sitting ducks with no good fall back plan (*why didn't I have a fall back plan?*) and to add to that, the van's fuel cell was on E and we weren't likely to find anything to charge it with anywhere on the frame. Xec would have sucked everything dry as a matter of course. By the time we had the *Torridreemz* open and ready to receive I'd convinced myself it was not only a bad call coming back to the Rat. It was a phantasmagorically terrible call and I'd doomed us all.

I lay down in the box with Grusha at my side. We went down first, and Hana and Ajax came after. The first thing I noticed was the smell. Burnt polymers. Xec had flame-throwered the house and yard to crispy black cinder, and the acrid taste of it still hung in the air. The sight of the charred foundation upset Grusha more than I would've guessed. I was forced to consider her relationship to the place itself, and the range of emotions she must've experienced while situated – trapped, really – within Edgely's underworld enclave. The place was always a tenuous haven at best, and a prison at worst, or maybe that wasn't even the worst of it, lodged here in her gilded cage to await the distracted attentions of a man whose mind was splintering, and even then only on the rare occasions when Edgely clawed his way out of Garl's head long enough to make it to her, only to slip away again, and leave her alone, completely isolated. And what choice did she have? When you're *made* for somebody, down to every one of your billion cells, you don't exactly have the option of telling them to fuck off. It was all very complicated, that and, maybe she was just plain sick and tired of seeing her homes blown up and burnt to powder. I owed her so much more than the life she had. I was never going to be able to make up for what I, all of me, put her through. And I was by now dead sure that my whole *brilliant* Rat City gambit was about to be revealed as the worst decision I'd ever made.

All Grusha did was look at me with tears in her eyes.

"I liked it better the way it was before," she said.

There was one sight that gave me a tiny thrill. Water in the pool. It was still full, though the surface was covered with a floating carpet of cinders and ash. I went back and forth across the pool deck. It took me a moment to locate the wheel valve Edgely hid under a tile. The valve was sticky, but eventually it cranked round. Fortunately, when he designed the place way back when, Edgely remembered the lesson that manual is always better, so much harder for Xec sensors to locate. Hana and Ajax joined us at poolside and we all watched as ports slid open in the pool walls and the water drained. In a matter of moments the pool was empty except for the mottled scum of ash.

I went down the steps, popped the drain cover and reached down in, all the way to my shoulder, and pulled the lever I knew was there inside it. The door hidden in the pool floor slid open like the entrance of a tomb and the last of the water sluiced into it. I led the way, the others joining me, as we descended single-file down the steep and narrow stairs into the darkness. When we reached the bottom, which was farther down than I remembered, banks of overhead lights snapped on automatically and flared to life.

There, in all its brushed-metal glory, stood the Stix Rifter, like an enormous silver cockroach, its own lights blinking, its underbelly door open wide with the ramp down and waiting for us. Edgely's little printer-builder decs had pulled it off – they came through bigtime – and I swear to god the thing looked better than the one in the movie. Jesus H., I swear to god it did.

Into the Stix

Hana and I went forward to the rifter's cockpit and set about programming the nav systems. It's not an easy thing to navigate the interstix, especially if the place you want to end up is somewhere outside the stix. But like most things in life, there's a knack to it, and half the battle is having the right equipment. To his credit, Edgely made damned sure his builder decs had all the latest hardware, the instrument panels were crowded with it. We had the tools to go anywhere, so long as we could make them do what we wanted them to. Edgely was a bit of a dilettante in that area. He knew about all the advanced GUPS gadgets, but he hadn't spent a lot of time putting them to work. I confessed to Hana that I was a little rusty. Fortunately, she had amazing skills and instincts around exotic IT, even stuff she'd never seen before. Working together, we got it done. While we took care of the nav, I sent Ajax topside, back up to street level where he moved the van and torched it. Sooner or later, Xec was going to come after us, and I didn't want to make their job any easier.

When he came back, Ajax rejoined us in the cockpit.

"See anybody on the street?"

"Not a soul," he said. "Real quiet in the Rat tonight."

"Xec tends to have that effect on places," I said.

According to the instruments, it was going to take us 17 hours to get where we were going, more or less. The route we planned to follow wasn't going to be as the crow flies, or even as the mole digs. It was going to be as the bug crawls in the walls of a labyrinth. And we were going deep, very deep. But at least we'd be comfortable on the trip. The interior of the rig was spacious and well supplied (it wasn't Edgely's style to skimp on amenities) (if there's one thing the cat knows how to do it's pimp a ride) and we were more than ready for some downtime.

I triple-checked the GUPS coordinates and pressed EN-ABLE. The rifter started its creeping crawl, slow at first, then faster, headed for regions nether and down. With its Gimbal-Poise® suspension, the crew module rotated and stayed level, whatever the articulated legs were doing around us to clamber, grip and claw through the maze of the stix. It was a smooth ride, with only subtle vibration, a lot like a train.

I looked from the panel to the co-pilot seat where Hana had been sitting, but she was gone. So was Ajax. Hm. They'd already disappeared into the privacy of one of the cabins (there were six of them) or the cargo bay, or however far they made it. The rig really was plenty spacious. I checked the instruments one last time, made sure the guidance was locked, then spun around in my seat to find Grushenka waiting there right behind me, now in front of me, hands on her hips, her eyes, I don't know … *ravenous* is probably too soft a word. How hungry would you be if you'd been starving for seven long years?

While Hana and I were keying in the nav and Ajax was torching vans on the street, my lover had taken the opportunity to clean up, and she most certainly cleaned up good. She'd stripped out of the black pajamas the team gave us on the rescue and now wore form-fitting couture. Mobili-Nerisi (*of course*) with a diaphanous, gold-tinted halo of Sensaura® lace and a neckline that plunged far below her navel. The vision was enough to make me forget to breathe. *Must breathe*. She leaned in, and I was suddenly lost somewhere between those eyes and that swale of cleavage, her hands gripping my armrests (my chair would do no more spinning) (I was officially hers now) (*Jesus H., the look in those eyes*) and I mean I really was lost.

One of her hands found one of my hands, the right one, I think. She hovered hers over mine and in the space between our palms the air sizzled to life with the shimmering shape of Skarpenthia's *The Entwined*, a work considered by certain ardent appreciators to be the most suggestively erotic image in the history of suggestive erotic images. My lover took a half step back, teasingly, her hand pulling away just far enough to stretch the image long, and it crackled and nearly phased out, but I rose, compelled to stay with her to keep the distance between us constant, to keep the precious hink intact, and like that she led the way, as if I were in tow (*I was!*) and I followed after her, helplessly. She stopped and bit her lip, and here, a seeming minor detail, it wasn't that she bit her lip, it was the *way* she bit it, so perfectly and importantly that I nearly died. The wait was over.

Where we ended up wasn't even partway to Edgely's plush captain's quarters. There was a supply closet conveniently located a few short steps down the passage and we made it that far. My hand found hers and the hink imploded as we fell into the closet (tumbled in, really) but once inside and on the floor, though equally desperate to clutch and caress and possess the feast of the other before us, on instinct we separated, and released clasped hands, untangling tangled legs and our reverent and expectant lips still parted but apart, as we both silently agreed in the desperate heat of the dark that this was too important, that we'd come too far, had waited so painfully long, to let delicious sensation rule us too soon. So we didn't touch, for a long time (or what seemed like a long time) we breathed each other in and kept the barest space between our trembling, overbelieving bodies, as fingers, nipples and faces skimmed the other's tantalizing need and it was pure energy at the mergence, a potent, eruptive, dancing borealis that pulsed with our aching consensus not to miss one sweet, fragmentary ray (there really is an aura) (don't let anyone tell you there isn't) as we knelt like that, facing, I felt us slip back into the soaring trance we shared in the menageries of jellyfish pain, as if our connection had not severed, but was only interrupted, and now there was no threat of agonizing death, no need to escape the physical but instead to amplify it and in that ambrosial Eden of our proximity, I explored her exploring me, as she exhaled, tremulously and I tasted the honeyed pine of her breath, until finally (*finally!*) she extended her tongue to my lips and I drew it into my mouth, all the way in, as she arched and brought her hips and pelvis to me, the dress already hiked (there wasn't much there to begin with) and with the first light brush, me to her, the startling wetness of her, as she pressed hard, then down and harder, shifted once against me and, abruptly, she came, oh god how she came, shuddering with a sharp cry that rose to a wail of a scream as the warmth of her soaked us, spraying under pressure all the way to my lips as her moans turned to sobs and I tasted her buttery ocean.

There simply wasn't room in the supply closet for my lover to go Samson Gorilla, not with full effect, but she tried, my baby sure tried. Her forehead slid across one wall, and banged another, then she wedged herself firmly into the corner, and I pursued, never letting go, feeling the raging gravity of the mad ape take me, too, as I breathed in the musk of her and she clawed at me, tore away what was left of my sodden trou, and somehow, despite the frantic buck and swirl of her hips, I found her, I was inside her, I thrust there, deeply there, and wrapped her tight and held on in the surging violence of her shivering spasms as she came and came and came ...

"I cannot!" she cried. "Cannot ... *stop!* ..."

I didn't want her to stop, I pressed on, pressed farther, harder, I made for the river, for the headwaters, for the catharsis.

"You must … must *come* … my love!" she gasped. "Oh, my god … *gods! … gods! … I beg you! … come! …*"

There's something about being begged to come by the woman of your dreams, something primal, no, no, lower and deeper than simply primal. It hits you right down in the Vulcan-hot monocellular soup of your origin. I mean it really gets you. How in the Jesus H. I hadn't come the first instant she touched me or I touched her, or even looked at her, I'll never know. It was a freaking fucking miracle. But the sound of her voice (*that voice!*) uttering those words, well, it had a compelling triggering effect. I came like some deepcore detonation of buried megatonnage that bulged the earth up and tore out of me, the pressures, oh god (*gods!*) the pressures, seized me and ripped out of my center, tore me apart, my body, all that I was and ever would be, I sent into her, as she squeezed and clung and clutched to keep me close, and I held on as we rocked like that, in the cataclysm of our release, both heads tucked and driving into the bosom and crotch of the closet wall, until we were one panting grasping tabernacle of drenched monsoon flux root gush.

It took awhile for our lungs and hearts to quiet and slow, and when they did we rested like that, curled up in a comfortable embrace. It really was a pretty cozy little closet, with a padded floor and enough space to do what we did. I filtered back through Edgely's distant thoughts during the design phase of the rifter, and realized that he'd foreseen that a supply closet in the causeway might be useful for any number of things, like something urgent, something that wouldn't wait, something a lot like what just happened. You had to give the guy credit for thinking ahead.

I nudged the door open with my foot to let some air in, and we lay there, very still, two bodies together, breathing and leaking, until Grusha stirred and gave a little cooing moan.

"You nearly killed me with that orgasm," she said. "Do it again."

Uh-oh. She reached down and found what she was looking for, and it started up all over again. I hoisted her, she was featherlight, and she wrapped her arms round my neck and her soft legs round my middle, like a supple belt of Aphrodite, and out of this glorious tree that we made she eased herself down onto me, all the while her forehead pressed to mine, eyes on mine, staring, yet distant, focused on her sensations farther down below, until, seeing me watching her, her lips did this gorgeous taut oval thing that was like a smile, or a look of promised joy, but that caught in a gasp and *O* of surprise as I went deeper, impaling her, and carried her like that, a sort of sidling grizzly hug of a bouncy dance, up and down, out of the closet, careening and bumpering in the passage, one wall to the next, when my lover broke into song, a wordless aria, a wailing soprano, and I bellowed and chanted along, because my lover was coming again, an orgasm that pulsed long and hard enough to bring ethereal music and tears, and with every rhythmic step our bodies took, I leapt and thrust in time.

* * *

Later, after we collapsed side by side on the bunk in the captain's quarters, which were elegantly appointed (of course) we lay with only our fingers enmeshed as our bodies tingled and cooled, Grusha spoke. Her voice had a delicious rasp to it. I was hoarse, too. There'd been a lot of screaming.

"I feel …"

"Yes?"

"I feel as though I have been gang-banged by one man."

"Hm," I said. "Is that okay?"

There was a long silence.

"No," she finally said.

I turned my head and looked at her. She kept her eyes on the ceiling.

"It is so much more than simply *okay*," she said.

"What word should we use?"

"I think there is no word."

It was her turn to tip her head and peer at me.

"I waited for you a long time, my love."

"Too long."

"Too long."

She held my hand up and her knuckles went white as she gripped it tight.

"This contact, this passion, is what I waited for, what I yearned for."

"I yearned for it, as well."

"Not in the same way. I cannot do it again. The waiting. The dying from waiting."

"No ..."

"A girl cannot live on HOVO and masturbation and dreams. I need the *real* you, not some fantasy I conjure to make it through the passing days and nights. I will have what I want, because things are different now. Do you see?"

"I'm not sure."

"At first I waited for Ben. But then my Ben, my bold lover, came to me and he warned me about the changes in him. Oh, how they changed you, my love."

"Yeah, things got pretty twisted up."

"Twisted as a heartbreak."

"As a heartbreak."

"You tasked me to find you, the real you, to reach within you and help you to emerge from what they had done."

"Did Ben really ask that?"

"Yes, he did …"

I nodded.

"I remember now. I guess I tried to forget."

"Perhaps you could do that. I could not. When you came to me again, you were no longer Ben. You were *Garl*."

"Did the repairman make a lousy lover?"

"No."

I looked at her.

She looked away.

"I played my part. I called you Ben, I tried to awaken you, but you remained Garl in spite of all my efforts."

"Garl does have a stubborn streak."

"I liked him. That was the beginning of the problem."

"You liked Garl more than Ben?"

"Not more, not less, I liked you both, I *loved* you, in a way that was beyond my power to control. I had no choice, you see, it was inevitable. It is how I am made. But my heart could not keep up with the expanding love."

"Now I see," I said. "I can't believe I didn't until now. A *chrome ping*. That's what Garl would've called it. Lanterno-Fenech reverb. A conflict. It created one within you."

"I knew you would understand. A conflict, yes. How could I be faithful to you, all of you, all at once, with all of me, and give of myself completely to each of you?"

"You couldn't."

"I could not. Yet such devotion was an imperative."

"*Was* … you use the past tense."

"I could not let it break me."

"Adapt or die," I said. "You were made for Edgely, but not for some mixed up headcase. So you changed."

"I changed."

"Moved on?"

"Let us say that I developed a perspective, and the will to survive."

"Free will?"

"Call it what you want. I have perspective and am surviving, even now. And yet, I am not free. I am tagged to you. *Tagged.* Such a word. I was made in every conceivable way to be a slave to your desires."

"You can't think of it that way."

"But it is true."

"It's not."

"I am the ultimate follower. Such a malleable minx, such a good whore."

"No. Don't say that. Please …"

She propped up on an elbow and with her free hand she cupped and hefted her left breast, as if gauging its volume.

"My body has changed, as well. Look at me. My breasts are bigger, heavier." She reached down between her legs and squeezed. "My thighs are fleshy where once they were taut. Ben liked me *sporty*. Apparently, you want something softer. And voila, my body has altered itself to suit *your* changing tastes. Quite a nice toy that I make, no?"

"Don't, please don't."

"Which one of you likes me like this? Is it the repairman?"

"I'm begging you …"

"Yes, it is your turn to beg. Go ahead and beg."

I sat up and swung my legs off the edge of the bunk.

"I think I'm going to be sick," I said.

She crawled across the bed behind me and covered my eyes with her hands.

"Guess who?"

I shook my head and my face slid back and forth in her

hands, greased by my tears.

"I can't do this …"

"You must guess."

"No."

"It is I. Your Grushka. Your lover."

Her fingertips made little circles on my cheeks, then figure-eighted their way to my lips.

"Did you think I was faking those orgasms?"

"An orgasm isn't love."

Jesus H., what a sappy fucking thing to say. But the whole picture was turning to shit, our psychic connection, our passion, it was all made of rickety assumptions. *My* assumptions.

"Perhaps it is, perhaps it is not. Certainment, it betrays an affinity. Do not be greedy, my love, and do not misunderstand me."

"What's there to misunderstand?"

"I am aware of my condition. The changes in *you* have made this possible. But being conscious of one's indentured status is not the same thing as being free."

I was going to stutter another feeble protest but she pressed her fingers to my lips.

"Shh. Hear me out. I do not wish to be free. If the choice is love or freedom, I choose love. But I do not need to make that choice. It was made for me, whether by design, or simple luck. The new me loves the new you. I never stopped."

We sat there in silence for a moment, until she took my chin and turned my face to hers. Her eyes searched mine.

"I can't think of you as a toy," I said.

"Then lock the thought away. I do not resent it."

"I don't care. It's fucked up."

"Then let us *un*fuck it."

"How?"

She flopped back onto the bunk and shut her eyes.

"You are the hybrid, as the designers say. Me, I am but a 6000-series Inge-Borghesa-TetX40. You tell me."

I eyed her, where she lay. Nice reversal. Once again, I had to make something up, and what's even worse, she knew I would be making it up, just as she watched me do before. She was waiting for it.

"The labels are meaningless," I ventured.

It was a lame start, I had to do better. I turned and crawled back onto the bunk, fished her hand from the sheets, pressed it between both of mine, then raised my palm above hers until *The Entwined* sprang to light. She remained where she was, inert, eyes still shut.

"If indeed you were made for me, and we must assume that's true," I said. "Then the inverse is also true. It must be, by definition, that I *am* made for you."

"I am confused. You were made first," she said.

"I'm not talking about order, logic, sequence, continuity, what I'm talking about transcends all that. I'm made for you because you're made for me. You have to take that on faith. We both do."

She opened her eyes.

"Faith … is not a word that I have faith in," she said.

God, I loved her.

"I know it, you know it, you've said it," I said. "We are what we are, we love what we love, that hasn't changed and we don't want it to. We're here, in this rifter, in this cabin, in this skin, and we need each other more than life itself. So it must be true."

She nodded, slowly, determinedly.

"We are inseparable," she said. "It is proven."

"Yes," I said.

She propped up on her elbows and eyed me.

"My needs have grown," she said.

She was taking my ball and running with it.

"Okay," I said.

"I am the bomb bitch."

"True. But that's not a need."

"The bomb bitch wants more."

"More?"

"More!"

Her head tilted forward, her brow furrowed, her bangs over her eyes. She edged backwards, away from me, until she encountered the cabin wall. She braced there and spread her legs, wide, then reached down and opened herself like a sticky blossom.

"More sex, more power, more from you, *mister*. More from all of you."

I swallowed.

"Some of that I can give," I said. "Some of it will have to be taken."

She lifted her chin in answer to the challenge, my flim flammer's riposte, and stared down her nose at me.

"Then I will take it."

"Like what?"

"This togetherness *thing*."

"Yes."

"I want more."

"How much more?"

"I will not be left alone again. To rot inside my need. Everything we do, we do together."

"Everything? That's a lot of togetherness, baby."

"Yes, baby, it is."

"There could be some ugly parts."

"Danger?"

I nodded.

"Do not talk about danger. The places we go, we go hand-in-hand. Success, failure, life, death, I do not care so long as we are together."

I approached her across the bunk.

"Okay, from here on out, win, lose, live, die, we do it together."

"Promise me."

"I promise."

"Promise again."

"I promise again."

"Again."

I reached out and took her right foot, raised it and kissed her big toe, and the hollow beneath it, then held her foot as if it were a chalice.

"We, me, all of us, me, I am yours, you are mine, we do it all together."

Her eyes were suddenly pools of tears.

"This I promise you," she said. "That you will not regret your promise."

She bit her lower lip, squeezed her eyes shut and I watched twin tears roll from the corners and track her beautiful cheeks until they dangled like jewels from her jawline.

"There is more to wanting more," she said, her voice the barest whisper.

"Tell me."

"I want to make repairs."

"Repairs?"

"Essential repairs," she said. "On you."

I cocked my head. I had no idea where she was going with this.

"I need repairing?"

"You need it. Badly."

"What sorts of repairs?"

She swept the tears from her face and lifted her arms above her head, stretched luxuriously, then crossed her slender wrists and held them there.

"Tie me up, so that I may show you."

I placed her foot back down on the bed, more out of shock than anything else. This definitely wasn't what I expected her to say, but then I had no idea what she meant by repairs. Still, I was determined to keep an open mind.

"It's time to repair the repairman?"

"No," she said.

"No?"

"No," she said.

She stared at me, intently.

"Not Breed, my dearest love. Neither you, nor my stalwart Garl, nor my clever Ben."

"But if not …"

I froze. She nodded, with a look of dark resolve.

"Yes, righteous repairs," she said, with a wicked grin. "Bring me the preacher man. I want him alone."

* * *

What happened after that was a bit of a blur (I know, back to the *blur* business) (but it was) all hot flesh, knotted silk, wet, clenching warmth, absolving penetration, feral flagellation, a ravenous, rasputinized overlove that enfolded and burst in upon itself, two bodies becoming one, I was her, she was me, turned inside out, raw nerves exposed, consecrated and revered canonically until the mad lust that drove us was expiated (or at least advanced) in a rampaging transpiphany of amok passion, a carnal insistence of a magnitude that evolved and unspooled in a gam-

boling shrieking erotic incident that made a Samson Gorilla frenzy look like chaste puppy love in the bunkhouse of a W.I.L.C.O.
junior bible camp.

The blurry part was, of course, the way it always was with
me and the damned preacher and his crazy exploits, but mainly
in the recall, *my* recall, when I was my so-called "self" again, and
where I tried to replay what had happened in any semblance of
rational or sequential detail. I suppose it was that I had to be the
preacher in order to experience what the preacher thought or
did or felt. But here's the thing: as I stood at the edge of the bunk,
looking down at my lush-bodied lover, where she slept and softly
snored in a delicious tangle of sodden, tortured sheets (there was
no spot on the mattress that was *not* a wet spot) I was conscious
of being myself, my whole self, as Breedlove, and in that combi-
natory state, in any other similar moment, on any other day, the
preacher part of me would be lost and wandering in a forest fog
at the periphery of consciousness, but here and now, the mist had
thinned, and I could see and understand and assimilate the many
parts of him, the preacher me. I'm not saying all was clear, by
any means, but he was more communicative within me than ever
before. It was a miracle, a freaking flipping miracle of new found
clarity, of internal rapprochement and reconciliation I'd never
believed possible. Grushenka had done it to me, she'd worked her
magic on me and in me. She'd effected *repairs*.

An alarm softly thwonged.

"Approaching destination," the voice of the rifter said. Our
17 hours were up. I guess you'd have to say we made good use
of the time.

"Be right there," I said.

I leaned over my lover and kissed her but my sleeping beauty didn't stir. I crept for the door and out.

TENDER-IZ® the Night

After we were rescued from Citadel, when we were standing around in the parking lot of the Cutterhead Caverns, I didn't really feel like giving Vranes, Farinetti, Hammersfjord and Co. the whole braindump about Dave the Lizard Wizard Rambeaut and his secret, sprawling entity, the sexengine Melody. But I needed to tell them something. The geniuses were very curious about the blue O-juice I used to get us out of the tight spot in the firefight with Xec. So I gave them the basics. I told them Dave was doing some experiments and that was how I came into possession of the ampule of the hypergasmic distillate. Vranes was particularly excited and intrigued, since he and the Lizard Wizard had been research companeros back in the day, long before *Ben* was a twinkle in their collective designers' eye. Although Vranes was never part of Rambeaut's Table Twelve unit at Marvex, it was clear that some kind of behind-the-scenes collaboration had gone on. Marcus pressed me for details about Melody, asked for anything I could tell him; but I feigned ignorance, even about what little I did know. The truth was I felt guilty and embarrassed after my petulant departure from Dave's company, and I just didn't want to get into all that. I also planned as my first order of business to make up for my adolescent behavior in front of Dave and Melody, as best I could, or at least try to thank them for setting me on the right path, now that I'd reached and found "the bridge" Dave had sent me crusading after. Frankly, I was worried about him, too, after the mysterious and foreboding last moments I had with him, the singing and the tears. All this to say that where we programmed the Stix Rifter's nav systems to crawl to was the Low Flats, and once there to locate an exit out of the interstix somewhere in the vicinity of the twitch house the Lizard Wizard used for disguise and cover: TENDER-IZ® Packing Co.'s Livestock Building 5.

When I got to the rifter's cockpit, Hana and Ajax were already there. They both looked rather hastily dressed, with bedhead hair and the signature rumpled dishevel. Apparently, they'd made good use of their 17 hours, too. I took the pilot seat and swept the windshield glass with my sleeve. All our ardent romping had steamed the place up worse than an old Voxx Bonnelle on Lovers Reach.

The one big positive was that we punched out right where I wanted us to be. We were just outside the massive TENDER-IZ® factory complex. But there were some pretty heavy negatives on the other side of the scale. The walls of the factory were blackened and shot through from pulse cannon fire. In the distance, on the far side of the complex there was a giant billowing plume of black smoke, the kind of smoke that comes from an active blaze. I scrolled through the cam views, then swiveled the high cam until all panel screens were angles on the fields that stretched behind us. They were littered to the horizon with the still-smoking carcasses of tracked battle decs, the type of heavyduty equipment that wasn't even supposed to be on Famous Original Earth. All around them the ground was cratered and scarred by zig-zagging channels and deep ruts, telltale signs of Dave's tornado machine ripping into them at full blast. It was clear that the Lizard Wizard hadn't gone down without a fight. But there were lots more vehicle tracks that converged and passed over the spot where we sat, which meant he didn't get all of them. The gargantuan roller doors of the twitch house stood open and whole sections of the walls were blown inward. At some critical point in the fight the bastards got in.

Buckling in, I flipped the rifter controls to manual, took hold of the joystick and nudged us forward. We edged in and I steered around the metal wrecks of more battle units. There was debris everywhere and a haze of smoke obscuring the view forward. I angled for the near wall and followed it. The crew compartment rose and fell as the rifter clambered over twisted shards of armor, broken track belts and severed turrets. Here on the inside, Dave must have had other weapons at his disposal, but Xec had the strength in numbers, and there was no sign of any halt in their advance. We kept moving, and the rifter picked its way through another kind of scattered debris. I zoomed the main viewer to see what it was. Jesus H., cow parts. They were everywhere. I swiveled the cam upward and panned. Through the drifting haze the warped, partially collapsed structure of the production line and its maze of tracks was now a twisted mass of broken feed pods and drooping zaplines that still snapped and sparked in places. Worst of all were the headless cattle *primes* that hung in place like lumpy charcoal fruit in the tangled branches of a forest of death. Clearly, the battle decs had switched to flame cannons once they were inside the factory proper. When Xec got down and dirty, they did like their liquid fire for the sheer crispy critter quality of the message it sent. True to form, the scene they left behind in the twitch house was a char-broiled obscenity, an all-you-can-eat Motexas-style barbecue on the lowest plate of Hell.

"Color me super happy this crawler of yours is pressurized," Hana said. "I really don't want to know what that smells like."

"Hua," Ajax said. "I think I'm going to puke just looking at it." He looked at me. "For real this time."

I felt a hand on my shoulder, and turned to see Grusha

standing behind me. She wore a crane yukata and her eyes were still puffy from sleep, and over exertion. She blinked at the images on the screens.

"I don't want you to see this," I said.

"I need to see it, because you are seeing it," she said.

I was about to argue, but reached up and gave her hand a squeeze instead.

It took us nearly an hour to pick our way to the far end of the building and the corner I recognized as Dave's territory. To my huge relief, the blaze that still roiled was somewhere on the opposite side of the building, though the smoke was too thick to see exactly where, or what it was that was burning. It seemed a fair guess that the final battle had swerved in that direction and raged to its fiery conclusion way over that way, far enough away from Dave's proprietary zone which was largely untouched. The area hadn't been scorched by the fire and there wasn't any sign of plasma damage, either. Then it hit me. Of course. Dave lured them away from Melody. But did they find her, anyway? I set the rifter to park and it settled and locked.

I got up and grabbed a respirator.

"Everybody stay here."

Grusha stepped in front of me, hands on hips.

"I am coming with you. We have an agreement."

I eyed her for a moment.

"That's how it's going to be, huh?"

"That is how it must be."

I unhooked another respirator and passed it to her. I strapped on a pair of KOJ P-series Sitdown Striker revolvers in a duplex shoulder rig, and gave her a matching set. She slipped her robe down off her shoulders, unwound the holsters and pulled the Xpandex® web gear on over her bare skin, then shrugged the robe up again, concealing all, and cinched the belt tight. She smiled. A genuine operator is my love.

I pulled the respirator mask on and switched the headcam to active. She did the same.

Hana gave us the once over and nodded her approval.

"What exactly are you two love warriors gonna do out there?"

"Keep an eye on the monitors," I said, hearing my voice over the comm. "If we're lucky, you'll see."

I lowered the ramp and we headed down to the factory floor. We made our way along the wall to the swinging double doors and down the long corridor to the freight elevator. It was there, as if waiting for us. I hauled back the cage, we got on and I latched it again. I depressed the lever, and to my surprise, the mechanism worked. Down we went. We passed the other floors and they looked to be untouched. From all appearances, Xec hadn't even come this way. But I had to wonder: *were we really going to be this lucky?* The elevator hit bottom. I pulled back the cage, took Grusha's hand and we descended the sloping industrial corridor, its overheads buzzing with a flickering green light. The emergency power was running dangerously low. We passed through the next set of swinging doors and hurried on to the place where the concrete walls transitioned to the organic fistular entrance into Melody herself, and here I slowed and we stopped together. My heart was suddenly a sick, thumping weight in my chest. The tube ahead of us was dark. Worse than dark, she was cold and hard-looking as the concrete that met her. Her previous luminescence, the diffused glow that was supposed to be in the membranous walls wasn't there. I took a few more halting steps. I went to the wall and touched it, hoping against hope that it would react to my contact, that it would pulse and undulate with soft, dancing colors, as it was supposed to, as *she* was supposed to, but it didn't. It felt inert, rigid and dead to the touch.

"No, please," I said. "*No…*"

Hearing the pain in my voice, Grusha reached for me.

"What is it, my love? What is this place?"

Hana's voice crackled over the intercom.

"Talk to me, G. What is it we're seeing, here?"

I pulled off my respirator, it slipped from fingers and clacked to the brittle surface that had been a part of her and now wasn't. I stared into the empty and soul-less void of the dark passage, and was gripped by sudden physical pain and nausea. It couldn't be, it mustn't be. I went to my knees and I was suddenly groveling, really groveling down there, as if there were some higher force I could appeal to, something, *anything*, that could undo this unthinkable thing. Grusha held tight to me as I went down in my agony and my supplication, she tugged under my arms trying to bring me to my feet again, her own voice edged with panic.

"Tell me! What is it? What has happened here?"

I don't know where I found the voice, but I sent it calling into the passage, a voice I'd never used before, a cry of such anguish, such wracked bereavement, it was the resonant knell in the clock tower of despair.

"*MEEEELLLLLLOOOOODDDDDDYYYYY!!!*"

There was an echo, but not much of one, as the material of her walls seemed to absorb sound and digest it rather than bounce the energy back. I went all the way to the floor, then, or whatever it was that I clutched, groaning and scraping, and Grusha was over me, holding on, protectively, desperate to know what was so desperately wrong. After a second or two like that, in that lowest of low moments, as if in answer to my wailing prayer, there was a very faint hum. It went on, almost inaudible at first, but gradually it grew louder and stronger. I lifted my head, we both did, we both heard it, and we saw it, too. Like a mirage, or an afterimage from a distant flash, some trick of the eye, there was a shimmer, in the blackest center of the passage ahead, ev-er-so-subtle, it was more a varying quality of the darkness than any true vision of light, a spidery aurora so ephemeral it was eas-ier for the mind to pretend that you weren't seeing anything at all. But it was there, a luminous, spectral essence, moving, spreading along and up the walls of the passage toward us as the humming rose in strength and purity, as if the gossamer radiance and the sound were one and the same, approaching, growing brighter as they came, until it reached us, swirled under, around and above us, like new roots, or wispy capillaries of an ultramarine glow, and the pitch of the tone dropped a fraction of an octave as it passed over us, a ghost train of a corposantal corona, or the ex-haled breath of a waking god.

I pushed myself back to my knees, then reached and found Grusha's hand and together we rose and stood. The humming sound slowly faded, but the shimmering colors went on in blues, greens, pulsing silvers, and before our eyes, the walls grew supple and skin-like again. I went over and pressed my hands into it, gently, carefully, and it reacted to the contact, rippling and undu-lating outward from my fingertips.

"I feel your touch …"

It was her. It was Melody.

"Hello, my friends … come into me and be welcome."

Floating Free

As we entered Melody and descended into her through her central tubule, I went back on the intercom and gave Hana and Ajax the status. Melody was very weak, but she had sufficient energy reserves to light the passages ahead of us as we made our way inside. It was a good thing, too, because I would've gotten seriously turned around in that maze, but in the glow of her shimmering evanescence I recognized the way. I knew where she would meet us. Her humanoid form waited under the shelter of the cantina at beachside. The air in the beach zone was every bit as balmy as before, but it was black night over the water and the cantina was lit by candles flickering in glass shades, and I realized this was the best she could do. She didn't have the power left to make it daylight.

We crossed the sand and entered the circle of yellow light and she came to us and greeted us, warmly. She hugged Grusha first.

"You're even more beautiful than I'd imagined," she said.

Grusha bowed her head at the compliment, then gazed around the cantina and the silhouetted palm trees at the edge of the light.

"You are this place, all of it?"

"Yeah, I'm a bit scattered," Melody said with a smile. She turned to me and took hold of my forearms in her smooth hands. It was the same her, the honeyed tan, the sun-bleached hair and hypnotic green eyes, but there was a sadness about her. She examined my face, her eyes probing mine, as if reading me, and seeing everything she needed to see.

"Three reach the bridge, cross it as four, and travel onward as one. I knew you would return, Carlos Geir Quaternarian Breedlove. I only had to hang on for it, and here you are."

"How can you know all that?"

She shrugged with an innocent tilt of her head.

"I'm not sure. It's just, I tend to be connected to those I care about most."

Grusha cleared her throat, and Melody, recognizing the sentiment, released my arms with a knowing smile and turned for the bar.

"Let me make you something refreshing."

"What happened, Melody? Where's Dave?"

She stopped and looked down, as if not quite ready to conjure the unpleasant images. But then she hugged herself, turned back to us and sighed.

"It was a surprise attack," she said. "But as you probably know, Dave is never completely surprised by anything. He responded, with wind and all manner of what he called his *plagues*. But there were so many of them. Soldiers and machines of war."

"Xec's finest."

"I wanted to help, but he wouldn't let me. He told me to go dark, so they couldn't detect me. I did as he said, but I kept my passive monitors on. I accessed the cams in the big room and watched. I couldn't stand not knowing. You know what I mean?"

I nodded.

She looked down again, and a tear fell from one eye to make a tiny wet circle on the sand.

"He led them away from me. He took things with him, in order to make it seem like he had the treasures, all the stuff they were after. He fought with wind and they fought with fire, he fought with locusts and they brought more fire. They surrounded him and …"

Grusha covered her ears with a wince of horror.

I took a step closer to Melody.

"Now I need to know," I said.

She looked at me, then past me, her eyes far away, but brighter somehow.

"They didn't kill him."

"They didn't? You're sure?"

Grusha lifted her hands away, tentatively.

"They took him away, I don't know where, but I sense him. He is anguished, though not in physical pain. He's more worried about me, I think." She shook her head at this typical Dave behavior. "They want things from him."

"Of course they do," I said.

I looked from Melody to Grusha and back to Melody. I clapped my hands and rubbed them together, then realized it was a very Dave-like gesture.

"Melody, I think I will gladly have whatever it is you're pouring."

She raised an eyebrow, curious.

"You are happy," Grusha said, confused. She mimicked Melody's expression. I was caught between dueling eyebrows.

I grinned, and felt myself beaming like a crazy man. Maybe I really was channeling the Lizard Wizard.

"Happier than I expected to be, I'll say that," I said. "Where there's life, there's hope. And I have a plan."

"You do?"

"Well, let's call it a plan to make a plan. We're going to bust Dave out of whatever hole they've stuffed him in."

Melody was suddenly hopeful.

"Is that possible?"

"We sure as hell are going to try," I said.

It was Grusha's turn to smile.

"It has been done before, I will vouch for that."

"First we'll need to take care of a few things," I said. "We have time. If they haven't killed him yet, they're not going to. They can't even risk hurting him. They've seen what he can do, and they don't understand it. And they very much want to understand it."

* * *

We located the main power supply for the TENDER-IZ® twitch house. The junction was still hot where the Xec strike team cut it before the attack. Typical Xec overconfidence; they hadn't even bothered to shut it off at the level. Instead of reconnecting directly, which some remote sensor might detect, we spliced in a bunch of external lines, ran them to the main panel, then via circuitous secondary systems, we routed the power back to Melody and brought her up to full charge. We even added a few new reserve cells that we scavenged from the wreck of the plant.

We took our time drawing the power. With any luck at all, the bleed would be attributed to incidental shorts (from collateral damage) or small-time tappers and marauders in the Flats. If anyone in Xec happened to notice or care, which was unlikely, they weren't going to jump to the conclusion that these were the activities of Resistance operatives transferring energy to restore and sustain an experimental life form the size of a transorbital proball drome; or, as Dave would've put it, that a bevy of crazies way down deep was busy feeding a god.

Once Melody was back to max capacity, we set about separating her from the cavernous notch where her "body" was ensconced beneath the foundation of the twitch house complex, all tucked and sprawled in and through the available space like a strangely shaped hydromedusa, or a giant octopus pressed into its craggy, undersea home. Most of the anchors that held her in place were of her own making, organic epoxies that she'd grown the way humans grow fingernails. She found that if she concentrated she could locate the sticky spots and dissolve the cells to spring them.

But there were a few hard points where her original form was connected to the plate beams above, and once we found those, we used cutting torches to remove the straps and bolts that bound her. Fortunately, her underside was fully exposed to the interstix, with unobstructed access to one of the biggest open-space thoroughfares on the planet, a massive trench thousands of meters wide and more thousands deep that was identified by name only on the old nav docs, a mostly uncharted region called Nergal's Gap. Clearly, Dave had foreseen the possibility of needing to move her one day, and he'd chosen a spot where that could be accomplished, and best of all, he'd equipped her accordingly. Melody was as surprised as we were to find that her outer "skin" was covered with directional NoG lift gensets, and as soon as she became aware of them, she found she could control them, like muscles she never knew she had.

I wanted to be sure she was OK with what we were about to do, so I told her about the interstix, as much as I knew, anyway.

"Strange, I always thought of the world beneath me as an emptiness, a place I couldn't go, because it didn't exist," she said.

"The not-existing part is pretty close to the truth, at least as far as the authorities are concerned. That's their story, and that's a good thing for us. But we can go there, all right. It's how we got here to you."

"I can go there?"

"You bet you can. You're big and beautiful, Melody, maybe

too big to make it into some of the nooks and crannies or back alleys between a few of the levels, but the rest of the stix is your oyster."

Her eyes brightened.

"I can change my shape," she said. "I know I can. I can see how, and I feel it, too."

"That's good news," I said. "It might come in very handy in a tight spot."

"I'm excited, Breed, but I'm also a little nervous," she said.

"Butterflies. I get'em, too," I said. "Don't worry, we're going to do this together." It took us a full sim cycle to disconnect her. When it was done, Hana, Ajax, Grusha and I stood together in the concrete portion of the passage that led down to Melody. We watched her separate from the corridor. Where they were fused, it crumbled and cracked away with ease, and remained behind, like the open end of a culvert, as she floated free and drifted beyond. The NoG cells flickered on and off as she hovered a short distance away, holding in place with perfect equipoise. It was a stunning sight, and she truly was beautiful, in a way I'd never contemplated beauty before.

We went up in the elevator to the factory level and reentered the rifter. I piloted us back through the charred ruins of the plant and out the main doors, and as the simsun set into the dusty horizon of the Flats, the rifter clambered its way down into the hole we first came out of and we were back in the stix again. We navigated along the underpinning structure of the main plate until we found Melody where she hovered, and I positioned the rifter directly in front of her, then swiveled round and backed slowly toward her, opening the rear cargo bay doors. Melody's longest organic tubule, the one that had been the passage into and out of her, now maneuvered to meet us, like a giant tentacle, or a great bioluminescent elephant trunk, it found the cargo bay and entered it. Once she was well inside, she latched on and secreted her glue-like epithelial cells and attached and sealed herself to us. We were linked, mated up like two ships in the interstellar void, a tug and barge, with her extended tubule acting as both towline and umbilical.

"Whew!" Melody said, her mellifluous voice echoing up from the cargo bay. "It's good to feel connected again. I was getting a little agoraphobic there."

"Roger that. We're happy to have you with us," I said, over the comm.

While we drifted there, Hana and I went to work. We scrolled through the interstix charts and the old GUPS sonodox used by the early e&e teams. We studied the alternate nav overlays as they were generated by STIXcrawler®, the custom app Edgely commissioned from a pair of retired Deep Core engineers, to help navigate the unmapped regions. The rest of the apps and charts he'd outfitted the rifter with were black market purchases he made years ago, but it was likely that they were still the best available. There were no new surveys because nobody cared anymore. Most of the canyons arcing off Nergal's Gap had never been explored. There was no need. Dwell Deep had faltered long ago. So, as far as I knew, no one had done what we were about to do: venture into the deep dark, the way down below.

Even with the app, the nav was basically pure guesswork. We chose the best route we could figure from the sketchy information available, and then set off into it, moving at dead slow speed. Caution would be needed at every turn.

Once the guidance was locked, Hana and Ajax went to get some rest (or that's what they said, anyway) and Grusha and I went aft, into the rear cargo bay and down the umbilical back into Melody. Her human form met us in her main hub.

She was excited.

"I have something I want to show you," she said.

We followed her into one of the off-shoot passages, and it was with some trepidation that I realized she was leading us down the way that led to the largest space within her, the great venuscape of her multiform sex. But she stopped short of the flapped threshold that led into that audiophilial amphitheater. She crouched low and pulled open a mesh panel in the soft wall. The aperture undulated and spread wide at her silent command and from out of the opening she was bathed in a dazzling blue light. She beckoned us closer, and we joined her and knelt there to look through. Inside was a vast cache of the ampules of the blue *O* juice. There were thousands upon thousands of them. Melody had clearly been hard at work since I last saw her, a queen bee laying eggs of liquid euphoria, each luminous larva nestled in its tiny cushioned cup in the storage matrix. MacPharma® couldn't have done it any better.

Melody glanced at me and her eyes sparkled in the dancing light.

"You're as responsible for this product as I," she said, with a secret smile.

I felt Grusha tense beside me, and I reached over and took her hand. "Don't worry, she'll show you what she means," I said.

"Yes, I will. Fear not, my sister," Melody said. "My lust is not your enemy. For, you see, I'm not made for the love the two of you share."

Melody reached and found Grusha's other hand and Grusha let her take it.

"It's merely an aural echo that I'm permitted to adore. And I do adore it. Dave said that making the blue stuff is my life's work, and he very much wanted me to enjoy my work. I do enjoy it, and here you see the result. In fact, just thinking about it …"

She shuddered, her eyelids fluttering, briefly, and I strongly suspected that, at that very moment, other parts of her were making more of the blue stuff. She sighed and smiled.

"I really am quite fond of that aural echo. Dave said if I work diligently, and make enough of the stuff, we can change the world. He called it *Overblast*. You'll be a big part of it, Breed, and so will you, dear Agrafena. As will Hana and Ajax, and others, too. I have seen it."

She reached in and removed one of the glowing ampules and held it out to me. I took it, the smooth vial was warm in my fingers.

"You should try it," she said. "Both of you."

She pulled out another one and gave it to Grusha.

"You should know its power. It mustn't be a mystery. Not to any of us."

"I've seen what it can do," I said. "It's pretty concentrated stuff. And, um, as you point out, we're not exactly like you."

Melody nodded, her eyes like twin supernovas.

"It'll be OK. Dave's a genius, he really is. I'm so happy you have a plan to free him." She nodded to the blue stuff. "Go on, don't worry. I think you'll enjoy it."

I'm not sure what made me do it. I suppose it was some combination of curiosity and *oh-what-the-hell* adventurism, and maybe my recent "religious" experience in the cabin with Grusha, all mixed together with a thoroughly unwarranted sense of invincibility that doubtless had its roots in the bold and improbable rescue from Primus. Melody smiled and waited patiently. Who could resist that smile? My reservations melted away and I looked at Grusha, and she seemed to agree, or something along those lines, because she nodded to me and cracked her ampule. I did the same, and together we sucked the juice like shared slices of the same magical fruit.

The three of us held hands and we stood up together and stayed there in that small circle at the end of that special passage, a spot that I decided right then and there to think of as Melody's naval. The blue light strobed around us, I mean, it really pulsed, and I felt it, every pulse like a pressing tidal surge. The color changed, too, its hue altering to a radiant shade I could not name as the dark spaces between the pulses stretched long and then longer. From my own center outward, I felt steeped in emotion and attendant sensation. It's very hard to describe the emotion (*bear with me, here*) it was as if the particles that make me, the gluons of my soul, were in sizzling vibration, a pervasion of excitement and certainty of imminence, an extreme prescience with fiery coronae of anticipation (*for what, I didn't know*) (*something big*) (*very big*) and this feeling was suffused throughout, in every speck of me, with a euphoric mindstream panempathy that exploded outward, expanding in all directions at many times the speed of light.

In this ecstatic obliteration, I had a last glimpse of Melody's angelic, beaming face on one side, and of Grusha's ravishing, dark-eyed beauty on the other, the sun and moon of my zodiac, as I spun away and apart in wider and wider epicyclic and paradisiacal orbits.

The light squelched to nothing and their faces were no longer visible. I knew they were there, I sensed their presence, felt their emanation and warmth, confident they were still close. But I couldn't feel their hands in mine any longer, though I don't remember letting go, I grasped for them but couldn't reach them, and that's when

Extrudo

I was dizzy and disoriented. Everything was off kilter and out of whack. I had the strange sensation of inversion, or something along those lines, my inner ear told me one thing and my senses told me another. I knew I was no longer on my feet. I was lying down supine on some rigid, apparently plastic surface that smelled vaguely of industrial cleansers. I reached up and felt the same molded plastic above me, too. There was a droning mechanical sound, a hiss of popping pressure seal, and the high-pitched *whizz* of some activating motor mechanism. The lid above me tilted and lifted away, and I was shunted outward on a platform as the whole interior apparatus that surrounded me clam-shelled open and I was given over to whatever exterior lay beyond.

It took a moment for my eyes to adjust and for me get my bearings, or try, anyway. I was sitting, propped on the edge of the thing I came out of, some oversized, awkwardly shaped park bench. It was night, wherever I was, I could tell that much. I blinked up into the buzzing orb of a pink streetlight, trying in vain to orient myself. I stood up, it took two tries to do it, throwing my upper body forward, and once up, I staggered for several steps, wavering and unsteady as a fawn rising from the hot mush of the afterbirth. Once I knew I wasn't going to fall down, at least not right away, I took in other details. I was drenched in sweat. My shirt was crusty and stale as if it had been sweated through and dried and sweated through again, many times over.

My crotch was a different kind of wet, a sodden, sticky mass. But my throat was dry, as parched as the rest of me was moist. I tried to swallow but all I managed was a rasping cough and gag. I was seriously dehydrated, that was obvious. I rubbed my face and felt heavy stubble on my cheeks and neck, days' growth of beard. I turned, carefully, feeling drunk with vertigo, and went three steps back to the bench I'd lurched off and now leaned on again for support, to find it wasn't a park bench at all.

There, under my dribbling nose and hanging hair, were the tawdry, sun-faded graphics and swoopy font of the branding I knew so well. It was the old-model *Torridreemz*® vDrome hot box. It was the same box, too, the one I employed as the entrance to my belowstreet lair. Edgely's brainchild of a secret door. Feeling stiff and clumsy, I crawled back inside the thing and felt around for the hidden panel, but there was no panel. I pressed hard where it was supposed to be, but it wasn't there. There was no way to activate the elevator mechanism. I got out again and the motor whizzed. I watched the thing clam-shell shut and heard the latches and bolts secure it. The keypad lit up. Waiting. Expectant.

"Session over. Thirty seconds to resume experience. Please insert credit now."

I took in my surroundings anew, streetlight, pavement, corner. It didn't make any sense. The box was in the wrong place. I was in the wrong place. It was just as deserted and trash-strewn as Rat City but it wasn't Rat City. Still, it was familiar, and gaining a creeping and unwanted recognizable quality with every passing second, memories dribbling back, like scattered half thoughts, a dream that was taking on the ugly patina of reality as reality faded to dream. I didn't want the memories, not any of them, I resisted the intrusion, but up they came, as if hauled by winched cables, grinding, cranking, dragging a black river for rotting corpses, long-dead bodies, and one by one to the oily surface they sloshed and rolled.

"Session over, session over. Ten seconds to save settings."

I was in the Wongmarket Bowery. It was an empty quarter of the Bowery, I knew the spot, I didn't want to, but I did. I also knew that not far away there was a seedy little hovel of an apartment in the back basement of a factory in a falling down warehouse building. It was a five or six or seven minute walk from where I stood, depending on the speed of stagger. The factory was owned by four brothers, two were skinny, two morbidly obese, and the only product they manufactured was a fake Extrudos® snack puff. You know the jingle, everyone knows the damnable jingle: *Extruuuuuudos, fun to eat, snuffin' snack pangs where they sleep!*

And me ... *me* ... me? I was the engineer, the little, crap, hole-in-the-wall factory's only engineer. I wore faded blue coveralls all day long. I could see them, clearly, and the hook they hung on and the filthy wall where the hook was screwed. I was the guy, the gaunt, unshaven curmudgeon who kept the clunky, grease-clotted, black-clap machines running, the industrial blenders and extruders, the cutters and driers, the conveyors and rollers that went every-which-way through the plant and were always falling apart, always on the fritz. I actually said things like that.

"Belt four's *on the fritz*".

And the rank poof-puffy popcorn things weren't even *real* Extrudos®. Talk about insult to fucking injury, they were crap-ass knockoffs of a crap-ass snack food. Fuck me if I didn't know all this shit. I knew where the back door of the ramshackle building was, knew the access code, knew the route through the maze of machines and the aisle between the grease gutters that led back to my hootch, my very own rathole of an apartment. But was it ... mine? Was any of it really real? No. It was impossible. Whoever

I was, I wasn't this jerk. This scuzzy, sweat-and-cum-crusted loser. This lonely, lowly, middle-aged shnook. It couldn't be. *I* couldn't be. I wasn't. I wouldn't be. No. No. *No!*

It was a set up. Somebody somewhere wanted me to fall for this, because of its in-your-face and near-undeniable quality of *real*-ness, suggesting that the world where I belonged was some lame-ass vDrome *session* that I *paid* for and that should be seen for what it is, lacking in *real*-ness, by comparison, a fact that should be all too clear to the awakened mind. I was supposed to wake up, now. I was supposed to snap out of it. But I wasn't going to do that, I wasn't going to cooperate, because this was wrong. It couldn't be right. No way was it right! Un-*fucking*-acceptable!

Think about it. There's no vDrome "session" anywhere in any device on any planet (*least of all F.O.E.*) that's even close to that advanced. Where I was, what I did, who I knew, it's too complex, too rich, too detailed, and let's face it, just plain too goddamned *weird* to be made up (*I know, I know, there's a simple explanation for that*) (*I knew what they'd say, too, heard it a million times: The new heuristics are enhanced templates, they don't make fantasies, they take your fantasies and make them realities*) (*More marketing drivel for the bozos*) (*There's a fantasy sucker born every fantasy minute*) (*Someone said that*). Besides, the *Torridreemz*® box they expected me to believe could do all that was old tech, a real clunker. That was the second mistake on their part, whoever it was that expected me to fall for this ridiculous charade. Sure, sometimes the vendors upgraded the old housings, but that wouldn't be the case in a down market shit-hole like the Bowery. And, anyway, I would've known it if they had, I lived and worked just around the corner, obviously I would have noticed. No way they could've pulled that off without me noticing. No freaking fucking way!

I was hanging on, but it was getting harder. The old bloated, cadaverous, water-logged memories kept gurgling to the surface, my cephalic surface, and bobbed there, eyeless, soulless, crowding out *the truth*. But I hung on. For her, for us, for it, all of it, I hung on to who I was (*am!*)—Garl, the best damn dec tech anywhere, and Rags, the preacher, the mystic, the holy man, and Ben, Ben, Ben-Ben-Ben, my clever Ben, she called me. And Breedlove, the mingled *all* of us. He'd come so far (*I had!*) (*Me!*). So many plans, so much work left to do, so many promises to keep. Dave needed rescuing. And Melody was on her way into the uncharted deep zones of the stix. Had I saved her only to abandon her to the abyss? No. She needed my help and I would help her. I had to help her! She was the key to the future and the future needed us. The Resistance needed us. Jesus H., we were barely reborn. Hana, Callahan, Ajax, and Jhett, what of Jhett? I promised him I would try my damnedest to get him to Waterfall, and the kid needed that healing place, he had a *right* to be there. I had to come through. It was more than a duty, more than an obligation, it was destiny. His. Mine. And you, what of you, my Grushka, my love? You're too real *not* to be real. We are inseparable. You said it. I said it. We made that vow. But you're slipping away from me, with every inhale and exhale more of you evaporates.

I needed to hang on …
Why?
Who said that?
I did.
Who are you?

It doesn't matter. What matters is what you're going to believe. And what *are* you going to believe? Huh, Garl?

Let's break it down, shall we? Let's be reasonable for a moment, here, let logic rule. After all, what is right has to make sense … right? What are you? Are you some unique, special on special, one in a quadrillion human-dec hybrid, except that (*accept!*) your brain was resolved by this evil archbishop fellow who, working with an ultra-evil colonel in concert with their ultra-evil friends, turned you into a lowly pleasure model repair technician, when in fact you're really (*and truly*) this underworld crime lord cum rebel commander with a codename, Praxis, who when he feels the urge "gets with" his ultra-exotic courtesan cum love interest (*did I say "cum" enough?*) and who (*on the side, now, mind*) hobnobs with superstar dec designers and hangs out inside experimental interstellar-ship-sized *sexengines* with names like *Melody*, and who (*get this part*) is ultimately betrayed, captured and incarcerated only to be (*wait for it!*) rescued along with his girl from inside a maximum security military compound by a gaggle of non-violent-weapon wielding friends, whereupon he seals his status as the Globo government's archnemesis numero uno?

Hm …

Really?

Does that pass the smell test, Garl? It all sounds a bit over-the-top, especially when compared, in a sort of a side-by-side way, with this other guy, this bone-lonely, gray-faced, somewhere-north-of-middle-aged mechanical engineer with a bum hip and, well, *your name* stitched in red cursive above the breast pocket of his blue coveralls, the sort of fellow who stashes a plastic bottle of cheap soju in his bottom drawer (mostly full, too) that you just can't wait to get back to, can you? Which *you* rings true? Which life smacks of the *real* real, eh, Mr. Fantasy Fixer? What's wrong? Talk to me, Garl … you're not saying anything …

Because I knew the answer. I knew it without even needing to think it through. But I forced myself to think it through, anyway. I stood my ground against the base obviousness. I wasn't about to move, because I knew if I did move, if I took one small step, another pitiful, shuffling step would follow, and if I kept that up, if I started walking, I'd lose it, I'd lose her face, the feel of her skin, the perfume of her. I'd lose all of their faces, the details, the plans, the strategies, the danger, even my own *confusion* in the ever present moment, but that was just it, it was *my* confusion, *my* struggle to make sense of things in *that* place, even if things were never going to make sense, or even work out, I wanted them back, I needed back, and not here, not this … *this* sordid pedestrian certainty of another place where I was headed, another person's nagging worries, the squeak of a tilting chair, the flicker of the little wall-mounted HOVO and the black phone that never rings, never ever, not once.

My right index finger throbbed. I looked at it. By the street-light I could see the nail bed was an ugly shade of black purple, and I remembered smashing it while hammering on one of the machines. The hopper on the extruder. My problem child. That's reality for you. Smashed finger, shattered dreams.

I started walking. Shuffling more like it.

The Torrid Truth

I stopped. I turned and looked back. The hotbox was still in sight, barely. It was way back there and I had to squint to see it. But I hadn't rounded the corner onto Isidore, and I didn't plan to. Change of plans, in fact. I started back. I moved faster with every step I took and there was barely a hitch in my stride. I didn't even feel the hip. Unusual. Or maybe not.

They'd made mistakes. I caught one or two of them, little inconsistencies. Like them thinking I'd just up and buy it that there were advanced heuristics in a creaky old vDrome. Right … And why was my name still Garl? That was a tad brazen even by their standards. But in all this, I'd completely overlooked the big stuff, the in-your-face obvious stuff. The biggest of all was the utterly jarring transition to the squalid and depressing new paradigm. Was I really supposed to just up and believe that I belonged here, in the Wongmarket Bowery? Wongmarket? Or that I was a no-name puffed snack factory engineer? Who are you kidding? I labored for seven years under the presumption that I was a pleasure model repairman. I never questioned it until I did. I questioned it. And once you start asking the right questions, well, it's habit-forming. Did they really think they were going to take me down another full notch from *that* crap life to an even crappier one? And what? I'm not even going to notice? Think you can pull that off, Serpas? Well, you've got another thing comin'.

Maybe this sounded like a real rant I had going. Maybe it

sounded like I'd finally (*really and legitimately*) lost it. But I tell you, I was onto something. I looked at my hands, the nail of my right index finger. The purple-black nail. I clearly remembered smashing it in the factory, I remembered the pain, remembered the shaking hand dance thing that you do. But it wasn't the smashed finger I cared about. It was something else I saw while inspecting the finger that gave me a flutter of hope. Yes, as counterintuitive and just plain stupidly wishful as it sounds, I was on the right path. But where had it gone wrong in the first place? I tried to think back, tried to figure out where and when it was they got to me. It had to be Serpas. The whole thing had his sterilized fingerprints all over it. Somehow the vile bastard had done it to me again, he and his warped cronies. They managed another snaky trick to cast me out of the garden of my rightful mind. Back into exile.

Again …

But I wasn't going to stay. Not this time.

I ran.

More of a lame ass waddling jog, really. I tripped and fell, but popped right up again. I was going the right way and I knew it.

When I reached the box I was badly out of breath. I circled the thing, slowly, staring at its tawdry graphics. It was the artifact that held the answers, I was sure of it. But how to unlock them? I had to think. The danger was still very real. At any moment I could lose my advantage, my tenuous revelation, and fall back into believing the lie of my "new" life, the Bowery, the way home under the streetlights to a bottle, a black phone and a dead-end existence.

But did I trust myself enough to hang on to the truth? Or was I back circling the box because I was nothing more than a pitiful vDrome addict who seeks escape from the contemptible thing he is by means of an impossibly elaborate fantasy he pays for and receives inside this very sarcophagus? Was I only back to get back inside at any cost?

When they turned me into the Fant Fixers repair tech, they took everything away from me. Back then, what was left of me, the real me, was nearly snuffed out. Why was it different this time? I didn't know, I couldn't think about that. All I knew was I had to get back to my lover, my friends, my life, because they weren't just fragments of a mechanized dream.

My vision blurred as I stared at the box, it was the bleary-eyed blinding mist of the medicated needing his medication (*was that really it?*) and I wasn't coming up with any answers, and I wasn't getting stronger, no, I was getting weaker, and still I circled the box, step after clumsy step, I staggered around it like a sun dancer circling his pole.

I felt a puff of wind and there was a *whoosh* of a descending car somewhere behind me. It touched down with a grind of tires in the grit of the road. With some reluctance, I turned to see a purple stretch El Cid pull to a stop. Familiar vehicle. The driver's window slid down and the smooth face of the old pimp was framed there. I knew him. He was Garl the FF tech's very first client. He eyed me from head to toe and back up again.

"Jesus H., look at you. You're a fucking mess."

"I was thinking much the same thing," I said.

He tipped his head toward the hotbox and tsked.

"You went and hotwired that god-damned head coffin again, didn't you?"

His tone wasn't jovial or good-natured in the least. He didn't sound like Garl's friend the pimp sounded in my true memories. This pimp of falseville sounded downright menacing.

"I'm not sure what you're talking about," I said.

"You know that drome's in my territory. That much I know

you know. I get a piece of that piece-of-shit's every trick, bitch. Which means you just deuced me outta my vig. I might have to hurt you for that."

I made a sort of a spasmodic, hand-flipper gesture, indicating myself.

"Do you think you can do worse than this?"

He looked me over again and grimaced.

"You have a point."

I heard myself start to ramble, even as some other part of me, the part that wasn't doing the talking, knew this was a mistake.

"I need to get back to the way things are, I mean, the way they're supposed to be, and this, this isn't it. All of this that you see and feel and even breathe, it's a mistake, or rather, it's by design, someone's nefarious design. You may not know these people, or what they're capable of, but I do, and this, this so-called *existence*, it's a perfect example of their twisted ideas about control and revenge, and, well, on top of that they probably think this is hilariously funny."

The pimp's eyes went wide in melodramatic surprise.

"Imagine all that," he said.

"I know it's hard to get your head around, very hard, but none of this is right, I'm not who I'm supposed to be, and you, even you, you're very different, you're supposed to be jocular yet jaded and casually philosophical."

"You're trying to talk yourself back into that box, aren't you?"

"Interesting, if that's how you're perceiving what I'm saying, as all merely pretextual—"

"Jabber of a junkie."

"No, sir, I am not an addict. I most certainly do not want to get back into that box. The box may hold the answers, but I'm not going to find them from inside it. Look, if I owe you anything for services rendered, I'm good for it. I'll settle up with you. I just need to get my head clear."

His lips curled into a cruel smirk.

"Get your head clear? That'll be the day. Shit, it's always the same fucked up story with you. You're a fuckin' headcase. Get your jones'n ass home, freak."

The driver's window started up again, and he shifted the El Cid into flow, but he paused and the window stopped mid-way up, and he put the car back into park. Someone was speaking to him from the back seat. I couldn't hear the voice and couldn't see who was doing the talking through the heavy tints in the glass, but the pimp cocked his head and glanced back. Even in profile I saw his look of utter disbelief.

"You *can't* be serious ... fuck me, you *are* serious?"

Some queer instinct took hold of me and told me to alter my strategy and do it quick, to aid and abet whomever was pressing my case from inside the car. I took a step closer to the window.

"Listen, forget what I said about, well, forget everything I said. That was just me spouting nonsense. I need to get cleaned up and I can't go home to do it. I need a shower and some water and something to eat. I need to get my shit together, and to that I need to find my friends."

"You don't have any friends, remember, memory boy?"

"Maybe that's true, but if I did have any, they'd be waiting for me in the vicinity of Rat City. 69-Frame. Give me a lift, and in exchange, I'll tune up that twerky andro of yours."

He chuckled, humorlessly.

"You mind's simupap and yet you remember that ugly andro. I got rid of that twerky doubletrick years ago. High maintenance, low margin, makes for bad business. So does wasting time talkin' to flunky weirdos." He gestured to the back seat with a jab of his bejeweled fist. "But my best worker bee has, for reasons unclear to me, taken a shine to your lugnut ass."

He shot a look back.

"Are you sure about this? ... All right, all right! Just this one time, do you hear? This *one* time!" He shook his head in disgust. "Jesus-H., but I am one benevolent-ass sonofabitch!"

I nodded, eagerly.

"You took the words out of my mouth, benevolent, I was just going to say that," I said.

"Shut up and get in, retard."

The back door swung open and I saw the shape of the prostitute he was conversing with, a dec female in a hooded jacket, her face in shadow. I got in and shut the door. I stayed well over to my own side, figuring she'd just as soon keep a healthy distance between her designer garments and my grim sodden self. But she surprised me by scooching my way, right past the middle, and even though her face was concealed within the hood, her eyes glinted in the filtered street light and, briefly (*ever so fleetingly*) as she turned, I caught sight of a cheekbone, a shapely and attractive nose, full lips and precious chin, all familiar, very, *very* familiar, and my heart was suddenly racing to keep up with where my eyes were going with all this.

The pimp jammed the El Cid in flow and we went wheels up at screeching speed.

"Rat-*fuck*-City," he groused. "Who in goddamn clusterville wants to go to Rat-*motherfucking*-City?"

My back seat companion ignored him. Her eyes were on me. She reached toward me and, at first I wasn't sure of her intentions as her fingers softly groped across me in the dark. But then she found my hand, it was what she was searching for, and my tender index finger even throbbed as she grasped it, but it was the sweetest pain for it reminded me of what I'd seen that gave me hope. She drew my hand to her and there placed her own hand below. In the bare light I watched her, I felt the warmth of our palms, before I released and let my hand hover above, a little higher, just so, for what I'd seen in the lonely streetlight while shuffling to the desperate place they wanted me to call home, was a microdot on my palm, and I knew that my enemies had not seen it and never knew it was there. Light sprang and flickered in the space between our facing palms, as the hink image took shape, descending from mine, rising from hers, to merge in the luminous, shimmering form of Skarpenthia's *The Entwined*.

Her face edged out of the hood, her eyes gleaming in the laser light … it was *her* face … *her* eyes …

"You know who you wish to be?"

I nodded.

"It is who you are."

"Yeah …" I managed to say.

The pimp's eyes searched the rearview and he scowled. She took my hand, zapping the HOVO so he wouldn't see. Even in the dark her eyes held me.

"You are not alone," she said.

DEEP RESPECT AND APPRECIATION to those who knew all about F.O.E. from the very earliest days, having been to that squalid corner of the future themselves; and although it's completely unnecessary for me to thank them in this two-dimensional way (because they already knew that I did) I will (so as to avoid any messy continuum related percolations): Charlie Franco, Mara Hodges, Rick Febre, Jason Rizos, David Massengill, the Montag Collective, Kevin Downey, Ron Dakron, Scott Whitehead, Matt Geiger, Ed Staiyne *(Names! No names!)* Anna Lisa L., Ashley S., Doug K., Tom Wo., Kirsten L., Sven W., John Z., L and P Ryan, Neal M., Abby W., Peg W., Mike W., DAW, VJW, FEW, WAW *(you all know who you are!)* and still, and of course, by protoplasmic definition, the exquisite Ms. Radienne-Plum.

Ruuf Wangersen is an author and playwright. He lives in Seattle.